The Mountain Man's Badge

*The Mountain Man Mysteries:
Book Three*

Gary Corbin

This book is a work of fiction. Names, characters, businesses, incidents, and dialogue are either drawn from the author's imagination or are used fictitiously, and are not to be construed as real. Any resemblance to actual events or persons, living or dead, is entirely coincidental.

To all of the brave, hardworking, honest
men and women in uniform
who keep us safe in our communities

CONTENTS

PART I

Murder

Chapter One

Lehigh fussed with the wide clip of his bolo tie and adjusted the fit of his black suit jacket, sweating in the July evening heat. He rang the bell and turned to take in the view of the McBride estate, a sprawling mansion at the peak of 50 acres of sloping, mixed terrain. A manicured four-acre front lawn lay before him, bisected by a meandering paved driveway and dotted with flower beds, shrubs, and standalone old-growth firs. On each side of the coliseum-sized lawn, thick clumps of mixed tree stands created a castle-wall effect, as if to stave off attacks by savage hordes. That impression struck Lehigh as appropriate, given the embattled state of retiring Senator George McBride's political career.

Given that the evening's event would inaugurate his own reluctant political career, it also struck him as a little bit ominous.

A smiling woman answered the door, wearing a black and white maid's uniform. The top of the dark bun on her head could not have reached five feet, despite her two-inch heels. "*Hola*, Señor Carter!" she said. "Please come in."

"*Gracias*, Consuela. It's good to see you again." He extended his hand to her.

She brushed it aside and crushed his tall, lanky frame in a tight hug, the top of her head barely reaching his shoulder. "The family is in the Great Room," she said, stepping back. "Would you like to freshen up before joining the party? Or perhaps a drink first? I just made fresh piña coladas." Her broad grin exposed dazzling white teeth, surrounded by bright red lipstick accenting the cinnamon tone of her skin.

Lehigh took off his sheriff's hat, allowing his long brown ponytail to fall onto his back, and stepped inside. The foyer felt a good ten degrees cooler than the mid-80s temperature still clinging to the evening air outside. "If I could enjoy one in the senator's den while I cool off, that'd be ideal," he said.

"You go in. I'll be there *en un momento*." She disappeared around a corner, and Lehigh slipped into the silent office alone.

The room reeked of the senator's privilege and success. Framed photos of George and his wife Catherine with various politicians and celebrities covered most of the fir-paneled walls not occupied by bookshelves, the largest a photo from his swearing-in as state senate president *pro tempore*. Behind the senator's huge desk, the head of an elk leered down at intruders, its snout hanging over a gun rack sporting four rifles, two of them antiques. Sharpshooting trophies on shelves below the rack reflected the dim light from the brushed-bronze desk lamp. More photos scattered throughout the room demonstrated the senator's firm support of the second amendment and the enthusiastic backing he received from gun-rights groups.

A burst of energy from the doorway startled him. "I have missed you!" Consuela said, handing him a drink. "You don't come by so much these last few months. I haven't seen you since your wedding!"

Lehigh accepted the drink and took a long sip. "Who knew that being interim sheriff of sleepy little Mt. Hood County would keep me this busy? And I've missed you. How is Manuel?"

"My boy says his mill misses your excellent lumber," she said. "When I told him this party was to raise money for your re-election, he tried to stop me from coming here!"

"I take it he didn't make a contribution, then," Lehigh said with a grin. He took a long sip of the ice-cold piña colada. Perfect.

She shook her head and adjusted his tie. "I'm teasing you. He would donate if he could, but he is still rebuilding his business. Three months he was in jail with no trial. It nearly ruined him." She teared up and hugged him again. "I never properly thanked you for releasing him."

"It was the right thing to do." A lump rose in Lehigh's throat. He'd had to clean up a multitude of messes in the first weeks after taking office, including Manuel's case. Ex-Sheriff Buck Summers' enemies suffered as much as his friends had benefited from the corruption he'd overseen in his twelve years in office. Unfortunately, Lehigh had only just begun fixing those problems.

"I'd better let you get in there," Consuela said. "Can I get you another piña colada? Or your usual, scotch on the rocks?" She took his jacket and hat and pulled him into the hallway.

"If the senator will part with it," he said with a grin. "Otherwise, another piña colada would be perfect."

"Scotch rocks it is." She hustled off, humming.

Lehigh nodded to the two buzz-cut men standing at attention on either side of the double doors of the Great Room. He recognized them as off-duty deputies and struggled to remember their names, failed, and hoped that a smile in their direction would suffice. They nodded back, but didn't return his smile.

He took a deep breath and pushed open the doors to the aptly named room, a spacious expanse with high ceilings and luxurious decor. A dozen crystal chandeliers cast bright light on an equal number of Roman-style marble pillars. Two dozen round tables, each capable of seating eight for dinner, surrounded an open space suitable for dancing or mixing. Sweet and savory aromas emanated from a long buffet table loaded with beef brisket, raw and roasted vegetables, and too many desserts to count. A four-piece jazz band occupied a small elevated stage in one corner. Lehigh's high school prom had taken less space and hosted fewer people.

"Darling!" Lehigh's bride of two months, Stacy Lynn McBride Carter, appeared in a knee-length dress that made his eyes pop. Burgundy in hue, the silk fabric hugged her slender form and revealed her amazing curves. Her long black hair sat atop her head like an ebony crown, complete with embedded jewelry that sparkled in the room's abundant light. She kissed him—a deep, passionate expression of love and longing, but only for a few moments—enough to titillate, but not enflame. She caressed the smooth skin of his freshly-shaved cheek. "You look fabulous."

"You too. And you smell even better." He took a deep breath of her scent, floral and sweet. Somehow she never seemed to perspire, even on the hottest summer days.

"No Pappy or Maw?" she asked.

"Pappy thinks fund-raisers should be illegal," he said with a grin. "And Maw thinks they already are."

"Well, thank God you made it," she said. "If I had to endure one more minute alone with these politicians, I'd—"

"There you are! Our guest of honor!" A rumbling baritone behind them betrayed the presence of Stacy's father, George McBride. Moments later his rotund frame stumbled into view. A broad smile split his white-capped, ruddy face. It didn't take a detective to realize the senator had enjoyed more than a few shots of his favorite scotch before dinner. Lehigh wondered if any remained and resigned himself to drinking lager.

"I wasn't sure you were here," Lehigh said, accepting his father-in-law's handshake. "I didn't see your New Yorker parked outside."

"My mechanic is working on it. Something about being out of alignment and needing new tires." George stepped between the happy couple and hooked their arms in his. "Anyway, as your campaign chairman, I could hardly miss a party like this! Now, my boy, I need to introduce you to some people. It is, after all, a fund-raiser, and we're starting your campaign late, very late!" He steered them through the crowded room, causing several collisions, spilled drinks, and mumbled apologies. "But not to worry. You're the talk of the town these days, Lehigh. The talk of the town!" He slung his arm around the shoulders of a well-dressed donor and whispered something in the man's ear.

"Folks must be awfully bored if they're wasting conversation on the likes of me," Lehigh said. "What-all would make people give a whoop about what I'm up to?"

"Don't be so modest, darling," Stacy said. "People love a

hero, especially a rogue like you who's finally cleaning up the dirty politics in this county. Dwayne Latner doesn't stand a chance of beating you!"

"That's why I leave the campaign stuff to you and your dad," Lehigh said with a grin. "I know barely enough about politics to vote."

"Will you be charging Latner with any crimes, as we've been hearing?" A tall, handsome man with a made-for-TV smile and haircut stepped in front of them, a half-empty martini glass held between loose fingers. Bruce Bailey, an investigative reporter for the town's sole local network TV affiliate, somehow managed to block the path of Senator McBride and both of his prisoners with his athletic frame. Bailey's dark blue suit made him look larger and even more fit than in his many TV appearances.

"Nobody gets charged with anything unless we have solid evidence," Lehigh said, scowling at Bailey. "And anytime we do, we'll share our findings with the press at the appropriate time and place." He narrowed his eyes and planted a palm in Bailey's chest, pushing him backward. "And this ain't it."

"I expect an invit—hey, watch it, Sheriff! You're spilling my drink!" Bailey stepped aside and dabbed at his own suit, then George's, with a napkin. "I'm sorry, Senator."

McBride pulled his arm away from Bailey, scowling. "Forget it. I'll send it to the cleaners. Dammit, Bailey, you've knocked off one of my cuff links. Keep an eye out, everyone! If it gets stepped on, it's a goner." He held up his free arm to display the remaining cuff link, a gold circle embossed with his initials, then grabbed Lehigh's arm again and tugged.

"You should go change, Dad," Stacy said. "You can't introduce him to donors looking like this!"

"No, no," McBride said. "It's almost time for the main event. Anyway, it looks fine."

Lehigh tuned out the rest of their argument. Stacy's preoccupation with clothes paled only in comparison to George's fanatical obsession with politics. Lehigh hated both.

"Now come on, Sheriff," Bailey said, trailing behind them. "Do you have news on the Buck Summers and Paul van Paten cases? Is Dwayne Latner implicated?"

"No comment for the press," Lehigh said. "And that goes double for you, Bruce."

"Lehigh, my boy," McBride said, turning back to him with a grin, "I believe we've finally found something on which we can agree. The less said about that skunk-rat Downey, the better."

"Is that so?" Bailey finished drying off his suit and dropped the napkin on the tray of a passing waiter. "I thought you and Ev Downey were old pals."

"Nonsense," McBride said, coughing into his sleeve. "You need to stick to the facts and ignore those ugly rumor mills, Mr. Bailey." He pulled Lehigh and Stacy past the protesting newsman toward a cluster of well-dressed couples whose gray hair and wrinkled skin hid beneath layers of makeup, hair coloring, and plastic surgery. "These are the people I want you to meet," McBride said.

"Dad, I've known these people since I was four," Stacy said.

"Not you, my dear. Your husband." McBride pushed Lehigh toward the group, who parted to create an opening for the inbound trio. "Ladies and gentlemen. Have you met my son-in-law, our new county sheriff?"

"I don't believe I've had the pleasure." The shortest of the men, a bespectacled, round-shouldered banker with thinning gray hair combed back over his scalp, extended a handshake and mumbled his name.

"Pleasure to meet you, sir," Lehigh said. He'd have to ask his name again later. "And this is my new bride, Stacy—"

"I remember Stacy very well," the banker said with an oily smile. "Didn't you once have short red hair?"

Stacy's face darkened and her eyes smoldered. "No, sir," she said, her voice icy. "Always black, and always past my shoulders." She slid around behind her father and grabbed Lehigh's arm, squeezing tight. Her fingernails dug into Lehigh's skin, even through his lightweight suit jacket.

"What the heck was that about?" Lehigh asked Stacy between handshakes with more donors. "Short red hair?"

"This isn't the time nor place for that conversation," Stacy said through a frozen smile.

After what seemed like a hundred more introductions, McBride spoke the words Lehigh longed to hear. "And last but not least," he said, "this is County Commissioner Desmond Mitchell. But I believe you two have met?"

A slender, light-skinned African-American man with light gray curls leaned his 6'4" frame forward, his right hand outstretched. "Indeed we have," Mitchell said. "I appreciate your work, Sheriff. Just don't forget about us poor farmers up in the northern part of the county."

"Not a chance," Lehigh said with a grin, shaking the commissioner's hand. "After all, we're kin, of sorts. I'm just an old tree farmer myself."

Mitchell laughed, an eruption of noise that drew attention from half the room. "Indeed we are, Mr. Carter. Indeed we are. Honey, did you hear that? Tree farmers is kin to us! Hah!" He tapped the shoulder of a much shorter, very talkative woman with straight, jet-black hair in a light pink backless gown, but she waved him off without turning. "Ah, well, once she starts talking about saving animals, there's no stopping her," Mitchell said with another laugh.

"Just my kind of gal!" Stacy said with a warm smile. "I knew there was a reason I liked her."

Mitchell nodded. "And likewise, Mrs. Carter. We love your animal clinic and we won't bring our pets to any other vet." He clapped Lehigh on the shoulder. "But tonight it's all about you. I'm thrilled with the work you're doing to root out the old boys network in this county. Keep up the good work, Sheriff." He shook Lehigh's hand and returned to his wife's side.

"That's five big donors I've lined up for you," McBride said. "Your war chest is off to a huge start tonight, my boy!"

"I don't want big donors," Lehigh said. "Stacy, didn't you tell him?"

"Tell me what?" George glanced at each one in turn. "Wait, *don't* tell me," he said. "You didn't—"

Stacy reddened. "We've decided to limit contributions to one hundred dollars." Her gaze fell to the floor.

"A hundred bucks? That won't even cover the cost of their drinks!" McBride said in a hiss. "Are you crazy?"

"Most folks seem to think so," Lehigh said. "That never slowed me down none."

"Well of all the stupid—! Unbelievable. I wish you'd have told me this sooner." He fumed, drained his drink, and clutched at his chest, wincing. "Well, we'll figure something out. A super PAC or something. Anyway, these people are important to your campaign. Be nice to them."

"I'm nice to everyone," Lehigh said, and Stacy burst into laughter.

"Even Paul van Paten, your wife's ex-fiancé?" Bruce Bailey popped up again in Lehigh's view, his martini glass refilled. "I heard he was going to file suit about the conditions of the jail you're keeping him in."

"Don't you have a crying baby somewhere to exploit?" Stacy said.

"I don't know. Does your father have a secret life I should know about?" Bailey asked. "Mistresses, or former female staffers with stories to tell?" He grinned and sipped his drink.

"You must be thinking of Ev Downey again," George said, pushing his way back into the mix. "No woman was ever crazy enough to marry Everett. Even his closest associates know he's a liar and a cheat, and they are all men. If you ever see him with a woman, you know she's bought and paid for."

Stacy grabbed her father's and Lehigh's arms and tugged them toward another well-dressed couple. "I think we should mingle."

"I think we are mingling," Bailey said. "We're having a delightful conversation about George's old pal, Everett. Is he here tonight?"

"Everett's old, but I wouldn't call him a friend," George said, looking around as if searching for someplace to spit. "I can't trust that man out of my sight. Unfortunately, I also can't stand the sight of him. So, no, Mr. Downey wasn't invited."

"Really? Didn't you sell him some property a few years back—the old McGowan farm, the one that the state bought for the new prison property?" Bailey stirred his cocktail with his finger. "I understand Mr. Downey made quite a profit off that sale. Did you benefit at all from that deal, Senator?"

"Not a dime!" McBride pushed to within inches of Bailey's smirking face. "I lost a small fortune on that deal, in fact. Downey swindled me!"

"Angry, aren't we?" Bailey said. "How interesting. Maybe I should follow up with Mr. Downey."

"Now, don't you go making something out of nothing," McBride said. "That was years ago. I'm over it. Win a few, lose a lot, I always say."

"Of course you do," Bailey said. "Well, would you look at that. My drink's almost gone. I guess I better go refresh." Bailey sauntered off toward the bar, draining the last dregs from his glass.

"Whatever you do, keep an eye on him," McBride said in a low voice to Lehigh. "He's nothing but a cheap muckraker."

"I know Bruce well," Lehigh said. "But thank you. I will."

At that moment, Consuela popped up between them. "Mrs. McBride sent me to remind you to take your medicines," she said to George. She held out a tray on which perched a saucer holding a tumbler of water and three pills of various shapes and colors.

"Later," George said, coughing. "I'm very busy right now."

"Mr. McBride, your pleurisy is not going to get better on its own," Consuela said. "I insist."

"In that case, you really have no choice." Lehigh grinned. McBride sighed and washed the pills down with one great gulp of water.

"Time for the main event," George said when Consuela departed. "Are you two ready?"

Stacy grabbed Lehigh's arm. "Come on up to the stage. It's time to give your speech."

"What?" Lehigh said. "I didn't prepare any speech! What am I going to say?"

"Don't worry, I wrote one for you," George said, handing him a few folded-up sheets of paper. "Standard crap. Just try to sound genuine, would you? Make them happy they're here. Don't forget to ask them to write you a check. A hundred dollars! What were you thinking? Go on now."

Lehigh stumbled toward the dais, studying the pages George had handed him. The text read like a stock political speech, full of meaningless sound bites. Crap. He hated speeches like this. The donors would hate it, too. And the press would eat him alive.

Speaking of which. He glanced around to locate Bailey again, but he had disappeared. Just great. The one moment he needed the TV reporter to show up and he was probably puking in the restroom.

Oh, well. Maybe that would limit the damage.

Or, as it turned out, not.

Chapter Two

The following Wednesday, Lehigh parked his pickup truck in the dusty, broken-gravel parking lot alongside Montgomery's Gentleman's Lounge, located on the main highway leading into and out of Clarkesville. About half of the central Oregon county's five thousand residents called Clarkesville home, yet somehow Everett Downey's strip club managed to fill its official capacity of 112 patrons most Friday and Saturday nights. Lehigh had never set foot inside, but Stacy had once worked there as a waitress, much to the chagrin of her conservative and once-powerful father.

Lehigh stepped out of the vehicle into the dry July heat of the foothills of the Cascade Mountains. It wasn't even 11:30 a.m., but already the day had turned into a scorcher. No shade, no breeze, no clouds, just the constant blaze of a white hot sun overhead. He wiped his brow, then turned when the crunch of tires on gravel sounded behind him.

He spotted the green Volvo wagon and smiled. Stacy had promised to make the meeting if she could, but had warned that her caseload at the Cascade Animal Clinic looked heavy that morning, and dying or suffering animals always took precedence over politics. She parked in a shady spot on the street, managing to block a "Latner for Sheriff" sign. Lehigh grimaced. Her father hadn't even printed Lehigh's campaign signs yet.

"I'm so glad you're here," he said when she got out of the car, and he gave her a massive hug and kiss.

"I'm not," she said, hugging him back. "I mean, I'm always happy to help you out, but I hate it here."

"Me too." He led her by the hand to the front door. "I'm not even sure why we're here."

"Protocol," she said. "I know it's distasteful, but just trust me. Stick to the plan, and we'll be fine. And fix your collar." She faced him, adjusted his tie, and dusted off the beige shirt of his sheriff's uniform. "You look amazing."

"So do you." He gazed down at her, over a half-foot shorter than his wiry, six-one frame, astonished still that this smart, beautiful woman had exchanged vows with him six weeks before. Her long black hair tumbled around her shoulders, her summer tan exposed by the blue sleeveless dress that finished off just below the knees of her strong, toned legs. But as beautiful as she looked, he appreciated her political savvy even more. If even she said he needed to meet with Downey, it had to be true. "Thank you for arranging this. I'd have never…"

"You're going to do just great." She smiled, took a deep breath, and pushed open the door to the bar.

A wave of cold air, reeking of stale tobacco, whiskey, and cheap perfume, pushed back at them. Stacy scooted through, Lehigh following. He blinked against the smoky air and waited for his eyes to adjust to the dim light of the small foyer. Then he held open the second set of doors for Stacy to glide through.

"So much for a smoke-free workplace," Lehigh said. "That's one law he's breaking already."

"Sh," Stacy said. "We have bigger fish to fry today."

The interior of Downey's club looked as Lehigh expected: dim light interrupted by flashing neon signs promoting cheap beer or outlining suggestive, if not outrageous, poses by long-legged, busty women. Small round tables topped with dark wood and crowded with chairs all facing the same direction. A woman wearing a purple wig, black fishnets and a smile gyrated around a floor-to-ceiling chrome-colored pole in the center of a small stage to the incessant beat of some timeless disco-like Europop song. A handful of middle-aged men scattered around the bar nursed straw-colored beers in undersized pint glasses and pretended not to care what happened on stage, except to toss the occasional crumpled greenbacks into the spotlight whenever the purple-haired woman slithered by to scoop the bills into her fishnets.

"Don't they have to wear G-strings or anything?" he asked Stacy.

She shook her head. "Not in Oregon. That's considered 'free speech' here." She grimaced at the stage. Lehigh could tell that the memory of her past employment still scarred her. Best not to press it any further.

As if summoned by his thoughts, a woman wearing just enough shiny, fur-lined fabric to cover her essentials greeted them. Everything about her screamed fake, from the platinum wig and inch-long eyelashes to her gravity-defying bustline, but she surprised Lehigh with her deep, gentle voice. "Two for lunch?" she asked with a sweet smile.

"We're here to see Mr. Downey," Lehigh said around a nervous cough. "He's expecting us."

She nodded and pointed a two-inch-long multi-colored fingernail toward the far corner of the room, away from the bar. "Can I bring you a drink? On the house, Sheriff."

Stacy shook her head. Lehigh smiled, tempted. "Just coffee, thanks."

"Shot of Irish Cream in it for you?" she asked.

"Not while I'm on duty." He tapped the badge on his chest, and she shrugged.

"Election season, I get it. You're the second one today. Don't worry, I'm not taking any pictures or talking to the press. Company policy." She disappeared into the dimness.

"I guess you're right," Lehigh said to Stacy. "Everyone needs Downey's support, but nobody wants to admit it. I wonder who else was in here? Maybe Dwayne Latner?"

"Could be anyone," Stacy said. "Half the County Commission is up for re-election. Plus, all the statewide offices are gearing up for next November. I know Ray Ferguson's been making the rounds, gearing up for his run for state attorney general. Come on, let's get this over with."

Lehigh and Stacy wended their way amidst the tables to Downey as the music ended and the purple-haired dancer scooped up the last of her cash, accepting some additional contributions from the hands of appreciative patrons. A new song began, much like the one before it, and a new dancer wearing a blue wig and a gauzy blue gown over a mini-bikini and high heels took her place.

"Doesn't anyone here have their own hair?" he asked.

She shook her head. "Wigs serve everybody's interests. The women maintain some sense of anonymity, the guys get their bizarre fantasies fulfilled, and this way, each dancer can perform several acts, each time as a different character. It's weird, but it works."

"Is that why that banker at the party asked about your short red hair?" he asked.

"Waitresses wear wigs, too," she said, nodding. "Those who want careers afterwards, anyway." She arrived at Downey's table a step ahead of Lehigh and extended her hand to her former boss, who stood to greet them.

"Stacy, my dear." Downey's bloated figure blocked a considerable fraction of the flashing neon light, but the tonic coating his thick white hair reflected the reds, blues, and purples blinking all around them. A toothy smile revealed multiple gaps between uneven teeth, which appeared stained even in the dim light of the bar, and his ruddy face gleamed with a fine layer of perspiration. He bowed from the vicinity of where his waist should have been and kissed her hand. "So lovely to see you. And Sheriff, I don't believe we've met before in person." He extended a clammy hand, and Lehigh shook it. A moment later Lehigh resisted the urge to wipe his hands on his trousers.

"Please, sit. Enjoy the show." He grinned again, expelling a burst of air reeking of tobacco, garlic, and gin. Lehigh's belly kicked him from inside. The urge to run nearly overwhelmed him. But, following Stacy's lead, he sat.

"I've been following your career," Downey said once their coffees arrived. "You have quite the future in politics, Mr.

Carter."

"I hope not," Lehigh said.

Stacy cleared her throat. "What Lehigh means," she said, her face flushing red, "is that for him, it's not about winning elections. It's about making sure justice is served fairly in Mt. Hood County."

"Can't get it done without winning, though, can you?" Downey laughed, his mouth wide, and his pink, snake-like tongue floated inside his mouth. Lehigh wondered if he'd evolved from a different species of man.

"Gotta win for the right reasons, though," Lehigh said. A waitress drifted among the tables, her perfume preceding her. He held his breath until she passed.

"Of course, of course. That's exactly why I wanted to meet with you." Downey reached into his suit jacket and produced a cigar, offered it to them. Lehigh shook his head. Stacy waved it away. Downey rolled the tip in his mouth, then held it while he spoke. "I don't ever recall seeing you in my club before, Sheriff."

Lehigh shook his head again. "Not my thing."

"Do you oppose the presence of establishments like mine?" Downey gestured with the cigar at the newest dancer, a young woman with orange hair, matching lipstick, tiger-striped high heels, and strategically placed body paint. Or tattoos, Lehigh realized, wincing.

Lehigh glanced at Stacy, whose intense gaze surprised him. He wondered how she would have answered the question, given her past. He met Downey's stare, cleared his throat. "Your business is legal. My job is to enforce the laws, not write them. So, do I support you? Not with my hard-earned money. But, so long as you obey the laws," and he paused a moment to stare at the unlit cigar, "I'm not aiming to shut you down, if that's what you're asking." He glanced again at Stacy, who winked, and her lips turned up at the corners.

"Good answer," Downey said. "And, not the one I got from the assistant district attorney, earlier today. *Or* your opponent, I might add." He pulled out a cigar cutter from his pocket and placed the unlicked tip into the notch, a quarter-inch from the end.

"Which opponent?" Lehigh asked. "As far as we've heard, the only one running an active campaign is Dwayne Latner. After his involvement with Buck Summers, his chances are slim to none, and Slim just left town."

Downey smiled, clipped the tip of the cigar, and inspected his handiwork. "One must always take a challenger seriously when we have a weak incumbent. No offense," he said, picking up a silver lighter from the table. "But you were appointed to fill in the unexpired term of a disgraced three-term office holder. There's always someone who feels the job should have been theirs." He put the cigar in his mouth, inhaled it, unlit. Lehigh stared at the tip and at the lighter in Downey's hand. Surely he wouldn't be so bold—

"No matter. I've always worked well with the McBrides," Downey went on, "and, my boy, you're a McBride now."

"Reckon I've been called worse," Lehigh said in a low voice, still watching the lighter. Stacy kicked him under the table and accompanied it with a muffled harrumph.

"Well, Sheriff, I'm a busy man," Downey said. "I'll get down to brass tacks. I can give you five thousand. Will that suffice?" He lowered his head, keeping his eyes on Lehigh, and brought the lighter, now aflame, to the tip of the cigar. He inhaled, and the tip of the cigar glowed bright red.

Lehigh, aghast, stared at the man, then coughed into his fist. The guy had *cojones*, he had to grant that. "Sir," he said, "I'm here to discuss issues of concern to you. I'm not seeking financial support—"

"Baloney." Downey enveloped them all in a thick cloud of blue smoke. "Campaigns cost money, son. And I want you to win. But I have limits. So, if this is a game to elicit even more from me—"

"Of course not," Stacy said. "What Lehigh means is—"

"What I mean is, put your checkbook away," Lehigh said, his temper flaring. "I don't want your money. I ain't taking big checks from anyone. Nobody's gonna own me. I'd rather lose the election than my integrity." He stood and glanced at the untouched cup on the table. "Thanks for the coffee. And Mr. Downey, in case you need reminding, smoking's been banned indoors in this state. So *if* you want to remain open, you'd do well to obey that law…and all the others." He gestured toward the dancers. "Keep 'em onstage, shall we, Everett?"

The two men glared at each other, the cigar dangling from Downey's mouth, for several long moments. "You're not threatening me, are you, Sheriff?" he said at last in an even tone. "Because I'm certain Dwayne Latner won't be turning down my money."

Stacy slid her chair a few inches closer to Downey's. "Nobody's threatening or bribing anyone," she said. "In fact, I happen to know how much the county appreciates your support of our educational system, Mr. Downey. And since you have some money to spend, might I suggest you donate it to the campaign for the school levy that will also be on the ballot this fall? It's a cause we all adore, and they're fighting an uphill battle. Wouldn't you like to show your support for the sheriff in a symbolic way, by supporting the county's schools?"

Downey scowled and pointed at the orange-haired dancer. "Do my employees look like they need a better education?" He sucked on his cigar and exhaled again. "Thinkers make lousy dancers."

"Mr. Downey," Stacy said. "You supported me years ago when I needed money for my education. It made all the difference in the world to me. Didn't that work out well?"

Downey shrugged. "For whom?"

"For me," Stacy said. "And today, for you. Consider it your expression of support for Lehigh—and the McBrides. Please?"

"But, if you'd rather," Lehigh said after a long silence, "we can ask the health department to look into *alleged* reports of indoor smoking on these premises. Maybe the liquor board, too. And who knows what else we'll find, once we start digging?"

Downey glared at him, puffed at his cigar again, then stubbed it out in the ashtray. Finally, he looked away.

"Send the information to my secretary," he said. "And get the hell out of here."

Chapter Three

Lehigh slammed shut the lower left drawer of the ancient county-provided wooden desk, sending an echoing boom down the hallway. He winced, knowing the loud noise would stir up a reaction among the sworn officers and civilian employees—whispers of concern about his temper, perhaps, or with his growing frustration with this job. Even though he only slammed the drawer because it had stuck. Again. For the fourteenth time in a week.

Still, the whispers would be justified. He *had* lost his patience more than once with the amazingly frustrating bureaucracy of Mt. Hood County government, the decrepit conditions of the building in which he worked, and the resistance to change exhibited by almost every employee under his supervision. Everyone knew his appointment expired soon after election day in November, just a few months away. Most figured they could wait him out until a "real" sheriff would be elected. Until then, foot-dragging on changes he'd tried to implement seemed the only principle unifying the work of his department.

"Everything okay, Sheriff?" Deputy Ted Roscoe, a clean-shaven, twenty-something man of below-average height and a little too much belly, poked his head in the door of Lehigh's office. The smell of stale tobacco smoke preceded him, as always. His auburn hair, short on the sides but longer and combed back in front, flaked dandruff onto the sleeves of his beige uniform, which he never seemed able to either prevent or remedy.

Lehigh grimaced and waved Ted in. "All's okay, Ted. Sorry to slam things. This old desk just drives me bonkers sometimes."

"You want me to requisition you a new one?" Roscoe asked. "That one's been here since before Buck first became sheriff, I think."

Lehigh shook his head. "It ain't in the budget. I'll make do." Plus, he didn't need the headache. Ordering a new, expensive piece of furniture would create the appearance, if not the reality, of extravagance and reinforce the impression already circulating that he expected to remain in this job for life.

He just might, but not in the way his detractors expected. This job might just kill him long before the election.

"I'll get someone from facilities to come by with some wax," Ted said. "Maybe that'll make it shut easier." He disappeared.

Moments later, Lehigh's desk phone rang. "Sheriff? Jim Wadsworth. I've got some bad news."

Lehigh groaned. When his best detective said he had bad news, any bad day was about to get far worse. "What have you got? More cost overruns? Another deputy quitting? Or has the Clarkesville *News-Clarion* skewered me on the op-ed page again?"

A breathy cough came over the line. "Nothing as easy as all that, Lehigh. This one's really bad."

Lehigh's ears perked up and he sat up straight in his chair. "How bad?"

"Real, bad, Lehigh." The line went quiet a moment, then: "There's been a murder."

***

Lehigh arrived at the murder scene an hour later, a sunshine-soaked patch of cleared forest a little larger than a football field, situated a half-mile hike from Brady Mountain Road. Forensics teams had marked off the area with yellow police tape, and the inside crawled with deputies, a few well-dressed men in dark suits swearing at the mud on their shoes, and a couple of frumpy detectives from his own office. He waved at his favorite, Detective "Gentleman Jim" Wadsworth, a man ten years his senior with a permanent five o'clock shadow. Dressed as always in a wrinkled gray suit and a tie that advertised that his last meal included some form of red sauce, a casual observer would never guess that Wadsworth had just celebrated 25 years of marriage to the same woman. At 5'10" tall and well over 200 pounds, the detective's stride lacked grace even in a meeting room, and he looked doubly awkward picking his way over to Lehigh through the underbrush.

"You in charge of this scene?" Lehigh asked him.

Wadsworth shook his head and coughed into his fist. "Just helping out Clayton." He pointed to a shorter, wire-framed man with a salt-and-pepper buzz cut and sun-weathered skin, conversing with a small team of deputies on the edge of the clearing. "I made him the lead, since I've been in and out of the office with this stupid cold."

"Can we trust him?" Lehigh asked in a low voice.

Wadsworth shrugged. "As much as anybody. He's a lifer, but a pro."

Lehigh nodded. Not a ringing endorsement, but it'd have to do. "Anyone from the district attorney's office here yet?"

"A few. Ray Ferguson's on his way," Wadsworth said. "Apparently he was up in Wyee Falls this week with his family."

"Wow. They're bringing out the big guns." Lehigh shielded his eyes from the sun, glaring over the treetops to the east. "What do you know so far?"

"Looks like Mr. Downey may have stepped in front of somebody's hunting rifle." Wadsworth coughed into his sleeve. "And whoever pulled the trigger was a damned good shot."

"Might it have been an accident?" Lehigh asked.

"Maybe, but I'm guessing not." The detective coughed again. "You don't often see accidental shots at point blank range to the chest."

Lehigh stared at him. "Point blank? I thought you said—"

"The first shot hit him in the leg," Wadsworth said, "guessing by all the blood. Looks like it must've hit a major artery. He might've bled out if not for the second shot."

Wadsworth pointed at a path wending its way across the clearing. "We found footprints matching these that weren't the victim's, over behind that patch of brush. Must be 150 yards. A *damned* good shot."

"When did it happen?" Lehigh asked.

"Herman tentatively put the time of death at between eight p.m. and midnight last night." Wadsworth wagged his chin toward the coroner, Herman Doskey, a round-shouldered, gray-haired man in gold wire-rimmed glasses, supervising a team preparing to move the body. Lehigh had spotted a county hearse at the trailhead parking lot when he arrived. "We'll know more after the autopsy," Wadsworth went on, "but it looked like a high-calibre rifle shot, at first glance."

"How can you tell?" Lehigh asked.

"The distance, and the exit wound," Wadsworth said. "The likelihood of hitting someone with a single pistol shot at that distance is pretty low. Plus, bullets shot from a rifle leave a cleaner exit wound due to their speed. And that," he said with a smile, "is as much as I remember about the subject. Anything more, you gotta talk to Herman."

"And the shooter wasn't after deer, or elk?"

Wadsworth scoffed. "With ammo like that, they could have brought down a bear. But it's not bear, or deer, or *anything* season right now."

"Another reason to believe it's not an accident, then." Lehigh shook his head. "Who'd want to shoot Ev Downey? And why here?"

Wadsworth coughed again, and this time didn't stop for several seconds. "Damned summer colds," he said at last. He cleared his throat and swallowed. "Downey had even more enemies than you do," he said in a raspy voice, then grimaced. "Sorry."

"No offense taken."

"He never married, so we can rule out a domestic dispute," Wadsworth said. "And as for why here—well, secrecy, I imagine. Downey sure wasn't here to hunt."

"You're sure of that? He didn't strike me as a man who'd

worry about rules and permits."

"Yeah," Wadsworth said, exploding into a new round of coughing, "but even Everett Downey wouldn't go hunting in a Brooks Brothers suit."

"No, he wouldn't," Lehigh said, more to himself than to Wadsworth. "What *would* he be doing here, then?"

"It's ironic, in a way, that he died here," Wadsworth said. "It's supposedly sacred burial ground for one of the tribes."

As if on cue, the coroner's team hefted the silent body onto a stretcher. Moments later they disappeared onto the half-mile trail through the woods.

With him, Lehigh realized, went all of his secrets, to the grave.

***

Soft hands interrupted Lehigh's focused stare at the computer screen, and he sank back into them with a sigh of relief. Stacy kneaded the tight cables of muscles holding his head upright in its rigid pose, causing blissful sensations of relief to flow down his neck and back. Soft lips pressed against the tiny bald spot forming at the top of his head.

"Dinner's ready, my love." She continued to massage his neck and shoulders. "Come on, hit 'Save' and close up. You've worked enough for today."

He leaned back into her and a tiny groan escaped from somewhere deep within him. "No fair with the mixed messages," he said, grinning up at her. "Part of me wants to jump out of this chair and go eat, but the rest of me doesn't want to move. Ever." He patted her hands, then reached behind her to pull her in close. "You're a temptress."

"I've got an even better temptation waiting for you after dinner." She spun his chair 180 degrees and sat in his lap. Her long black locks cascaded over his shoulders and the scent of his favorite perfume emanated from her deep plunging V-neck dress. She planted a lingering kiss on his lips and resumed the neck massage.

"Let's just skip dinner, then," he said, wrapping her up in a tight embrace.

"Aren't you hungry? I made your favorite. Italian sausage lasagna."

"Starved," he said, "in so many ways. And lasagna is great cold." He slid his hand up her thigh.

She slapped it away. "But it's much better warm, and I spent an hour and a half slaving over it. Come on, before the dogs eat it all." She jumped off his lap and led him by the hand from his makeshift home office into the kitchen of their split-level ranch. Sure enough, Lucky and Diamond, their adopted three-year-old Lab-hound mix and eight-month-old border collie puppy, respectively, dropped their front paws from the counter and slunk away in guilty crawls out of the kitchen.

"I don't suppose they were after the salad," he said with a grin.

They filled their plates with lasagna, fresh greens, and Parmesan-crusted garlic bread fresh from the oven and plopped down together on the living room sofa in front of the TV. An ad for Dwayne Latner ended with a soft-focus image of the candidate looking resolute, with his slogan, "Experienced and Professional," plastered across the screen. Lehigh groaned. "Change the channel, please," he said.

Stacy picked up the remote and skimmed through channels while sipping wine. "I wouldn't worry about his TV ads," she said. "I knocked on a lot of doors today and made dozens of calls. Most people who know you, love you."

"Most people who know me don't vote," he said, scooping lasagna into his mouth.

The local news came on, and the anchor, a forgettably adorable bleached blonde reading a teleprompter, introduced a breaking story. "With more on the Everett Downey murder," she said, "here's KMTH's Bruce Bailey."

Stacy groaned. "Shall I turn the station again?"

"No, let's watch," Lehigh said with his mouth full. "I'm curious about what he considers 'breaking news.' What does he know that I don't?"

"Nothing," Stacy said around a mouthful of salad, but she turned up the volume.

"Thanks, Amanda." Bruce Bailey stood with his back to the taped-off murder scene off Brady Mountain Road. A few out-of-focus people in dark uniforms or suits moved around in the meadow behind him. "Mt. Hood County Assistant District Attorney Raymond Ferguson led an investigative team today looking into the apparent murder of local businessman Everett Downey. The crime occurred here in a secluded area on the outskirts of Clarkesville best known as a favorite site for elk and deer hunters," Bailey said. "But it appears that this time, the prey was human."

"How melodramatic," Stacy said.

"At least he's not making stuff up, for a change," Lehigh said, scooping up red sauce with a chunk of buttery bread.

The camera panned back, and the bald, fit figure of "Reverend" Ray Ferguson towered over Bailey, with his name and title captioned at the bottom of the screen. "The victim died of multiple gunshot wounds late last night," Ferguson said. "While we can't rule out accidental death, all signs at this time point to foul play." The Reverend scowled at the conclusion of his remarks, his bushy salt-and-pepper eyebrows curled above his eyes like bicycle handlebars.

"What a gold-bricker," Lehigh said. "Last one on the scene, first one on TV." Stacy giggled, half-choking on her garlic bread.

"Any suspects yet?" Bailey asked Ferguson.

The Reverend's scowl deepened. "Unfortunately not," he said. "We'll be working cooperatively with the Sheriff's Department to analyze available evidence. We fully intend to apprehend the culprit and prosecute him—or her—to the full extent of the law. Punishment will be swift and severe."

"Any timeline on that?" Bailey asked.

"Not at this time."

The camera shifted so that only Bailey's face occupied the screen, wearing a grim expression. "The investigation is hampered, some officials say, by the inadvertent contamination of the crime scene by first responders from the Sheriff's office," he said.

"What?" Stacy said with a gasp.

"Baloney!" Lehigh shouted, choking on a mouthful of pasta.

"Incompetence of this kind has been a frequent complaint aimed at the Sheriff's office since the rise to power of Lehigh Carter, who took office with little to no background in law enforcement," Bailey said. "Only this time, the impacts were fatal. Back to you, Amanda."

Lehigh's shoe struck the "off" button on the TV with amazing precision, having left his foot only a moment earlier from six feet away. The screen went blank. "What a crock of pig manure!" Lehigh said, followed by a string of colorful curses.

Stacy winced and edged away from him. "I'm sorry, honey." She rested a hand on his knee. "Bruce Bailey's nothing but a muckraker. He's been filing baseless reports like this against my father for years."

"Bailey's an idiot, but he's not who I'm worried about." Lehigh shoved another chunk of garlic bread into his mouth and chewed with angry vigor. After washing it down with a gulp of red table wine, he went on. "Someone filled his ears with that 'compromised crime scene' nonsense. That's who I'm mad at. And I have a strong feeling the man responsible goes by the nickname *Reverend*."

Chapter Four

Lehigh squirmed in the hard wooden chair provided for witnesses in the Mt. Hood County Commission hearing room. Built in 1901, the building's high domed ceiling framed a dozen long, narrow windows that allowed sunlight to brighten the otherwise dull proceedings in its dusty, hallowed halls. The windows also allowed the sun to heat the non-air-conditioned room beyond anyone's comfort level, even without the added distress of being grilled by angry politicians.

"Twenty-two years we've gone without a wrongful death in this county," said the white-haired, bulbous-nosed man occupying the luxurious leather seat elevated two feet above the seat that Lehigh occupied. The nameplate in front of the man read, *Hon. E. Jackson, Chairman.* "Then you come on the scene," he continued, "and we have two murders in less than a year. When are you going to do something, Sheriff, to keep the people of this county safe?"

The chairman, a beach ball of a man six-and-a-half feet tall, wore a dark blue pinstripe suit that pinched tight under the armpits and wouldn't button shut even if he succumbed to that fancy of fashion, which he apparently did not. Nor did he believe in buying suits in a larger, better-fitting size.

Lehigh loosened the collar of his khaki shirt and wished the standard uniform of the Sheriff's department didn't include the solid black wool tie that choked off all oxygen to his brain. He wiped sweat from the side of his neck and dipped his head toward the mic. "All due respect, Mr. Chairman, the first murder you mentioned happened on my predecessor's watch. That said, I—"

"None of them happened before you started hanging around downtown Clarkesville," said County Chairman Elliott McBride Jackson, first cousin to Lehigh's father-in-law, George McBride. Jackson had cast the sole dissenting vote in Lehigh's appointment by the Board to fill the unexpired term of former sheriff Buck Summers. Rumor had it that Jackson decided his vote the moment he heard that the senator had endorsed Lehigh and embraced him as a member of the family. The storied rivalry between George and Elliott went back decades—to infancy, according to the old wags who told the story at the slightest provocation on Saturday mornings at Dot's Diner. Jackson's antipathy to anything connected to George intensified whenever political points came up for grabs, and a public grilling of the inexperienced sheriff proved too tempting a target for the county chairman to ignore.

"Yes, sir," Lehigh said. "Me and the actual murderer, who was also my sworn enemy—"

"I wasn't done talking, Sheriff!" Jackson's eyes bulged and dark blue veins pulsed along his temples. "I always doubted the wisdom of appointing a layman with no criminal justice experience to head up our fine, dedicated corps of law enforcement professionals in the sheriff's department. I believe this incident proves my reservations well-justified. But I'm a man of open mind," he said, glancing at the three silent, white-haired colleagues to his right, and then to an equal number on his left, "so I'll let you prove me wrong if the facts so warrant. Along those lines, let me ask you, Sheriff: have you arrested a suspect?"

Lehigh stared down at the black-topped table. Every set of eyes in the hearing room focused on him at that moment. The room held over a hundred people when filled to capacity, although that had happened only twice before, according to official county records. The first time occurred during a visit by 1932 presidential candidate Huey Long. The second time occurred during the aftermath of the World Trade Center bombing, when area residents came together to console one another and worry *en masse* about political terrorist attacks in Oregon. The building's granite block construction on the exterior reassured most residents of its ability to repel almost any attacking horde.

This was the third such occasion.

He gazed around the room. The dark cherry panels on the interior walls provided a serene feeling of safety to the dozens of fearful faces gathered inside, so long as they occupied the comfortable pews in the gallery rather than the hot spotlight of the witness chair, where Lehigh sat. He cleared his throat.

"We have not yet arrested anyone, no."

"As I suspected!" Jackson bellowed in outrage—real or mock, it mattered not at all to Lehigh. The commissioner raised his voice further to be heard above the buzzing voices filling the room. "Why, your predecessor, in a similar circumstance, had a suspect in custody within hours of discovering a body. What, besides your own *incompetence* and lack of professionalism, prevents you from doing the same, Sheriff?"

Lehigh took a long, calming breath and kept his voice even. "All due respect, Mr. Chairman, my predecessor arrested an innocent woman to cover up his own role in that murder."

"Dallas Summers served this county selflessly and faithfully since you were in kindergarten, young man," Jackson said in a condescending, booming voice, once again shouting down the din of voices surrounding them. He pointed a chubby finger at Lehigh and arched his white bushy eyebrows. "You'd best speak with respect for the man who built the legacy of the department you inherited from the sweat of his brow!"

Lehigh sighed. Dallas "Buck" Summers had left a mess of cronyism, laziness, and corruption for his successors to clean up, entrenched in the hiring of a cadre of deputies loyal only to Buck and largely untrained in proper police procedure. Jackson had so far blocked Lehigh's every attempt to correct the problems he faced, and his meek, election-minded fellow commissioners had been unwilling or unable to override him.

"My deputies," Lehigh said, "are working night and day to investigate this heinous crime."

"And what about you?" Jackson said with a snarl. "Your predecessor would have personally led such an investigation. What have you done while your diligent, professional deputies do the actual work of this department?"

Heat rose in Lehigh's collar, and not from the tight wool tie. "Mostly," Lehigh said, "I seem to attend County Board meetings, answering pointless questions from grandstanding politicians." He stood, knocking his chair to the floor behind him. Gasps arose from the gallery and the dais alike. One commissioner, a white-haired retired schoolteacher that had taught Lehigh in third grade, even set down her knitting to peer over her glasses at him with a disapproving stare. Lehigh didn't bother to register the expressions of her colleagues. He strode toward the exit, jaw clenched.

"You are not dismissed!" Jackson shouted. "Where are you going? Get back in that chair before we rule you in contempt of the Commission!" Jackson pounded his gavel to punctuate his protestations. His face turned beet red, and Lehigh, glancing back at him, wondered if he might keel over.

He stopped a few feet from the door and faced all seven commissioners, arms folded across his chest. "Ladies and gentlemen," he said, "by a show of hands, how many of you think this here circus sideshow is worth even five more seconds of your time or mine?"

The chairman stared at him, mouth agape, apparently too stunned to answer. The other six commissioners exchanged furtive glances, but kept their hands by their sides. Desmond Mitchell hid a grin behind the palm of his hand.

"You see, Mr. Chairman? Nobody finds this useful—not even you. So let's cut the crap and let me get back to work." He pushed open the heavy wooden doors and strode into the lobby, ignoring the buzz of voices stirring behind him.

***

Lehigh stayed below the speed limit the next morning during his drive up Brady Mountain Road, a thin ribbon of asphalt winding through the forest in the foothills of the Oregon Cascades. Not because of the five-pointed gold star he wore on his beige uniform, nor because of the doleful stares of Lucky and Diamond reflected in his rear-view mirror. Living his entire life in the area had acquainted him with the hidden risks that lurked around its many tight curves and steep embankments. Sudden drifts of fog, leaping deer, and deep ruts ground into the surface by a steady stream of logging trucks created hazards for the unaware. But as a long-time resident of Brady Mountain, he'd also grown to appreciate the challenge and beauty of its many surprises.

He would have preferred to head to his own property, but this morning's errand took precedence: a visit to the site of Everett Downey's murder, a state-owned patch of land off Brady Mountain Road, a few miles closer to town. Local hunters who found the body at first assumed Downey had been the victim of a hunting accident. But Downey had been dressed in a suit, and the late estimated hour of death—between eight and ten p.m.—made it unlikely that he'd been hunting or hiking for fun. So did the lack of a hunting rifle and ammunition in his possession, or gunpowder residue on his fingers.

Lehigh parked at the trail head that led to the site and filled his lungs with fresh, pine-scented air while the dogs relieved themselves in the tall grass. Then, dogs at his heels, he walked the perimeter of the parking strip, a flat patch of dirt and gravel on the side of the highway, unmarked by any signs. He started at the opening to the trail at the center of the lot and walked along the edge of the greenery to the end, looking for anything unusual on either side. Finding none, he strolled in the opposite direction, past the trail head to the other end. Just as he was about to turn back, Lucky stopped and sniffed at something shiny in the dirt.

"Come, Lucky." The hound glared at him, a stare that told him that what she'd found interested her far more than whatever treat he could bribe her with. He leaned closer and let out a low whistle. He snapped a picture with his cell phone, then picked up the shiny object, careful to touch it only by the edges. Looked it over.

A gold cuff link, embossed with three letters. Initials, he guessed.

G.L.M.

A perfect match of the ones worn by George Lindsey McBride.

He searched his memory for any other locals with the same initials. He could think of none who would wear cuff links, least of all to a hunting site.

After several moments, he reached an inescapable, unfathomable conclusion: his own father-in-law and campaign chairman had left incriminating evidence at a murder scene.

How? And why?

He hated the answer his mind provided, and hated even more the prospect of sharing that information with his colleagues—and his wife. His breakfast churned in his gut.

Had George finally discovered—or admitted to himself—Stacy's history with Everett Downey, and come to take revenge?

Lehigh pocketed the cuff link and followed the dogs back toward his truck, lost in thought. The cuff link *proved* nothing. But it lent strong credence to the notion that George McBride had been to the trail head. How recently, and whether he came armed and with malicious intent toward Everett Downey, remained to be seen.

Diamond, the young border collie, stopped at the edge of a drying mud puddle lining the edge of the pavement and lifted his leg. Way too close to the road. "Not there, Diamond," he said, snapping his fingers. The dog glanced at him, lowered his head, and trotted off to the tall grass closer to the woods. Lehigh looked closer at the puddle. At the edge, someone's vehicle had left deep tracks, as if the car's wheels had spun for a few seconds, removing the layer of gravel that should have covered the spot. A similar rut appeared about six feet to the right. The muddy contents of the ruts surprised Lehigh. Typical of summers in the

Cascades, it hadn't rained in several days, since a freak thunderstorm passed through a few nights before the murder. The gravel covering the rest of the parking lot had dried. He pushed some aside with the toe of his boot. About an inch deep, the gravel gave way to mud, just like where he'd found the tire ruts.

Still, the gravel covering the ruts could explain the lack of evaporation there. The puddles, exposed to air, should have dried further.

Except.

He glanced up at the tops of the Douglas firs and lodgepole pines creating a thick, tall wall of forest at the opposite edge of the gravel lot, then at the similar scene lining the opposite shoulder of the highway. Behind the trees, about midway up, droplets of sunlight trickled through the thick bramble of branches, stippling the highway. He followed the trajectory that the sun would follow and the line of trees that shaded where he stood. Only at high noon, give or take an hour, would the sun's glare shine unobstructed on the edge of the highway. At this elevation, too, the heat of day wouldn't reach the scorching temperatures suffered by the scrub-desert ranchers living 50 miles east. A burst of rain could take several days to dry out, particularly if any other precipitation came along to refresh the dowsing.

Overnight fog, too, extending well past sunrise, often coated vast expanses of the Cascades. He'd dodged enough frightened deer on the highway to know that.

But if someone had stopped here to, say, wash mud or blood off their hands, that would also explain the puddles. Of course, they'd have had to know in advance to bring a jug of water. But a person with premeditated murder on their minds might do just that.

He knelt by the puddle and focused on the tire tracks left in the mud. The tread pattern appeared...unique. Not the typical zig-zag of most all-weather tires. Deep, V-shaped ridges flared out from a half-dozen ribs, shallower on the side farthest from the highway—what should be the inside of the tire. He checked the other puddle and found a similar pattern, but in reverse, again on the inside of the tire. Shallower ridges indicated uneven tire wear—a car out of alignment.

Like George McBride's classic 1990s New Yorker.

Which sported custom, imported tires.

That needed replacement.

Lehigh grimaced, letting it sink in. Without a doubt, George had been to this site in recent days. He'd gotten out of his car, lost a cuff link, and had been in too big of a hurry—or it had been too dark—to retrieve it.

He thought back to the campaign fundraiser. He closed his eyes and summoned the image of George McBride. Hadn't George lost a cuff link that night? Had he ever recovered it?

***

Lehigh returned to his truck and slid the cuff link into a sandwich-sized plastic bag he'd now grown accustomed to storing in the back seat of his pickup. He'd started the habit when he all too often found himself lacking for doggie scoop bags. Until now, he'd never had to use one for preserving evidence.

He closed the door of the truck, locked it, and crossed the gravel lot back to the spot he'd found the cuff link. He stepped into a clearing in the brush, the dogs one step behind on either side. He followed a series of gaps in the brush and trees, along what appeared to be a lesser-used path roughly parallel to the main trail off to his left. A few hundred yards in, a stream interrupted their path. On the main trail that he'd taken the first time to the murder scene, state land managers had installed and covered a culvert to allow the current to flow under the trail, allowing both hikers and water to continue uninterrupted. On this makeshift path, however, the stream widened to a slow-moving shallow pool some five feet wide. Lehigh could easily hop across without getting wet.

But a shorter, older, heavier man? Probably not.

The dogs splashed into the stream, lapping up the cold

mountain spring water on their way. Again, Lucky stopped on the far bank, her nose almost inserted into the mud. Diamond bounded into the woods, oblivious. Lehigh hopped across to the far bank, next to Lucky, and spied her discovery: a well-formed footprint of a man's dress shoe, size 8 or 9, an inch or so deep into the mud. The kind of print an older, heavier man would make if he'd, say, tried to jump across the stream, landed short, then hopped forward to spare his expensive shoes from being ruined in the chilly stream.

He freed his own stuck boot, shooed Lucky out of the way, and snapped a photo of the footprint with his cell phone. Then another, this time placing a pair of business cards from his wallet in an L-shape near the heel, for scale. And another, just to be sure, with the cards placed near the toe.

He picked up the cards, wiped off the mud, and jotted down the date, time, and rough location on the back. Slipped them into his hankie, then put the hankie in his back pocket. He sighed. He'd need to check with the forensics team to see if they'd been over this way. If not, they'd need to.

The dogs followed Lehigh deeper into the forest, toward the clearing where the deputies had found the body. The welcome smell of pine needles and damp vegetation cleared his sinuses. He loved the smell of the forest: home, for Lehigh, and much preferred to the stink of polluting cars, perfumed boutiques, and antiseptic department stores that filled even small cities like Clarkesville. And he loved the quiet.

He paused to listen. Birds chirped and cawed in the skies overhead. Squirrels chattered in branches rustling in the light breeze. Somewhere nearby, a ground critter scampered for cover. The sounds of silence, of nature. Of home.

Chapter Five

Deputy District Attorney Raymond Ferguson, a.k.a "The Reverend" to his detractors, studied the coroner's report on his desk with a skeptical eye. While he had no particular beef with Dr. Herman Doskey, or reason to doubt his competence, he had strong reason to doubt that the coroner would capture all of the relevant details of the case.

For one thing, Mt. Hood County's murder rate had maintained a steady level of zero for most of the past two decades. Having two murders in a single year amounted to a veritable crime wave. The good doctor's private practice thrived, based on his ability to give flu shots, set casts on broken bones, and refer more complex cases to specialists in Bend or Portland. His forensic skills, though, had likely gotten rusty in recent years.

Second, Ferguson had, as he liked to think of it, obtained some insider knowledge of the case.

Then again, how complex an analysis could anyone expect? Two gunshot wounds, the first to the leg—*had* to have been first, the coroner noted, given all of the bleeding—and one to the heart, at close range. A first-year med student would have seen that.

Or, an experienced prosecutor with inside knowledge.

Three raps on his office door interrupted his concentration. "Mr. Ferguson?" The voice of his legal assistant, Ginger Michaels, leaked through the door.

"Come in, my dear." The door opened halfway, and Ginger's

abundant red curls and even more abundant smile became visible in the space of the doorway. "Come in, come in," he said. "Don't be shy."

Ginger ducked her head but pushed the door wide, then closed it behind her. She wobbled across Ferguson's office in three-inch spike heels, with which the top of her puffy 1980s hairdo might have reached an elevation close to five feet six— four feet six of it legs, by Raymond's estimation. Long, toned, and pale, they seemed to reach up to her chin.

He shuddered at the thought. *"A man who looks at a woman with lustful intent has already committed adultery with her in his heart,"* sayeth the Lord.

He sighed. Office rules mandated that dresses and skirts reach below the knee, but Raymond could not bring himself to admonish his assistant over the dangerously high hems and low necklines she seemed to prefer. After all, she worked hard, and minded her own business. Who was he to complain if she wanted to share her God-given gifts with the world?

She stood in front of his desk, hands fidgeting in front of her pale blue dress, and pushed her oversized blue-framed glasses back up the bridge of her nose. "Commissioner Jackson is here for your two p.m. meeting," she said in a weak, nasal voice. "Shall I show them in?"

"Them?" Raymond tore his gaze away from her legs for a moment. "The commissioner brought a colleague with him?"

"Not another commissioner, sir. Miss McBride."

Ferguson feigned surprise. "Stacy McBride? Why?"

Ginger's face reddened. "N-no, sir. Not Stacy. Her cousin, Teresa. The fire chief's daughter?" Her expression shifted, as if she'd just tasted something bitter.

Raymond suppressed a smile. Good. Jackson had questioned his request to bring the young assistant along, but Ferguson had his reasons.

For one, her position and personal connections in the county gave her access to information and people he needed in times like these.

Two, the petty feud between Ginger and Teresa amused him. But he preferred to conceal his mirth, lest he offend his dutiful aide. The Good Lord knows, finding a replacement for her as competent, loyal, and pleasing to the eye would be as likely as discovering another murder in quiet little Clarkesville. "I'll never understand," he said instead, "how she became secretary to the County Commission. A girl so plain and slow-witted."

Ginger stepped closer, checked her surroundings, and whispered, "It's her name, sir. Her whole life she's traded on being a McBride. Everyone says if her name had been Smith or Jones, I'd have been named Lumber Queen instead of her."

"I've heard that as well," Raymond said, crossing his fingers under his desk. "But perhaps we've kept them waiting long enough?" He closed the coroner's report and gestured with an open palm toward the door. "Please invite them to join me. Perhaps you could bring in a tray of coffee and tea for our guests?"

Her eyes narrowed. "Sir, I have cases to research. Are you sure this is an appropriate assignment for me?"

He wiped a bead of sweat off his brow. "I thought you might like to join us in the meeting," he said. "But if you'd rather I ask someone else—"

"No, no, of course not." A proud smile crossed Ginger's face, and she glided out of the room. Ferguson chuckled, wondering what foreign substance might find its way into Teresa McBride's coffee. In any event, the errand would keep her busy while making her feel included. Perfect stagecraft.

Moments later, Chairman Elliott Jackson strutted into the room with a young woman close behind. Her slight frame and jet-black hair could not have contrasted more against Jackson's white-haired, voluminous presence. The Chairman's trademark pinstripe suit, at least one or two sizes too tight, reminded Raymond of a globe, appearing to widen at his equator-like waist and converging on his snow-capped head and shiny white shoes. Teresa McBride, even more slender than her older cousin, looked ready to fly away like a kite in the slightest breeze. Her almond-colored knee-length dress exaggerated her minimal curves, and shoulder-length jet-black hair shone against her smooth, porcelain-white skin.

"Raymond, my friend, thank you for seeing us on such short notice." Jackson extended a pudgy palm. Ferguson gripped the wet, clammy paw and gave it a firm shake. Jackson gestured toward his assistant, urging her forward. "And I believe you know the commission's secretary, Ms. McBride?"

"I've had the pleasure." Raymond gestured them into seats perched in front of his desk. "Ginger," he called out to his assistant, "are the refreshments ready?"

Ginger appeared in the office doorway with a dark grimace on her face, her gaze averted from him. She set a tray on an oak table against one wall of the office and her eyes shot angry darts at Teresa. In a restrained voice, she asked, "How do you like your coffee, Commissioner?"

"Black, please."

Ginger poured and brought full cups to Jackson and Ferguson, then stirred cream into a third, took a small sip and headed toward a chair.

Raymond cleared his throat. "And for Ms. McBride?"

Ginger stared at Raymond. Pure poison.

"I'll have green tea, please," Teresa said with a plastic smile.

"Oh, dear," Ginger said, no hint of a smile remaining. "I'll need to run back to the break room for a tea service. It might take a few extra minutes." She sped out of the room before anyone could reply.

"Well, then, now that the room is *secure*," Teresa said, "we can get down to business."

Ferguson and Jackson exchanged glances, and let the moment pass.

"Commissioner," Raymond said, "I do appreciate your coming this morning. We need to discuss the murder investigation. I think we have a jurisdiction problem."

Jackson smiled. "I agree. And I'm getting a lot of heat from my constituents." He sipped his coffee. "They're anxious to see this killer brought to justice. And, I'm afraid, our new sheriff had little progress to report at our hearing yesterday."

The Reverend nodded. This pleased him very much. "That, I'm afraid, is what we must expect when we put amateurs in charge of such sensitive and vital operations. Now, I like Mr. Carter, but—"

"You do?"

Raymond paused and smiled. "He's agreeable enough."

"He's an idiot," Teresa said. She did not cower when both men turned to stare at her.

"That's not an unpopular opinion," Raymond said with a chuckle. "But he is well-liked, and the local population seems to trust him."

"They're idiots, too," Teresa said.

"Now, now." Jackson shrugged at Raymond. "I apologize for my assistant. She can be a bit impolitic."

Ferguson cleared his throat. "I have my own people working on the case. We're, uh, cooperating with the sheriff, of course, as the taxpayers have a right to expect."

"While exercising appropriate discretion, I hope, to avoid leaks and misperceptions?" Jackson's tone grew foreboding. "I wouldn't want our new sheriff to run off half-cocked, arresting the wrong people based on rumor or insufficient evidence."

"I assure you, we are constructing our case carefully, and only sharing information that we can verify and which constructs a plausible narrative." Raymond adjusted his sitting position, suddenly unable to find a comfortable posture in the chair.

"On that front, I am curious," Jackson said, "as to whether you've come closer than our novice sheriff on identifying a culprit?"

"We are pursuing some very promising leads, but haven't yet—"

"My uncle George did it!" Teresa's words exploded out of her. "He hated Ev Downey for what he did to his daughter—or what he thinks he did. God knows, Stacy never had a problem getting naked in front of men!"

The two men exchanged glances, Jackson's one of apparent

surprise. Ferguson guessed that his own expression matched the chairman's. "Do you have evidence supporting this claim?" he asked. "Other than the obvious motive."

"Uncle George owns dozens of guns," Teresa said. "And he's a crack shot. I bet dollars to donuts he owns the gun that killed Downey—and that he pulled the trigger!"

"Has the murder weapon been found?" Jackson asked.

"No," Ferguson said with a cough, "but ballistics believes they've identified the weapon. A 30-30 Winchester hunting rifle, common among elk and deer hunters in this area." Ferguson paused, not wanting to disclose too much. "Two shots—the fatal one being a shot to the heart."

"A professional, then, perhaps?" Jackson asked, appearing surprised.

Ferguson shook his head. "No. One to the heart, following a wounding shot to the leg. No head shot, but evidence of a fine marksman, at that distance." No need to reveal just yet that the second shot was point blank. "Not inconsistent with what young Ms. McBride here claims."

"Senator McBride is both an excellent marksman with a rifle, and the furthest thing imaginable from a professional hit man," Jackson said, nodding at Teresa.

"Uncle George tried to put Mr. Downey out of business early in his career," Teresa said. "He always went on about how we didn't need 'his kind' around here."

"I don't doubt his motive," Raymond said. "But he is hardly alone in having a reason to want Mr. Downey to disappear. The question is whether there is any physical evidence connecting him to the crime." Which, Raymond knew, there was, and plenty.

"Check his guns," Teresa said. "I'm telling you, it was his gun."

"I'll need probable cause," Raymond said.

Jackson scowled. "You're sounding like Lehigh Carter now, making excuses."

"Don't compare me to that bumbling amateur!" The

Reverend's voice took on an edge of steel. Fire and brimstone, some might say, and this time, he might not disagree. "And don't tell me how to do my job."

"Why not?" Teresa said. "Everyone tells Commissioner Jackson how to do his!"

"Now, Teresa," Jackson said. "I've told you before: as an elected official, that just comes with the territory." He plastered a campaign-trail smile across his face and returned his attention to Ferguson. "In my zeal for prompt justice for our unfortunate victim, I can tell that I've overstepped my bounds. Please forgive me."

"Nothing to forgive, Commissioner. I value your input."

Jackson nodded and stood. "I think we've accomplished our mission in coming here today. Please keep us apprised of the situation as it develops. You know you have my support in conducting your investigation, wherever it may lead. If it leads you cross-wise with our *acting* sheriff, well, rest assured, I will support the county's long-term *professionals* over inexperienced interlopers every time." He bowed his head, extended his hand, and helped Teresa out of her chair. "And do thank your young assistant for the coffee."

"It's a shame," Teresa said with a hard smile, "I wasn't able to thank her for the tea."

They saw themselves to the door, where Ginger met them, carrying a tea service. "Oh, am I too late?" she said, a tinge of disappointment in her voice.

"Next time, we'll talk slower," Teresa said with a sneer, "so you can keep up."

"I'm sorry. Our teapot is dreadfully slow." Ginger slid aside so they could leave.

"I wasn't talking about the teapot," Teresa said. "But if you're going to eavesdrop, don't wait by the door. Next time, just come on in."

Ginger watched them leave, seething, then spun toward Ferguson. "Pity," she said. "I wasted a perfectly good mouthful of spit on her teacup."

She stormed out of the room, and Raymond burst into

laughter.

***

The crime scene stood out in the forest, not only from the bright sunshine concentrated in the golden-brown grasses, tufts of seeding dandelions, and dying milkweed, but also from the glaring reflection of sunshine off the plastic yellow tape that still roped off the area. "Police Line—Do Not Cross," read the block letters on the tape, over and over for hundreds of yards, even in the tight double loops it formed around trees on the perimeter. Lehigh ordered the dogs to sit and stay, then stared at the edge of the scene, looking for clues, or maybe ideas—he really wasn't sure which. Something to give him a new direction in the case.

But nothing came. The scene had been scoured by the forensics team, every square foot examined and photographed. Lehigh realized that he stood in the area where the gunman had pulled the trigger, according to the investigative team. They'd recovered one shell casing, taken plaster casts of footprints, and recovered a few strands of fabric snagged by the brush. The victim had fallen on the opposite, western edge of the clearing, near where it intersected the main trail. The lead detective on the case, Clayton Maddox, had surmised that the killer ambushed Downey as he entered the clearing, shooting without warning from a distance of about 150 yards. Ballistics would need to confirm his theory of a rifle shot, but at that distance, even a rifleman would have needed a scope. A shooter with a handgun would have needed blind dumb luck. The casing from the bullet responsible for the second wound hadn't been found, and nobody had found evidence of a miss.

The question plaguing Lehigh, and hampering the investigation, remained. *Why?* The ambush suggested premeditation. Someone had lured Downey to the spot somehow, and had had enough advance knowledge of his arrival to set up the ambush. The late hour of the murder suggested an arranged meeting, an invitation—a ruse. No spontaneity about this case. None.

He closed his eyes, imagining the scene in darkness. The winding, rough path he'd followed, with its many obstructions—the stream, the switchbacks, the fallen logs— would have made the hike treacherous at night, particularly for someone carrying a rifle in his hands. That would have handicapped him—or her—in moments where climbing over or moving obstacles became necessary. Someone who planned a careful ambush would, therefore, either carry a flashlight— another item to occupy the hands—or would have had to come before sunset. But even then, he—or she—would have had to make their escape in the dark. And, having just killed a man, they'd want to leave in a hurry.

He was missing something. Something obvious. It gnawed at the back of his brain, but remained hidden, like the ground squirrels whose chatter subsided as he passed.

What was it?

***

"What do we have on the Downey case?" Ray Ferguson stretched his legs and set them on a low table tucked into the corner behind his desk. He glanced sideways at his young legal assistant. Fresh-faced, eager, innocent, and... So. Darned. Pretty. That red hair, and that dress—wow. Hard to imagine she'd lost that beauty pageant years before—unless she'd worn those horrible blue-framed glasses that obscured her entire head.

Ginger was capable enough. She'd graduated tenth in her class two months before from Lewis & Clark Law School in Portland, although she hadn't distinguished herself among her peers in any way: no law review articles, no mock trial victories, no volunteer service. Just a studious, nose-to-the-grindstone student, smart but introverted, ambitious but suffering from self-esteem issues. Perfect, in other words. Raymond needed cheap help, and top-of-the-class attorneys brimming with confidence didn't often submit resumes to tiny public law offices in the Oregon Cascades. Luckily, she'd returned home after graduating to stay close to her family.

"We don't have a lot," Ginger said, pushing her glasses back up to the bridge of nose. Her nasal monotone made Ferguson wince inside. Despite her pleasant appearance, he could never let this woman present an argument in court—certainly not to a jury. "We have some fabric—threads, really—recovered from the crime scene that need to be analyzed, some man's size eight-and-a-half footprints, a bullet casing being evaluated by Ballistics, and a few tire tracks that could match a thousand vehicles in the area. No witnesses, and a lot of people with motives."

"Give me those," Ferguson said. "Start at the top."

"Downey has only one surviving relative, a niece in California he hasn't seen in twenty years." She wrinkled her nose. That made her glasses slide down again, and she pushed them back up with an unpolished fingernail, then continued reading from her file. "He has over two dozen known business partners with whom he owned over fifty properties—and rumor has it, the list of unknown partners is a lot longer than the ones we know."

Ferguson nodded. "That's a fact. Downey had his fingers in everything around here."

She scrunched up her face into a look of disapproval. "Some of the businesses, even the known ones, were kind of shady. Strip clubs, casinos, cheap hotels—I can't imagine what he'd hide, if those are what he claimed publicly."

Ferguson chuckled. "Good point," he said. "Now, tell me what we've got on Senator George McBride."

She blinked. "N–nothing, sir."

He set his feet on the floor, leaned forward with his elbows on the desk, and fixed her with a hot stare. "Well, then. That's something we need to change."

Chapter Six

Though Lehigh couldn't have imagined how, the morning newspapers brought Bruce Bailey's recent sensationalist charges about him to even more ridiculous heights.

"SHERIFF INVOLVED IN COVER-UP?" the two-inch headline blared above the fold, with a fifteen-inch story below it and more on the inside pages.

"What the hell would I be covering up?" Lehigh shouted at the *Clarkesville News-Clarion* unfolded in his hands. "And what's this got to do with George McBride?"

Stacy appeared in her robe behind him in the doorway leading to their front steps, holding two mugs of fresh coffee steaming slightly less than Lehigh. "They're linking my father to this?" she asked, pushing the storm door open with her foot. "How? And more importantly, why?" She handed him a cup of coffee. Diamond and Lucky bounded out the door into the yard and found their favorite bushes, then chased each other around the side of the house, barking as if an army of squirrels had invaded the backyard. Which, Lehigh realized, might well be the case.

He sipped the delicious brew and showed her the paper. Under the headline appeared a photo of George with his arm around Lehigh, a picture taken, judging by Lehigh's jacket and tie, at the recent fund-raising gala kicking off Lehigh's election campaign. The caption under the photo read: "New Sheriff Protecting Family From Suspicion?"

"That's crazy!" Stacy grabbed the paper from him and sat on the two-seat swinging rocker perched to one side of the small front porch. Lehigh joined her.

"It says I'm suppressing the release of evidence to the District Attorney's office," Lehigh said, reading over her shoulder. "What a load of crap! I give them everything we've got—which, admittedly, isn't much."

"I don't get why they say my father's implicated in the Ev Downey murder." Stacy unfolded the newspaper to full length. "Dad avoided Downey like the plague. Ever since—uh, oh." She pointed to a paragraph buried deep in the article. Lehigh read the text:

> *Reliable sources, who asked to remain anonymous, assert that among Downey's few enemies was the recently disgraced Senator George McBride, who was quoted publicly describing Mr. Downey as a "smut dealer" and a scourge that should be removed from the community.*

"Few enemies?" Lehigh said. "The guy didn't have a true friend outside of the state penitentiary. Maybe a few in the legislature, but they're practically the same people."

"Hush." Stacy gave him a playful slap. "This is serious. This newspaper is implying that my father wanted Ev Downey killed. That's ridiculous!"

"Well, your dad did let his tongue get a little loose the other night," Lehigh said, "at the party."

"Lehigh Carter! This is your father-in-law we're talking about!"

Lehigh held his breath. She was near tears, and her bewilderment tempted him to tell her about the cuff link and tire tracks he'd found at the scene. But he hadn't yet logged that evidence, or shared it with Wadsworth or Maddox. He eased the air out of his lungs and met her gaze. "Sorry. I'm not saying he did it. Just that he gave them a little too much material to work with. But that ain't evidence of anything."

"He's a public figure," she said. "Every move he makes gets

hyper-analyzed and second-guessed. That doesn't make him a murderer."

Again, he suppressed the gut reaction to respond with what he knew. Instead he read further into the article, and soon his own blood boiled.

"Favoritism? What a crock!" He smacked the newspaper out of Stacy's hands to the floor. Stacy snatched it up and spread the article in front of her.

"How ridiculous!" she said. "They're insinuating that the only reason my father's not in jail is that you're holding the keys—and that you can't be trusted to keep him in there if he *was* arrested, because you two are so close. That's wrong on so many levels!"

"They sure as hell never listened to us at dinner at your mom's house, if they think that," Lehigh said.

"Maybe they should join us at dinner," Stacy said. "They'd wonder how you both survived this long."

"Bite your tongue," he said. "The more of them, the less there is for me. Besides, I never want to break bread with the likes of Bruce Bailey and his dopey mimics here in the *News-Clarion*. Even your father's better company than those yahoos."

"Hey, careful. You were just getting back on my good side."

He grinned, the tension easing out of him, and wrapped an arm around her narrow waist. "All sides of you are good."

"Yeah, but you like to play favorites," she said, grinning.

"Indeed I do." He nuzzled her neck and planted kisses along the loose neckline of her robe. She laughed and pushed him away. "I've got to get to work. And so do you. You've got to figure out who really committed the murder and get the media off my father's back."

Lehigh sighed and followed her inside to the living room. "Unless it has the opposite effect," he mumbled.

"What's that?"

He cleared his throat. "I, uh, said I'd much rather we both called in sick today."

"Don't you dare!" She darted into the bathroom. "The minute you let down your guard, you know these goons will succeed in their witch hunt. My father needs you—and I need you—to find the true culprit. Come on, Lehigh. A killer's on the loose. What if he kills again?"

"If the victim's name rhymes with Goose Gailey, I might be okay with it." He stood in the doorway of the bathroom, watching her adjust the shower temperature. "But I can tell, your mind's made up. So, off to work we go."

She grinned, dropped her robe and sashayed into the shower, giving Lehigh another moment's distraction from the grim work that lay ahead.

He went outside to retrieve the dogs, still thinking about the news article. The public had a right to be frustrated. He had no leads, other than George McBride, as weak as that one was. Or, he had too many, which amounted to the same thing. Everett Downey had earned a reputation for ruthlessness in business, and even Lehigh's cursory review of the many lawsuits filed against the man over the past two decades yielded a virtual *Who's Who* of Clarkesville's business community. He also had engaged in behind-the-scenes politics, and his personal life remained obscure: he had no family, few close friends, and kept his own name out of the press, until recently. Few people had liked Ev Downey, but fewer admitted publicly to hating him.

Except, recently, George McBride.

Lehigh sighed. Off to work, indeed.

***

The discoveries at the crime scene and questions they raised preoccupied Lehigh while he drove up Brady Mountain Road to his property where his house once stood. The cuff link in particular bothered him, not only because it put George McBride at the scene, but because it contradicted everything Lehigh had said and believed about his father-in-law. Lehigh had stumbled onto evidence of McBride's campaign finance fraud a year before, destroying his gubernatorial bid, and the senator had gone to war against him, but had stopped short of personally engaging in violence.

He'd had no problem farming it out to others, however. His overzealous minions had reduced Lehigh's home to cinders almost a year before. But today, the months of waiting for the insurance settlement, designing a new house, getting permits, and finding a suitable contractor would end. The day had come when the contractor would begin work. Lehigh had confirmed their planned eight a.m. start the night before, by phone. His truck clock read 8:15. He'd hoped to get there before the contractor—no point in having them wait around for him to arrive—but the newspaper stories had distracted him much more than he'd realized.

He turned off the highway onto the gravel drive leading to his property. Low-hanging branches brushed the roof of his pickup. He'd neglected to trim them back since the fire—he'd need to get on that so the larger construction vehicles could pass without breaking them, or damaging the vehicles. That is, if his job ever allowed him a day off to get the trimming done.

His mood lifted in expectation of beginning the construction of the new house. The old structure, a 1950s ranch, had suffered from age, despite his diligent upkeep. Old pipes, old wiring, old wood siding, and three layers of asphalt roofing couldn't have withstood the damp Oregon weather much longer anyhow. The fire had disrupted his life and cost him plenty, but it also created an opportunity to start fresh and give his bride the joy of living in someplace new.

He had very little new in his life, materially speaking. He drove an old truck—always had. He seldom bought new clothes, and Stacy had given up on buying anything for him, since he never wore what she bought. He preferred calculators and manual typewriters over computers and soft, broken-in sofas and mattresses. His TV, lost in the fire, had knobs and buttons he actually had to touch to change channels or volume. Even his toaster was a hand-me-down.

Hell, even the new things in his life were old. Stacy, his new bride, was an old flame from twelve years before. Lucky, who he'd adopted a year ago, was four or five, middle-aged for a dog. His job felt old the second day he sat at the desk. Only Diamond, the border collie puppy, had yet to celebrate a birthday.

But soon he'd have something new: a house.

Or, he realized when his job site came into view, not.

He parked his truck at the end of the driveway. His *empty* driveway. No contractors to be found.

He pulled out his cell phone and speed-dialed the contractor.

"Hey. You've reached Melvin of Crabb Tree Construction. I'm sorry I can't take your—"

Lehigh pressed the "pound" key, resisting the urge to actually pound the phone. After the beep, he said, "Mr. Crabb, Lehigh Carter. I'm at the site, thought you'd be here waiting for me. Did plans change?" He left his number and hung up.

He got out of the truck, breathed in the crisp mountain air. He missed being able to do that every morning, living in Stacy's suburban home. Her two-acre property, while large for an in-town location, still felt cramped and crowded by too-close neighbors. Before moving in with her, Lehigh had never lived closer than a half-mile to his nearest neighbor, an experience Maw had characterized as "city living." Any place where he could hear the neighbor's car backfire was too crowded for Lehigh.

He circumnavigated the charred remains of his house. Most of the walls, and all of the roof, had collapsed in the rainy months following the fire. It would take the contractor days, maybe weeks, to clear the rubble before they could rebuild. Already they ran the risk of not finishing the exterior shell before the rains came in fall. A delayed start would almost ensure it.

That damned cuff link just bugged him. He needed some resolution there. On a whim, he speed-dialed the McBrides. "Consuela?" he said upon recognizing her voice. "May I speak to George?"

"He is not in, Señor Lehigh. Is there a message?"

Perfect. Maybe he could find out without alerting the senator to his snooping. "Consuela, do you happen to know if George ever found that cuff link he lost the night of my fund-raiser?" Lehigh asked.

"I don't think so," she said. "I will ask him this evening if you like."

"No, no," he said. "I, uh, was thinking maybe I'll replace them for him, as a surprise for his next birthday."

"He would like that!" Consuela said. "I will keep your secret."

He called Melvin Crabb again, and again got voice mail. This time he didn't leave a message. He needed to get to the office anyway—the County's law enforcement business would not wait. He cursed his decision to take the damned job and returned to his truck. He found paper, jotted down a quick note for the contractor, and taped it to the once-intact section of dark brown siding on the front of his house. The bright white paper stuck out like a pimple on the cheek of the Lumber Queen. Hell, NASA could probably see it from space.

He drove to the sheriff's office, breaking most of the speed limits the county paid him to enforce, still wrestling with guilt over not sharing the evidence of the cuff link and footprint he'd found. If it came out that he'd sat on his findings, his critics' claims of him hiding evidence would look pretty believable.

He made it to his desk before nine-thirty. Deputy Ted Roscoe followed him from the reception area to his office up the hall.

"District Attorney's office called," Roscoe said. "Five, six times. They said it's urgent."

"Did they say that on the fifth call or the sixth?" Lehigh hung his hat on the rack in the corner and booted up his stupid computer.

"All of 'em. I reckon they expected you sooner."

"Yeah, I reckon that too. Did they say what it's about?"

"Something about a ballistical report."

"*Ballistics.*" Lehigh sighed. "Did they send one over?"

"Uh, I'll go check." Roscoe hurried out. Before the door closed behind him, Lehigh's desk phone rang. Two quick rings—an internal call. "This is Lee—uh, Sheriff Carter."

"Sheriff, this is Julia at the front desk. The, uh, District Attorney's office is on the line. He's called several times—"

"Yeah, I know. Patch him through." Something was eating The Reverend up this morning. Might as well find out what.

"Mr. Carter? Ray Ferguson."

"You've been busy this morning, Raymond."

"Did you get my messages? About the suspect? We need to make an arrest, ASAP. Now, I understand if you—"

"Slow down, Ray. Who's the suspect? What's the sudden interest in locking someone up? Do you know something I don't?" Lehigh cringed at his unintended open invitation for a cheap shot, but Ferguson didn't take the bait.

"Have you seen the ballistics report?" Ferguson said. "I've been in touch with Detective Maddox and he's ready to go, but given the, ah, sensitive nature of this case, we didn't want to proceed without you knowing."

"Not yet." Lehigh circled his desk, pulled open his office door, and craned his neck to give himself a wider view of the hallway. No sign of his deputy. He covered the phone. "Roscoe? You got that report for me?"

"I'll give you the Cliff's Notes version," Ferguson said. "The report identified the weapon as a Winchester 30-30 rifle. Very unique set of identifying marks on this weapon. Probably an antique."

"And?" Something gnawed at him. He should know why this was important, but he couldn't bring it to mind.

"And there's identifying records on file. We have an exact match. We must test it again to confirm, of course, but I have no doubt about who owns and possesses this weapon." The Reverend cleared his throat. "We've got a warrant for a search of the owner's home, but, well, we wondered if you wanted to be present. There's a very strong likelihood it will lead to an arrest."

"Of whom? Who owns a gun like that?"

Lehigh waved Roscoe in, who'd just reappeared in his open doorway. Roscoe handed him the report and Lehigh scanned it. He turned to the page containing a photo of a Winchester lever-action 30-30. He'd seen this type of weapon before. Recently, in fact.

On the wall of the den in the house of—

"Your father-in-law," Ferguson said. "Senator George Lindsey McBride."

Chapter Seven

Lehigh's phone rang in the middle of a tough afternoon spent writing a summary report of open cases due to the County Commission the day before. He hated writing and struggled with it. No doubt the two facts were related, but report writing was an important part of the job—another aspect Jim Wadsworth had failed to mention when he recruited Lehigh for the post a few months before.

He hated interruptions almost as much as writing reports—*almost*. He slid the keyboard aside and picked up the receiver. "Carter here."

"Sheriff, it's Bruce Bailey. How are you doing today?"

Lehigh grimaced. A bad day was about to get worse. He suppressed a silent curse at Julia for letting the call through and put as much pep in his voice as he could muster. "Still on the right side of the black bars, so I guess I'm okay. You?"

Bailey guffawed. "Good one, Sheriff! Can I print that?"

Lehigh cringed. When reporters acted like sycophants, they needed information that they should not have. "Only on the funny pages. What can I do you out of, Bruce?"

"Do me out of—hilarious!" Bailey brayed again. "You know, Mr. Carter, if this law enforcement thing doesn't work out for you, you could give comedy a try."

"I'll keep it in mind. So, did you call just to compliment my stand-up routine, or is there some higher purpose to this conversation?" Lehigh hit *Save* on his document and wondered why Julia hadn't sent this call to voicemail. What a waste of time. A window popped up, asking for a filename, defaulting to

"Document1."

"I like that, Mr. Carter—you're all business. Okay, let's see. Got my notes ri-i-ight here." Paper shuffling noises sounded in the background. "Yes, here we go. On the Downey murder—"

"Bruce, you know I can't comment on an ongoing investigation."

Bailey's voice took on a pleading tone. "Come on, Sheriff. Just some basics. Do you have a suspect?"

"If we had a suspect, would I tell you? I might as well tell the suspect himself."

"Oh, so you think it's a man?" Scribbling noises and more shuffling of paper.

"Mr. Bailey, don't put words in my mouth."

"Aren't they almost always men?" Bailey breathed into the phone. Lehigh had a sudden urge to clean his ear.

"I wish you'd all have thought of that when you dragged Stacy through the mud earlier this year on the Jared Barkley case." A message popped up on his computer screen: he had a meeting in fifteen minutes.

"Proves my point," Bailey said. "She wasn't guilty after all. Now, speaking of the McBrides, I've been told her father is the subject of your investigation. Can you verify that?"

Lehigh swore under his breath and clicked *Sleep* on the meeting notification. "Who told you that?"

"I don't divulge my sources. You know that."

"What I know," Lehigh said, "is that your sources are often unreliable."

"Are they in this case?" Bailey asked.

"No comment."

"I see. Well, Sheriff, were you aware that Mr. Downey and Senator McBride had business dealings in the past—"

"Everybody's had business dealings with Downey. He owned half the town."

"—And the two men met secretly shortly before the murder?"

"Again, where are you getting this information?" Lehigh's blood pressure rose another notch. Nobody had told *him* about any secret meeting.

"And the coroner found elevated levels of alcohol in Mr. Downey's blood, is that correct?"

"So? He owns like ten bars, doesn't he?" Lehigh shook his head. Conspiracies under every rock with this yahoo.

"Speaking of which, can you confirm that Mr. Downey had applied for new liquor permits, allegedly for a string of new strip clubs he was planning?" Bailey asked.

"Where did you get—Look. Bruce. Again. I'm sorry. I can't comment. Okay? I have to go." The meeting notification reappeared on his screen.

"Just one more quest—"

Lehigh hung up and clicked his mouse on the notification window. Nothing happened. He clicked again. And again. The computer didn't respond. He pounded a few keys—

The screen flashed. The notification window disappeared—along with his document. The report that he'd slaved over for hours. The one he hadn't yet saved, much less backed up, and that had taken all day to write.

Gone.

His head dropped into his hands. His temples throbbed, and he massaged them, to no avail. A headache loomed at the front of his skull.

His computer beeped. Against his better wisdom, he glanced at the screen.

"Crime Report Meeting with County Commission: Overdue."

He sagged into his chair, defeated.

***

Lehigh arrived to work the next morning well before his habitual 7 a.m. start. His many years in the logging industry had ingrained in him the early-to-bed, early-to-rise habit—or, rather, reinforced the practice Pappy and Maw raised him on. He loved the quiet of the morning before the noise of civilization intruded and, as an added bonus, he loved sunrises.

Arriving before the day watch gave him quiet time in the office to tend to the hard tasks of the day, those that required intense concentration. Thinking time, as Pappy called it. At the moment, he had plenty to think about, most of it centered around rebuilding his burned-down house and solving the Ev Downey murder.

He'd called the missing building contractors on the drive in, taking advantage of their own tendency to start early, and elicited apologies for their no-show the day before and new unreliable promises to begin work right away. That left the even-less fun murder topic for the rest of the morning.

The smell of a fresh, dark roast lured him into the break room, and he poured himself a cup of coffee before heading into his office. While stirring in the cream and sugar, a voice in the hallway caught his attention. A voice, he realized, that didn't belong.

The voice of Assistant District Attorney Raymond Ferguson.

"I've requested the information several times," Ferguson said. "Detective Wadsworth knows I need the file. I don't understand why it takes so long to get information these days. When Buck Summers was sheriff—"

"Sheriff Carter does things *different*," came the sarcastic reply. A male voice, fading, as if moving away from the break room. "But if there's any way I can help, you let me know."

Lehigh's ears perked up. The deputy, whose voice he could not identify, seemed to be promising to provide information outside of proper channels. Or was he? He sipped his coffee and took a step toward the break room doorway.

Ferguson's voice came again, also fading away. "I like the way you think. The law is the law, and we're all *partners* in enforcing the law, don't you agree, Deputy? *Judge your neighbor fairly,'* saith the Lord."

Something about the way he said it sounded suspicious. As if he meant something very different than the spoken words...and that he expected the deputy to understand. Speaking in code only they would understand—and not someone listening in from, say, the break room.

"I do agree," the deputy responded. "I prefer when we do things the right way—professional and cooperative, you know? Like we used to."

The voiced faded away. Lehigh stepped into the corridor and glanced in the direction of the voices, just in time to spot Ferguson exiting through the heavy double doors to the lobby. A tall, broad-shouldered deputy with a dark buzz-cut, screened by Ferguson's own tall frame, slipped out of view a moment later. Lehigh took long, quick strides down the hall, but the door shut behind them long before he reached it. He pushed the door open with his free hand and glanced around the lobby.

Empty.

He crossed the lobby and exited the glass doors to the parking lot. A black sedan slithered past, driven by the assistant D.A. Ahead of it, a black and white Crown Victoria, its license plate and vehicle ID obscured by Ferguson's car, exited the lot and sped away.

Lehigh returned inside. The reception desk remained unstaffed. Odd. He hadn't noticed that when he first arrived. He pushed through the heavy double doors leading to the interior corridors and strolled down the hallway, checking offices and meeting rooms as he passed. All vacant. Nobody had shown up to work yet. Why? Even the graveyard shift should have a few uniforms on duty.

A door opened behind him. He turned to discover Jim Wadsworth exiting the men's room, wiping wet hands on his slacks. "We're out of paper towels again," he said. "What does it take to get the facilities crew in here once in a while?" He pulled a handkerchief from his pocket and blew his nose. "Stupid cold. Can't seem to get rid of it."

"Forget facilities. Shouldn't someone be at the front desk?" Lehigh asked, louder than he intended.

"I saw Julia out there earlier," Wadsworth said. "Roscoe should have been here a half-hour ago to take over. Where is that boy?"

"Probably out for a smoke." Lehigh spun around to check

the area, but saw no sign of Roscoe, nor of his administrative assistant, Julia.

"I took one day off to try to get better, and look what happens." Wadsworth blew his nose again.

"I just saw somebody pulling out of the lot, after talking in here with The Reverend, of all people," Lehigh said. "I didn't see who it was, though."

"What's Ray Ferguson doing here at seven in the morning?" Wadsworth hitched up his slacks, sagging below his bulging belly. "Usually he's at church at this hour."

"I was hoping you'd know. He was pumping someone for information about a case." Lehigh waved Wadsworth closer and continued in a quieter voice. "I don't know which one, but I'm willing to bet it's the Downey murder."

"In that case, it could be anyone," Wadsworth said. "Most of the department's helping out on it. I can't get any help on my own investigations, and nobody's working traffic anymore. And people are noticing. Just yesterday, I saw four people going sixty in a forty-five, and—"

"Where's the duty roster?" Lehigh said. "Usually it's here on the bulletin board." He pointed to a wall-mounted cork board on the wall beside them. The "Now On Duty" section remained empty.

"Julia must be reprinting it," Wadsworth said with a shrug. "I vaguely remember a few deputies went home sick yesterday. Some sort of summer flu."

"Yeah. The flu." Lehigh shook his head. "Angler's flu, no doubt. I hear the fish are biting."

Wadsworth grimaced. "Better not be. Damned cheaters. I'll write them up so fast—"

"Easy, Jim. The last thing I need right now is to give everyone around here another reason to hate me." Lehigh gestured with his coffee mug toward the break room. "Let me buy you a free cup of coffee."

Wadsworth grinned and clapped him on the back. "Last of the big-time spenders."

They walked side by side the short distance to the doorway.

Lehigh waited in the corridor while Wadsworth filled a cup from the pot. "Has Ferguson made a habit of hanging around here, mornings?" Lehigh asked.

"Not to my knowledge." Wadsworth leaned against the counter and sipped his coffee. An apple Danish somehow materialized in his other hand. "He's been getting regular briefings from the investigative team as we learn things, so far as I know. My impression is, we don't have a lot to give him."

"Have they returned the favor?" Lehigh asked. "Are they sharing what they know?"

Wadsworth shrugged and swallowed a bite of Danish. "Probably. They usually do. You'd have to ask Clayton."

Lehigh drained the rest of his cup and stepped in to the room to refill it. Movement behind him caught his attention, and he glanced around in time to see the slightly rounded figure of a brown-haired, forty-something woman strut past, clutching a sheet of paper.

"Julia, is that today's duty list?" Lehigh called out to her.

Julia poked her head around the doorway. Two long strands of hair fell in front of her face, and she blew them away with a quick puff of air. "Oh, hi, Sheriff. Detective. Yes, would you like to see it before I post it?" She handed Lehigh the paper.

He scanned the page and let out a low whistle. "Only four deputies on patrol today? And nobody at the desk? What gives?"

"Lots of guys called in sick," she said, "and Detective Maddox has four helping him on the Downey case. I thought I'd offer to work reception, if that's okay."

"Sure, sure. But we can't afford to put that many on Downey if we're this short-staffed. Reassign DuPont and Peters to patrol. And Julia, send Maddox in to see me as soon as he gets in. I need to make some changes, and I want him to hear it from me." He handed the page back to her.

She lowered her eyes, casting a quick glance at Wadsworth. "Yes, sir. You say so." She turned to leave.

"You have a problem with that?" Lehigh regretted his sharp tone and softened his voice. "I mean, why the long face?"

"I got no problem with it," she said. "But Detective Maddox is already out with Deputies Drummond and Kinney on patrol, interviewing witnesses."

Lehigh checked the clock. "At seven fifteen in the morning?"

Julia reddened. "It wasn't my doing, sir. W-would you like me to call them back in?"

Lehigh gritted his teeth. Always one step behind. "No. I'm sorry. Go ahead and post the duty sheet. But from now on, please let me see it first, before it gets posted."

"Yes, sir." She shuffled down the hall.

"You got any issues with that?" Lehigh asked Wadsworth.

The detective shook his head. "About time someone made some changes around here."

***

"What's this about a cuff link?"

Lehigh held the phone away from his ear, too late to salvage his aching eardrum. Raymond "The Reverend" Ferguson's loud rant continued, a torrent of syllables interspersed with the occasional recognizable word: "evidence... secret... inept..."

"Do you hear what I'm saying?" The Reverend concluded at last.

"I think they can hear you in New York," Lehigh said, "but unless you slow down and take a breath, ain't nobody gonna understand you, here nor there."

That set Ferguson off again, so Lehigh set the receiver down on his desk and went back to reviewing resumes of applicants for his open deputy positions. Twenty-two people applied for four jobs. In the forestry business it would have thrilled him to get six applicants to choose from, but at least half would have qualified for whatever job he'd offered. From this list, he'd be lucky to find four worth interviewing.

"So I want these questions answered, and now!" The Reverend's second rant ended with a giant intake of breath.

Lehigh picked up the phone and cleared his throat. "Mr. Ferguson, I'm always more than happy to share all of our evidence with you, on this and every case, as soon as it's been properly logged into our sys—"

"Logged, *shmogged.* You're sitting on evidence, Carter, and it's hampering the investigation. But that's what you want, isn't it? To protect your father-in-law? Well, it isn't going to work with me, Sheriff. I have eyes and I have ears, and my eyes and ears see and hear what's going on. And what I see and hear, I share with the people that need to know. The public. The County Board. The press. Am I making myself clear, Carter?"

Lehigh sighed. Ferguson's threats couldn't be less subtle. "I'm sure my detectives are preparing a full report disclosing all evidence to you as we speak. Give them a break—I just briefed them late yesterday after they returned from their little field trip—with you, Mr. Ferguson, to God-knows-where. Now, is there something in particular you're looking for?"

"I'm looking for *everything* in particular! For instance, I hear *you* went snooping around *my* crime scene—"

"*Your* crime scene?"

"—and found monogrammed cuff links belonging to George McBride. Why wasn't I the first to know this? Huh?"

"Mr. Ferguson, I—"

"I'll tell you why. You're withholding evidence, that's why!" Ferguson's breathing grew loud and ragged again.

"No," Lehigh said. "It's in the report we're preparing. Which, if I recall, we're scheduled to share with you in a meeting at ten this morn—"

"I shouldn't have to wait for a damned report!" Ferguson's shouts rose to eardrum-piercing levels again.

"Apparently you don't," Lehigh said with a sneer he wished The Reverend could see. "But since you already know about it, maybe we should both—"

"And footprints. Why don't I have those photographs? We need forensics out there, taking casts—"

"Underway. Which is why you don't have it yet."

"And tire treads—"

"Reverend, if you already have all of the information, why—"

"*Don't call me Reverend!*" Ferguson punctuated his shouts with the sound of his phone slamming into its cradle. Then a dial tone.

Lehigh blew air out between his teeth and hung up his own phone. Great. On top of having a megalomaniacal assistant D.A. who hated him, Lehigh also had deputies leaking premature findings to the angry fool, and God knows who else.

Which meant that Ferguson had moles inside the Sheriff's office. His "eyes and ears."

And those moles seemed dead set on undermining Lehigh.

Chapter Eight

Lehigh woke at the sound of a *thump* coming from somewhere outside, followed by an immediate eruption of barking so loud he wondered if it came from inside his own head. "Shush, dogs," he said in a whisper so as to not wake Stacy, sleeping beside him.

Of course, if the dogs hadn't woken her, his spoken voice wouldn't either. Sure enough, Stacy responded by snoring once and rolling over in bed.

He trudged downstairs, tugging on a bathrobe as he went, let the dogs out back, then checked the front steps. Sure enough, the invasive, pernicious attack that had so enraged the dogs for twenty seconds was the delivery of the morning newspaper, the *Clarkesville News-Clarion*.

He scooped it off the step and breathed in the morning air. The sun hadn't yet peeked over the tall arborvitae rimming the eastern edge of Stacy's property, blocking the view of her neighbor, a cranky old auto mechanic with way too many cars parked on his lawn. Lehigh brought the paper inside and skimmed it while a pot of coffee brewed on the counter. The front page focused on the ridiculous shenanigans in Washington, DC and in the state capitol, neither of which interested him. He flipped to the local news in Section B. The headlines there focused on the County Commission's debate on a new sewer fee and the school district's proposal to refurbish the football stadium. He yawned, wishing the coffee would finish brewing, and flipped the paper to scan the stories that landed beneath the fold. A brief headline almost escaped his attention:

Downey Shopping Center Sold

"How," he wondered aloud, "could Everett Downey have sold a shopping center from the grave?" No doubt his estate had yet to go through probate. Something didn't add up here.

The story jumped to a middle page, where a large photo accompanied the bulk of the text. The tale that emerged answered his first question. As it turned out, Downey had formed a holding company to develop the land a decade before. The original plan included a number of small stores and commercial spaces, and, as Bruce Bailey had suggested, another strip club. When unnamed investors joined the project, the plan evolved to favor larger department stores. Also, despite the name, Everett Downey owned less than a fourth of the company, having sold off shares to other investors. The article named a few of the partners, mostly well-known developers in the county.

Mostly.

One of the names, mentioned near the tail end of the story, surprised Lehigh. The man was not known for his real estate investments, nor for any other business engagements in the area. The man, in fact, had made quite a fuss about divesting his private sector holdings when he entered public office decades before, amid solemn declarations about the importance of putting the public's interests ahead of his own. A man for whom conflicts of interest could devastate his political ambitions, if he had any hope of rehabilitating his foundering career.

A man who, until recently, had few public connections to the murdered Everett Downey.

The man named was Oregon Senate President *Pro Tempore* George Lindsey McBride.

***

County Commission Chair Elliott McBride Jackson smiled at Assistant District Attorney Ray Ferguson, seated to the right side of Jackson's dark-haired young assistant, Teresa, at the long black-topped conference table. Ferguson had brought along two junior attorneys, both nondescript white men with short dark hair and blue suits, and thankfully not the redheaded woman who so enraged Teresa on contact.

"The reason I called this meeting," Jackson said, "is to help foster stronger cooperation between our law enforcement agencies." He scowled at Interim Sheriff Lehigh Carter, seated opposite the lawyers in his khaki uniform, accompanied by Detective Clayton Maddox.

Maddox was a white-haired, hard-faced man whose once-pale skin had turned the same burnt sienna color as the hard-scrabble ranch on which he'd been raised in the south of the county five decades before. He had earned his reputation as a no-nonsense investigator whose dogged pursuit of the truth made up for a lack of obvious intelligence and an even more obvious lack of formal education. These traits conspired to make him perfect for his current assignment as lead investigator on the Downey murder.

"I applaud your personal attention to this matter," Ferguson said with an oily smile. "We in the District Attorney's office are always seeking to improve interdepartmental communication within the County. Having fresh eyes on this matter can only benefit the public."

Carter rolled his eyes. Jackson narrowed his. Lehigh Carter had a reputation for going rogue, even before he took over the Sheriff's office. He needed to keep this bumpkin on a short leash.

Carter smiled at Jackson and Ferguson in turn. "I ain't gonna argue with the need to cooperate. In fact, I've got a few suggestions—"

"We'll all have opportunities to brainstorm ideas," Jackson said, keeping his voice even despite the urge to strangle Carter. "First I suggest we define what the problems are and explore some of the root causes. Mr. Ferguson?"

Ferguson nodded to one of the suits. "Mr. Williamson will brief us on the process."

The lawyer to Ferguson's right opened a folder and shuffled a few pages. "We've suggested a process for this discussion, rooted in the principles of Appreciative Inquiry—"

"Oh, for heaven's sake," Carter said.

"What Mr. Williamson here is getting to," Jackson said, "is that perhaps, Mr. Carter—if I may be so bold as to suggest this—perhaps you'd be better served by *listening* than by jumping to preconceived solutions." He glanced at Ferguson, who flashed him another oily smile. Jackson returned it, then turned his gaze back to Carter.

The sheriff's face puckered, as if to vomit. He glanced sideways at his detective, whose eyes widened. In worry, or feigned innocence? No matter. Everyone knew their lines here, except the rogue sheriff, of course. And he'd learn his, soon enough.

Carter fixed his gaze back on The Chairman. "Should I just bend over now, or should I send out for some lube first?" Lehigh said.

"Outrageous!" Teresa said, more of a gasp than a shout.

Ferguson's face turned crimson. His two suits looked as if they wanted to crawl under the table. Jackson leaned over, eyes narrowed, elbows planted. He spoke with slow deliberation, emphasizing every syllable. "I beg your pardon, Sheriff?"

Jackson waited for Carter to continue, but the sheriff remained silent.

"Mr. Carter, this is not one of your logging crews," Jackson said, his lip curled in disgust. "The *lady* and gentlemen in this room are professionals and deserve to be treated as such."

"I apologize for my language," Carter said, "but not for the sentiment. If you expect me to sit here and listen to you yahoos chew me out and explain my job to me, you're gonna spend the next hour talking to an empty chair. I ain't sitting through that, and neither would you."

"Mr. Carter," said the other suit with Ferguson, "do you know who you're talking to?" His nasal voice grated on Jackson's nerves almost as much as Carter's did.

"Yes, I do." Somehow Carter kept his tone even, almost

calm. Impressive. "So far as I can tell, four people in this room are civil servants. Two of us are elected." He turned to The Chair. "Which makes us equals, by my reckoning."

The nerve! "You were *appointed* to your position—"

"By the Commission. *Without* your support, if I remember right. So I owe you nothing. And if I decide I want to keep the job, I'll have to make my case to my real bosses. The voters. Come November, they'll decide whether I stay or go, not you." He pushed his chair away from the table and stood. "But whatever the voters decide, I don't, and won't, answer to you about how I do my job." Carter glared at each one of them in turn around the table.

Jackson fought for words, but they stuck in his throat. The nerve of this redneck fool, coming in here, talking like that to him! No wonder the sheriff's office had turned into such a mess. This idiot had to go. He'd have to pay. There'd be investigations, oversight, audits, maybe worse. After all, the voters had elected Elliott Jackson to the highest office in the county, Chair of the Commission. They'd put him in charge of defending their interests, which included their safety and their pocketbooks, and he wasn't about to let this interloper, this rogue hayseed, come in here and tell them how to run things.

But he needed to make sure Carter didn't get in the way. Which meant, for now, appeasement.

"Sheriff," he said, "believe it or not, we're here to help. We're all on the same team here. And all of us—" He paused and locked eyes with Ferguson for a moment. His next comment needed to come off as truthful, no matter how much it was not. "We *all* want you to succeed."

They waited.

***

Lehigh glanced around the room, weighing his options. Run, fight, or—the new option—*trust*. He knew none of the other five men in the room well. Pappy had drilled into his naturally skeptical soul that he needed to trust people more, that people would do good if he gave them a chance. Maw had taught him the opposite: keep a safe distance, lock the doors, and keep the powder dry.

But Maw was paranoid and half-crazy. He'd always wished he could be more like Pappy. Following his pride and instincts had kept him alone in life for 37 years. Trusting in Stacy a year ago had turned all that around. She'd made him a happy man. Frustrated, at times—like this very moment—but much happier.

"All right," he said. "We've got a murder to solve. You've got ideas on how to solve this case, I'll listen." He dropped his hat on the table and took his seat. It felt lumpy and hard, a bit off-balance, and his Maw side suspected they'd given him the uncomfortable seat on purpose. He banished the thought, channeling Pappy. *Trust.*

"One of the difficulties we've been having," Ferguson said, looking to his assistants for support, "is the slow pace at which information on the case has been shared between our departments. We each have people investigating different facets of the case, and getting the information all in one place has been, uh, *problematic.*"

"We've tried to speed things up," Detective Maddox said, speaking for the first time in the meeting, "but our computers are kind of old, and—"

"We understand that you need better technology," Jackson said. "I'm familiar with your budget requests. Unfortunately, funds are tight, and we won't be able to make the necessary improvements in time to benefit this investigation."

"That's an area in which we might be able to help," Ferguson said. "In fact, that's very consistent with my overall point here today. We've had better results when our teams have worked together. In an integrated fashion, so to speak."

"Other jurisdictions work this way," Jackson said. "They form a sort of task force across departments."

"It's best practice," said the younger of Ferguson's assistants. Williamson. All eyes turned to him. He flushed red and stared at his lap.

"We haven't had many murders in Mt. Hood County in the past," Jackson said. "So it stands to reason that we haven't had many opportunities to work this way. But I have to say, from my perspective as the County's highest elected official, it makes a lot of sense to me." His chest seemed to puff out.

Lehigh considered Jackson's words…and his body language. Trust became harder and harder. "So you want to combine forces, then," Lehigh said. "Work as a team."

"Exactly." Jackson's grin appeared genuine this time. "One, happy, unified team." He gazed over at Ferguson and his assistants, whose smiles flickered, faded, and appeared again.

As if they were nervous about something. Waiting for the other shoe to drop.

Lehigh glanced to his right, reading the more subdued reaction of his deputy. The detective looked away, his fingers twitching, restless.

The other shoe, Lehigh decided, was about to become a boot. One that matched Lehigh's wood-soled, leather-lined size twelves. He smiled. Two could play this game.

"I welcome your staff's addition to my investigative team," Lehigh said. "They'll report to Detective Maddox, effective immediately."

"Ah…" Ferguson coughed into his fist. "Actually, we had a different arrangement in mind."

"Seeing as the District Attorney is legally in the lead of the investigation," Jackson said, his voice as condescending as Lehigh had ever heard, "and, technically, senior to you in longevity and civil service status, if not in rank, we feel it best if your deputies and detectives report to his staff on this case." He flashed the world's oiliest smile. "That way, all of the evidence collected will flow directly to—"

"What a pile of crap." Lehigh stood again. "This is nothing but a power grab."

"I assure you, it's temporary," Ferguson said. "Just for the duration of the discovery part of the case."

"It's standard practice in other jurisdictions," Jackson said.

"Even in larger cities, police get detailed to special task forces investigating high-profile and complex cases. You're quite welcome to call your colleagues in other counties if you'd like to verify this for yourself."

"Standard practice, statewide," Ferguson said, not meeting Lehigh's hot stare. "On matters like these."

"Is that so." Lehigh checked in with his detective, who nodded once, then shrugged.

"So I hear," the detective said. "It's my first murder case. Wadsworth took the last one."

Ferguson coughed. "We followed a similar strategy on that case," he said. "Our office took the lead—"

"And investigated *me*. And my wife." Lehigh leaned over the table, his flushed face inches from Ferguson's. "And look how that turned out. Just like last time, you've got a bug up your butt to prosecute a member of the McBride family. Last time, my fiancée. This time, her father. Coincidence? I. Think. *Not*." He punctuated his final words with well-timed slaps on the table.

"We follow the evidence, as we're doing now," Ferguson said, his voice weak.

"In fact, that's another reason to do it this way," Jackson said. "There is at minimum the appearance of a conflict of interest with your involvement in the case, Sheriff. You'll have to recuse yourself, no matter what else we do."

Lehigh straightened, adjusted his shirt. He'd wondered when they'd get to this. As much as he hated to admit it, they had a point. Besides, removing himself from the case could keep him out of Stacy's doghouse if the evidence continued to incriminate her father.

"All right, then." He nodded to Maddox. "Keep Jim Wadsworth up to date on everything."

Maddox nodded, head down, unable or unwilling to meet Lehigh's gaze.

So much for teamwork. Time for Plan B.

Chapter Nine

"You sure about this?" Detective Jim Wadsworth leaned back in the guest chair in Lehigh Carter's office, watching the sheriff pace about the spacious room. He inhaled, enjoying the ability to take a deep breath again after fighting his stupid cold for two solid weeks. "This might not be the best time to create a whole new investigative team, right after detailing Maddox's squad over Reverend Ray's way. Especially since you want them to work on the same murder case."

"I know it looks bad," Lehigh said. "But I don't trust those guys as far as I can throw 'em. And I never was any good at playing quarterback." He picked up a stapler off his desk and gave it a vacant stare.

"Well, there's that," Wadsworth said. "Plus the fact that we're short-handed so many guys. Because of, well, you know." Heat flashed across his brow. He'd just brought up his boss's most sensitive topic. Idiot.

"Since I got half the department bounced out of here for conspiring to lock my fiancée in prison for the rest of her life?" Lehigh set the stapler down and chuckled. "Yeah, I know. Well, all that means is, I'm gonna have to fill those slots. The County Commission will have to approve funding now. With the ones I got fired and Maddox's squad all working for Ray, that puts us down eight. I can't function on half of a department."

"Well, it's not *quite* half. Not when you consider all of our units across the county." Wadsworth cringed. His wife Gwen often complained that his obsession with accuracy made him do dumb things like contradict his superiors. No wonder he never made lieutenant. He steeled himself for a reprimand. But, he discovered yet again, Lehigh Carter was not Buck Summers.

"True," Carter said. "But with four guys working for the D.A., the Clarkesville unit is down eight out of seventeen. They at least gotta let me fill the vacancies."

Wadsworth smiled at his boss. Gotta love the guy's optimism. "Maybe, but where are you going to find five men with police training in Clarkesville?" he said. "Heck, try to find five who haven't been arrested at least twice."

"Who says they have to be men?" Lehigh said. "There's plenty of women cops. And I bet we can steal a few from Deschutes and Jefferson counties. Maybe even Hood River. Last time I checked, we pay better."

"Yeah, but who wants to move for a deputy job? I don't know, Lehigh." Dammit. He hated being the naysayer. But Carter didn't seem to mind. He seemed to enjoy the debate.

As if on cue, Lehigh grinned. "Care to wager?"

Wadsworth flushed again. Carter had a plan. Cagey, this one.

"I've been putting out some feelers." Lehigh handed Wadsworth a stack of loose pages of varying shades, textures, and thicknesses. On each page, candidates listed their qualifications and experience, some with considerably more than others. Some, Wadsworth noted, looked like they spent more time in County lockup than the guards.

"Have you looked at these?" Wadsworth asked after skimming the pile. "I only see two that have any formal training. And I've never heard of either one."

Lehigh shrugged. "Yeah, I figure they're automatics for interviews. That'll tell us whether they have three heads or eat their young. The others in there will help us mix it up a little in terms of who we hire. The old boys' club is going out of business. Look at the resumé at the bottom of the pile."

Wadsworth moved a canary-colored page from the bottom to the top of the stack and scoffed. "It looks like it's written in crayon. Hell, man, this kid's barely out of high school."

"Perfect. We can train him our way."

Wadsworth laughed. Carter was irrepressible. "He's a farm

boy," Wadsworth said. "Probably just learned to read."

Lehigh smacked his desk with an open palm. "Dammit, Jim. This is what I'm talking about changing—attitudes like that. Prejudice. Exclusivity. Hell, a year ago, what did you think of me? Honestly. Tell me."

Wadsworth sighed and sat in the chair he'd been leaning against. "I see your point."

"No. That's not good enough. I want to hear what you thought about me." Lehigh stared at him, eyes blazing.

Wadsworth's face warmed. He was probably blushing, a legacy of his Scottish ancestry. He'd overstepped, for sure. "I thought you were a recluse. An anti-social loner."

"Which I was. And still am. What else?"

"Kind of crude."

"Ditto. And?"

A deep breath. "Uneducated. Okay, ignorant. And maybe a little, I don't know, crazy perhaps."

"And now?"

Wadsworth smiled. He really *did* want to hear it. "Still most of that. Just not the ignorant, uneducated part."

"What I am," Lehigh said, standing and pacing again, "is the guy *you* recruited to fill in this stupid job after twelve years of crooked, rigid, same-old same-old from Buck Summers. A job *you* didn't want because of how much time and effort you'd have to spend dealing with corrupt politicians and rooting out deputies on the take. Well, I'm in this cesspool, and I don't like what I see. I'm gonna fix this place or get run out of town trying. If it means doing things differently than how they've been done in the past—if it means bending a few rules that only serve to perpetuate the crooked way business has been done around here all of our lives—well, all the better, I'd say." Lehigh stopped pacing, his arms thrust wide, as if he'd just knocked down a football team's entire offensive front with a clothesline tackle.

Wadsworth flipped through the resumes again, this time from the perspective of Carter's "clean-it-up" approach. Not a single person in the pile had any connection whatsoever to anyone currently wearing a badge. He nodded. "Sheriff," he said, "if that's what you're about, I have only one thing to say." He stood and extended a hand. "When do we start interviewing?"

***

Stacy downshifted. Which one rarely needs to do with an automatic transmission, even less often with a Volvo station wagon driven mostly by suburban families to and from soccer games. But dropping it into low gear allowed her to accelerate in a hurry, even in her old Volvo. And, on this bright, warm summer morning in late July, Stacy was already ten minutes late to a house call on Mrs. Altmayer's sick, and possibly dying, Australian riding pony.

The car ahead of her, a small SUV loaded with antennae and men whose uniforms bore the same five-star symbol that appeared on the front, back, and sides of the vehicle, chugged along at twenty-five miles per hour. Five *below* the speed limit, for heaven's sake.

She checked the left lane, stomped on the accelerator, and zoomed past the deputies' vehicle in a matter of seconds.

Bright blue-and-red lights flashed in her rear-view mirror. "Damn it!" she fumed at the mirror. "I passed you at the speed limit!" She considered stomping on the accelerator again, but resisted the urge. She hoped that Percival, the pony, could hold on a few extra minutes. She slowed and pulled over to the shoulder.

Two deputies emerged from the vehicle, both at least ten years younger than her. Both sported buzz cuts and aviator sunglasses under their hats, with downturned mouths that defied any hint of humor. The driver towered a good six inches over his partner. Broad-chested, muscular, with a thick neck, he reminded her of a football player, but not slender like Lehigh. More like a fullback.

The other guy stood maybe 5'7", 250, and probably shopped at the Big and Tall store, right next to the Country Buffet. And not in that order. White as a daisy, he could easily be mistaken for one of Dot's Diner's large powdered donuts.

"Afternoon, ma'am." The driver stood outside her open window. Heat poured in, replacing the air-conditioned comfort her Volvo provided. "Do you know why we pulled you over today?"

"Officers," she said, "I don't believe I was speeding, but I am in a bit of a hurry. One of my clients is very sick, and—"

"You're a doctor, Ma'am?" The driver deadpanned his delivery, but he cocked his head in apparent surprise.

She sighed. "No, officer. I'm on an emergency call to Mrs. Altmayer's horse farm—"

"You're a veterinarian, then?" the other deputy asked.

"Not exactly," she said. "I own and run the Cascade Animal Clinic, but I never got my degree. Have you heard of us?"

The two deputies exchanged glances. She knew the look: "Oh, not one of *these*." She checked her watch: fifteen minutes late. *Hold on, Percival!*

"Are you in an emergency situation, ma'am? Are you, or any of your passengers, in need of a hospital or medical attention?"

She turned in slow motion, indicating the empty passenger and rear seats. "As I already mentioned, officers, Mrs. Altmayer's pony is in need of emergency attention."

The athletic one cleared his throat. "Don't most vets carry one of those black doctor bags, ma'am?"

"What *color* is the pony?" the short one asked.

"What color? I'm not sure, I—"

"How tall is it?"

"How *tall*?"

"Male or female?" "How old?" "What's the name of the siring stud?" "Does it compete in any shows?"

Stacy blew air out from pressed lips. Unbelievable. The pony lay suffering in a barn three miles away, and these guys needed to quiz her credentials? "Officers, really. Is this your usual routine, asking bizarre questions of women driving alone?"

The one on the driver side straightened, looked off in the distance toward the rear of the car. "I'll need your license, registration, and proof of insurance."

She dug them out of her purse and handed over the paperwork, along with her clinic ID, then read their name badges. Sergeant DuPont, the athletic one, had her license. Deputy Peters, the round one, guarded the passenger door, as if he suspected her of planning an escape down the side of the highway.

"Ms. McBride?"

She returned her attention to Sgt. DuPont. "It's Carter now. See there, on the license? The new registration card hasn't come in yet."

"Hmm." DuPont flipped between the cards. "Any relation to Sheriff Lehigh—"

"My husband." His face blanched, and she flashed him a wicked grin.

DuPont kept her license in his hands, considering her. "Seems a sheriff's wife might want to be a little more observant of county speed limits. Set a good example and all, y'know?"

She breathed a sigh of relief. If he intended to ticket her, he wouldn't waste time with the lecture. "That's excellent advice, Sergeant. I'll relay your concern for my safety to my husband tonight at dinner. Now, may I tend to my client's sick animal, before it's too late?" She held out her hand, hoping her expression showed the concern she felt for Percival.

DuPont placed the paperwork on her open palm and signaled his partner. "Drive safely, ma'am."

***

Back in their patrol car, Deputy Evan Peters and Sergeant Dale DuPont held their silence until Stacy McBride Carter pulled away from the curb in her Volvo. "Dammit. I should've written her up," DuPont said.

Peters pivoted his head to stare at him. "Oh, sure. You want to be the one to explain to the new sheriff why we wrote his wife a $400 ticket?"

DuPont threw his hands up in the air. "She broke the damn law, that's why! Speeding, crossing a solid yellow strip to pass—"

"Yeah, and every time you take a coffee at Dot's without paying, it'll go on *your* record. And mine. No, thanks." Peters slumped in his seat.

"Still." DuPont signaled and steered the patrol car back onto the highway, his voice gaining energy. "This is favoritism. Cronyism. It's exactly what's wrong with Mt. Hood County, and always will be. Why'd we bother getting this outsider as sheriff? To 'clean things up,' he said. Huh. Nothing's changed. Nothing ever will."

"Yeah, yeah," Peters said. "Go tell it to Bruce Bailey."

DuPont stared at his partner for several long seconds. "You know, *somebody* ought to do just that."

***

"What *is* this nonsense?" Lehigh slapped the newspaper down on his desk, knocking over an Oregon State Beavers mug full of pens and pencils and scattering them across the floor. He kicked a few that landed near his feet for good measure. "I avoid watching TV news anymore so I don't have to hear that smug idiot Bailey blather on with his made-up crap. But now they just print it all in the daily paper?"

"Gentleman Jim" Wadsworth grimaced in the guest chair on the other side of Lehigh's desk. "Is there anything to it?"

"Of course not!" Lehigh tossed the paper onto the detective's lap, then stood and crossed his arms, leaning against the wall behind his desk. "I never ordered anybody to let my wife or family members go busting the law and get away with it. I never even hinted at it. Nothing of the sort!"

Wadsworth scanned the story under the two-inch headline. "They're making a big thing out of nothing and trying to link it to you not wanting to arrest her father."

"I can't arrest the man without evidence of probable cause!" He threw his hands up in the air. "I've been on the wrong side of that one, as you no doubt remember. I won't repeat the mistakes of my predecessors!"

"Easy, boy. Don't shoot the messenger. I'm on your side,

remember?" Wadsworth read further into the article. "What's this about your wife threatening to get a couple of deputies fired, just to get out of a ticket?"

Lehigh spun his chair with a vicious shove. "It's baloney. If she got stopped for a traffic violation, it's news to me."

"It looks bad, Lehigh." Wadsworth set the paper down on Lehigh's desk. "It looks like nothing's changed from when Buck was in charge. New faces, same old crap."

"I know. And that's what makes me crazy." He sighed and plopped hard back into his chair. "I've been trying to change things, but every time I try to do anything, Elliott Jackson screams and hollers about me 'taking over the county.' If I ask for a dollar for paper clips, I'm a wasteful incompetent. Make a decision, I'm a fascist dictator. Try to run a fair and professional investigation and I'm playing favorites on behalf of my friends and family. In his eyes, I can't do anything right. I hate this damned job!"

He looked up at Wadsworth and noticed movement over the big man's shoulder. In the doorway stood his administrative assistant, Julia, frozen in place, a look of shock and horror plastered across her face. Lehigh's heart sank. No doubt this would make the rumor mill before the next coffee break.

"Is this a bad time?" Julia asked, holding a sheet of paper between her fingertips.

"It's always a bad time these days," Lehigh said. "What's up?"

"I have the approval from Human Resources here to fill four deputy positions. You said to bring it right away." She took two baby steps into the room and held the sheet out in front of her.

Lehigh spread his hands wide. "What the—?"

"I sent the request to H.R. after our talk yesterday, asked them to expedite," Wadsworth said. "Pulled a few strings. I figured why bother the Commission with asking permission when we've got bureaucrats already in place who owe me favors? *And*," Wadsworth added with a grin, "I did it under my signature, rather than yours. No one can complain about you overreaching this time."

Lehigh grinned. "You're a bureaucratic genius. Let's get hiring!"

Chapter Ten

Lehigh poured himself a cup of strong black coffee and set a glazed donut on his napkin. He tested the creamer carafe, found it empty. Ditto the sugar. He shrugged. The coffee smelled good. He tore off a piece of the donut and dipped it into the coffee. Perfection.

He turned from the refreshments table and faced the room, a small meeting space in the Grand Cascade Hotel in Wyee Falls, a tiny tourist trap on the north side of the county overlooking the Wyeast River. The wood-paneled room featured glass on two sides, affording a spectacular view of the snow-capped mountains rising up above the whitewater flowing alongside the hotel. Inside the room sat his new investigative squad, classroom style. He glanced at each in turn. Not the team he'd envisioned, but a good group, overall.

Jim Wadsworth sat in the front row on the far end of four chairs lined up abreast. Lehigh trusted him to lead the effort and keep the team's activities under Ray Ferguson's radar. In fact, Lehigh trusted him completely. Period.

"Good morning, team," Lehigh said with an uneasy smile. "As of this morning, you are all assigned to the Special Investigation Unit of the Mt. Hood County Sheriff's Department."

"I feel special already," said Donnell Winthrop with a grin. Sitting in the back row with two other new recruits, he personified the many contrasts of the group. His bright smile, easy laugh, and friendly demeanor belied his intense stare, multiple piercings and hints of tattoos emerging from his loose shirt collar. Slender of build and standing just under six feet tall, he wore a red bandana over his tight black curls, explaining that he preferred to cover his prematurely balding scalp against sunburn. "Bright red don't go with midnight black," he said with a loud laugh that would make a southern good-old-boy proud. He'd aced every written test, despite an appearance that most suburbanites would mistake for a street drug dealer. When his paperwork went through, Lehigh was astonished to learn that the department had hired only white males to deputy positions in its 150-year history.

The other recruits chuckled at Donnell's wisecrack, except one, a guy who sat two seats away from Winthrop. Bobby Wills, a dough-faced fireplug with short, sandy brown hair, a button nose, and a waistline that nearly disqualified him from service, seemed irritated by the joke. Which struck Lehigh as odd, since Wills cracked more dumb jokes in any ten-minute period than a bad late-night sitcom.

"Before we begin," Lehigh said, "do any of you have any questions?"

"I do," said Ted Roscoe, seated at the far end of the row from Wadsworth. Lehigh had made Roscoe the final member of the task force only that morning, mostly because he was the only uniformed deputy carried over from the Buck Summers era that didn't seem to hate Lehigh on sight. Besides that, he had demonstrated earnestness, discipline, honesty, and loyalty, if not high intelligence, in the few months Lehigh had worked with him. Lehigh had grown to like Roscoe and depend on him for his candid assessments of how the other sworn officers felt and thought of Lehigh's decisions and leadership style. So far, Roscoe hadn't disappointed.

"What is it, Ted?" Lehigh asked him.

Roscoe stood and brushed dandruff from his shoulder. "Why are we meeting way the heck out here in a hotel in the north part of the county? We've got plenty of meeting rooms in Clarkesville." The other deputies nodded in agreement.

"Good question," Lehigh said. "We have a number of

reasons. One, we serve the entire county, not just Clarkesville." Eyes rolled. Okay, so nobody bought that one. Time to cut the politically correct crap. "Second, we wanted an off-site meeting to keep you focused on the business at hand, rather than your emails, phones, and regular distractions."

A few heads nodded. Better. And he'd saved the best for last.

"And three, what we're doing here needs to remain strictly confidential."

The deputies, most of whom had been slouching in their chairs, sat up at full attention. "Cool," said a thirty-something Native American deputy under his breath. Martin Lightfoot's hulking size, thick brows, and brooding expression created an imposing presence at first, but his honesty and quick, broad smile won over the other recruits before they finished their first coffee. In a nod to the department's standard of above-the-ears hair length for men, he'd cut his dark hair to collar length, a compromise Lehigh decided he could live with, particularly since Lehigh's own ponytail hung halfway down his back.

"So we're on some sort of secret mission?" asked Bobby Wills. "What are we going to investigate around here, a bunch of cows?"

"I'll let Detective Wadsworth explain, if there are no other questions," Lehigh said. Nobody stirred. Lehigh nodded once to Wadsworth, who stood and faced the group.

"As you know, the investigative team we assigned to the Everett Downey murder case has been detailed to assist the district attorney's office full time," Wadsworth said.

"Lucky them," Wills said, not quite under his breath. Wadsworth glared at him and the deputy shrank into his chair.

"The Downey investigation had a big problem," Wadsworth said. "Discipline." His gaze swept around the room, pausing for a moment at each new face. Lehigh noted which ones met his gaze and which looked away. Only Wills and Lightfoot could not meet Wadsworth's intense stare.

"On our team, that won't be a problem," said a woman's voice. It belonged to the department's first-ever female sworn deputy. Ruby MacArthur, who went by "Ruby Mac," sat behind

Wadsworth's empty chair with her arms crossed. Lehigh had stolen her from the ranks of nearby Wasco County, where she'd earned the rank of Sergeant after a decade of service. Besides Wadsworth, she had the most experience in the group. Despite her small frame—she listed her numbers as 5'5", 135 pounds— she had excelled in every physical test, running a crazy-fast 4.6-second 40-yard dash and bench pressing almost 200. Her short black hair formed a tight helmet around her round head, and dark black eyes contrasted with her bright white teeth. She could flash a dazzling smile or fierce snarl with equal speed.

"That's right, Ruby," the detective said. "That's because each of you were chosen or recruited for this assignment because you demonstrated the ability to work as a team *and* keep confidential information out of the wrong hands. Both of those traits are critical to our mission."

"And here I thought it was because of our crack skills at looking under rocks," Winthrop said. Ruby Mac, Roscoe, and Lightfoot grinned.

"The only crack around here is what you've been smoking," Wills said.

For a moment, silence hung in the air, as if all sound, even the air itself, had been sucked out of the room. Lehigh took a deep breath and got ready to intervene. The last thing he needed was tension and race-baiting among his team.

A loud guffaw broke the silence. Winthrop reached over and slapped Wills on the back, with more laughter spilling from his wide-open mouth. "Good one, Meat Loaf!" he said and clapped. "The 'crack you been smoking.' That's funny, man."

"Meat Loaf!" someone repeated and laughed. Low-level chuckles and wide grins filled the room. Wills rubbed his shoulder blade where Winthrop had slapped him, but maintained a sheepish grin. Lehigh relaxed. Donnell could take care of himself.

"So, you were saying," Winthrop said to Wadsworth, "how brilliant we were."

"I thought he was saying we were all such good boys," Wills

said with a nervous grin.

"Not all of us are boys, dummy," Ruby said without looking around.

"Sorry, I couldn't tell," Wills said, his grin growing wider. He looked to his companions on either side for support, but both looked away. When he glanced up again, Ruby Mac filled his view. She grabbed him by the shirt and pinned him to the wall one-handed, his feet dangling.

"Care to repeat that?" she said.

"Take it easy," Lehigh said, moving toward the two of them. Wadsworth stopped him with a raised hand. *Let this play out,* he mouthed. Lehigh stopped, waited.

"Hey Mac, don't hurt him," Winthrop said. "We're counting on Bobby to find all of the best donut shops."

Ruby smiled. "You're bringing the donuts tomorrow?" she said to Wills.

"Donuts, sure. Hell, I'll buy you lunch. I'll buy everybody lunch," Wills said, gasping for breath. "Put me down, awright?"

Mac let him slide to the floor, then brushed off his shirt with her hands. "Chocolate glazed," she said. "With sprinkles."

"My favorite," Wills said.

Lehigh let out a silent breath and everyone returned to their seats. On the way to her chair, Ruby noticed Donnell staring at her and cocked her head.

"My eyes are up here, my friend," she said.

"Girl, I ain't staring at your chest," he said. He tapped his left bicep. "I was checking out your guns. You play football or something?"

"Softball, Oregon State, Pac-12 home run champion," she said with a grin. She accepted Donnell's high-five and returned to her seat.

"Back to business, then," Wadsworth said. "Anyone here have a problem with maintaining strict confidentiality regarding your cases? Only discuss them with other members of your team. No one else—not even your wives, husbands, girlfriends, no one."

"You hear that, Wills?" Winthrop said. "No telling your wife *or* your girlfriend." The room erupted into laughter, including Wills. He slapped Donnell on the back—not quite as hard as the blow he'd earned, though.

"That goes for you, too, Mac," Winthrop said to Ruby. "No telling your wife or your girlfriend."

"At least I got one," Ruby Mac said, and "woo-hoos!" echoed around the room.

"All right, quit horsing around," Wadsworth said. "I'm serious. Anyone have issues with keeping your work on the QT?"

"What if other deputies ask?" Roscoe said. "We've got to tell them something."

"Tell them you're on special assignment," Lehigh said, standing. "If they want to know more, tell them to ask me."

"Works for me," Roscoe said. Heads nodded around the room.

Wills raised his hand. "Can we take our patrol cars home?" he said. "I don't have my own car right now."

"No personal use of county vehicles," Lehigh said. "Do you have a way to get to work?"

"Yeah," he said in a sullen voice. "My girlfriend can drop me off."

"Ooh, Bobby's got a girlfriend!" Donnell said. "What grade is she in?" Howls of laughter filled the room.

"If there are no other questions, we'll partner up now," Wadsworth said. "Mac, you'll partner with Lightfoot. Winthrop, you're with me. Roscoe, you've got Wills. Ruby Mac's my number two on this team, so if anyone needs something and I'm not around, she's your go-to. Everybody got it?"

Heads nodded again. Wills seemed less than enthusiastic, but said nothing.

"I've got a question," Martin Lightfoot said. All heads turned toward him, no doubt as surprised as Lehigh that the man opened his mouth unprovoked. "I understand the murder happened in the old Wasco burial ground. I know that place well. That's sacred territory for our tribe. Has anyone contacted the tribe about reconsecrating that site?"

Lehigh looked to Wadsworth. Another complication! His detective took the cue. "No one is allowed in there until the case is resolved," Wadsworth said. "But we will, I promise."

"I thought we had a suspect already?" Wills asked. "How much more resolved does it need to get?"

"Innocent until proven guilty, Bobby," Ruby Mac said, shaking her head.

"The sooner we can get this case figured out, then, the better," Martin said.

"On that note," Wadsworth said, "let the training begin!"

Chapter Eleven

At the end of two grueling days of team-building and training, Lehigh checked out of his hotel, confident in his new team and the leadership provided by Wadsworth and Ruby MacArthur. Wills, Winthrop, and Lightfoot showed energy and intelligence, but made mistakes that only experience would cure. And experience they would get—fast.

"Was everything to your satisfaction?" the preppy male clerk asked while ringing up his bill.

"Very much so," Lehigh said. "As expected. Oh, that reminds me. Credit Ray Ferguson with the referral for this. He stayed with you a few weeks back and raved about you."

"I'll do that," the young clerk said. He clicked some keys, then frowned. "What was Mr. Ferguson's first name again?" he said.

"Raymond."

The clerk shook his head. "I don't seem to find him in our database."

"Maybe it's under his wife's name," Lehigh said.

Another head shake, then a shrug. "No Fergusons in the last two months at least. Well, I'll look into it later, Sheriff. I don't want to hold you up."

"Probably my mistake," Lehigh said. "Don't worry about it." He didn't know of any other hotels in town. He'd have to remember to check back with Ferguson later.

***

Lehigh made the hour-long drive back to Clarkesville and

dropped Ted Roscoe off at his well-kept manufactured home in a small trailer park outside of town, then returned home. He slept like the dead and rose at dawn while Stacy continued to snooze, a vision of beauty with her long black hair sprawled over the bright white sheets of their queen bed. He downed a cup of coffee and a piece of toast and headed into work.

When he arrived, a slew of suits stood waiting for him in the small lobby. He counted noses: six, all of whom looked like they shopped at the same men's wear store. He checked the time: a few minutes after seven. Not exactly rush hour for lawyers in Mt. Hood County.

In the center of the group stood Ray Ferguson, wearing a grim expression that barely covered a smile. Lehigh recognized two of the suits from the "coordination" meeting with Ferguson and Commissioner Jackson, and another who looked out of place in his cheap blue pinstripes and wrinkled white shirt. Detective Clayton Maddox, on loan to Ferguson from his own staff, appeared not to have so much combed his mop of white hair as molded it with a gallon of hair gel. Another pair of uniformed deputies, also assigned to the task force, lingered on the fringes behind the suits.

"Is this a funeral, or are all of you just late to my wedding?" Lehigh asked. "If so, you can drop off gifts in the break room. Follow me." He pushed his way through the crowd toward the double swinging doors that led to the secure inner sanctum of the sheriff's office.

"We'll need a large meeting room, stat," Ferguson said, a step behind him. "We have important business to discuss."

Lehigh caught the eye of Ted Roscoe, emerging from the reception area. "What have we got, Ted?"

"The big meeting room's reserved for you and Clayton," Roscoe said. "I got coffee in there already."

Lehigh barreled through the swinging double doors to the hallway, waving the others on behind him. "I'm guessing this is about the Downey case," he said when they'd all filed into the room. Three tables had been pushed into a U shape, and Lehigh took the center chair at the bottom of the U. Ferguson's crew took over both sides, leaving Lehigh alone in the middle.

"I'll cut right to the chase," Ferguson said. "We'll lay out the case for you in a moment, but we have a suspect in the murder, and we want him arrested."

Alarm bells rang in Lehigh's head. He indicated Detective Maddox and the two deputies assigned to the task force, Peters and DuPont. "You've got sworn officers of the law at your disposal, so I'm guessing there's some reason you didn't just go get that done?"

"Out of courtesy to you," Ferguson said, "we didn't want to make a high-profile arrest without your knowledge."

"High-profile, huh?" The alarm bells rang loud and fast now. His heart thumped and his ears felt like fire. "I'm guessing you don't mean the victim, but the suspect?"

Ferguson's eyes narrowed and the corners of his mouth twitched upward. "You know who it is, Sheriff. At least, I hope you do. And no matter what you think of it, it's your duty to arrest him." His firm, cruel smile sharpened. "No matter," he said, "that he is your father-in-law."

***

The small caravan rolled single-file up the long, tree-lined driveway toward the sprawling McBride home, a classic English-style array of tall peaked roof ridges atop interconnected, blocky tentacles clad in brick and wood placed by builders from generations long past. Willow branches drooped in the heat, brushing the antennae of the Crown Victoria cruisers and official SUVs of the convoy, and the leaves on the maples had already begun to turn brown from the heat and drought. McBride's gardeners had some catching up to do.

The lead car, a cruiser driven by Deputy Peters, pulled in behind McBride's vintage white New Yorker, blocking his unlikely escape. Ferguson's black Crown Victoria pulled up next to the New Yorker, followed by another sheriff's cruiser with Lehigh at the wheel and Jim Wadsworth to his right. Detective Maddox brought up the rear, with Deputy DuPont driving him.

Not just an arrest squad. A veritable army.

Lehigh turned off the engine and blew air out between his lips. "Well, Jim," he said, "here goes the end of my marriage."

"Were you able to reach her?" Wadsworth asked.

Lehigh shook his head. "I left three messages on her cell phone and at the clinic, each one more urgent than the one before. I guess they had some sort of emergency she can't break away from. I didn't dare say why I was calling."

"Good," Wadsworth said. "If she had alerted George, and he ran—well, you'd be the shortest-tenured sheriff since, well, Dwayne Latner, I guess." He emitted a forced laugh, one that evoked no response from Lehigh. Latner had filled in for a few days after Jared Barkley's murder several months before, until the County Commission voted in Lehigh.

"This is going to suck," Lehigh said.

"We don't have to do it this way. Any of those deputies out there could do it. I could. Hell, I should. Let me."

Lehigh shook his head. "It's on me. If anyone's going to believe in me making changes around here, I've got to—"

A knock on his window interrupted them. He rolled down the window. Deputy DuPont bent over and spoke in a low voice. "We should go ahead and get this done, Sheriff."

Lehigh nodded. "I reckon." He rolled the window back up, drummed on the steering wheel. "I guess it's time."

Wadsworth pulled the lever to open the passenger side door and swung his legs out, then glanced back at Lehigh, who hadn't moved. "You coming?"

Lehigh stared at nothing for another moment. Nodded again. "Okay, then, let's go arrest my father-in-law for murder."

Chapter Twelve

Lehigh got out of the car and took a deep breath. Ferguson waited at the walk-up to the McBride's front door, flanked by his assistants and the two deputies, Peters and DuPont. Lehigh took every step with slow deliberation, dread rising with every inch of ground he covered. He took in the grim expressions on the faces of the entourage—except one. Sergeant Dale DuPont sported a satisfied smile, a small moment of malicious joy over his hated boss's predicament. Or maybe DuPont was just remembering the last time he'd pulled the wings off of flies. Hard to say. Lehigh had never been much of a mind-reader.

Ferguson and his contingent let Lehigh take the lead on the slow trudge up the walkway, lined by golf-green grass on each side. In contrast to the parched trees lining the driveway, the manicured lawn and garden featured bright flowers in black, loamy soil, with white and yellow roses climbing the estate's red brick walls. Occasional droplets of moisture dotted the azalea leaves and blades of grass. Beautiful in appearance, but extravagant to the point of arrogant.

Just like George McBride.

Lehigh winced. Try as he might, he couldn't work up enough anger to make this easy.

"Sheriff?" Ferguson appeared at Lehigh's side. Without realizing it, Lehigh had stopped a good six feet from the front steps. He met The Reverend's gaze and considered resuming his inventory of the McBrides' garden. But no sense delaying this any further. Hesitating here would show weakness in front of the crew, each, except for Wadsworth, already doubting his resolve.

He trudged onward to the steps and reached for the doorbell. Before he could ring it, however, the inner door, a wide, heavy wooden beast with inset patterns of stained glass, swung inward. Through the glass of the white-clad storm door appeared the short, matronly figure of Catherine McBride, wearing a simple print house dress. No Consuela today, he noted with disappointment.

"Lehigh?" Catherine pushed open the storm door, her hazel eyes ablaze. "What are you doing here? Who are these men?"

"Morning, ma'am," he said. "Is George home?"

Catherine leaned out and looked over the entourage. "Is that Raymond Ferguson from the District Attorney's office? Mr. Ferguson, what is the meaning of this?"

Ferguson stepped forward, placing himself to the handle side of the doorway next to Lehigh. "Morning, Ms. McBride. I—"

"Don't you 'Ms.' me, Raymond Ferguson!" Catherine wagged a delicate finger at him in front of her half-closed eyes and pursed lips. "I spanked your bottom in kindergarten often enough for you to remember my proper name. Now use it, young man!"

Ferguson blinked twice in silence, then coughed into his fist. "Yes, ma'am. *Mrs.* McBride. I believe your son-in-law has some, ah, *information* to share." He glanced at Lehigh, who returned a puzzled stare. Ferguson rolled his eyes. "The warrant, Sheriff?"

"Oh. Right." He reached into his jacket, fished around in his pocket. Bingo. Pulled the pages out, unfolded them. He held the pages out to the door. Catherine stared down her nose at them.

"Really, Lehigh? A warrant? *This* is how you deliver such news—to your own family?" She shook her head. "Tell me. What's the warrant for? Your goons have already tromped through here looking for God-knows-what."

"Warrant? What warrant?" A red-faced, white-haired barrel of a man in a white button-down shirt and black dress pants with a crisp crease appeared behind her. George McBride elbowed his wife aside and pushed open the door. He grabbed the warrant but didn't so much as glance at the contents. "I assume this is for me."

Lehigh bowed his head. "Yes, sir."

McBride scanned the pages and his flush-red face turned as white as his hair. His mouth gaped open. "Are you *serious*?"

"What does it say?" Catherine stretched her neck over his arm to read the text.

"Say it, Sheriff," Ferguson said under his breath. "You've got to say the words."

Lehigh let out a long breath and met George's fierce gaze. "Senator McBride, you are under arrest for the murder of Everett Downey."

***

"Unbelievable!" Stacy threw her hands up into the air and turned her back on Lehigh. Tears welled in both eyes. Unfortunately, she couldn't put any further distance between them in her twelve-foot-square office. Not without tossing Lehigh out, anyway.

Which felt very tempting, at that moment. But for now, she resisted the urge.

"I tried reaching you," Lehigh said. He stood, hat in hand, midway between the edge of her desk and the door, which, although closed, provided almost no privacy should anyone want to listen from the hallway. In Clarkesville, and in particular the insular world of the Cascade Animal Clinic, eavesdropping amounted to a near-certainty—no matter that Stacy owned, managed, and founded the clinic six years before, and paid the salary of every last one of the potential spies. In a small town, people often valued good gossip over a steady paycheck.

She kept her back to him. "It's not about reaching me. It's about whether you arrest a man you know to be innocent—a member of your own family—or whether you keep your promise to end the long-standing tradition in Mt. Hood County of harassing powerless victims of ingrained corruption that keeps this town in the dark ages. My own father, for God's sake!" She tossed her hands skyward again and stole a glance back at Lehigh.

He took a deep breath. "He is not exactly powerless. He's the president *pro tempore* of the state Senate, and until recently—"

"The now *outgoing* senator and, I might add, the honorary chairman and chief fundraiser for your campaign. Can't you afford him the least bit of dignity as his political light fades?" Her voice cracked and tears ran down her cheek. Dammit! She did *not* want to cry at that moment. But imagining her aging, proud, accomplished father sitting in a jail cell with common criminals and thugs tore her heart in half. She could only imagine how her poor mother felt.

"So, what are you saying?" Lehigh spread his arms wide. "I should only arrest the rich and powerful at the peak of their power? I should ignore the evidence and let my friends and family get away with whatever crimes they want, like the papers are saying anyway? And like Buck always did?"

"Of course not." She crossed her arms and took a breath. "All I'm saying is, my father's not in control of the party machine anymore. He's at the weakest point of his political career. I thought that the weak and powerless were the people you wanted to protect as sheriff, not the arrogant good old boys in the D.A.'s office."

Lehigh held his hands out to his sides. "It is, hon. But I had no choice. I need to enforce the law and follow the evidence. I resisted as long as I could, but even I had to admit—it's looking bad."

"My father may be a lot of things, but he's no killer! And you know it." She whirled about to face him, took a step to reduce the distance between them.

"I'm sorry, Stacy. Like I said, I had no choice. The evidence—"

"The evidence is cooked!" Her voice reached peak volume, and footsteps outside the door told her that plenty of clerks and interns had heard it loud and clear. "Why can't you just throw the fake evidence out and tell those goons in suits to find the real killer?"

"That's not how it works," he said. "The D.A. decides who to charge, and the grand jury rubber-stamps it. Once they do that, I have to do my duty, whether I agree with their decision or not."

"Is that so?" She leaned closer and poked his chest with a chipped fingernail. "And is it your *duty* to arrest my father personally? To make it as humiliating as humanly possible?" She punctuated the end of her speech with another poke in his chest. Suddenly, she found her wrist encased in his steely grip in front of her.

"I did it personally," he said, his voice low and menacing, "to make it *less* humiliating. To put a familiar face on it—"

"Flanked by four deputies, six lawyers and an entire fleet of cop cars?" Her voice pitched high and loud again. "What did you think he was going to do, attack you with a battle axe? Did you really need to bring a damned army?"

"Stacy, it wasn't up to me—"

"Nothing's up to you, is it? For God's sake, you're sheriff. You have some authority around here, don't you?" Spittle flicked onto Lehigh's cheek. She felt bad about that. Even worse when the bright red color rose in his cheeks. She knew then that she'd gone a step too far.

***

Lehigh glared at his wife, then heaved away from her, thumbs hitched in his pockets. "What do you think, Stacy?" He fought to keep his voice steady and low-volume. "You think I wanted to arrest your father? You think I enjoyed one second of that? *Do you*?" He wagged his head side to side, eyes narrowing. "Because I have to tell you, that was one of the worst moments of my life. Worse than having my own house burned down last year—partly because of *him*, I might add—and worse than having your ex-boyfriend point a gun to my head. *Almost* as bad as you dumping me twelve years ago—"

"For God's sake, Lehigh. Am I the cause of *all* of the problems in your life?" Her voice cracked, and more tears welled up in her eyes. "Are you trying to tell me you'd be better off without me?"

"No, Stacy." Again he kept his voice steady and calm. "It is *not* what I'm saying at all."

"Then what are you saying?" Sadness and anger shone from her eyes.

He took a deep breath, exhaled. "I'm just saying, your dad created some of the mess he put himself into here. He's done some shady stuff—"

"To you."

"Made some enemies—"

"Again, you!"

"And it looks…bad."

"Again—to you!" She bit her lip, then flinched. He waited. No more words came.

He stared at her, crossed his arms over his chest. "Not just to me," he continued in the mildest tone he could muster. "To the entire law enforcement community around here. Of which I am now, partly thanks to you, a leading member."

"Stop blaming me!" She stepped toward him again. "It's not my damned fault."

"I'm not blaming you," he said. "But I am going to do my job."

"No matter what it means for me and my family?" She breathed through her teeth, seething.

He fought to remain calm. Someone in this conversation had to. "If that's how you need to think of this," he said, "then there's nothing I can do to convince you otherwise. Is there?"

"Don't make this about me!" She whirled away from him again and crossed her arms.

He stared at her back. He understood her anger. Why couldn't she see his own pain in this situation? Why must she blame him for this mess instead of her careless, reckless father? Why the blind loyalty to her old man? It's not like he'd always treated her all that well. Certainly she could see the tough spot Lehigh found himself in.

After several moments, he broke the silence. "What would

you have me do, Stacy?"

She turned to face him again. "I'll tell you what you should do," she said. "Let my father go. Even if you think he's guilty, you know he's not going to go anywhere. He doesn't need to sit in jail like a common criminal."

He sighed. She had no idea. "I can't do that, Stacy. It's up to the courts now. They decide on bail and custody."

She clenched her eyes shut. "Why the hell not? Buck Summers never worried about any of that. None of his friends ever spent ten minutes in jail."

"Because I'm *not* Buck Summers! What the hell is wrong with you?" He cursed himself and clamped his mouth shut. He'd tried so hard to keep his temper, and now he'd gone and snapped at her. Stupid, stupid.

"You must think I'm an idiot," she said, almost in a whisper.

"You just took those words right out of my mouth," he said. "About me, I mean."

She paced behind her desk. "You must be able to do something. Sheriffs have pull. You can tell the judge—"

"Stacy, *I can't free him!* Don't you get it? He's been charged with murder. This is serious!" He gripped the edge of her desk. How many different ways could he say this?

She glared at him. "You think that's serious? Well, so am I. Listen to me. If you don't have the courage to stand up to these cretins and keep a man you know to be innocent out of jail—"

"Do we know him to be innocent, Stacy? Do we, for real? Because the evidence is there. It looks pretty bad, Stace." Keep. Voice. Calm. No matter how hard the heart pounds.

Tension filled the air between them. She glared at him as if he had three heads. "Is that how you feel?" she said. "That he actually *may* be guilty of murder?"

He cast about, spread his hands wide. "There's evidence. There's motive. He has no alibi. What am I supposed to think?"

Her jaw dropped. She steadied herself against her desk. "I'll tell you what you can think," she said. "You can think about finding yourself another place to sleep tonight. For as long as you keep my father sleeping on one of your rat-infested cots in a locked jail cell, you can forget about sleeping in *my* bed."

He cocked his head. Had he heard her right? "Are you telling me," he said in a raspy voice, "that because I did my job and arrested your daddy, I got to sleep on the couch?"

She shook her head. "No. Let me clarify. You're not sleeping on my couch, or anywhere in my house. Not sleeping, eating, or brushing your teeth. Until my father is a free man again, I don't want to see you on my property."

Dizziness swept over him. Because he was performing his duty, in a new job that he hated, his two-month-old marriage could be over.

Part II

Enemies Within

Chapter Thirteen

Lehigh flipped through the pages of the report on his desk, ignoring the impatient grunts from his most trusted colleague, Jim Wadsworth, sprawled out in the uncomfortable guest chair in front of him. The D.A.'s report, an updated summary of evidence on the Downey murder, recapped mostly old information. But a separate report, compiled by Lehigh's internal team, contained some new findings of interest.

"I see we've got some witnesses placing George near the scene just before the time of death," Lehigh said. "What dry swamp did they crawl out of?"

Wadsworth frowned. "Bobby Wills found them. Just good old-fashioned investigating. Beating the streets and asking around until someone talks, I gather."

"And another report claims he recently did some target shooting at the Twin Falls marksman's club?" Lehigh shook his head. "That's odd, since George has a private range on his own property."

"McBride denies it," Wadsworth said, "but his signature appears on the sign-in sheet. The range operator confirms the signature came from George. Donnell Winthrop found that piece."

"It just seems like a stupid thing to do if you're planning on shooting someone," Lehigh said. "George is a lot of things, and not all of them good, but I've never known him to be so unsophisticated."

"Ninety percent of the time, crooks get caught by being stupid," Wadsworth said with a wry smile. "Maybe ten percent of the time it's because of brilliant police work. I wish those figures could be reversed, but I'll take a stupid crook's mistakes any day."

"Sure, sure." Lehigh shook his head in wonder. He had tripped up the idiots who'd tried to set him up the year before because of their own sloppy mistakes. He skimmed through the pages. "Forensics matched the tire treads?"

Wadsworth nodded. "And the footprint. Eight and a half, just like your father-in-law. It all looks pretty bad for George."

"Have we checked to see if they match anyone else's tires?"

Wadsworth grunted. "Underway. It's a slog, tracking that stuff down."

Lehigh sighed. The exhaled breath shuddered out of him. "My wife's not going to be very happy. She already thinks I've got it out for her father. Some sort of revenge thing for his shabby treatment of me when we were dating."

Wadsworth straightened in his chair. "You're not telling her any of this, are you? Leaking that to anyone outside of the department or the D.A. would be a serious breach—"

"No, no." Lehigh waved him off. "Hell, I don't talk to her at all right now. You know she kicked me out, right?"

Wadsworth's eyes lowered. "I heard you've been sleeping at a motel. I...didn't want to pry."

Lehigh stood and arched his back. Sore muscles resisted his attempt to stretch. "Sleeping? I wish. I haven't slept a wink since the day of the arrest. That stupid motel is a waste of money I ain't got. Hell, even if I could sleep, the damn bed's so lumpy, I might be better off on the floor. Except the floor's even more disgusting." He stretched again and his lower back muscles barked at him. He sat back in his chair. "Sometimes I wonder why I ever took this job."

Wadsworth turned away. "I'm sorry. I feel like I got you into this."

Lehigh's heart fell into his gut. He couldn't let Wadsworth take the blame for this. "Aw, Jim, it's not your fault. I came into this with eyes open. And I'm still hanging onto the belief that we can make a difference here, clean this place up. I'm not giving up on that yet."

Wadsworth faced him again, his face brightening. "Glad to hear it. Now, do you want me to join you at the meeting with Ferguson today?"

Lehigh shook his head and stood. "Nope. I want you to steer clear. Let him take his shots at me. Speaking of which, I'd better hustle over there. I'm late as it is."

Wadsworth stood and shook his hand. "Thanks, Lehigh. And good luck."

Lehigh grinned. "I'll need it."

***

A knock on Ray Ferguson's office door startled him. He'd asked his secretary to leave him undisturbed until his meeting with Lehigh Carter at ten a.m. No, not asked. He'd left *strict* orders. Why would she—

"Ray? You in there?"

The voice of his top aide on the Downey case, Aaron Williamson, floated in through the door. That meant he'd probably found something new on the case. Something urgent.

Maybe something bad.

Speaking of which...

He folded the pages in front of him top to bottom and slid them into an unmarked yellow envelope, then locked them in the bottom drawer of his desk.

"Yes?" he called out. "Come in, Aaron."

The young attorney strode in, dressed as always in a black suit, white shirt, black oxfords, and a monochromatic tie. Today, crimson. Otherwise he could have been dressed for a funeral. In other words, perfect.

He closed the door behind him and sat in the guest chair in front of Ferguson. "You told me to report to you immediately if I heard of any developments in the Downey case, especially if they came from, er—"

"The other team. Yes." He hated to interrupt, but he could afford no slip-ups. Not on this case. He never knew who might be listening. "Go on," he said.

"Our sources say that, uh, *people* have been asking questions of potential witnesses." Williamson shifted in his seat. "It appears they're trying to poke holes in the case against the, er, accused. From what I gather, they've been unsuccessful, but I thought you should know what they're after."

Ferguson nodded. No surprise there. He didn't expect Carter to sit still while his father-in-law rotted in a jail cell. "Any specifics?"

"His whereabouts around the time of the murder, and leading up to it. His apparent visit to a rifle range a few weeks before. Stuff like that."

Ferguson smiled. Good. The information he'd expected to come to light had done so. Some of it, anyway. "What about forensics? Any news there?"

Williamson's eyes widened. "Um, yes, as a matter of fact. The footprint and tire tread match. As you predicted."

Ferguson smiled. "Indeed. As I predicted. Thank you, Aaron. Good work."

Chapter Fourteen

"Mr. Carter?" said the young man outside Lehigh's motel room door. "I'm Jackson Pitt. How are you today?"

Leaning one shoulder against the edge of the open metal door, Lehigh rubbed sleep from his eyes and took in his visitor's appearance. About 5'10" tall, wearing black slacks and a white polo shirt that hugged his wiry but athletic build, he looked like a distance runner. Probably in his mid-to-late twenties, with light brown acne-free skin, wavy black hair trimmed around his ears, all neat and professional. The name and logo for "Hood Trail Motels" stood out above his chest pocket. Lehigh recalled meeting the man once or twice at the front desk over the course of his stay at the roadside inn.

"I'm fine, but it's a bit early. Unless you're here to bring me coffee." He remained in the doorway, blocking the young man's view—or attempted ingress—inside.

"Well, sir," the young man said, his cheery smile fading, "we were running your charges against your credit card, and, uh, well, sir…the charges were declined."

"Say what?" Lehigh folded his arms, then freed them up to search his pockets. Which he didn't have, because he'd pulled on only a pair of sweatpants and a plain black tank top when he crawled out of bed to answer the door a minute before, at oh-dark-thirty. "Hold on a sec. I'll be right back." He crossed the room to where his uniform rested over the back of a chair at the too-tiny-to-be-useful desk unit built into the wall next to the TV. He searched his pockets and located his wallet. When he turned, he discovered that Jackson Pitt of Hood Trail Motels had followed him into the room.

"I thought I told you to wait outside," he growled, fishing the credit card out of his wallet.

"Did you? Out loud?" Pitt scanned the room. If he was trying to be discreet, he'd failed.

"Get outside while I call my bank," Lehigh said, pointing at the open door. "I'd like some privacy."

"I'm sorry, sir, but technically you haven't paid for the room."

"Listen, Jack," he said, "I—"

"Jackson."

Lehigh blinked. "What?"

The young man leaned against the wall, picking at a perfect fingernail. "Jackson. My name's Jackson, not Jack."

Lehigh sighed, counted to ten, managed to keep his blood pressure under control. "Fine. Jack-*son*. I need you to give me a minute." He picked up his phone and dialed the toll-free Customer Service number on the back. Jackson watched him, unmoving.

"You deaf?" Lehigh said, his voice as sharp as a hunting knife.

"Uh…yeah. Okay, I'll just, uh, go back to the office. When you get this straightened out, you give me a holler, okay?" Pitt shuffled to the door, his pace quickening with each step under Lehigh's glare. Lehigh kicked the door shut behind him, just in time to be put on hold by Customer Service.

***

Shuffling back to the motel's shabby office at the center of the sprawling two-story building, Jackson hummed an old, familiar country song he'd heard on the oldies station, an old ditty by Juice Newton that his parents used to listen to in his youth. Something about not being really smart, and the joker playing with the queen of hearts, or something like that. A stupid song, but it wouldn't leave his mind, so he hummed along. He felt kind of like the foolish joker, having been outplayed in his conversation with the sheriff a moment before, but the song's peppy melody put a spring back into his step, and he reached the office in time to answer the ringing phone on the counter.

"Hood Trail Motel. This is Jackson. How may I—"

"Is he gone?" asked the voice on the other end without so much as a "Hello, nephew."

Jackson cleared his throat. "N-not yet, sir. I just let him know about the credit card—"

"No matter what you have to do," his uncle said, "you make sure he's gone, you got that?"

"Y-yes, sir, I—"

Dial tone interrupted his response. He slammed the phone into its cradle and swore. Some days, he hated his uncle. And some days, this town was just too damned small.

***

An hour later, Lehigh gave up on trying to convince his credit card company to raise his debt limit and hung up in disgust. He had almost no cash, and his bank wouldn't open for at least an hour or two, so they'd be no help. Frustrated, he pulled on his uniform and trudged to the office, a museum of chipped Formica, scuffed linoleum, and bland paint, where he found Jackson Pitt reading something on his computer screen.

"I'll need to get my bank to wire a payment to you," Lehigh said. "If I can just keep my things here until—"

"I'm sorry, sir," Pitt said without looking away from his damned computer. "We need a valid credit card on file with available capacity to hold your room. Company policy."

"It'll have plenty of capacity in a couple of hours." Lehigh's face grew hot. "For heaven's sakes, kid, it's just a few hundred dollars. I'm good for it."

Pitt shook his head. "I'm sorry. As it turns out, your room is unavailable after today anyway. The rodeo has us booked solid through the rest of August."

"Rodeo? Oh, for the love of—! Look. Just give me a few more days so I can find another room." His sweat glands poured cooling moisture over his hot skin. He'd paid no attention to the local entertainment schedule lately. The rodeo tended to take over the whole county for weeks on end. He'd never find another room if he didn't get right on it. Plus, he hadn't scheduled his deputies with any overtime to cover it. He'd have to scramble to get back in front of this.

"I'm sorry, sir. How will you be settling your final bill? Cash, or bank check?"

Lehigh slapped his card on the counter. "Credit card, dammit. Or wire. Just keep the room open for me!"

Pitt shook his head. "I'm so sorry, sir. Checkout time is ten o'clock—about two hours from now. Please remove your belongings and have payment ready." Eyes still glued to his stupid computer.

Lehigh leaned over the counter and waved his hand in front of the screen. "And if I don't?"

Pitt finally glanced his way. "Then I'll have to call the sher—Oh."

Lehigh laughed. "*Now* do you understand the predicament you're in?"

***

Lehigh returned to his room, took one very long final shower and shave at Hood Trail's expense, and changed back into his uniform. Something about this whole situation stunk, and not just the moldy bathroom. The local TV news confirmed Pitt's assertion about the rodeo's impending invasion, reporting that competitors had booked every motel room, bed-and-breakfast, and campsite for a hundred-mile radius. So much for his initial conclusion that the kid had lied to him.

He considered testing the motel management's resolve. He *was* the sheriff, after all. But he dispensed with that idea in one shake of a squirrel's tail. For one thing, if the kid did call the cops, his own deputies would no doubt take great delight in hauling Lehigh's skinny butt out of the room, preferably with TV cameras rolling. Second, a stunt like that is exactly what Buck Summers might have pulled. Exactly, in other words, the sort of behavior he was trying to eliminate from county government.

He stuffed his few spare clothes into his duffel bag and tossed it into the back of his pickup, then glanced toward the office. Through the window he spied the kid still staring at that confounded computer screen. Pitt, he'd said his name was. Jackson Pitt. The name rang a bell. A Jackson Pitt had made a big splash on the Twin Falls football team a few years back, breaking the single-season conference touchdown record as a wide receiver. The record, he recalled with a smile, that Lehigh had set in his own senior year, the last time Clarkesville had taken the conference championship. Some reporter had called once, asking him to comment, but he'd never returned the guy's calls.

What did he care about such things? Records were made to be broken. He'd read the story in the paper when it came out, the kid surrounded by his proud family, a mix of brown and white faces all beaming at the camera. It was a big deal in Mt. Hood County, celebrating a family like that. There weren't many interracial marriages in this conservative part of Oregon, even in the twenty-first century. Even more remarkable, his family on his white mother's side was politically connected—

Lehigh froze, his hand still turning the key in the ignition of his truck, the starter whining its complaint.

Jackson. The kid's mother was Julianna Pitt, neé Julianna Jackson, the younger sister of County Commissioner Elliott Jackson.

Damn it all to hell!

Chapter Fifteen

Moving his stuff took most of the morning and put him in a foul mood. He'd thought about camping, but he had no way of securing his belongings from people and weather when away from the site. Plus, now that he had an office job, people expected him to do things like shave and shower and wear unwrinkled, laundered clothing. How he missed his days in the forest.

The timing of it all put him at the rear side of the sheriff's office, where jail cells held prisoners awaiting trial, just before noon. Lunchtime. An idea struck him when he spied Ted Roscoe just inside the door, pushing a cart laden with covered trays toward the secure area.

"Let me take this for you," he said, blocking Ted's progress down the hallway.

Roscoe stopped the cart and blinked. "Okay. You know the layout? The trays are marked for each inmate."

Lehigh scanned the tray covers, recognizing all of the names—all there because of him. "Yup. Been back there several times. Enjoy your own lunch, okay, Ted?"

Roscoe grinned and whistled down the hallway, a harsh, tuneless noise that echoed off the concrete walls. Lehigh winced. Someone needed to give that boy music lessons. He pushed the cart to the heavy metal doors and entered his access code. A loud click sounded and the doors swung toward him, banging into the cart and pushing it into his midsection. Damn. He'd forgotten which direction they opened. He pulled the cart out of the way, then rolled it through and entered the code to close the doors. They groaned shut behind him. His eyes watered at the familiar harsh aromas of urine, sweat, and bleach assaulting his sinuses. He took a deep breath through his mouth and held it.

He'd sat in one of those cells once before, after Buck had arrested him for burning down his own house, a crime Buck knew he hadn't committed. He'd also made it a policy to visit each occupant at least once while they awaited trial. The one person to whom he still owed a visit sat in the last cell on the right.

He stopped at the first cell, occupied by a couple of tools named Brockton and Thornburgh, two goons that had worked for Lehigh's worst nemesis, Paul van Paten, a former Portland lawyer who sat in the next cell down on the left. All three awaited trial for conspiracy to murder former interim sheriff Jared Barkley, attempted murder of Lehigh, reckless mayhem, and a half-dozen other charges. None of the three said a word to him when he slid their trays through the slot, letting their angry glares do their talking for them. The second cell on the right held the white-haired form of Buck Summers, a man built for comfort rather than speed. Buck mumbled a brief hello and thank you, then sat facing away to attack his lunch plate. Alone among the prisoners, Buck never complained about the food. He didn't dare, since he'd been responsible for providing it for over a dozen years as sheriff, and probably longer as a deputy.

The third and final cell on the left remained empty. Across from it stood the 6' tall, barrel-shaped figure of George McBride, dressed in the same orange jumpsuit as the other four. His face fell when he spotted Lehigh.

"Lunchtime, George," Lehigh said, setting the tray in the slot. George remained at the bars, his eyes focused on his toes.

"Did you *have* to do this?" George said, gripping the black bars of the cell door. "After everything else you've done to me...now this?"

Lehigh's heart fell into his stomach. "I owed you a visit—"

"What you owe me is my freedom! And my good name!"

George shook the bars, or tried to—the thick iron, lodged deep into the concrete, refused to budge. "Will you be returning to bring me those? Huh?"

Lehigh sighed. He couldn't begrudge the man his anger. "If I could open these doors, believe me, I would," he said.

"You can, but you won't!" Spittle flew from McBride's mouth, landing on Lehigh's uniform. "You've always hated me. Ever since Stacy broke off your first engagement twelve years ago. You've always blamed me for that. Don't deny it, I know it's true. You've wanted to get back at me ever since, and here you have the opportunity, and you take it. Get away from me!" He slapped the tray of food back through the slot, and it clattered to the floor. Grilled chicken, mashed potatoes and bright green peas splattered onto the concrete walkway between the cells.

Lehigh took another deep breath, exhaled it. In his peripheral vision he spotted the other inmates staring through the bars of their own cells. A few of them laughed—Brockton and Thornburgh, of course. He wondered if they'd be tried as adults or juveniles for their crimes.

He squatted, picked up the tray, and used a dustpan stored on the bottom tray of the cart to scoop up the lukewarm food. A sponge in warm soapy water, also stored on the tray, mopped up the wet remains. George, clearly, wasn't the first prisoner to toss away his lunch in anger.

He stood and faced George, who glared back at him in apparent defiance and triumph at having reduced Lehigh to the role of janitor. "I'm sorry that I had to be the one to arrest you," Lehigh said. "I thought it would be beneath you to be arrested by anyone of lower rank. You are, after all, the president *pro tempore*—"

"I know who I am!" George shouted, again shaking his arms against the unmoving iron bars. "The question is, do you know who I am? And what I am to you? Do you? I chaired your damned re-election campaign—correction, *first-time* election, Mr. *Interim* Sheriff. And this is how you repay me?"

Lehigh took a moment to let George's anger and sorrow seep

into him. He'd miscalculated, arresting McBride in person, that much had become clear. Damage he couldn't undo. He met George's furious gaze and surrendered the tiniest nod of his head. "Again, I'm real sorry. If there's anything I can do—"

"I've told you what you can do. Let me out of this moldy prison cell. Now!" He coughed, as if on cue, for several seconds. "I can hardly breathe in this place."

Lehigh frowned and shook his head, a slow, remorseful wag. "That's up to the courts, now, sir. But if it means anything to you, I hope they do release you."

"Bull hockey."

Lehigh sighed. He couldn't convince George of his sincere wish for justice, but perhaps he could find another way.

"Senator," he said, knowing the honorific would appease his father-in-law at least a little bit, "there is something I'd like to ask you. About the evidence—"

"So-called evidence, you mean." McBride scowled and turned his back on him.

"Something puzzles me about it all," Lehigh said, "and I thought maybe you could clear it up. It's about the marksmanship reports from the Twin Falls rifle range. It strikes me as odd that you'd go practice there, seeing as how you have a private range on your own property."

"I haven't been to the Twin Falls range in ten years," McBride said with a growl. "Whoever says otherwise is lying."

"The range provided the target with your signature—"

"Forged!" McBride roared. "They're liars, I tell you!"

"Okay then. Now, there's something else, and I'm sure the lawyers have been over this with you, but if you'll indulge me a moment…that cuff link that appeared on the scene—"

"I have no idea how that got there," George said. "I was never there. Not once."

"And the tire tracks—"

"Sheriff, did you come here to insult me? Or to run up my legal bills? Because any further conversation is going to require the presence of my attorneys!" George stood and shook his finger at Lehigh, then pointed down the hallway. "Now get out of here, you lying skunk! And stay away from my daughter. Do you hear me? You are *not* a part of my family. You will regret this, do you hear me? Do you?"

Lehigh braced under the force of McBride's words. He had to admit, they stung, especially the part about Stacy. He turned the cart around in the hallway, then paused to glance at George again. Tried to think of something to say. Nothing came. A cool draft gave him the shivers. Or, something did.

Finally, the mess on the cart gave him words. "I'll, uh, bring you a new lunch."

George spat. The stream of saliva landed on Lehigh's shoe. "Send one of your minions," he said. "I don't want to see you ever again."

Lehigh nodded and rolled the cart toward the heavy metal exit doors, ignoring the gleeful stares of his orange-clad audience.

***

"Gentleman Jim" Wadsworth paused outside the sheriff's office door before knocking, gripping the manila folder in his free hand. The pages didn't tell the story that worried him and would without doubt give Lehigh Carter fits. They simply created the excuse for the impromptu closed-door meeting they needed to have, stat.

His heart rate increased as his knuckles paused inches from the thick wooden door. He couldn't explain his apprehension. Unlike his predecessor, Carter had never shown any tendencies toward "killing the messenger" when bad news showed up on his doorstep. Buck Summers, by contrast, had punished bearers of bad news with graveyard shifts, duty reassignments, disciplinary write-ups for "insubordination," and worse. But where Buck lashed out at others, Lehigh seemed to internalize problems. Sure, he cursed a bit, had broken a few staplers and kicked over a trash can or two. Before becoming sheriff, he'd even clocked a few deserving thugs with a solid right cross. But not for telling him what he didn't want to hear.

Still, Wadsworth had a sense that something had gone wrong. Something, that is, besides the bad news he had to deliver to his boss in a moment—something he couldn't quite name.

Maybe it was just the bad news bugging him. And maybe, just maybe, someone had already told him. Doubtful, but possible. He shook off the foreboding and knocked.

"Who is it?" Lehigh's voice sounded distracted rather than upset. That meant he didn't know yet. Which meant the duty of upsetting his boss remained Wadsworth's.

"Got a minute?"

"Come on in, Jim." He sounded almost pleased.

Wadsworth turned the handle and pushed open the door, expecting to see Lehigh seated at this desk, the usual spare furnishings perched nearby.

Which he did. Except for the "spare" part.

Lehigh's desk, normally set deep into the room, now sat spitting distance from the office door. The two guest chairs rested off to one side rather than in front of the desk. Behind him, boxes stacked three or four high lined the wall. In front of the boxes, on the floor, rested an old soft-sided suitcase with a plaid fabric design. A rolled-up sleeping bag rested against the pile off to one side.

He stared at it all for a few seconds, taking it all in. He coughed.

"Shut the door, would ya?" Lehigh said.

Wadsworth nodded and pushed the door closed. "You're living in your office now?"

Lehigh grimaced and pointed to a chair. "It seems the local motels are all booked a week early for the upcoming rodeo. And my wife's still not keen on letting the man who arrested her father sleep under her roof. So." He waved an arm at his belongings.

"Does anybody else know about this?" Wadsworth slumped into a chair.

"Hell if I know. Who cares? I gotta sleep somewhere."

Lehigh sipped at his coffee mug and gritted his teeth. "Cold coffee. Ugh."

"You might want to keep this quiet," Wadsworth said. "If Commissioner Jackson or that moron Bruce Bailey found out, it could get ugly."

"It's already ugly." Lehigh chuckled and set his coffee mug aside. "What's up?"

Wadsworth rubbed his temples. Great, just great. Not only did he have to deliver bad news—he had to spoil one of Carter's rare good moods. "A buddy of mine in the D.A.'s office just tipped me off to something you'll want to know." Wadsworth sighed. In for a penny, in for a pound. "Why our own men on the task force won't tell us anything is anyone's guess."

Lehigh waved a hand in the air, as if swatting a fly. "No mystery there. Every one of them hates me." He grinned again. "So, what's the big news? You're killing me with the suspense."

Wadsworth grimaced. "Your father-in-law's bail hearing is today. I'm guessing Ferguson didn't tell you?"

Lehigh's head fell into his hands. "Of course not."

Wadsworth sighed. "The odds of him getting out are pretty much nil. Ferguson has him profiled as a flight risk, and as wealthy as he is, he's got a point. Plus his active passport." He paused, shaking his head. "Lehigh, I'm afraid we're going to be hosting your father-in-law for the foreseeable future, until his trial."

Lehigh's face fell into his hands. "Thanks, Jim. I guess I'd better call Stacy."

Uh, oh. That bad feeling returned again. "If you're thinking of getting involved in this," Wadsworth said, leaning forward in his chair, "I have only one word of advice: don't."

"I was just going to warn Stacy—"

"I repeat: don't," Wadsworth said, louder. "My instincts tell me, you should stay away."

"Dammit, Jim. He's family."

Wadsworth sighed. Carter could be so damned stubborn. And he *was* the boss. "Okay. Don't say you haven't been warned." He stood, hitched up his belt, and gazed down on

Lehigh, deep in thought. No doubt he'd already cooked up one of his clever schemes that always seemed to surprise people— and get Lehigh in trouble.

But if he wanted trouble, that was his prerogative. Jim had done his job. With a nod that his boss ignored, Wadsworth trudged out of the office and shut the door behind him.

**

The slamming of his office door shook Lehigh out of his reverie. He'd come up with an idea that might shake some things loose on this case. It meant taking some risks, and the downside, if it didn't work, would look pretty bad for him. Maybe cost him the election. But that thought, rather than causing depression, lifted his spirits a little. Stupid election. Winning would mean staying in this rotten job four more years. That sounded like a death sentence.

Besides, he'd only want to stay in the job if it meant pursuing truth and justice. Breaking up the cronyism that plagued not just the sheriff's office for the past few decades, but the whole county government.

He sat at his desk, debating his next move. Odd that his so-called partner in this investigation, Ray Ferguson, didn't alert him to the court proceedings. In fact, Ray Ferguson had withheld far too much of the truth from him all along, and that seemed contrary to justice. If nothing else, he needed to arrange for prisoner transport from the jail. Hiding basic operational details like this showed either an uncharacteristic sloppiness on Ferguson's part—or an even greater level of distrust than Lehigh had feared.

It stunk. And it needed to be answered.

So far, all of the evidence pointed to George. *All* of it. Which seemed too pat, too neat—contrived, even. It didn't square with what Lehigh knew about his father-in-law. People might call him biased on behalf of his family, but truth to tell, he'd never really liked the man.

Like him or not, though, George McBride built his long,

successful career on words and promises—and, yes, more than the occasional convenient lie, like any politician—but he'd steered very clear of taking direct action. Like, ever. Even when he'd tried to silence Lehigh when he'd stumbled onto illegal campaign contributions during McBride's run for governor, he worked through surrogates. He might very well have conspired to kill Everett Downey, but he almost certainly didn't do it himself. He had help, and as long as he stayed in jail, his cronies would keep their distance. That might suit Ferguson's purposes, providing a single suspect and a clean case against him, but not Lehigh's. With George on the outside, something would shake loose. Someone, somewhere, would make a mistake—and, with luck, Lehigh and his team would find it.

If George didn't do it, he didn't belong in jail. But only the court could order his release. For that, they'd need a strong argument. He was, after all, a murder suspect with many resources at his disposal.

A thought struck him. Something George had mentioned when Lehigh had brought him his lunch. About the mold. County inspectors had cited the facility on numerous occasions for mold and spores. Buck had ignored the reports for years, one of the many things Lehigh had been meaning to change, but other priorities always won out. And he'd read somewhere that mold can aggravate certain medical conditions...

He picked up the receiver on his desk and dialed Stacy's cell number. Before pressing the final digit, though, he paused. Wadsworth's warning flashed through his mind again. He'd learned to trust the big man's experience and instincts, and the warning couldn't have been clearer.

Okay, new plan. He hung up, then dialed a different number.

Chapter Sixteen

"Richards, Stephens, Bullock, Attorneys at Law. How can I help you today?" The officious-sounding male voice carried none of the friendliness to which Lehigh had grown accustomed growing up in Clarkesville, or even in his experiences in larger Oregon cities like Portland. It reminded him of the brusque snobs he'd seen on TV cop shows based in New York or Los Angeles. He'd always hated those people, fictional or not.

"This is Lehigh Carter. May I speak with—"

"Good morning, Sheriff. A pleasure to hear from you again." The man's voice transformed into a soft, harmonic ooze. Like wet velvet, except fake. More like a polyester towel smeared with margarine. "How may I direct your call?"

"As I was saying," Lehigh said, a little more gruff than he'd intended, "I'd like to chat with Constantine Richards, if I could."

"I'm sorry," the receptionist said. "Mr. Richards is in court today. Can one of our other partners assist you?"

"Yes, but we'll need to hurry," Lehigh said.

***

Lehigh considered hanging out by George's cell until his escort arrived to take him to court, but decided against it. Both sides, he reckoned, would take that the wrong way, and explaining would only tip his hand. Instead, he slipped out of the office around 9:30 a.m. and drove away in his truck, right past the courthouse about a block away and beyond. He sipped a weak cup of coffee at Dot's Diner, grimaced at the taste and dumped in more cream and sugar. "You know what they say about Dot's," Wadsworth once joked with him. "No beans were harmed in the brewing of this coffee."

He sat alone at the counter. Nobody approached him, although conversations buzzed whenever he looked in the opposite direction of whatever cluster of diners huddled in each corner. He wondered what topics in his life fascinated them more: the negative stories in the press about how bad of a job he was doing as sheriff, or how much his deputies hated him, or his political weakness and ineptitude. Or maybe they focused on the personal, like his troubled marriage to a former employee of the murdered Everett Downey, a woman who'd spent much of the year in jail on charges of murdering Jared Barkley—a man they all thought she'd been sleeping with. Or how a group of conspirators burned down his house and framed him for it, then tried to kill him, and damn near succeeded. Take your pick, he wanted to tell them. It was all as juicy to chew on as that Canadian bacon on their greasy plates.

At five minutes before ten, he left enough cash to cover his bill and a generous tip and left the diner. Less than ten minutes later he parked in his usual spot at the office. Minutes later he entered the building a block away and slid into the back row of the gallery of courtroom number two, unnoticed by almost everyone. Only one person acknowledged him—the person he cared about the most.

Stacy waved to him from the second row of the gallery, then turned back toward the judge. He recognized the worry in her eyes, masked by the confident smile she'd put on for her father's benefit. George sat in front of her, wearing a dark suit, contrasting with his red scalp visible between thick combed rows of white hair locked into place with gel. She whispered something to him and patted his shoulder. George nodded and bowed his head. Beside Stacy, her mother Catherine sat in stoic silence.

The lawyers conferred with the judge at the bench, their backs to the courtroom. Judge Petros Geroux, a thin, bespectacled man with thin black-and-white hair and black-framed glasses perched on a long, pointed nose, whispered in turn to each attorney with curious skepticism. Ferguson clenched and unclenched his fists as the defense attorney answered the judge's inquiries, then interrupted. The judge held up a hand as if to silence him. Lehigh smiled. The Rev could get pretty wound up, particularly in court. Most judges in Mt. Hood County put up with it, but not this one.

The judge waved them away, and both men returned to their respective benches. Ferguson looked unhappy, and doubly so when he spotted Lehigh. Lehigh responded with an aw-shucks wave. Surprise, Reverend. Company.

Constantine Richards, a man of patrician bearing despite his Albert Einstein-like shock of white hair, huddled with George and an aide, speaking in quiet voices. He straightened and winked at Lehigh, then set his half-lens glasses atop his long, Roman nose and faced the judge. George turned to face his wife, his eyes wide and mouth moving. Catherine responded with a start, her hand covering her mouth. Stacy spun in her seat, and her mouth formed an O when she caught Lehigh's eye.

He smiled at her. She cocked her head to one side and, as though lost in thought, turned her attention back to the proceedings.

"Very well, then. I understand you have something to offer, counselor?" the judge said, his gaze sweeping the defendant's side of the courtroom.

"What's this?" Ferguson said. "Your honor, it's far too late for the defense to be—"

"I'll decide what is permitted or not in this court," the judge said, pointing a finger at Ferguson. "Now wait your damned turn. Mr. Richards?"

Richards stood and cleared his throat. "Yes, your honor. The defense petitions the court to order a compassionate, immediate release of the defendant, on grounds that the condition of the facilities aggravates a documented and potentially fatal medical condition." He handed some papers to the judge, who scanned them and nodded.

"You have copies for the prosecution?" Judge Geroux asked.

Richards held up more papers, and the clerk delivered them to a sputtering Ferguson at his own team's desk.

"Our firm has represented dozens of clients before this court, many of whom have been detained in county facilities pending trial," Richards said. "Our history shows that the county jail facilities are conducive to the growth of molds and spores, which in turn contribute to or aggravate symptoms of pleurisy, bronchitis, arthritis, and other breathing disorders. These conditions can be life-threatening, and the court has taken these factors into account in past bail and custody rulings. The defendant's personal physician has signed an affidavit attesting to Mr. McBride's history of pleurisy, and our brief details how the defendant could suffer unwarranted, serious, adverse health consequences from his continued detention there. In short, your honor, unless our client is released immediately, he may not survive until trial."

Lehigh kept his eye on Ferguson during the defense attorney's speech. As expected, the prosecutor grew agitated, hopping from foot to foot, anticipating an opening. "I object!" he said when Richards paused for breath.

"Settle down, Mr. Ferguson," Judge Geroux said. "You feeling ill, George?"

McBride coughed, convincing in ferocity if not in timing. "I've been better, your honor," he said. "Thanks for asking."

"May I approach?" Ferguson asked.

"Counselors," Geroux said in a weary voice, motioning for both lawyers to gather at the bench. Ferguson made it there in double-time, already jawing at the judge before Richards could even leave his seat. Lehigh's attention, though, focused on the dark-haired wonder seated behind the lawyer, who'd affixed Lehigh with an open-mouthed stare from the moment Richards had risen to speak.

"You?" she mouthed. A smile hinted at her lips.

Lehigh stood, winked at her, and left the courtroom with a spring in his step. There were things to like about being sheriff after all.

***

The ruling didn't take long. Nor did it take long for the heat to rain down on Lehigh's head.

"What were you thinking?" Ferguson's voice echoed off the walls of Lehigh's office—even over the phone. "Why did you even involve yourself in this?"

"Well, hello to you, too, Raymond," Lehigh said into the receiver. He turned the handset 90 degrees so the earpiece extended in front of his face, saving his eardrum from the Rev's crushing volume. "I take it the judge has made a decision?"

"Don't play coy with me!" Ferguson's voice grew hoarse despite dropping about ten decibels in volume. "You know as well as I do that his jail cell remains empty. You needn't try to continue your deceptions with me!"

"Deception? I'm afraid I don't follow."

"The entire county knows you fed that report to his defense team today," the Reverend said, his voice rising again. "Did you really think we'd be so stupid as to not put two and two together?"

Lehigh smirked, glad Ferguson couldn't see him. "You don't want me to answer that." He chuckled while the line went silent, knowing that Ferguson was doing everything he could to stop himself from saying something he'd later regret.

"Just whose side are you on, Carter?" Ferguson said after several seconds. "Or is it too much to ask for you to try to keep murderous criminals off the streets just once? To speak nothing of your oath of office, and your duty to the community? What makes you so blind, Carter? Family? Fear of McBride's position in the community? *Do not pervert justice; do not show partiality to the poor or favoritism to the great,*' the Bible says. I know you can't be bothered to go to church on Sundays, but I know your parents are God-fearing. Didn't they raise you on scripture, boy?"

Lehigh took a breath. Despite the religious rant, or perhaps because of it, Ferguson had calmed to the point that Lehigh could hold the phone against his head, and that only meant that the Rev once again had full control of his mental faculties.

Ferguson had earned a well-deserved reputation for his ability to bait witnesses into saying too much, and Lehigh vowed to stay out of that trap.

"I'm on the side of justice, Raymond. Which, in our system, means we lock up the bad guys—and only the bad guys. Which means," he said, rushing on to keep Ferguson from interrupting, "in our system of innocent until proven guilty, being accused doesn't mean you've done it. Or did I get that backwards? Help me out, I'm new around here."

"Don't give me your high school civics lesson," Ferguson said with a nasty edge in his voice, his volume rising. "You pulled a fast one to help your father-in-law. I get it. But mark my words, Carter. If he doesn't show up for his trial—if he so much as walks in a half-minute late—he's going to prison for contempt. And so are you. Not to that rinky-dink vacation home of a jail you run over there, either. You're going downstate, where the hard-time convicts split heads just to stay in shape. Have I made myself clear?"

Lehigh shook his head in amazement. When the Rev got wound up, he could lay it on hard. "Raymond, if George is guilty, I promise to help you lock him away, and I'll throw away the key myself. But until then, I don't intend to treat him any different than any other person accused of a crime. Am *I* being clear?"

After a loud breath, Ferguson responded. "Be careful about protecting him, Carter. If your father-in-law walks because of your help, you will pay. Remember: 'God stores up the punishment of the wicked for their children. Let him repay the wicked, so that they themselves will experience it.' Job twenty-one nineteen."

Lehigh gritted his teeth. "Yeah? Well, *you* best be careful too, Reverend. Remember, *'Fools give full vent to their rage, but the wise bring calm in the end.'* Proverbs, twenty-nine."

The line went dead. Lehigh brought the headset back to its receiver, and noticed, to his own surprise, that his hands were shaking.

Chapter Seventeen

Stacy slid into the booth at Shirley's Cafe with her back to the wall and one eye on the door. It meant sitting too close to the swinging saloon-style doors and the cacophony of the kitchen, but it guaranteed that no one could enter or escape without her seeing them.

"Coffee, hon?" A heavy-set waitress with a brown tower of curls atop a round, ruddy face turned Stacy's cup right-side up in its saucer and splashed light brown liquid halfway to the brim. "All by yourself today, or will a tall-dark-and-handsome be joining ya?"

"There'll be two of us. That's enough coffee, thanks." Stacy opened three thimbles of cream and dumped them into her cup, turning its contents snow white. "I'll wait to order until he arrives."

"Gotcha." The waitress winked. "Good thinking. Men like ordering for you. Makes 'em feel smart." She hustled away, the heels of her flats clapping an uneven beat on the dingy brick-red tile floor.

Stacy stirred fake sugar into her coffee and stewed over the waitress's inappropriate comments. She couldn't care less about making men, or anyone, feel smart—including the man already five minutes late for what she'd hoped would be their first make-up date since their big fight. Men didn't need women calling them smart. If anything, they needed reminders of how clueless they acted most of the time.

Most men, anyway. Lehigh seemed pretty grounded and self-aware most of the time. Maybe that's what drew her to him—

the self-assured way that he took on the world, always on his own terms and without pretense. "It is what it is," he always said, a wisdom he'd gained from his salt-of-the-earth parents. Despite her anger over him arresting her father, she missed him. A lot. But, as hard as she tried, she couldn't forgive what he'd done to her father. George had emerged from his few weeks in jail a broken man, shamed and afraid, his fragile health weakened by the ordeal. Not the strong, confident man who'd raised her.

But then Lehigh had helped him. Maybe she had reason to hope. Heaven knows, she wanted a reason. She couldn't decide which made her more sad: waking up each morning alone, or eating microwaved dinners in front of the TV with the sound turned up loud enough to drown her loneliness until she nodded off. Or trudging upstairs to bed, knowing that she wouldn't sleep a wink without his strong presence lying next to her.

The front door opened with a whoosh, and a tall, broad-shouldered man in a khaki uniform shuffled through. Her hopes rose—then fell. The man removed his aviator sunglasses, met her gaze, and smirked. He took off his hat, revealing a conservative black buzz cut, and ambled over to her table.

"Dining alone today?" Sergeant DuPont asked. He smelled like spicy gym socks, reminiscent of the cheap aftershave her grandfather used to wear when grandma went out of town.

"For the moment," she said.

"That's a shame," he said. "And risky. You never know what kind of trouble a pretty woman like you could attract in a town like this." His tone grew even slimier. "Word's out that you're single again. Wouldn't you rather have the company of a strong man beside you?"

"I will, soon," she said. "Until then, I'd rather be left alone."

"Now, let's not be all unfriendly." DuPont edged closer. Too close. "I'm just looking for some company myself."

She thought about sliding away from him, but he might take that as an invitation. Instead she glared at him with false bravado. "What's the matter, Deputy?" she asked. "Have you run out of defenseless women to harass on the streets, or are diners your preferred venue for annoying private citizens?"

His eyes darkened and he leaned over the table, his large frame casting an imposing shadow over her. He put his face inches from hers, overwhelming her with the aroma of moldy laundry. "You know," he said, "your husband isn't gonna be sheriff forever around here. Maybe not even six months from now. You might want to reconsider who you want as friends when he goes back to hunting squirrels for a living."

"I don't kill squirrels. I eat 'em alive, like I do misbehaving deputies."

DuPont froze, his snarky smile fading like the color in his face. Over his shoulder appeared a lanky, long-haired man, disgust apparent in his downturned lips and furrowed brow. Despite the current tensions with her husband, Stacy couldn't help but smile at Lehigh's strange humor.

"I–I–" DuPont shuffled aside, a hang-dog look overtaking his face. "I didn't expect—"

"You never know what to expect from a wild mountain man who eats rodents, do you, Deputy?" Lehigh glared at his employee and slid around him to sit in the booth opposite Stacy. "Now, don't you have some actual criminals to arrest somewhere?"

"Y–yes, sir," DuPont said. He stared at his shoes, hat in hand, and backed away from the booth. After a few steps, he bumped into a waitress carrying a tray loaded with stacks of sandwiches, drinks, and deep-fried treats. He mumbled an apology and hustled out the door.

"I can see why your deputies love you so much," Stacy said in a teasing tone. "With a bedside manner like that, maybe you should become coroner next."

Lehigh glared at her. "You're welcome."

Stacy flushed. Uh-oh. She'd misjudged his mood—again. When in a take-no-prisoners frame of mind, Lehigh's rough edges could leave a wide path of destruction in his wake.

"I'm sorry. Thank you. Tough day so far?" She tried on a smile. It didn't fit, and from Lehigh's reaction, he could tell.

"Every day. What's up with DuPont? Is he still bugging

you?"

She shrugged. "This is the first time since the traffic stop. After this, I don't suspect he'll bother me again."

"You let me know if he does." Lehigh signaled the waitress for a cup of coffee. "Have you ordered?"

"No, I just got here. Are you pressed for time?" He seemed fidgety. Nervous. As if he wanted to leave—or not be there in the first place.

"No."

They sat in silence for a time. After what seemed like hours, Lehigh picked up the menu and stared at it.

"The lunch menu's on the other side," Stacy said.

He lifted his eyes over the top of the menu, gazed at her several seconds longer. "I've got a hankering for some pancakes. Breakfast all day here, right?"

She took a heavy breath. "Right. Of course. Pancakes for dinner?" She managed a smile.

His gaze did not waver, nor did his expression. "Lunch. Unless this is a longer meeting than necess—er, expected."

Heat flashed over her face. Her fingers trembled on the edges of her own menu. "Longer than necessary, huh? I should think that—"

"Stacy, I didn't mean—"

"Saving our marriage is worth—"

"I have a meeting—"

"A few minutes out of your precious workday—"

"I can make a few calls—"

"Of the job you *hate*!"

Her voice echoed off the walls of the suddenly quiet restaurant. Not so much as the "ting" of a fork touching a plate disturbed the silence. Every set of eyes in the busy cafe seemed to stare at her.

Including Lehigh's. But unlike the others, which expressed curiosity or pity, his blazed with anger.

"Thank you," he said, setting down the menu. "Now every soul in town knows how I feel about being sheriff. That ought to go over well in the November election."

"Lehigh, I—"

"I wonder if Bruce Bailey's here? Maybe we could see a replay of all of this on the six o'clock news." He grabbed his hat and slid across the booth. But before he could exit, the brown-haired waitress returned, blocking his escape.

"Are we ready to order?"

"Yes!" Stacy blurted out the words before Lehigh could object. "I'll have the chicken Caesar salad, light on the dressing. He'll have the pancakes. Right, honey?"

He fixed his eyes on her, his face darkening, a harsh breath escaping through his lips. "Reuben. *Extra* dressing. Fries. And I believe I already asked for—"

"Coffee?" A curly-haired, freckle-faced boy dressed all in white, save for the smorgasbord of food stains on his apron, held a cup and saucer out to Lehigh from the waitress's blind side, his hands as shaky as his customer-service smile. "Will you need—"

"Cream and sugar." Lehigh nodded.

"I'd like some more coffee as well." Stacy fought to keep the edge out of her voice, but probably failed, judging by the boy's frozen stance, with a cup and saucer poised inches above the tabletop. Lehigh sideways-eyeballed the kid and extended an index finger in Stacy's direction. The boy slid around the waitress and reached out again with the saucer, this time in front of Stacy, his hands shaking more than ever. Coffee splashed from cup to saucer to placemat, creating brown rivers rushing to encircle the condiment containers spread across the center of the table.

"Oh my gosh, I'm so sorry! I'll go grab a rag." The boy disappeared in a white blur toward the kitchen. The waitress clucked her tongue, rolled her eyes and wiped up the mess with a brown-stained rag.

"Can't get good help no more," the waitress said, clacking her gum. "I'll run and get you both some fresh coffee and cream and get your orders in. You all sit tight." In a flash, she, too, disappeared behind the swinging saloon-style doors.

Stacy stared at the wet, brown-streaked table, then lifted her eyes to Lehigh's. His eyes seemed sad, filled with resignation and regret. She imagined hers did, too.

And then, to her surprise, his eyes brightened, and the lines around his eyes and mouth deepened. Not lines of worry or anger, though.

He was laughing.

At first, it was just a chuckle. More of a snort, followed by a choked-back guffaw, unsuccessfully suppressed as the irony of their situation overcame the inappropriateness of his reaction. Then giggles, his hand covering his mouth. Tears, even.

To her even greater surprise, she found herself laughing, too. Not just polite expressions of amusement, but loud, uncontrollable high-pitched peals of ridiculousness. He responded in kind, laughing loud and hard, and in moments they'd lost all control of their laughter, like drunks telling obvious lies about fish caught, touchdowns scored and royalty kissed in outer space. They laughed until their tension evaporated, their anger spent, and their coffee, which had somehow appeared without notice, had gone cold.

For a moment, all went quiet again. Then:

"I love you," he said.

"I love you too," she said. Then, as quickly and forcefully as they'd laughed, she cried, tears bubbling forth like geysers, and through the blur she saw he'd started crying, too. Then he held her hand, both hands, and they sat there, crying, until both of them somehow knew it was time to stop.

***

"Well, ain't this great," he said, minutes later when they could speak again. "Ain't no one gonna vote for no crybaby sheriff." He smiled, not that he felt the least bit happy, but to let her know that he was joking.

"I will." She smiled too. Not joking.

Their lunches arrived and somehow that got them down to business.

"So, about my father," she said, scooping up a bite of chicken onto her fork. "Thank you for helping to get him released."

Lehigh dipped a French fry in ketchup and stuffed it into his mouth. He hated ketchup, but Sheila's fries were inedible otherwise. "Just doing what's right. But, you're welcome."

"What can we do to get them to drop the charges?" she asked.

He shook his head. "It's out of my hands. It's up to the D.A. and the courts now. But if it helps, I don't think we had enough evidence to arrest him—yet."

"It does help," she said. "But if that's the case, why *did* you arrest him?"

He picked up a fry, set it back down. He'd lost his appetite. "Once the D.A. decided to charge him, it's my sworn duty to take him into custody."

"So you take that oath more seriously than our wedding vows?"

His breath caught in his throat. She could be impossible sometimes. "I take our wedding vows as seriously as you do. Which is why you surprised me by kicking me out. For better and for worse—"

"Faithfulness matters!" Her volume soared.

He took a deep breath, exhaled it out his nose. "I haven't been unfaithful to you."

"You're being unfaithful to my family. *Our* family. Arresting my father! Putting him in that disgusting jail cell! For murder of all things!" She tossed her napkin onto her unfinished salad and turned away from him.

"Are you listening to me? For Pete's sake, Stacy. The D.A. charged him, not me!" He picked up his untouched Reuben, stared at it, set it back onto his plate, and ate another awful French fry instead.

"You're an elected official. Seems to me you could show a little political backbone." Still she refused to look at him.

"I'm an *interim* public servant, *appointed* to fill an unexpired term by a corrupt sheriff who played favorites. Do you want me to just follow in Buck's footsteps and land myself in jail?"

"Better you than my f—"

She stopped, a hand over her mouth, eyes wide. "No, I mean—"

"I know what you mean." He stood, grabbed his sandwich off his plate, and slapped a twenty and a five on the table. "And I'm very glad I understand how you feel now. For better or for worse, my ass!"

He stomped out the exit, ignoring her protests. He strode over to his truck, unlocked the door. Footsteps crunched the pavement behind him. Hand on the open door, he took a deep breath. "Stacy, I don't think this is the time and place to—"

"Sheriff?" A familiar male voice surprised him. He swiveled to find an old high school pal, Phil Reardon, approaching.

Lehigh calmed and even managed a weak smile. "S'up, Phil?"

The balding man, a few inches shorter than Lehigh with the build of an out-of-shape linebacker, coughed into his fist. "I just wanted to say, Lee. I–I think you're doing a great job as sheriff."

"Why, thanks, Phil. What brings this on?"

Phil shuffled his feet and put his hands in the back pockets of his jeans. "I saw what went on in there with your wife. I know arresting your father-in-law couldn't have been easy. But you did the right thing, in my opinion."

"Thanks." Lehigh smiled and shook his hand. "Unfortunately, I think you and I might be alone in holding that point of view."

Phil shook his head. "Nope. A lot of people around here feel that way. It's just that—well, after putting up with Buck and his gang for so long, people are fed up, but still scared of what might happen."

"What do you mean?" Lehigh studied his old classmate's face, wrinkled with worry. "Scared of what?"

Phil looked around as if checking for spies, then stepped closer and lowered his voice. "In the bad old days—six months or a year ago—people didn't dare stick their necks out around here. Anyone who did found themselves on Buck's bad side, and then..." He looked around again. A young family exited Sheila's and waved to them. Phil waved back and shook his head. "Let's just say, nothing good ever came of talking to the sheriff back then." He dipped his head and shuffled away.

Lehigh stared after him. Somehow, he needed to find a way to make it easier for people like Phil to do the right thing in this county. To speak up and help stand up against the people who kept good, hard-working citizens like Phil living in fear—even if it cost Lehigh his marriage.

But how?

Chapter Eighteen

Wadsworth greeted Lehigh at the door to his office wearing a grim expression with a TV remote in his hand. "I feel like I'm always the bearer of bad news," he said, "but you need to see this."

Lehigh followed him into the detective's office. A small TV sat atop a video recorder on a file cabinet. Wadsworth turned it so Lehigh could see it from the guest chair in front of the desk and flicked it on.

"Midday soaps?" Lehigh joked.

Wadsworth's expression grew even darker. "I'm betting that you haven't seen the news." He clicked "rewind" and waited for the images to blur by in reverse.

"I try to avoid that habit every day," Lehigh said. But then he caught up with Wadsworth's implication and his good mood vanished. "Don't tell me," he said. "Babbling Bruce?"

Wadsworth exhaled noisily and hit "play."

Lehigh's heart pounded in his chest. What had he done now to get the media all into a frenzy? He half-expected to see his argument with Stacy at the start of lunch pop up onto the screen, but instead, Bailey's smug, maddeningly handsome face filled the screen, somewhere outdoors. Wadsworth hit the *Pause* button and faced Lehigh.

"I wish I didn't have to show you this," he said, "but better that you know what's happening than not." Wadsworth took a deep breath and hit *Play*.

"Breaking news in the Everett Downey murder investigation!" Bruce Bailey announced from the TV. His face appeared somber, but no amount of makeup could hide the joy shimmering in his bright blue eyes. He stood in front of the courthouse just a few blocks from where Lehigh sat, his face lit by morning sun. A few curious passersby gawked into the camera behind him.

"What breaking news?" Lehigh asked. "Nobody's told me—"

"Sh!" Wadsworth said. "Listen."

Lehigh growled, but obeyed. So far the day had been an emotional roller coaster, and everything pointed toward it getting a whole lot worse.

"Sheriff's department investigators revealed today that contamination of the murder scene may have compromised physical evidence linking Senator George McBride, the defendant in the upcoming murder trial, to the crime," Bailey said. "This revelation could spell big trouble for the prosecution, inside sources say."

"What in the hell is he talking about?" Lehigh said, his voice too loud. But he didn't care. This was crazy. "We didn't contaminate any murder scene. And who—"

"Listen!" Wadsworth said again. "Talk after."

"However," Bailey went on, "prosecutors say that DNA evidence—"

"What DNA evidence? Why don't I know about this?"

"Apparently, ours," Wadsworth said, his face turning red. "Listen, will you *please*?"

Lehigh opened his mouth to reply, then thought better of it.

"—confirms that McBride was at the scene," Bailey said. The image shifted to the wooded area off of Brady Mountain Road, with yellow tape still visible through the trees. "Insiders suggest that the defendant may have been responsible for the contaminated evidence, and in any case, that evidence was at best, quote, supportive and circumstantial."

"Oh, for the love of cheese," Lehigh said. "Are they trying to say that because we let George out—"

"Hush!"

Lehigh growled at Wadsworth but obeyed. He was worse than Stacy, always shushing him when they watched TV.

"The investigators," Bailey said, his silly mug once again filling the screen, "who would not speak or be identified on camera, speculate that further charges could be filed—"

"What the hell?" Lehigh jumped to his feet and ignored Wadsworth's protestations. "Who's talking to the press about the case? Didn't we instill the fear of God into the hearts of everyone on the team? Or did I attend a different meeting?"

Wadsworth shook his head, frustration and sadness competing for primacy in his facial expression. "We did," he said. "But someone didn't listen."

"Are you sure it's one of ours?" Lehigh said.

Wadsworth just stared back at him in silence.

"We turn now to County Commission Chairman Elliott Jackson," Bailey intoned from the television, and Jackson's white mop and bulbous nose appeared next to the reporter, wearing, as usual, a sausage casing of a blue suit too tight around his beach-ball body. His expression seemed to scream both anger and triumph, a smile and a frown competing for dominance in the middle of his ruddy face. "Commissioner," Bailey said, "what does this mean for the investigation?"

"What would he know about it?" Lehigh said. Wadsworth shrugged.

"It means that the corruption, ineptitude, and cronyism in our sheriff's department has hit a new low," Jackson said. "I warned the other commissioners about the risks of putting our law enforcement in the hands of amateurs, and now we reap what we sow."

"Will you consider removing him from office?" Bailey asked.

"*What?*" Lehigh's screech actually moved papers on Wadsworth's desk.

"Nothing is off the table." Jackson glared at Lehigh from the TV screen. "We'll do what we must to return professionalism and competence to our law enforcement leadership. It will be my top priority."

Wadsworth clicked off the TV. Lehigh swore and closed his

eyes. Damn this job all to hell.

"For what it's worth," Wadsworth said, "none of this came from me, and in fact, I think it's a load of bunk."

"Thanks, Jim," Lehigh said, eyes still closed. Of course he hadn't suspected the detective, or anyone on the team. But clearly someone was yakking.

"I mean, okay, you're not the most experienced law enforcement guy in the county," Wadsworth went on, "nor the most skilled administrator around. And when it comes to politics, you're, well, kind of a fish out of water."

"Jeez, Jim. Are you sure you're on my side?" Lehigh said, opening his eyes.

"But," Wadsworth said, rushing his words, "you're honest. You've got principles. You work harder than anybody I've ever met, and that's saying something. None of that could be said for Buck Summers or either of the guys I worked for before him. In fact, as far as good sheriffs go, in my lifetime we've had you, and Jared, and that's it. There's less than six months of decent law enforcement in over four decades."

"I bet you say that to all the lumberjacks," Lehigh said with a grin. But he did feel better.

"Unfortunately," Wadsworth said, motioning to the TV, "I seem to be in the minority."

"You know, Jim," Lehigh said, "this may be the worst pep talk I've ever heard."

"Sorry. You know me. I calls 'em as I sees 'em."

"The worst thing is," Lehigh said, pacing the room, "these leaks only set us back on finding out who killed Ev Downey. If all we do is chase our tails, we'll never find the evidence pointing to the real murderer."

"You really don't think McBride plugged him?" Wadsworth asked.

"No. At least, not alone," Lehigh said. "And it bugs me that so many people want to shut this down and keep us from asking questions that might lead to another suspect. Doesn't it bother you, too?"

"It does. And you're right. We'll never get anywhere if people keep cutting our feet out from under us." Wadsworth stared at his feet, shaking his head. "We're going to have to investigate and chop off a few heads. The moment Ray Ferguson sees this—"

A knock sounded on the door, followed by Julia's timid voice. "Sheriff? Detective? Are you in there? The deputy district attorney is here, and—well, I think you'd better talk to him."

Lehigh clenched his eyes shut. He'd been right about one thing. This day just kept getting worse.

***

"These leaks have got to stop!" Ray Ferguson had yet to take a seat in the cramped meeting room, despite having nowhere to go. Lehigh considered starting a tally of how many times he pushed aside an empty chair that blocked the attorney's path as he paced behind his assistants seated opposite of Lehigh, Wadsworth, and Ruby Mac. Instead he jotted down a reminder to have it checked and repaired later—and to bill the D.A.'s office for it. Ferguson had pushed it too hard more than once, smashing its rollers into the legs of the table and the wall, rendering it immobile and lopsided.

"I agree," Lehigh said. "And the sooner you get control of your staff—"

"My office maintains strict protocols controlling information access and release!" Ferguson plowed over the chair again in an attempt to reach Lehigh. Luckily the chair, in its crumbling condition, served better as a blockade than as a missile. "Your department is responsible for this. Always has been, Sheriff. Even under Buck Summers—"

"*Especially* under Buck Summers," Ruby said below her breath.

"All due respect, Mr. Ferguson," Wadsworth said over her, "our people don't even have access to the information Bruce Bailey reported." The ever-patient Wadsworth had remained quiet for the first twenty minutes of the meeting, mostly, Lehigh suspected, because Ferguson had dominated the first nineteen with his crazy ranting.

"Of course you do," Ferguson said, whirling to face the detective. "We brief your deputies daily. Don't we, Clayton?" He pointed to Detective Maddox, seated alone at the far end of the table. He'd stayed so still and quiet, Lehigh had forgotten he was there.

Maddox nodded. "Yes, sir. Morning briefings of the task force. All hands present."

"The problem, Raymond," Lehigh said, fighting to keep his voice calm, "is that the task force doesn't share that information with us. The first I heard of it was on the news."

"And if these leaks continue, I'll see that you get even less!" Ferguson's veins throbbed on the side of his head, and his face turned as red as an unripe marionberry.

"If we're not getting any information now, how could we get any less?" Ruby asked, deadpan.

"The point is," Lehigh said before Ferguson could respond, "the leaks are a problem. We can all agree to that, right? Not least because it distracts us all from doing our job—gathering information that leads to a conviction of the murderer."

"George McBride," Ferguson said.

"Or whoever it is," Lehigh said. "I know you're convinced, and it's your job to be."

"He's the killer, Carter," Ferguson said. "I understand why you don't want to believe it, which is why the task force is under my direction. But it's true, and the sooner you accept that, the better."

"Regardless," Lehigh said, giving up on keeping Ferguson's mind open, "We don't want George McBride tried in the press."

"Not least because he's got a better lawyer than we do," Ruby said, this time not quite under her breath.

Gasps hissed from the attorneys' side of the room. Ferguson's mouth gaped wide, his eyes widening, face getting even redder. Lehigh wondered if he'd survive the insult, expecting the veins on the side of his head to pop at any moment.

"What my deputy means," Lehigh said, hand raised to shush Ruby from any further outbursts, "is that Constantine Richards will exploit any loophole, any technicality he can, to win for his client." An idea popped into his head that he hadn't considered before. It shocked him, and went straight to his mouth. "This raises the question: did the leaks come from *their* side? Was the information Bailey reported shared with the defense?"

Ferguson whirled to face his assistants. Assistant D.A. Williamson coughed and nodded, then shrank into his chair.

Lehigh pretended to write something on his notepad, letting the moment linger. He'd surprised the prosecutors with that idea as much as himself. Which meant he had one new advantage on this front: initiative.

"Well, then," Lehigh said, his eye on Ferguson in case he literally exploded, "We know who to talk to next. And I might know just who to ask."

He glanced at Wadsworth, whose jaw had dropped nearly to the table. He nodded once, confirming what he knew Jim suspected. Yes, he'd just volunteered to investigate his own wife's interference in the case. And it would not be any fun at all.

***

""So, Jim. Are we the problem?"

Several minutes before, Ruby had escorted Ferguson's team, including Clayton Maddox, out of the building and returned to her regular duties. Only Lehigh and Wadsworth remained in the cramped meeting room. Lehigh had defended his team with vigor against Ferguson's attacks, but he had to concede one point to the Deputy D.A.: the sheriff's office had, over the years, earned its reputation as corrupt and untrustworthy. He'd suffered at their hands himself not long before.

"If we were talking about the folks who ran this building a year ago, I'd say yes," Wadsworth said, a glum expression on his face. "People around here couldn't be trusted to keep things confidential. Not if it served their purpose to keep Bruce Bailey's face on TV."

"I wouldn't have trusted them with a load of dog crap," Lehigh said, trying but failing to lighten his own mood. "As I kept discovering, the foxes were guarding the henhouse, and nobody believed it, even when their mouths were full of feathers. But what about now?"

"Now?" Wadsworth drew a deep breath, exhaled, cocked his head this way and that. "It's...*better*. The worst of the bad apples are gone, and you've brought in some good new people. I trust Ruby Mac implicitly. Martin Lightfoot is honest to a fault. The others—well, let's just say there's a range."

Lehigh's ears tingled, and he found it hard to breathe for a moment. "Wait. *All* of the others?"

"I'm not saying they're bad," Wadsworth said, his words rushing out like a spring brook after a heavy rain. "They're just...untested. And I don't know that I'd bet on all of them passing a test."

Lehigh gritted his teeth. That meant that over half of his new team could be culprits. Then a light dawned as he realized the implications of Wadsworth's comments. "Wait. You're suggesting that we test them somehow?"

Wadsworth hesitated. "Maybe not all. Maybe just the most likely candidates."

"Namely?" Lehigh's pulse quickened. He had his own suspicions, but wanted to hear those of his most trusted and experienced colleague first.

"I'd narrow it down to three. Roscoe, Winthrop, and Wills," Wadsworth said, his gaze level.

Lehigh nodded. "I agree with Wills. Winthrop, maybe. Both are loose cannons, although as different as milk and whiskey in every other way. But, as unlikely as this may seem, I trust Ted Roscoe. Maybe because he's a little too simple to get involved in such schemes."

Wadsworth chuckled. "He isn't the sharpest tool in the shed, that's for sure. Now, between the other two, we should pick one to focus on first. Test him with some 'information' we don't give anyone else." He made air quotes with his fingers on "information" and winked.

"And see if it leaks?"

Wadsworth nodded.

"Jim," Lehigh said, unease spreading over him, "do you think anyone on the inside—our team, or Ferguson's—may be, you know, in on it?"

"On the leaks, the murder, or the cover-up of the murder?" Wadsworth asked.

Lehigh shrugged. "All of the above."

Wadsworth scowled. "The leaks, certainly. The cover-up, doubtful. The murder?" He stared hard at Lehigh, then shook his head. "No way. I know some of these guys are Neanderthals, and I realize Buck Summers is a great counter-example of what I'm about to say, but I don't think the rot goes that deep. Cronyism and favoritism, sure. Incompetence at times, you bet. But I've worked with these people for ten, twenty years, in some cases. Hired a lot of them. Do I think they'd stoop to murder? No, I do not."

Lehigh weighed his words, letting them roll around in his brain. Wadsworth was right, of course. "So, we should focus on what we can control. The leaks."

Wadsworth nodded. "You okay with setting a trap? Even if it means firing someone you just hired to help clean things up?"

Lehigh pondered the idea. It seemed risky, but so did placing blind trust in the entire squad of newcomers who hadn't firmed up their loyalties to anyone yet. "Okay," he said. "Tell you what. You pick."

"Which part? Who we tell, or what we tell them?"

Lehigh smiled. "Both. And don't tell me in advance. I want to be surprised—and more important, I want to remain unbiased. The last thing I need is to give the game away."

"Will do. Now, what about Stacy?"

Lehigh's smile faded. "I guess," he said, "she and I need to talk."

Chapter Nineteen

The screen door opened. The wiry frame of a sun-weathered, white-haired man in baggy overalls and a red flannel shirt appeared. He thumped his boots across the peeling gray paint of the wooden porch and sat in an old wicker chair in the corner, face to face with Lehigh.

"You're early," Pappy said, fishing a pouch of tobacco and cigarette papers from the top pocket of his overalls.

"Just appreciating the sunshine. Is Maw here?"

"Cooking lunch." Pappy spread tiny bits of brown tobacco in the crease of his rolling paper, his eyes focused hard at the task. In spite of his obvious concentration, about a third of the precious weed floated like snowflakes to the deck.

"What's on?" Lehigh sniffed the air, came away with nothing but pine needles.

"You didn't come here to talk food." Pappy's eyes never left the task at hand.

Lehigh smiled and nodded. "But I'd never turn down a home-cooked meal."

Pappy paused in his cigarette manufacturing operation and glared at Lehigh from the top of his eye sockets, his eyes barely visible through his bushy white brows. "It ain't been offered."

Lehigh let the comment float away in the gentle breeze. The offer would come. Pappy's harsh pretense would melt faster than ice cream lost to the summer sidewalk. And if his didn't, Maw's would. "So, as I said on the phone, I gotta ask you something."

Pappy licked the edge of the paper and rolled the cigarette

into a perfect, skinny cylinder. He shoved one end into his mouth, staring at Lehigh. He lit the other end with matches that appeared out of nowhere and disappeared just as fast. Smoke escaped from the corners of his mouth and rose up the front of his face. He sucked some of it back in and waved the rest away with a gnarled hand. "About your wife, I reckon."

Lehigh started in his seat, catching his breath. "Y-you know?"

Pappy inhaled, exhaled, and gazed through the blue plumes surrounding his head. "People around here talk, son."

Lehigh hung his head. He'd tried to keep his separation from Stacy quiet, but that was next to impossible in a small town. He wondered what Pappy had heard, a man who shunned people whenever he could. Or Maw, who socialized at church and bingo, but whose mental faculties had long ago begun to decline.

"It's not just Stacy." Lehigh sighed. "This job. It's killing me."

Pappy eyed him through the smoke, then pulled the cigarette out of his mouth and exhaled over the dried rose bushes pushing spindly limbs between the porch rails. They needed deadheading, and some trimming, too. Maw didn't used to get behind on such things. Maybe he shouldn't have come. Pappy had enough to contend with, keeping her safe from herself.

"Son," Pappy said at last, "you ain't thinking of quitting, are you?"

The statement rolled over him like a tractor. Lehigh stared at him, numb. The worst thing a person could do, in Pappy's world, is quit. He struggled for a reply. "I–I don't know, Pap. This job is ruining my life."

Pappy spat. "Every job I ever had ruined me. You're no different than anybody else."

Lehigh winced. If he'd expected Pappy to make an exception just this once and sugar-coat his advice, he'd once again underestimated the old man. But then, that's why he'd come to Pappy in the first place. Straight talk.

"This one *is* different, Pappy. It's wrecking my marriage."

Pappy chuckled. "Every man has the same complaint, son.

And every woman. Except the ones who don't want to be married in the first place. Which is what I thought of you, for a long time." Another long drag on the cigarette, another blue plume.

"Yeah, me too. But most people's jobs don't make them arrest their father-in-law."

Pappy laughed, then broke into a fit of coughing. At first Lehigh thought it would end quickly, but the coughs grew harsher, louder, more raspy. More out of control.

"You okay, Pap?" Lehigh stood and reached out to pat the old man's back. Pappy waved him away, coughed a few more times, then stopped, bent over at the waist, his chest parallel to the ground. After several seconds he straightened, tossed the cigarette to the deck, and stomped on it.

"Son," he said, "you know damned well George McBride didn't shoot Ev Downey." Pappy wiped his lips with the back of his hand. "He's a sleazy sumbitch, and a liar, and he ain't got the morals of a naked mole rat. But he's also rich and powerful, son, and if there's one thing I know about the rich and powerful, it's that they don't do their own dirty work." He coughed and laughed again. "They get ordinary grunts like us to do it for them."

"Not pulling the trigger doesn't—"

"But you didn't come here to ask me to play detective." He fixed Lehigh with one of his patented intense stares, freezing Lehigh in his tracks. That stare always reminded him of the time, as a kid, when he poached a dollar out of Maw's purse and tried to sneak out the back door to go buy candy. Pappy never said a word. Just stared at him from way out in the vegetable garden, a hundred yards away, leaning on his shovel. He'd somehow known what Lehigh had done, and what he intended. Or so it felt, anyway, with those icy blue eyes pinning his feet to the turf, then somehow forcing him back inside so he could sneak the dollar back into her purse. Pappy sealed the deal a few hours later with a few brief words: "You put it back?" For a brief moment Lehigh considered bravado and denial, but the same icy stare dashed his resolve, and he'd slunk away, defeated.

"No, Pappy," he said, finally. He took a deep breath. "I never thought I'd say this, but I'm here to get your advice on a woman."

Pappy choked again, as if he'd swallowed his cigarette. He coughed another blue streak, leaning one arm against the porch rail, never taking his eyes off his son. When Lehigh stepped toward him, Pappy held his hand out in a stop signal.

"You all right out there, Caleb?" Maw called out from somewhere inside the house.

"I'm fine, Irene," Pappy said between coughs, and wheezed some deep, uneven breaths, hands on his knees. His breathing calmed, and he straightened a little.

"Lunch is almost ready," Maw called again. "Come wash up."

"I'm talking to Lehigh," Pappy said. "Give me a minute."

"Lehigh's here already? Why didn't you say so?" Maw appeared in the doorway, a blue checked apron tied in front over a plain yellow ankle-length house dress. "I didn't make enough for three. Give me a few minutes and I'll fix you a sandwich. Fried ham okay?"

"That's okay, Maw. You don't need to feed me."

"Baloney. I'm your Maw. Maws feed their boys." She tightened the knot in her apron strings and huffed back her shoulders. "Especially when I know you ain't getting fed at home. Now, no argument. Lunch will be ready in five minutes." She disappeared inside.

"So, you asking *advice* from me? On a *woman*?" Pappy coughed again and cleared his throat. "Well, that's a first."

Lehigh smiled, as much in relief that his father survived the coughing fit as in appreciation of his dry humor. "Not since high school. And you know how that came out."

Pappy made a sour face. "You ended up marrying her anyway. Not my fault it took you twenty years."

"Well, anyway. Same gal, different question." He braced himself for another cutting insult, but Pappy surprised him.

"When you and your brother, God rest his soul, were still in diapers," Pappy said, "I bought a hundred acres of forest land on credit. Your Maw just about killed me. And you know as well as I do, I don't exaggerate when it comes to your Maw."

"Did she actually load the gun and point it?" Lehigh asked with a horrified smile.

"Pulled the danged trigger. Near shot my foot off." Pappy shook his head, a faraway look in his eyes. "To this day I'm grateful she's a bad shot."

Lehigh stared at him in wonder. He'd never seen an iota of evidence that his parents ever fought. Nor had Pappy ever admitted as much. That struck him like a hammer. Pappy was *sharing*. As in, personal stuff. As the daytime talk show hosts might say, they were having a "moment." He ought not to blow it. He waited, but Pappy seemed done talking.

"So, how'd you get through it?" Lehigh asked after a while.

"I did the only thing that ever satisfies an angry woman," Pappy said. "Just like you oughta."

"Which is?"

"Just go tell her you're a fool and you're sorry," Pappy said. "And make sure she ain't armed."

"I tried that," Lehigh said. "It didn't work. Anyway, I'm not trying to convince her to take me back…yet. I'm just trying to get her to talk to me."

"So call her." Pappy stood. "That all? I'm hungry." He stepped toward the door. The moment, as far as Pappy was concerned, appeared to be over. But not for Lehigh. He stood and blocked Pappy's path.

"No, that's not all. Pappy, I put her old man in jail. Then I helped spring him when I probably shouldn't have—the press is eating me alive for that. And now it looks like he, or someone working for him, may have tampered with the evidence. Maybe even *her*. If they did, well, they could be in a whole heap of trouble—and me, too."

"So…?"

Lehigh locked eyes with his father. "I need to find a way to ask her what she knows…without her divorcing me." His voice cracked, and any further words he had planned got caught in his throat.

Pappy rested a hand on his shoulder, looked him in the eye from his vantage point a few inches shorter. Still he seemed the bigger man, a giant talking to a little boy. "Son," he said, "do you believe she did it?"

Lehigh thought a long moment. His head said maybe she might have, but...

"No, Pappy." His voice sounded like sandpaper. For a moment, he wondered if Pappy heard him. He opened his mouth to repeat it.

"Then tell her that first," Pappy said.

Lehigh absorbed the words, tried it out in his head. "I don't think that's enough."

Pappy leaned closer, pulling Lehigh's head down to his level. "If she loves you, it is."

Lehigh inhaled, his eyes watering. Must be from the sting of Pappy's sharp tobacco. Another breath shuddered out of him. "And if it ain't?" he asked in a whisper.

"In that case," Pappy said, "you've learned all you need to know." He gripped Lehigh by both shoulders and looked at him a moment, his face resolute. "And if that's the case, you can always come back here. And not just for lunch."

Lehigh nodded. No words would form. He followed his father inside to the comforting aroma of home-cooked food.

***

Lehigh paused in front of the front door of Cascade Animal Clinic, drawing in a deep breath. The acrid smell of smoke pinched his sinuses, an all-too frequent occurrence lately with the dry lightning storms igniting the parched forests surrounding Mt. Hood County. Still, he took another deep breath. Better the smoke outside than the fire waiting within.

Finally he pulled open the door, and the air-conditioned interior chilled the sweat gathering on his scalp. A short, white-haired matron with black pince-nez glasses smiled at him from behind the Formica counter in reception. "Well, howdy,

Sheriff!" said Anne-Marie, the clinic's most faithful volunteer. "You bringing Lucky in for a visit today?"

Lehigh kicked himself for forgetting the obvious ploy. Diamond, too, needed a check-up. He improvised. "Well, I thought I'd see what your calendar looks like for bringing them both in soon," he said. "I'm sure they're due for some shots, or something."

Anne-Marie clicked on her keyboard. "Well, let's see…huh. Nope. They're both up to date. I guess that's the advantage of being married to the owner, huh?" She smiled, showing her perfect plastic teeth. Lehigh remembered her crooked smile of a few years back. He preferred her real teeth, but enjoyed Anne-Marie's pride in her falsies even more.

"Huh. Well, what do you know. I guess I need to speak to that woman," Lehigh said. "Is she in?"

"She's with a patient," Anne-Marie said. "I mean—well, you know what I mean." She grinned again, and this time her plastic teeth clacked together. Lehigh cringed and wondered if the ivory version made as much noise as the cheap plastic ones. "She's assisting Dr. Lewis with Mrs. Huckaby's Bijon-Frisé. They should be out any minute."

"Maybe I should come back later," Lehigh said. Relief propelled him back to the door. He reached for the handle—

"Lehigh?" Stacy's voice drifted in from down the hall. "Is that my husband out there, Anne-Marie?"

"It sure is, Mrs. *Carter*," Anne-Marie said. Lehigh froze in mid-stride. Anne-Marie's use of Stacy's married name, rather than her professional one, and the emphasis she put on it, revealed just how much office gossip Stacy had to endure. Lehigh wasn't the only one.

He turned, and Stacy appeared in the reception area behind the older woman, dressed in a white lab coat, her dark hair pulled tight behind her in a bun. She stopped in her tracks, and their eyes met. Hers seemed a tad bit misty. Or was that his?

"Hey, Stacy," he said.

"Hello to you, too," she said, her voice soft. "Would you like to come in? To my office, I mean." She lifted the hinged counter to allow him through.

He took slow steps toward her, then slid past. The counter thumped back in place, and he felt her presence following him down the hallway. He knew the way, but he kept a slow pace, in no hurry to have this conversation. She slid around him as they reached her office and pushed open the door.

"Come in," she said, holding it open for him. His chest tightened. He entered, turned—

And couldn't breathe. Because his fierce, unpredictable, beautiful, crazy wife had him in a body-crushing hug and lip-lock, squeezing out of him every last drop of air.

"Thank you for coming," she said after an eternity of kissing. "I've missed you."

"I've missed you, too," he said. They held hands, a foot apart, looking at each other, neither, apparently, knowing what to say.

"So," she said after a hundred years. "What brings you here today, besides the need to kiss me?"

He exhaled noisily, which surprised him. He didn't know he had any air left in his lungs. "Can't a guy just come visit his estranged wife at work because he misses her?"

Her smile faded at the word "estranged," and he wanted to kick himself. She pulled back and looked down, off to the side, biting her lip. "Sure," she said without enthusiasm. "Thanks."

"Stacy, I—"

"No, you're right." She edged away and leaned back against her desk. "It's just not like you."

He sighed, nodded. "Well, maybe it should be."

She cocked her head. "I wouldn't argue with you on that."

He surrendered an uneasy smile, remembering Pappy's wisdom. "I also wanted to tell you I'm sorry. I've been a fool."

She smiled. "Say hi to Pappy for me. How's Maw?"

"She's good. She'd like to have us over for dinner sometime."

Stacy's smile faded. "Look, Lee, I appreciate and accept the apology, but we have a lot more work to do before I'm ready for anything like that."

"Yeah. I know." He tried to hold her gaze, but couldn't, and stared at his shoes instead. Moments ticked by in silence.

"So, aside from an apology and a quick make-up kiss, there really isn't any other reason for this visit?"

He drew in a breath and held it. Caught. Stupid, stupid. He forced a crooked smile. "Well, while I'm here, I thought maybe I could ask you about something. It's about your father."

She crossed her arms over her chest and nodded. "Of course. Anything that will help him, I'm all over it."

He winced. Dammit. Why did these conversations never go the way he imagined they could? "I'm not sure if it'll help or hurt, but I need to ask anyway."

She waited, lips tight.

"So," he went on, "the D.A.'s office claims that someone visited the murder scene and disturbed some of the evidence. They're claiming it points to a cover-up of some kind."

"Any idea who might have done that?" she asked.

"Well," he said, and his legs grew wobbly. He looked for a place to sit, then realized she'd then be staring down on top of him, and changed his mind. "*They're* thinking maybe it was, you know, George."

"He would never do such a thing. You know that."

"I would sure like to believe that," he said. "But can he prove it?"

"My father hasn't left his property since his release," she said. "I'm sure his security tapes will bear that out."

"Excellent," he said. "And I hate to ask this, but I gotta. Have you…?"

"Me?"

"You haven't been—"

"Lehigh, don't be ridiculous!" She stomped around her desk and sat down. He sat in the guest chair opposite her, relieved that he hadn't fallen down. She clicked on her mouse and keyboard, then glanced up at him. "For God's sake. You're asking me whether I committed a felony. Seriously? I'm your *wife*, Lehigh. You know me. You shouldn't have to ask."

"It's just that—"

"And my father wouldn't do that either. He doesn't have to, Lee. He's innocent. He didn't kill that man. And I can't believe you're still trying to prove otherwise." She glared at him, nostrils flared, mouth set in a line. Her dark eyes smoldered. Her hands shook on the mouse and keyboard.

He measured his words and spoke in a dead-even tone. "I'm not trying to prove otherwise. I'm just trying to get to the truth."

"The truth!" She rubbed her temples with her palms. "The truth, Lehigh? The truth is, you're on a mission here to get back at my father for all the grief he's caused you."

"No, Stace—"

"And I admit, there's a lot. He's never treated you well. He hired thugs to silence you when you caught him taking funny money last year, and they burned down your house. His allies even tried to kill you. I get it, you have a gripe." She stood and planted open hands onto the desk. "But listen to me, Lehigh. *My father did not kill Everett Downey.* Nor did my mother, or me, or anyone in the McBride family. Got it?"

Lehigh sighed again, staring at his hands. He understood her anger, but why couldn't she understand the position he was in? He met her gaze. "Yeah. I hear ya. Thanks." He stood and turned toward the door.

"Lehigh."

He turned back to face her. She straightened. "You need to end this witch hunt against my family. *Our* family. You hear me? It needs to end *now*."

"Again, I'm not—"

"If it doesn't end," she said, "mark my words. Something else *will* end. Us. Because I can't stay married to a man who would do this to his own family."

They stared at each other for several long moments. He reached for the door handle. "If that's how you feel," he said, "I guess there's nothing left to say." He opened the door—

Only then did he remember the rest of Pappy's advice. Dammit. He turned back to her.

"If it makes any difference to you," he said, "I agree with

you. I don't believe George killed Ev Downey."

"Then why are you still pursuing this?" she asked, her voice breaking.

"Because, honey," he said, "I still have to do my job, whether I believe the accusation or not. Even if it means investigating a possible cover-up, by him—or," and he drew an unsteady breath, "by his family."

"Get the hell out of here, *Sheriff*," she said, and she sat back at her desk.

He left and closed the door behind him. Down the hall, the stout figure of Anne-Marie disappeared around the corner. She'd probably heard every damn word.

Chapter Twenty

"Are we ready?" Ray Ferguson asked when the young man pulled the make-up pad away from Ray's face and inspected him for perfection. They'd taken twenty minutes longer making him pretty than he'd spend on camera. The price he paid for keeping the public informed.

"One more thing," the make-up man said. He brushed a black crayon-type thing across Ray's eyebrows, then smoothed them with his finger. "I think that'll do it." He dabbed a wet finger on a stray hair at Ferguson's temple, then stood behind him so they could both inspect his work in the mirror.

"Who the heck is that guy?" Ferguson said with a grin. "That face looks younger than my son, and he's a college freshman."

"Eastern Oregon U, right?" the make-up man said. "I'm a Mountaineer myself. Class of '14." He ran his fingers through his own hair, a preppy do, short on the sides and thick up top. A pin on his lapel sported some Greek letters that Ferguson couldn't quite make out. He rested his hands on the attorney's shoulders, smiling. Almost flirting.

Raymond squirmed in the chair. Bad enough the guy touched him here, there, and everywhere. Now he knew where his kid went to college? "I think I'm ready," he said.

"Okey-dokey," the young man said. "I'll walk you to the studio."

"I know the way," Ray said. "Been there many times." He tossed off the plastic bib that protected his suit from errant flakes of make-up and straightened his tie, then strode down the hallway of the local TV station until he reached the door of

Studio Two. The "on air" light remained unlit, so he pushed through the door.

"Right on time," Bruce Bailey said, looking up from his notes. "We go on in fifteen. Take a look at these questions before we go on."

"Already have," Ferguson said. "Let's chat."

Ten minutes later, he sat on an uncomfortable stool next to Bailey in the well-lit recording studio surrounded by cameras. Music blared and a director counted them down. Bailey smiled into the little red light and prattled on for a while about how excited he was to have Ray on the program again, blah blah. The guy never shut up.

Finally, his cue. "What new developments can you share about the Everett Downey murder case?" Bailey said.

"Well, I can't discuss the specifics of a matter in pending litigation," Ferguson said, "and I'll be the first to point out that whoever is leaking information on the case to the press is doing the public a great disservice—as well as committing a felony. We will find the source of this leak and we will prosecute, I promise you."

"Understandable. But can you share with us the *type* of evidence you have, or what sort of case you intend to bring?" Bailey's eyes widened, as if to beg, *Give me something juicy, please!*

"We have a very solid case against the accused," Ferguson said. "Means, motive, and opportunity. Plus a significant body of physical evidence placing the defendant at the scene."

"Such as DNA evidence?" Bailey asked.

Ferguson frowned. "I heard your report on that, and I have to say, that concerns me," he said. More like alarms and terrifies, he added to himself. Exaggeration, if not pure fabrication, mixed with a whole lot of wishful thinking. Yet he couldn't refute it on-air without doing even more damage to his case.

Bailey waited for his reply, and Raymond realized he'd just wasted several seconds of dead air time. "Information of that sort should not have been disclosed to the public," he said. "It could do great harm to our case, as do the other leaks you noted in your opening remarks."

"In light of these developments, Mr. Ferguson," Bailey said, clearly enjoying this, "what can we do to prevent further leaks about pending cases like Everett Downey's?"

"First off, let me say that the District Attorney's office takes leaks very seriously," Ray said. "I'm proud to say that not once has a leak ever been traced back to our team."

"Very impressive," Bailey said. "So, where are they coming from?"

The little red light to Ray's left blinked a few times, his cue to turn to face the second camera. "As you all know, we've had a lot of change over at the sheriff's department in recent months," he said, keeping his voice somber. "With all the shifts in personnel, it's understandably difficult to keep a tight wrap on everything going on. So we're not *blaming* anyone, but it just stands to reason—"

"And those new personnel—that includes the man at the top, am I right?" Bailey asked with a grin. The grin meant the smug mongrel knew he was not on camera. "Sheriff Carter has been in office, what, two, three months?"

"I believe the sheriff is a good man," Ray said the way he'd rehearsed it a dozen times earlier that day. "But he's not a trained law enforcement officer. Nor has he run a large organization before. He faces a difficult situation."

"Would you say he's incompetent?" Bailey asked with a gleam in his eye. The smug grin had disappeared. The conceited charlatan wouldn't miss a chance of being on camera for this.

"I wouldn't use such harsh words," Ferguson said. "As the Gospel commands us, '*Judge not, and you will not be judged.*' What I would say is, there's room for improvement, for greater *professionalism*, in the department, yes."

"How much of this would you say is driven by Sheriff Carter being the accused's son-in-law?" Bailey asked in his most serious tone. Not like a few minutes earlier, when he'd rehearsed the line off-stage, practically howling with delight. Damned muckrakers.

"We can't ignore that possibility," Ferguson said, deadpan.

Let the viewers draw their own conclusions.

"Has there been any issue of cooperation from the sheriff, or, shall we say, a lack thereof?" Bailey asked.

The light blinked again, this time to his right. Ray turned to face the new camera. "There have been issues," he said. "I can't say whether the sheriff *intentionally* withheld evidence or obstructed the investigation, but there have been moments when they could have been forthcoming."

"Thank you, Mr. Ferguson. We need to take a quick break here." He shifted to face the center camera. "Again, this is Deputy District Attorney Raymond Ferguson, who some say may be the next Oregon attorney-general. Might we discuss a bit of politics when we come back?"

"Well, I, uh, suppose," Ferguson said. Acting humble was not his strong suit. Thankfully, the music filled the studio, and moments later, the lights dimmed.

"How'd I do?" Ray asked Bailey.

"Beautiful," Bruce said with a grin. "You know the script for part two?"

"I do," Ferguson said. "And I much appreciate it."

"Thank me later," Bailey said. "After your election to state attorney general next year, around the time you look around for a press secretary."

The second segment of the interview went as rehearsed. Bailey asked him innocent-sounding questions about the "tough issues" that an attorney general would face, and Ray responded with the type of law-and-order replies his pollsters had told him would sell in Oregon. When the lights went down for the final time, Ferguson felt larger than life. Almost immortal.

Still, something bothered him. Back in the staging area, he turned to Bailey. "You know, it's ironic," Ray said. "You asking me about leaks."

"How so?" Bruce picked lint off his suit.

"You broke the story," Ray said. "Shouldn't I be asking *you* who leaked it?"

Bailey's expression darkened. "That's not how the game is

played, Mr. Ferguson," he said. "Remember how this works? I need stories. You need air time. We play together by the rules, and everybody wins."

Ferguson stepped back, hands raised. "Understood. I apologize."

Bailey paused a moment, then put on his made-for-TV smile. "No apology necessary. Call it a learning opportunity. And, Mr. Ferguson? Thank you for *not* asking that question on the air."

Bailey strode out, and Ferguson wiped his brow with his sleeve. Too late, he remembered. He checked his arm.

Covered in that stupid make-up.

***

"Deputy?" Jim Wadsworth waved at Donnell Winthrop from his office doorway, several doors down from the break room where the young deputy emerged with a fresh cup off coffee. "Can I see you for a moment, please?"

"Sure thing," Donnell said with a grin. He sipped his coffee, then proceeded to Wadsworth's office at a brisk pace. "What's up, boss?"

"Close the door, please," Wadsworth said. "I have some, er, sensitive information to share with you."

"Whoa," Winthrop said. "Secret stuff? Cool." He shut the door and slid his long, lanky body into the guest chair. He leaned forward, holding his paper coffee cup in his fingertips by the top and bottom rims. He whispered, "Is it about the murder case?"

"Yes," Wadsworth said in a low voice. "I've gotten a new lead I want you to check out. Normally, as your partner, I'd do it with you, but I'm buried in paperwork. Are you up for it?"

"Yeah, yeah, sure," Winthrop said. "I got this. What is it? A new witness to interview? A stake-out? I'm good at stake-outs, man. I can blend right in where nobody can see me. Especially at night," he said with a big laugh. "One time in college, I—"

"It's not a stakeout," Wadsworth said. "I need you to do some digging for me."

"Digging?" Winthrop said, his smile fading. "Like, with a shovel, in the dirt, and all?" He removed the red bandana from his scalp and wiped sweat off his forehead.

"No, no. Research, I mean. Checking some records. Can you do that?"

"Oh, *that* type of digging. Sure, sure. I'm great at that. What ya need? Fingerprints, mug shots—"

"This." Wadsworth slid a manila folder across his desk to Donnell.

Donnell scanned the bogus paperwork on top of the file. "I don't get it," he said.

"It's a record of a business transaction," Wadsworth said. "By Everett Downey."

"Oh, yeah, I can see *that.*" Winthrop grinned again. *"Obviously.* What I meant is, how is it relevant to the case?"

"I want you to trace it," Wadsworth said. "See who it leads back to. It might point us to his killer."

"Whoa, like a smoking gun type of thing?" Winthrop said. "Man, that's cool. Sure, I'll get right on it." He stood and replaced the bandana over his short black hair.

Wadsworth stopped him with a raised hand. "Don't share this information with anyone but me," he said. "Not Ruby, not the sheriff, no one. Got that? This is super-sensitive. Just you and me, okay?"

"You got it," Donnell said. "My lips are sealed. And I think I know right where to start."

"Good man," Wadsworth said.

Donnell downed his coffee and strode out.

The trap was set.

Chapter Twenty-One

The sun dipped low on the horizon. Soft rays filtered through the columns of timber and occasional tufts of underbrush, giving Lehigh just enough light to drive the stakes securing his two-man tent to the hard-packed soil. Perched atop an embankment overlooking a babbling brook bisecting his property, his new temporary lodgings provided a clear view of what would someday, he hoped, become the construction site for his new home.

If the contractor ever showed, that is. They'd provided nothing but excuses and broken promises for weeks now, and he'd run out of patience and hope.

But at least it gave him a quiet place to camp, and think, while he waited for Stacy to cool off. He hoped that would happen soon. He missed her, he missed sleeping in a warm bed, and he missed home-cooked meals. His stomach growled, reminding him that he'd still not done anything about dinner.

He straightened and tossed another log onto his campfire, and that cued his best remaining friends on the planet all the excuse they needed to jump up and lick his hands and face. "Easy, Lucky! Diamond, get down, boy!" The dogs jumped up and down, spinning in circles, clearly anticipating treats and attention. He laughed. They knew him too well. He found chunks of dog biscuit in his shirt pocket and tossed them to the happy pups.

"How do you like our new home, dogs?" he said, watching them chew. Lucky finished first and found a stick for him to throw. He laughed again and tossed it into the brook. Both dogs tore through the trees, jumping into the stream and reaching the stick at the same time. They returned together, each with their teeth buried deep into opposite ends of the stick, walking at an angle toward him with playful, noisy growls.

He tossed the stick a few more times, his mind drifting to the Downey case. The "DNA evidence" cited on the news story still bugged him—mostly because he hadn't seen any, neither from Ferguson's reports or his own team's. Aside from the mysterious cuff link, the other tiny bits of physical evidence found at the scene—some fiber strands caught in the underbrush—couldn't be matched to anything in George's wardrobe. In fact, the forensics team had concluded that the fibers probably came from clothing worn by the investigation team—the only "contamination" of the scene documented anywhere. The footprint wasn't definitive enough, either. Really, right now, they had nothing solid on anyone.

The dogs returned, in a growling tug-of-war over the stick, which they each held in their mouths. He laughed. "One more, then I gotta get dinner," he said. He reached for the stick, but before he could grab it from them, the dogs erupted into an angry torrent of barking, dashing off at top speed into the woods again. In a moment he spied the object of their attention: a fat squirrel, chewing on a chestnut, had strayed too far from the safety of the nearest tree. Too late, the rodent dropped the nut and made a mad dash for safety, but the dogs were too fast. Before the squirrel could reach the first branch, Lucky leaped into the air, snapping jaws and swinging paws like a cartoon animal. Through sheer determination and luck, she knocked the poor critter to the ground. The rodent rolled to his feet, but stayed put a moment, stunned by the attack. Diamond, just a few steps away, had the squirrel in his mouth a moment later, swinging him side to side, the smaller animal's long tail whipping the air in frightened fury.

In less than a few seconds, the squirrel lay still on the ground. Diamond and Lucky stood over the inert body, pawing at it and whimpering.

Lehigh forced himself to move. He shooed the dogs away from the poor little animal, but it was too late to save it.

Lucky and Diamond sat nearby, their heads bowed. Whimpers escaped them every few moments. Neither would look at Lehigh. Instead they focused on the animal at Lehigh's feet.

"Now look what you've gone and done," Lehigh said. The dogs lay down, still whimpering. Lucky barked once, then lowered her head again.

"What do you want? No, I ain't gonna throw it," Lehigh said. "It ain't a toy. Even if it were, you already broke it."

Lucky raised herself to a sitting position. Barked again. Diamond followed suit, a dumb puppy mimicking his older mentor's example.

"Well," Lehigh said, picking up the dead squirrel, "I guess that solves the question of what we're having for dinner."

The dogs lay down, disappointment covering their faces like a blanket.

***

Of all of the public buildings in Mt. Hood County, Lehigh hated the Mt. Hood County Commissioners office and meeting hall the most. Not because of its architecture, which was among the most elegant in the entire region, or because of any problems with the structure. It was the occupants.

He loathed them. Particularly, Mt. Hood County Commission Chair Elliott McBride Jackson.

"If you don't *know* where the leaks are coming from," Jackson raged from his Chair-upon-high, "then how can you be sure they're not coming from your ranks?" Jackson turned his body from side to side, as if appealing to a shared sense of outrage among his colleagues on the Commission. Desmond Mitchell, seated at the far end to the Chair's right, held up a feeble hand, the signal for requesting the floor. Jackson ignored it.

"I am doing everything I can to discover the source of the leaks," Lehigh said. "If they are coming from my department,

I'll know soon. But I suspect—"

"Everything?" Jackson said, far too loud. His booming voice echoed off the walls, unmuffled by the presence of no more than a handful of spectators, most of them county staff, dotting the seats in the gallery. "What *specific* steps have you taken to root out the malcontents who would risk sabotaging a murder investigation by leaking sensitive information to the press?"

"We're taking steps," Lehigh said. He knew his evasion wouldn't satisfy the Chairman, but he didn't want to let on that he'd delegated the task to Wadsworth—in effect, deliberately keeping himself in the dark. "I'm not at liberty to disclose—"

"Not at liberty? Why not? You *are* in charge, aren't you?" Jackson again exchanged glances with fellow commissioners, and again ignored Mitchell's request for time.

"Of course," Lehigh said. "But—"

"Then enlighten me," Jackson said in triumph.

"I'm afraid that could compromise the investigation," Lehigh said.

"Don't give me these flimsy excuses," Jackson said. "In a minute, Desmond!" He turned and glared at his colleague, huffing and puffing loud enough for the spectators in the back row to hear. "I have the floor, and I will let you know when I am willing to yield." He waited for Desmond to lower his hand and look away, then turned his attention back to Lehigh. "We can't let this continue, Sheriff. It's intolerable!"

Lehigh's already short supply of patience grew dangerously low. He took a deep breath to calm himself. "I agree, Mr. Chairman. We can't let your cousin be tried in the press."

At the mention of the word "cousin," Jackson's face flushed beet red, and for a moment he remained speechless.

Commissioner Mitchell seized the moment. "If I could ask the chairman's indulgence," he said in his laconic vocal cadence, "could someone, maybe staff, share with us what information has been inappropriately leaked?"

"No, we can*not!*" Jackson fumed in his chair, practically bouncing in his seat. "It's bad enough that it's all over the press.

Discussing it here in a public meeting would only make things worse!"

"Begging the chairman's pardon," Mitchell said with a drawl, "if it's already public knowledge, how would—"

"It just is, that's all," Jackson said, a bit deflated.

"I'm just a little bit confused," Mitchell said. "How's the sheriff supposed to know what leaks to track down if we don't tell him which ones are of concern to us?"

Jackson spun in his chair to face his colleague again. Veins pulsed on the side of his skull. Lehigh wondered if he might have an aneurysm on the spot. "Just what are you trying to prove here, Desmond?" Jackson said. "Are you on the side of the leakers, or on the side of prudent, professional law enforcement?"

"I'm not on anyone's side." Mitchell winked at Lehigh. "Just trying to get at the facts."

Lehigh smirked. He had few moments of joy when testifying before the commission, and fewer still when a commissioner went to bat for him against the chair. He'd have to remember to send Mitchell a nice bottle of Oregon pinot noir for Christmas.

"Okay, you want facts? Here's the facts behind the leaks," Jackson said, scanning the dais to meet each commissioner's gaze in turn. "The defendant's attorney has been crowing in the press about contaminated evidence. How would they know about contaminated evidence unless someone in our sheriff's department told them? Huh?"

"Could any of the leaks have come from the prosecutor's office?" Mitchell asked, facing Lehigh.

"Well, that's *always* a possibility," Lehigh said. More than a possibility, he wanted to say. A damned certainty.

"And there's tire track impressions that, to my understanding, has led the defense to issue subpoenas to every tire and car salesman in the county, wanting detailed, confidential sales information, at *great* cost," Jackson went on. "And witness testimony that puts the defendant in the area at the time of the murder—" He stopped, as if remembering something. "Well, never mind that, but those other things—"

"What's that about a witness?" Lehigh asked, but his question got lost in the burst of voices surrounding the Chair, as every commissioner on the dais suddenly had something to say about this revelation.

"They saw him?" one asked. "Who saw him?" asked another. "Did he have the gun with him?" "Was he covered in blood?"

The banging gavel brought the cacophony to a halt. Jackson stood, towering over his colleagues. "I can see that we've lost all sense of order and propriety here." He glared at each elected official in turn. "Clearly we won't be getting anything else done here today. Sheriff, I expect you back here in a week with a detailed report on the steps you're taking to put a stop to these leaks. Understood? Good. Now. The commission is in recess for ten minutes. I gotta go to the men's room." Jackson rushed past his colleagues through a side door heading to their offices.

"A witness, huh?" Lehigh mumbled. "What else do I not know about this case?"

***

Wadsworth greeted Lehigh at the door to his office when he returned from the Commission meeting, a sour expression on his face. "Got a minute?" he asked.

Lehigh noticed the big man's concerned expression and waved him into his office. "What's up?"

Wadsworth furrowed his brow. "Where's all your stuff?"

Lehigh grinned. "I decided you were right. I can't risk any more negative press, so before Bruce Bailey could do another exposé on how I'm getting a free place to live on the county's dime, I moved everything back to my place."

"You're living in your house? I thought it burned down."

Lehigh shook his head. "Nope. Camping. Right on the hill above my house." He took a deep, satisfied breath.

"That sucks."

Lehigh laughed. "No way. I love it. I haven't slept this good in months. So what's on your mind?"

Wadsworth sighed and sat down. "Have you heard about the

Everett Downey real estate scandal?"

"Another one?" Lehigh said. He searched his memory. "No, but I haven't exactly been glued to the TV. What happened?"

"Nothing," Wadsworth said. "That's the problem."

"I don't understand."

Wadsworth grimaced. "I set up our man with some bait. He didn't bite."

Lehigh blinked. Finally he remembered their plan to uncover the mole. "Winthrop, or Wills?"

"Donnell. I set him on a research task. He reported back to me, as I instructed. No word to anyone else." Wadsworth shook his head in disgust.

Lehigh spun around once in his chair. "That's good, right?"

"Well, it's good for Donnell," he said. "Unless he was on to me. But I don't think so."

"Okay. Good, he's clean. So, on to the next one?"

"I guess so," Wadsworth said. Silence hung in the air a few seconds.

"It sucks, trying to trap people," Lehigh said.

"Big time."

"Do we have another option?"

Wadsworth shrugged. "We could just wait and see."

Lehigh considered it. "I'm getting killed by Jackson, and I'm pretty sure Ferguson is feeding him his bait. Waiting's not a good option. We've got to figure this out."

Wadsworth nodded, his expression glum. "Okay." He stood. "But if it isn't Wills—"

Lehigh snorted. "Then it's one of our most trusted people…and I have much bigger problems."

Chapter Twenty-Two

The drive up Brady Mountain Road held no appeal for Lehigh that evening, partly due to the fact that he had yet to stock up on food, and the prospect of repeating his dinner of squirrel stew held no appeal. He'd had his fill of Shirley's Cafe for lunch on an almost daily basis, and hated the chains along the highway. That didn't leave him much to choose from.

His phone rang as he considered his options, reverberating over the speakers the County had installed along with some fancy hands-free gizmo that gave him directions, answered phone calls, and showed him images of whatever was behind him when he backed up. He read the Caller ID on the dashboard screen: Julia's cell phone.

"Yeah, Julia? You working late?"

"I'm on my way home, but I just heard something I thought I should tell you. Do you know that Chinese restaurant near the motel?"

"Yang's? You bet." Chinese sounded good, actually. Much better than squirrel. "Something happening there? A fight or something?"

"Not a fight, Sheriff. But...let's just say, you should stop in and see who's in there...together."

"Any clues?" He spotted the restaurant's neon sign ahead in the distance.

"Let's just say, it might explain a few things. Gotta go, I'm driving." She hung up before he could press her any further.

He pulled into the lot and parked near the exit, facing out, in case he needed to engage in hot pursuit. With the night cooling down, he left the windows rolled down and gave the dogs a couple of biscuits to tide them over, then headed toward the restaurant's front door. Before he got within 50 feet of the door, a couple exited the restaurant, arm in arm. They looked familiar. No surprise there—everyone knew everyone in Clarkesville—but the combination of this particular man and woman did surprise him. In a heartbeat he knew this was the couple Julia had called him about.

He ducked between a couple of SUVs in the parking lot to get out of their plain line of sight and peeked through the windows of one to get another look at them.

The man, round in shape, wore a beige deputy's uniform. Lehigh recognized him in an instant: Bobby Wills. Not someone he wanted to bump into on the street at the moment.

But the identity of the woman on his arm made the trip worthwhile. Average height, slender to the point of stick-thin with flowing dark hair, people often mistook her for her cousin—a mistake that would infuriate both women.

Teresa McBride, the secretary of County Commission Chair Elliott Jackson. Stacy's much-younger cousin.

Lehigh ducked down to avoid being spotted but kept them in view. The couple walked closer, arms wrapped around each other's waist, engaged in conversation in low voices, punctuated by giggles. Bobby pulled her close, kissed her, and said something in her ear that made her giggle louder and swat him. "You're so bad," she said, but her tone of voice said otherwise.

"I'm *so* bad," he said. "And so, so good."

"Stop!" She giggled again. "At least wait until we get home." They walked further, right past a crouching Lehigh, their bodies close together top to bottom. "Anyway," she said, "I need you to tell me that thing again. Before I forget."

"Hush!" Bobby glanced around, but apparently didn't spot Lehigh. "People might hear you."

"No one's here," she said. "Come on, just tell me. So I can get my mind off of it. And onto you." She giggled again and kissed him. He giggled, too, and whispered into her ear.

"What was that?" she said. "I don't understand."

"You don't have to understand," Bobby said. "Just remember. Okay? Now tell me. *Whisper.*" He held his ear close to her mouth. A moment later he nodded. "Good. Perfect. Just like that, okay?"

"I will," she said. "Now take me home already, will you?"

They moved out of earshot, then got into a brown Chrysler four-door sedan the size of a small yacht. Typical McBride vehicle. Bobby got in the passenger side, and Teresa got in behind the wheel. Moments later they exited to the main drag toward downtown.

Lehigh waited until they left to stand. What he'd just seen confirmed it: Bobby *was* the mole. He made a mental note to thank Julia and placed a quick call to Wadsworth.

***

"We need to prove it," Wadsworth said when they met in Lehigh's office the next day. "Conclusively."

"Agreed," Lehigh said. "And soon. What's the plan?"

"Same as before. We plant information that only he knows—something juicy, something he can't resist—and let him hang himself."

"Like?"

Wadsworth smiled. "What does Jackson care most about in the whole world?"

Lehigh drummed his fingers on the desk. "Besides himself, you mean? The leak, I guess."

"Exactly," Wadsworth said. "We tell him that we've found the source. But we don't say *who.* Then we wait for Jackson to pounce, and boom, they're caught."

Lehigh smiled. "You're devious," he said.

"That's a good thing, right?" Wadsworth said, in a mock-hurt tone.

"That's a *very* good thing," Lehigh said.

***

"Sheriff?" Julia poked her head in Lehigh's office door. "There's some gentlemen here to see you from the district attorney's office."

Lehigh shook his head. "I believe you misspoke, Julia," he said. "There are no gentlemen in the D.A.'s office."

Her eyes widened, and shadows filled the space behind her. Moments later, Ray Ferguson burst past her into the room, flanked by his usual cadre of bland, short-haired men in dark suits.

"You're going to fry for this, Carter!" Ferguson stabbed a long finger in the air at him. "Fry, I tell you!"

"Good morning to you too, Ray." Lehigh closed the files he'd been working on and darkened his computer screen. "Please, come in."

His sarcasm appeared lost on Ferguson, who leaned over Lehigh's desk, finger still stabbing the air. "This isn't a laughing matter, Sheriff. Aiding and abetting a fugitive is a felony offense, and you're going down for it if it's the last thing I do!" His face flushed red, and his eyes appeared ready to pop out of his head. Behind him, his suited lackeys slid into chairs, leaving one in the center for The Reverend.

"What fugitive? What the heck are you jabbering on about? Julia!" Lehigh craned his neck around Ferguson's tall frame but couldn't see if his secretary had remained in the doorway. His phone rang a moment later, ringing once for an inside line, and he gestured to Ferguson. "'Scuse me a sec."

"Don't you take that—" Ferguson paused and took a deep breath. Lehigh pointed to a chair and turned away from him.

"Sheriff," said the voice of Julia on the phone, "Portland federal marshals are on the line. They say it's urgent. It's the chief himself, all the way from Portland!"

"Oh, no," Lehigh said, a sense of foreboding washing over him like a wet mattress. "Put him on."

"This is hardly the time for a phone call!" Ferguson reached out to grab the receiver from Lehigh's ear. "We have urgent business to discuss here!"

"You either need to shut up," Lehigh said, "or get the hell out of my—Oh, hello, Chief. What can I do for you today?"

"We have a man here in custody in Multnomah County," said

the marshal in his ear, "from your part of the world. According to our information, the man is under travel restrictions by court order. He was attempting to flee the state—had a flight booked to Washington, D.C. We can hold him a day or so, but then we'll need to arrange his transfer to you."

Pounding pain seared from one side of Lehigh's head to the other. This couldn't be happening. Not now. Please.

He hated to ask the next question, as he already knew the answer—as did, he suspected, Assistant District Attorney Ray Ferguson. But he had to hear it to confirm his worst fears.

"What's the name of this fella you apprehended at the airport?" Lehigh asked, staring at Ferguson. Surprise and recognition lit up in Ferguson's eyes, and a cruel smile crossed his lips.

"According to his ID," the marshal said, "the man's name is George Lindsey McBride. You know him?"

Lehigh dropped his face into his hands. "Know him?" he said with a sigh. "I guess you could say that."

***

"Well, at least you convinced Ferguson that it wasn't your doing," Wadsworth said once the D.A.'s pinstripe-suited army left Lehigh's office. "What the heck got into your father-in-law, anyway? Running off to the east coast for a 'fundraiser' at a time like this? What was he thinking?"

"If I only knew what made that man tick," Lehigh said, slouching in his chair, "my life would be a lot simpler pretty much all the time."

"Folks like him just think they can live by different rules, I guess," Wadsworth said.

Lehigh scoffed. "Old George has spent most of his life making up the rules. I guess he thinks he can just make up new rules now."

"Well, speaking of breaking the rules," Wadsworth said, "I've seeded our boy with some 'top secret' information. We'll see how soon it hits the light of day."

Lehigh nodded. So far as he could tell, Bobby Wills hadn't caught on to the fact that they suspected him of the leaks. "What kind of info did you lay on him? Nothing too prejudicial, I hope."

Wadsworth shook his head. "He 'found' a copy of a sales receipt to an ammo store in Twin Falls with George's name on it," Wadsworth said. "A store that doesn't exist, in a file labeled 'Top Secret—Sheriff's Eyes Only.' My guess is he'll leak it first, ask questions later."

"Are you sure that's wise?" Lehigh said. "Seems like a lot of people would be inclined to believe a story like that—and it might be awfully hard to convince them otherwise."

"Nah," Wadsworth said. "I've got the whole thing documented in a sealed file. Ruby witnessed it for me, and I trust her implicitly."

"She knows?"

Wadsworth shrugged. "I felt I had to bring her in on it. He does report to her, after all."

"Hmph. Okay." Lehigh sat up straighter in his seat, but an unsettling suspicion nagged at the back of his mind. He couldn't put a finger on what bothered him, exactly, so he shook it off. "Okay. So now we need to arrange a transport for him. It'd look bad if I go, so how would you feel about a day trip to Portland?"

Wadsworth's face curled into an ugly frown. "I was afraid you'd lay that one on me. Okay, I'll take Donnell with me." He stood, and gave Lehigh a long look. "You gonna be okay?"

Before Lehigh could answer, his phone rang. "Depends," Lehigh said with a wry grin, "on who this is."

Wadsworth shuffled to the door. "Better you than me, my friend."

Lehigh let him exit before answering the phone. "It's your wife," Julia said. "Shall I take a message, or—"

"No, patch her through."

Moments later, Stacy's voice greeted him. "What's this I hear about my father being arrested in Portland?" she said without preamble.

"He tried leaving the state, apparently," Lehigh said, "despite being under court order not to leave the county."

"He told me that you said he was free to go wherever he wanted," Stacy said.

"Never happened," Lehigh said.

"Something here doesn't add up," Stacy said. "My father wouldn't just lie about this."

Lehigh stared at the phone in disbelief, then returned it to his ear. "You're saying your father, a life-long politician with ambitions to higher office, who's been accused of murder one, wouldn't lie? I'd put him at the *top* of the list of people with motive to lie."

Stacy's voice took on a more conspiratorial tone. "This looks like a setup to me." She paused. "Why would he say that you told him he could leave?"

"I don't know, Stacy."

"I don't know either, Lehigh." She paused, and her voice took on a worried tone. "It just seems that every time I turn around, it looks like you're somehow involved in something that hurts my father and my family."

"That's not true, and you know it."

"The only thing that I know is what I see," she said in an even tone. "It's like, how did you put it with regard to the evidence against him? 'It looks bad.' Well, it looks bad for you, from where I sit."

Lehigh's heart sank, and he let out a deep sigh. "I hear what you're saying. But things are not what they seem. Okay?"

The line remained silent a long time. Finally Stacy broke the silence. "If my father goes to prison because of you," she said in a voice that sounded near tears, "I will never be able to forgive you."

The line went dead, much like the feeling creeping into Lehigh's heart.

Part III

Fake News

Chapter Twenty-Three

Ruby Mac blocked the doorway from the break room as Lehigh turned to head back to his office, his oversized mug filled to the brim with his favorite elixir.

"He's on the move," Ruby said in a low voice. "In a squad car, heading downtown."

Lehigh nodded. Ruby had kept a close watch on Bobby Wills since they'd set him up with the fake evidence, so he needed no further explanation. "Where to? The D.A.'s office?"

"The press. He's going public with it." Ruby jangled keys in her right hand. "Come on. I'll drive."

Lehigh took a big gulp of coffee, then set the mug down. "Can we catch him?"

Ruby laughed. "That's why I said I'll drive."

They hustled out to a squad car, motor running in a no-parking zone in front of the building. "Setting a fine example for the community, I see," Lehigh said with a smile.

"You want this guy nailed, or what?" Ruby gunned the engine and spit gravel behind them, tearing out of the lot. Once they hit solid pavement, she peeled rubber down the busy street, siren wailing.

"I see we've opted for the stealth approach," Lehigh said.

"We're a mile behind him," Ruby said. "Hold on." She slammed her foot on the accelerator and took a tire-squealing right turn at a red light. "Where'd all this traffic come from?" She zoomed around a slow truck pulling a full load of freshly baled hay. Lehigh dared not open his mouth to reply for fear of ingesting stray cow patties flying off the truck.

She turned off the siren a minute later and slowed to merely breakneck speed, pulling into the parking lot for Channel Six TV and parking in a handicapped spot in front. "Emergency parking," she said before Lehigh could object.

Lehigh scrambled out of the cruiser and scanned the lot. Bobby Wills, still in uniform, stopped in his tracks, interrupting a fast-paced stroll toward the TV station's front doors. His gaze rested on Lehigh and Ruby, and after a moment of hesitation, he broke into a run.

"Request for backup at Channel Six!" Ruby shouted into the radio mic. Bobby dashed along the side of the building and seemed certain to get around the corner before they could reach him. "What are you waiting for?" Ruby said to Lehigh.

Lehigh shook himself out of observer mode, jumped out of the car, and broke into a sprint. Though never a track star, Lehigh's speed and height earned him a starting position as wide receiver as early as sophomore year—and double duty as a defensive back, covering his opponent's fastest runners on pass plays. Years of working outdoors, felling trees, chopping wood and hauling debris had kept him in good shape. He gained ground quickly on Wills and thought he had a chance to catch him before he reached the entrance.

But he couldn't match Ruby's speed. She breezed by Lehigh and tackled Bobby a few steps past the corner of the building.

"Gotcha!" She slammed Bobby's body to the ground and landed on top of him. Bobby let out a loud grunt as he sprawled face-first in the hard dirt, and a large yellow envelope skittered out of his hand.

"What—the—heck—" Bobby gasped for air and rolled to his back to look up at Ruby. "What'd you do that for?"

"Suppose you tell us," she said, breathing hard and pointing at the envelope. "Or should I just look for myself?"

"Easy, Ruby." Lehigh snagged the envelope off the ground and tore it open. He scanned the pages, confirming his suspicions that they contained copies of the bogus information Wadsworth had planted in the files.

"I can explain," Bobby said.

"Best wait for your lawyer before you do," Lehigh said. "Because you, my friend, are in a whole lot of trouble."

***

"This is an outrage!" Commissioner Elliott Jackson slammed his open palm on the long black-topped table of the meeting room in the Mt. Hood County Commission Building. The table could seat at least a dozen people, but at the moment it held only four: Lehigh, Jackson, Ray Ferguson, and a thin, balding, bespectacled man with pale skin and a long, crooked nose whose name Lehigh had forgotten immediately. He hadn't said four words other than his name since the start of the meeting, but those words had said plenty. He was a lawyer, representing the union of county workers—in this case, Bobby Wills.

"Unconscionable," Ferguson echoed. "I'm shocked. Shocked, I tell you!"

"It is outrageous," the lawyer said, breaking his silence, "that an officer of the law can be assaulted in public by a fellow officer with impunity!"

"You mean," Lehigh said with growing impatience, "a suspected *felon* was apprehended while attempting—"

"You had no reason to suspect any such thing!"

Lehigh stared at the lawyer, shocked to hear the words coming from his mouth while his mouth remained closed, lips unmoving. Only after the sound of the speaker's voice registered did he realize that the person speaking was not the lawyer, but Elliott Jackson.

He turned to face Jackson, confirming the source of the words. "With all due respect, Commissioner, we had been watching Deputy Wills and had it on good authority that he—"

"Entrapment," the lawyer said.

"Disgraceful!" Jackson shouted.

"Definitely not proper procedure," Ferguson said, shaking his head.

"What the hell?" Lehigh faced each man in turn, not believing his ears. "We had him dead to rights, attempting to leak information—"

"Falsified information, by your own admission," Ferguson said.

"Planted," the lawyer said.

Lehigh counted to five, calming himself. He imagined actual steam coming out of his ears and wondered why they didn't react to such a sight. Keeping his voice low and even, he addressed Ferguson. "You were the one who insisted we do something to *stop* the leaks."

"The true leaks, yes," Ferguson said. "Not this 'fake news' that you're planting. Why, Deputy Wills clearly was trying to expose the cronyism and incompetence that surrounds our professional, sworn officers of the law on a daily basis. Isn't that right, Felix?"

The lawyer, whose name, Lehigh gathered, was Felix, nodded, a somber expression on his face. "That's correct, Ray. Absolutely."

"You practically invited him to share the data with the press," Jackson said with a snarl. "A bombshell like that, which hadn't been disclosed to either side in this case, sitting in a 'secret' file in your office—what would you expect from a young man with a strong sense of justice and police procedure?"

"Strong sense of *what*?" Lehigh nearly came out of his chair. "The guy was heading straight to Bruce Bailey!"

"You don't know that for certain," the lawyer said.

"Oh for heaven's sake." Lehigh collapsed back into his chair. "This is ridiculous."

"It certainly is," Jackson said. "And you're going to make this right immediately. Mr. Anderson, I'll personally make sure that Deputy Wills' suspension is wiped off the books and that the sheriff reinstates him without prejudice or break in service. Will that satisfy your client?"

"I'll make the offer," the lawyer replied. "And as for the sheriff?"

"We'll take the proper disciplinary actions," Jackson said.

"Discipline? On *me*? Are you nuts?" Lehigh's gaze swept from one man to the next in the room. All lawyers, except him, and none of them represented him. He kicked himself mentally for not bringing an attorney of his own. They'd ambushed him, and he'd played right into their hands.

But he refused to concede this time. He knew he was right, and no way he'd let them steamroll him. He pushed his chair away from the table and stood.

"Sit down!" Jackson shouted, also rising from his seat.

"*You* sit down." Lehigh pushed Jackson's chest with one flat paw. The commissioner thumped into his chair, his mouth agape. Lehigh leaned over the table, his face hovering above the other three, and pointed a long finger at each in turn. "Okay, guys. I see what's going on here. You want to run this town like a circus, you go on ahead and call in the clowns. You want Wills reinstated, you can do it yourself. Pass an ordinance, do whatever. I'll have no part of it."

"It's your duty as sheriff," Jackson said in a half-hearted rumble.

"My duty is to enforce the law," Lehigh said. "Which I can't do if you guys are constantly in my face, begging favoritism for your cronies and minions. No, don't deny it. Here's the deal, guys. As long as I'm in this job, I do it my way. You want it done different, you replace me. Until then, shut your damn trap."

The union lawyer snuck a peak at Ferguson, then at Jackson. "I, uh, think we're done here," he said. Ferguson nodded. They gathered up their papers and shuffled toward the door. Jackson stared at them both in shock. He followed them out the door with one long, nasty look back at Lehigh just outside the doorway.

Lehigh leaned against the table, rubbing his aching temples. The conspiracy, he realized, ran even deeper than he'd ever thought.

***

A Blake Shelton song blared from the open doors and windows of The Roadhouse as the sun dipped below the tops of the Lodgepole pines and Douglas firs on the slopes of Brady

Mountain, loud enough to hear from the highway. The smell of barbecue, fries, and grilled burgers drowned out the negative imagery otherwise invoked by lyrics celebrating the time-honored traditions of digging in the dirt, chewing tobacco, and spitting, which somehow made men more successful at chasing women. Or so the song claimed. Lehigh didn't care. The only thing on his mind was eating something besides roasted squirrel. That, and having his first beer in over a week.

He parked at the far end of the gravel lot and sauntered over to the entrance, passing two "Latner for Sheriff" lawn signs along the way. He stole a glance in the windows so he could scan the cowboy hat-wearing men and women cheering each other on around the pool tables. He'd found trouble in The Roadhouse before, more often than not, and steered clear of it for that reason. But the aroma of ribs and deep-fry drew him in like a fish on a line. Trouble or no trouble, he was hungry.

He didn't recognize any of the pool-table rowdies, male or female, but kept to the other end of the L-shaped bar anyway, and scooted up on a tall stool with empty seats on either side. The bartender, a skinny, ponytailed brunette with lines on her leathery face and a low-cut blouse so tight that it had to be constricting her smoke-filled lungs, slapped a cardboard coaster on the counter. "What'll it be, handsome?"

He squinted at her, wondering if she remembered him. "Gimme one of them pale ales you got, and a plate of ribs with jojos."

"Coming right up." She slipped a pint glass under the tap and filled it about three-quarters with foam and one-quarter with beer. She thumped it onto the counter, not bothering to wipe up the spill. Yeah, she remembered him, all right.

"Thanks, Babs," he said, and the edges of her lips curled into a smile.

"I'll get your food order in." She sashayed away, neon reflecting off the rhinestones studding the waist and sides of her jeans.

Lehigh sipped his beer and let the television distract him. He had stopped watching TV in recent weeks, not least because he didn't have one anymore, but also because the news coverage frustrated him to the point of distraction. A Mariners baseball game wound down its final half-inning, a lopsided affair that nobody, including the players on the field, seemed interested in. After the final out, a brief interview with the opposing team's star cut away to local news.

Oh, crap.

"Babs?" He craned his neck around the cash register to see where she'd gone, but he saw no sign of her. "Anyone back there got the TV remote?" he called out, but no one answered.

Moments later, the news anchor's face filled the screen. With the sound off, Lehigh couldn't make out the top story until a caption appeared at the bottom of the screen.

And then he *really* groaned.

"Corruption, scandal, and cronyism in sheriff's office," it read. The screen split, and Bruce Bailey's smug grin dominated half the screen. The anchor continued talking as Bruce nodded, clearly anxious to begin his report.

"Want me to change the channel, Sheriff?" Babs appeared before him with a wet bar rag, spreading the spilled beer thinner and wider across the counter.

Lehigh debated with himself for a moment, then sighed. "Actually, if you could put the sound on, I'd be much obliged."

"Happy to." She found the remote under the counter and turned up the volume, just in time to hear the start of the story.

"A recently hired deputy in the Mt. Hood County sheriff's office claims to have been fired in retaliation for whistle-blowing," Bailey said. "Deputy Bobby Wills alleged today that interim Sheriff Lehigh Carter physically tackled him to prevent him from revealing damaging information about cronyism, favoritism, and corruption to the press."

"What the hell?" Lehigh shouted before he could stop himself. "That yellow, lying mongrel, I ought to—" He caught himself and clamped his mouth shut, realizing that everyone in the bar was now staring at him and watching the newscast—the exact opposite of what he wished would happen.

"The deputy claims to have uncovered evidence in the investigation into the Everett Downey murder that Sheriff Carter was, for unexplained reasons, hiding from the prosecution that would support the conviction of Carter's father-in-law, Senator George McBride," Bailey went on. "When Wills attempted to share this information with the appropriate parties, he says, the sheriff attacked him, publicly, and threatened him further bodily harm."

"Liar!" Lehigh shouted before he could stop himself.

A heavy figure thumped onto the bar stool next to him. "Or, not," the man said to nobody in particular.

Lehigh turned toward him. He didn't recognize the man's face or voice. "What do you know about it?" he asked.

The man shrugged. Long, greasy hair, parted in the middle, hung to his beefy shoulders and blended in with his bushy beard and sideburns. He smelled like an ashtray that had just farted. He turned and his bright blue eyes fixed on Lehigh. "Only what I saw," the man said. "And I saw it pretty darn clear."

"Saw what?" Alarm bells rang in Lehigh's head. He replayed the scene in his own mind and admitted to himself that, on appearance, the scene might have looked pretty bad to a bystander.

"Saw you and that lady cop run him down and open-field tackle him like a linebacker," the man said. "And I saw that you were armed."

"We had good reason to arrest him," Lehigh said.

"Did you now?" The man smiled and gestured to the television. "I don't suppose you shared it with them folks?"

Bailey's voice emerged again in the quieting din of the bar. "Attempts to contact the sheriff today for comment were unsuccessful," Bailey said. "Back to you, Steve."

"What crap," Lehigh said. "Nobody tried contacting me!"

"Maybe," the man said, "they called your lawyer." He stood and leaned closer to Lehigh. "Maybe you should do the same. *Sheriff.*" He ambled over to the pool tables and picked up a cue, never looking back.

Lehigh's food arrived, but he'd lost his appetite. All he could

think about was the man's advice to call his lawyer.
It sounded like advice he might need to take.

Chapter Twenty-Four

Ray Ferguson pushed his way through the glass front door of Dot's Diner and scanned the room. It took effort to see past the blue haze of smoke that flowed freely from the bar to the kitchen, smelling of grease, salt, and weak coffee, but after blinking his eyes a few times, he spotted the broad back of his breakfast companion in the corner. He smirked at the man's weak attempt at disguise. He couldn't decide which parts were most ridiculous: the dark wig mostly hidden by a wide-brimmed hat, the bushy moustache, or the outfit of brand-new boots, black studded jeans, and a red rodeo shirt that had never been worn within a hundred yards of a steer or horse, except for photo-ops. The man's size alone would give him away, never mind the fact that his face appeared every four years, like clockwork, on campaign billboards around the county.

Minus the fake sideburns, of course.

He strode to the table, all business, and sat opposite County Commissioner Elliott McBride Jackson, facing the room. Not the safest seat in the house, but at least he could see anyone coming at him. Empty tables surrounded them. He felt safe removing his own rarely-used cowboy hat.

"Did you watch the news last night?" Jackson asked him. The Commissioner took a sip of coffee and winced. "Damn, that's awful."

Ray signaled the short, Brillo-haired matron behind the bar, and she set to pouring him a cup. "Yes, I watched. Remind me to send Bruce Bailey a good bottle of Scotch whiskey for Christmas this year."

"Was that your doing?" Jackson tried another sip of coffee and pushed it away.

"It was my understanding," Ferguson said with a smirk, "that the good deputy did it on his own volition, pursuing truth, beauty, and justice."

"In other words, yes."

"In other words, ask your secretary," Ferguson said. Damn him, playing innocent. "She might have some pillow talk to share with you. Officially, I've got nothing."

"I would never pry into the private lives of my staff," Jackson said with a glint in his eye. "So, let's get down to business. How's the case?"

Ferguson eyed him with caution. He didn't trust politicians as a rule, and this one in particular. As much as he'd fumed in public about the leaks in the case coming from Carter's shop, he harbored at least as much suspicion about Jackson, if not more. But, too late now. He'd cast his lot with the Chairman, and Jackson could help his own political career far more than the idiot hayseed sporting the sheriff's badge at the moment.

"It's going well," he said. "We have a few loose ends to tie up, but the fact that he tried to flee helps with the optics. I expect he'll beg for a deal, long before we go to trial."

"And will you give him one?"

Ferguson shrugged, decided to play it coy. "We'll consider anything that serves the public interest."

"The only thing that would serve the public interest is if that man hangs by his neck in the public courtyard!" Jackson slammed the table with his fist, and coffee spilled out of his cup onto the table.

The wiry frame of the waitress reappeared out of nowhere, finally delivering Ray's coffee. "Sorry for the delay—had to wait for a fresh pot. I'll get a rag to wipe that up." She vanished, giving Ray only enough time to read the name stitched into her blouse. Dot, the owner.

Ferguson sipped his coffee, grimaced at its harsh acidity, then stirred several thimbles of half-and-half and three doses of sugar into it. "Tell me," he said, "why are you so gung-ho to see your cousin go down for this murder? Not that I doubt that he did it," he added. "Not for a moment."

"Isn't his guilt enough? I tell you, if that man walks on this charge, after all of the crap he's done and gotten away with over the years, it'll be a grievous injustice. No, more than that. A travesty. A *scandal*." Jackson glared at Ferguson. "Don't let that happen, Raymond. You hear me? Don't. Let. It. Happen." He stabbed the table with his index finger with each word, as if to drive each one into the Formica.

"Don't worry, I won't." Ferguson smiled. "I have my own reasons to want to win this one."

"Like getting elected Attorney General of Oregon next year?" Jackson smiled for the first time since Raymond arrived. "Yes, a case like this could do wonderful things for a law-and-order candidate in this state." He started to lean forward and lay his arms on the table to make another point, but just in time he noticed the spilled coffee.

"Let me get that spill wiped up for you," Dot said from behind Raymond. She hummed tunelessly, pushing the brown liquid into her palm with the rag, leaving a wet river of grease behind. "There we go. Can I get you fellas any breakfast?"

"Eggs over easy, hash browns, toast," Jackson said.

"Same," said Ray, although he'd already eaten. Anything to get rid of the eavesdropping hag.

She moved over to another table, where a lone man had taken a seat, his face buried in a newspaper. Jackson cleared his throat. "What of our other, uh, priority? Anything new to report?"

Raymond lowered his voice and leaned toward Jackson. "With the TV news from last night, that ought to keep Carter's attention off of our business. He'll be fighting these leaks all the way to November. By then, we'll have McBride's conviction well in hand. I'm confident the voters will see fit at that time to return a law enforcement *professional* to head up the sheriff's office. The polls I've seen already trend in that direction."

Jackson frowned. "I don't like leaving this matter in the

hands of the public. Trust me, I know how fickle they can be. We need *insurance*."

Ferguson sighed. "Outside of beating him at the ballot box, there's little that I can do. Unless I catch him red-handed with his hand in the cookie jar—and, like it or not, Carter's too careful, and too honest, to get himself mixed up in any of that."

"What about him beating up that young deputy?" Jackson asked. "Couldn't you charge him with assault?"

"That woman deputy actually roughed him up," Ferguson said. "And we can't start busting every cop who gets a little physical with perps. Think of where that would lead." He shook his head. Courts and politicians already had placed too many silly restrictions on law enforcement without adding the chilling effect of an assault charge.

"There must be something we can do to Carter," Jackson said with an impatient growl. The man had no sense of humor. "He was accused of a cover-up. Can't you press charges on that?"

Ferguson shook his head. These pols could be so thickheaded sometimes. "That's a civil offense, if anything. You know as well as I do, those charges won't go anywhere in court. No, the only solutions are political. Which, I believe, is *your* area of expertise."

"I don't want to wait until November. Think of the damage he could do to this town!"

A rustling of paper distracted Ferguson for a moment. He glanced around. The closest person, the man with the newspaper behind him, seemed absorbed in his sports page. He faced Jackson again. "That's not the only political solution. He was appointed by the County Board, after all. You could remove him."

"I checked the charter. We'd have to impeach him, and my colleagues on the Board don't have the courage to do that. Hell, most of them *like* the guy, for whatever reason." Jackson scowled and picked up his coffee, thought better of it, and set it down. "We'd need to have something on him. Something big.

Something he can't weasel his way out of."

"Like?"

Jackson narrowed his eyes. "A felony, for example."

Ferguson rolled his eyes. "Carter's not likely to go out and rob a bank."

"I'm not talking about that." Jackson lowered his voice to a whisper. "The man has a temper, I'm told."

"So I've heard."

"And he's separated from his wife."

An uneasy stirring boiled in Ferguson's gut. "So?"

"So, estranged couples have been known to argue. And cheat." Jackson smiled, a cruel smile. "And men of his type have been known to let their emotions run away with them."

"You *want* him to beat up his wife? Your own damned *niece*?" Ferguson could hardly keep his voice down.

"No!" Jackson scanned the room again. "I'm saying, we might find someone willing to do a little *acting*, so to speak. A woman, say, whose occupation might lend itself to, uh, extra-curricular activities…?" He smiled again.

Recognition finally dawned. "You mean, perhaps, one of Mr. Downey's employees at the nightclub?"

Jackson nodded.

Ferguson considered the idea. "Not bad," he said. "This could help with our other objective as well. I've heard that the establishment has fallen into harder times since Mr. Downey's demise. Staff leaving, business being down. This could help drive the dagger into the heart of those awful places."

"And we'd be rid of them for good. And I mean, for *the* good—of the county, that is."

Ferguson grinned. "It's ingenious. *If* we can find someone."

Jackson shrugged. "You realize, of course, that some of the most frequent visitors to Mr. Downey's establishments work on your task force…so I've heard."

Raymond bristled. "That's absurd."

Jackson shook his head. "I have it on good authority. At any rate, they've been involved with enough arrests there over the years to have the whole staff on speed-dial. I say we use that resource, and quick. We should strike while the iron is hot and Carter's attentions are drawn elsewhere."

Ferguson relaxed. While Jackson more often than not infuriated him with unsubstantiated claims and pointless public posturing, Raymond had to admit that the deputies on his task force frequented the strip clubs—and probably had developed both personal and professional relationships there. Why not use them to his advantage?

Before he could respond, Dot appeared with plates in hand and set them in front of the men. "More coffee?" She picked up a pot she'd somehow stashed on the next table.

"Nothing more, thanks," Jackson said with the sweet smile of a campaigner.

Raymond waited until she'd moved away, then nodded at Jackson. "I'll look into this," he said. "It's a good plan."

Jackson nodded and took a bite of his breakfast, then dropped his fork. "These are the worst eggs I've ever had," he said.

Raymond shook his head. Spoiled brat of a politician. Nothing was ever good enough.

***

Phil Reardon hid behind his newspaper, waiting for the two men to leave the diner. They'd groused about the coffee, the food, the service, the grease—everything except the diner's most important flaw: its complete and utter lack of privacy.

He'd heard every word of their conversation, and it disturbed him.

It also surprised him. Jackson, though well-known as a liar and scoundrel, had always struck him as being more careful than this. Speaking in public about a plot to unseat one of his political enemies seemed reckless, even wearing that awful disguise. He'd survived in local politics by bullying most opponents and cutting deals with the rest, usually at taxpayer expense, but he also held a job few others even wanted. Phil, like most people, remained willing to let him do it if it meant he didn't have to.

The Assistant District Attorney's complicity shocked him more. Ferguson had a reputation for intelligence, hard work, adhering to Christian values, and a passionate zeal for enforcing the law. But if he'd heard this right—and he had no doubts about it—Ferguson was conspiring to break the law. Commit perjury, even, or at least convince someone else to do so.

He understood, even if he didn't agree, why they'd want to go after the strip clubs. As a father, he'd always despised the clubs and harbored secret fears of finding his daughters' friends (never *his* daughters!) on stage someday. That alone kept him out of the clubs, despite the loneliness he'd suffered since his divorce. But their zeal for going after Lehigh Carter he didn't understand. Lehigh went rogue at times, but he was honest to a fault. The independent streak they loathed was what most people liked about him. He couldn't be corrupted like Buck Summers—or, for that matter, Jackson.

"More coffee?" Dot refilled his cup without waiting for an answer. Phil lowered his sports page and noticed that the two conspirators had left. "Thanks, Dot. Busy morning, huh?"

"About the usual. Some new faces, though." She turned her head toward the now-empty table in the corner. "Normally I'd welcome a new customer, but..."

"Lousy tippers?"

Dot made a sour face, then nodded. "Two bucks on a twenty-five dollar tab. How's a gal supposed to earn a living?"

Phil shook his head. "Can't say I'm surprised. They're not the nicest of guys."

Dot cocked her head and rearranged the sugar bowl, creamers, and salt and pepper shakers on the table. "How d'you mean?"

"I shouldn't say anything. It's none of my business." He went back to reading the newspaper.

Dot swatted at him with her towel. "Those are public officials. Everything they say is our business. Come on, what'd they talk about?"

Phil grimaced. He'd always been taught to keep his mouth shut, his nose clean, and his powder dry. He hated wading in to someone else's business uninvited. But Dot kind of had a point about them being public employees, and Lehigh, a good guy, needed help against these goons.

"They seem to have it in for Sheriff Carter," he said. "Talking about trying to get him out of office. Before the election, I mean."

"Why?" Dot cleared the plates from their empty table onto a tray and paused by Phil's side. "What'd he ever do to them?"

"I dunno. I guess they think he's not up to the job, or something."

She scoffed. "Compared to what we used to have, he's a genius. But anyway, what can they do to him? He doesn't answer to them, does he?"

"No, but…" He looked around and lowered his voice. "They're talking about setting him up to take a fall on something he didn't do. Get some stripper or something to say he beat her up. It's all part of a plan to shut down the clubs. Sick, huh?"

"That's terrible!" Dot set the tray down on the next table over and sat down across from Phil. "Are you sure that's what you heard?"

Phil nodded. "Pretty sure. I could hear them pretty good."

"You have to tell the sheriff," she said. "Warn him, before they—"

"No, no," Phil said. "I couldn't do that."

"You have to, Phil. You can't let them get away with that!"

"Dot, I have my own problems, okay? My wife won't let me near my kids, she's draining me of all my money—I got too much on my plate already." He pulled out his wallet and dropped some bills on the table, including a generous tip. Hopefully enough to keep her from squawking too much about all this. "Look, just forget I said anything, okay?"

She shook her head. "This is serious business. You've got to do something."

"Do something, like what? Get cross-wise with the rich and powerful? Yeah, right." He stood and slid out of his chair. "That's how people around here get killed. Just ask Jared Barkley and Ev Downey. I don't want to be next. My kids need their daddy, even if their mother doesn't think so." He turned away from her and headed to the exit.

She caught up to him at the door, her face tense. "You sure about what you heard?"

He paused a moment, thought about it, and nodded.

"Well," she said, "I ain't got no little ones to worry about, and my husband would just as soon I go to jail as come home at night. So if you won't do nothing about this, I will."

Sweat broke out on Phil's brow. "What are you gonna do?"

She lifted her chin, straightened her posture. "I'm gonna tell the sheriff the truth. What you do about it is up to you." With that, she spun on her heel and strode into the kitchen.

Phil stared after her, cursing himself for opening his big, fat mouth.

Chapter Twenty-Five

Julia wobbled into Lehigh's office wearing two-inch heels and smelling of fingernail polish, or possibly polish remover, a clue that she'd had a pretty slow afternoon, as had Lehigh. She paused just inside the door, clutching an oversized yellow envelope. "The report from that independent lab you asked for came in just now," she said. "I thought you'd want to see it right away."

"Hold on a sec." Lehigh looked up from his monthly crime report, a brief document dominated by bar fights and domestic squabbles, both numbering in the single digits despite the intense August heat. He waved Julia onward, hitting *Save* on the spreadsheet, a step he'd missed too many times, to his frustration. How many late nights had that mistake cost him? He took the report from her. "Thanks, Julia. You're the best." She remained standing in front of his desk, her eyes pinned to the floor. He cleared his throat. "Is there something else?"

She brushed her hand through her long brown hair, which looked a little brighter and fuller than usual, and shifted her weight from one foot to the other on her uncharacteristically high heels. He feared at one point she might tip over, but she righted herself. "Sheriff, I wondered if it might be okay…well, it's our anniversary, and my husband wanted to take me out to dinner, but we could only get reservations at five, so—"

"Of course, of course. Enjoy yourselves. Where's dinner at, anyhow?"

"Wilkinson's, up in Wyee Falls. It's an hour's drive, so he was hoping to pick me up at four."

"With my blessing. Enjoy." He waited for her to wobble back out of the office, then opened his web browser on his phone. A few taps on the screen later, he had the number he needed.

"Wilkinson's, how may I help you?"

"I'd like to buy a bottle of wine for a friend dining with you tonight." The entire transaction took only a few minutes. Then he tore open the sealed envelope and found the section he needed.

The results startled him, even though it confirmed the suspicion he'd had that caused him to pursue the independent lab's opinion in the first place. He sat back in his chair, contemplating the report's implications.

The lab's analysis showed that, without a doubt, George McBride's 30-30 rifle could not have fired the bullet that killed Everett Downey.

He retrieved the county's ballistics report from his file and scanned the report's conclusions. That report declared a perfect match between the fatal bullet and the test bullets fired for the analysis. He scanned back into the detail of the report and examined the photographs of the bullets used.

Something didn't add up.

He returned to the independent lab's report. Checked the detailed analysis, and the photographs. Checked the other photographs.

They didn't match.

He needed more information. An expert. Luckily, he had one he trusted nearby. He picked up the phone again.

Moments later, Jim Wadsworth closed the door to Lehigh's office behind him. "What's this about a new ballistics report?" he asked, shuffling over to a chair.

"I sent for it the other day, while you were fetching George back from Portland." Lehigh handed him the report. "Read it."

Wadsworth flipped through the pages and landed on the one he needed, then scanned it, nodding. "Where'd this come from?"

"A private lab in Hood River. Here's the county's report."

He showed that one to Wadsworth. The next few moments seemed like eons. He'd learned a lot in the few months since becoming sheriff, but wouldn't call himself an expert on ballistics. Maybe he read it wrong.

"Okay, here's what I see," Wadsworth said. "Ballistics, first of all, is an inexact science. More of an art, really. Lots of subjectivity, despite what you see on TV."

"It's just opinion, then?" Lehigh asked, his heart sinking.

"I didn't say that," Wadsworth said. "Just that there's some interpretation involved. Having said that, there are two things everyone agrees on. One is that rifles leave striations on the bullets they fire, and no two guns' striations are the same."

"So, they're unique, like fingerprints?"

"Unique, but unlike fingerprints, they can change over time," Wadsworth said. "Unlike fingers, guns show wear with use. It's subtle, but traceable."

"Okay." That didn't sound good. He sighed. "You said two things. What's the other?"

Wadsworth set the reports side by side on Lehigh's desk, open to the photographs of the test bullets. "See the indentations on the tail end of the bullet there, and there? Those come from the firing pin. Those also can vary from weapon to weapon, and also with the age and use of the gun."

"They look different. I mean, the one in this report—"

"Doesn't match the one in the other. Right. Even though the bullets tested *within each report* are the same. In other words, the fatal bullet—the one that killed Everett Downey—is different in the two reports."

Lehigh shook his head. "I'm confused. How can that be?"

Wadsworth thought a moment. "Where did the bullet come from that the private lab used?"

Lehigh shrugged. "The evidence room downstairs. The gun, too. They had the originals, just like the country forensics office."

Wadsworth stared hard at him. "How good is this lab?"

"The best, according to my research."

"Would this lab have any reason to lie?"

"Of course not. They'd go out of business so fast—wait. Are you saying what I think you're saying?"

Wadsworth sat back in his chair and crossed his arms over his chest. "My friend, it's not what *I'm* saying. It's what this report says, which is: George McBride's 30-30 was *not* the weapon used to kill Everett Downey."

Lehigh let out a long breath. "I had a sneaking suspicion," he said, "which is why I hired these guys for a second opinion."

"The implications are just crazy," Wadsworth said. "I mean, what we have here is proof that the county ballistics report was falsified. The question is, why?"

"The other question, and maybe the more important one," Lehigh said, "is, by whom?"

***

"Would you *please* stop withholding evidence from me?" Ferguson shouted, shaking a sheaf of papers in his hand at Lehigh. The papers, Lehigh noticed with a small amount of pride, reflected the watermark of the nearby Twin Falls Paper Mill, the company owned by Consuela's son Manuel, who bought a substantial part of its pulp lumber from the co-op to which Lehigh belonged. Apparently, the D.A.'s office had a "buy local" policy.

"I'm not withholding anything," Lehigh said. "I just haven't gotten it to you yet. Hell, I haven't even had a chance to make a spare copy myself."

Ferguson slammed the report down on the table, a copy of the independent lab's ballistics report Lehigh had ordered. How Ferguson had gotten a copy so fast, he had no idea. But he'd need to find out soon. It wasn't Bobby Wills this time, though. Bobby was still on paid leave, a reward for the "trauma" of being accused of leaking information.

"Well," Ferguson said, "I shouldn't be getting reports like this from anonymous sources. I should be getting them from you—immediately, not whenever you get a chance."

Anonymous. Hmmm. "Let's focus on the contents of the

report," Lehigh said. "It seems to indicate—"

"—That McBride has more guns at his disposal," Ferguson said. "Don't worry. We're on our way to his house right now, and to every gun shop in the four-county area. We'll find this weapon, don't you worry. And when we do, your father-in-law is going down. As are *you*, if you continue to protect him!"

"I'm not *protecting* him." Lehigh pushed away from the table, but stayed in his chair. At his insistence, neither man had brought any other staff with them into the meeting, out of concern for leaks. He wished now that he'd brought Wadsworth in—Ferguson seemed to trust him more. "I'm just trying to do my job."

"As am I. And mine is to put a guilty man behind bars— which you seem hell-bent on preventing." Ferguson scooped up the report again and rifled through the pages. "Whatever possessed you to buy your own ballistics report, anyway?"

"I had a hunch," Lehigh said. "Which turns out to be correct. Someone falsified the original. Why aren't you as upset about that as I am? Aren't you concerned about going into court with cooked-up evidence? Couldn't that cost you the whole case and let a potentially guilty man go free?"

Ferguson glared at him a moment, then calmed, nodding. "Yes, of course I am," he said. "You're right. I'll look into that situation as well. But, dammit Carter, we need to work together on this stuff. No more of you running off on your own, understand me?"

Lehigh stood and met Ferguson's accusing gaze with one of his own. "That goes both ways, Ray," he said. "And remember: I don't work for you. I'm responsible to the voters. Nobody else. Do *you* understand *me*?"

Ferguson sneered. "We'll see how long that lasts." He shoved the report into his briefcase and headed to the door.

"Hey, Ray?" Lehigh waited for Ferguson to turn. "Don't let me find out that you were responsible for that false ballistics report," he said. "Because you know what? This badge here? It empowers me to arrest anybody…including district attorneys."

Ferguson gasped. "Are you accusing me—"

"How's that feel, Ray?" Lehigh crossed his arms and smiled. "Being accused of something before there's even a shred of evidence against you. Feel good? No? Well. I'm glad we now understand each other."

Ferguson slammed the door behind him. Lehigh's smile faded. As good as it had felt to push Ferguson's buttons in the meeting, the truth remained: Lehigh still had a serious problem with moles in the department. As long as that problem persisted, he'd never get to the truth behind the murder of Everett Downey. He had to solve that problem, fast.

***

Damn that redneck Pharisee!

Raymond Ferguson gripped the steering wheel of his black county-issue Crown Victoria with white knuckles, his hands in the proper ten-and-two-o'clock positions as he'd been taught at the age of sixteen by his stern, tight-lipped father. Archibald Ferguson had brooked no exceptions to conformity of any kind, who expected "perfection, or better," as he used to quip, the man's only attempt at humor in Raymond's memory. Father often came to mind in moments like these—moments of quiet crisis, of careful review of his recent actions, searching for possible missteps. Mistakes were inevitable but never excused in the Ferguson household. One always paid a price, in repentance if not in worldly sums. Always.

In this case, the mistake had been to underestimate his opponent. Lehigh Carter appeared to many as ignorant, if not downright dumb, and it led people to believe he could be easily fooled. Ferguson had fallen into that trap a few times now, allowing Carter to exploit Raymond's own weakness, the sin he could not seem to forbear: the sin of pride. What his enemies called arrogance. Enemies who seemed to multiply in number daily—or was he becoming paranoid in his advancing years?

The second mistake—sloppiness—compounded the first. He should have spotted the error before the sheriff did, and taken steps to correct it. But the tidiness of it all had pleased him too much, meshing with the other evidence to not only implicate McBride, but make him overconfident for a career-boosting slam-dunk conviction. Now he'd have to work a little harder, with a more thorough and—Father would approve of this—more disciplined approach.

Speaking of discipline, not all of the mistakes were his. He'd trusted people who had not earned it, and they'd disappointed him. For them, too, there must be consequences. Punishment, even. But what punishment fit that crime?

He pondered options, each more onerous than the last. God had punished Everett Downey's lifetime of wickedness with what some might call the ultimate punishment. But those with a more disciplined perspective—there was that word again—knew otherwise. Ashes to ashes, dust to dust. All men suffer the same ultimate fate. He shuddered to think of the punishment Downey would receive in the Final Reckoning.

An old hymn bubbled up in his throat, and he hummed its tune as he drove. Then the lyrics came to him: "*The wicked like the driven chaff are swept from off the land,*" he sang. "*The way of sinners, far from God, shall surely be o'erthrown.*" A smile crept onto his face, and his hands relaxed on the wheel.

Perfection, or better.

Father would be proud.

***

The second independent forensics report came in even faster than the first. Now that they'd established a relationship, the firm took on new work with just a phone call and a courier drop. This project, a simple matter of matching fingerprints against those of the deputies and employees working in the Clarkesville office, took only a day to turn around.

Lehigh spread the report's summary pages before him and scanned the report's conclusions. The analysis showed that only four people in the department had handled the ballistics report and left fingerprints on its glossy cover: Lehigh, Wadsworth, Julia…and one other deputy.

Not the name Lehigh had expected.

He gathered up the pages and locked them in his desk drawer, then made his way down the hall to the reception area. Ruby Mac sat behind the desk, studying a report.

"You're not on patrol today?" Lehigh asked her.

"I'm pulling a double shift," Ruby said. "Earning some extra money while we're short-staffed. I go out on patrol in twenty minutes."

"I see. And where's your partner right now?"

She jerked a thumb over her shoulder. "He just came in. I suspect he's getting a cup of coffee. Why?"

Lehigh winced. "You might need to work alone today. Stay here." Lehigh reversed course and headed straight to the break room. Nobody there. He checked the meeting rooms—all empty. Hmm. That didn't leave many places a deputy ought to be found inside the building.

But maybe he wasn't where he ought to be.

Lehigh hurried down the hall, toward the administrative office, where Julia managed the files and phones. "Julia," he said, breathing hard when he arrived at her desk, "have any deputies come by here today?"

She nodded. "Almost all of them. They pretty much have to pass my desk when they go in or out."

"Anybody ask to see any files?"

She shook her head. "Gosh, no. They all know better than that."

"Good. So, where would you have filed that ballistics report that came in a few days ago? The one from the private lab?"

"That's in the secure area," she said. "In evidence lockdown."

"Did you send that report down by interoffice mail, or did you walk it down yourself?"

"I walked it down. You said it was *very* confidential." She nodded, as if confirming in her head what Lehigh's exact instructions had been. "I locked it up there myself."

Lehigh leaned closer to her and lowered his voice. "Anybody see you do that?"

"Of course. There's always a deputy on duty."

"And who was on duty the day you brought that report to the evidence locker?"

She shrugged. "One of the new guys. I think his name's Marvin…?"

"Martin Lightfoot?"

She brightened and snapped her well-manicured fingers. "That's him. Indian fella. Very sweet guy. Why?"

Lehigh sighed. "Have you seen Martin today?"

She nodded. "I see him right now, in fact. Right down that hallway."

Lehigh spun on his heel. Martin Lightfoot, all 6'2", 250 pounds of him, stood 30 feet down the hall, staring at Lehigh.

And then he ran.

Chapter Twenty-Six

Lehigh caught up to Martin at reception, where, to his surprise, Ruby Mac had him trapped in a corner. If not for the seriousness of the situation, the visual of little Ruby, holding big Martin Lightfoot at bay with nothing more than a ball-point pen, would have pushed Lehigh into spasms of uncontrollable laughter.

"How the heck did you manage this?" Lehigh asked when he recovered from his surprise.

"Julia buzzed me, told me to lock the door," Ruby said, grinning. "Then Marty here comes barreling through and runs smack dab into the door, head-first. What's up?"

Lehigh looked again at Martin, and only then noticed the big man's dazed look. "Your partner's in trouble, Mac. Help me move him, and then come back and unlock the door."

Moments later, Martin sat in Lehigh's guest chair, wiping tears from his eyes. Ruby scowled at him from behind with arms crossed.

"I swear, Sheriff," Martin said. "I didn't do anything with that report. I held it for a minute, maybe less, when Julia was fussing with the locker. Then I never saw it again. Honest." He sniffled and coughed into his fist, then met Lehigh's stare with a pleading look.

"Why'd you run just now, then?" Lehigh asked.

Martin shook his head, mouth open. "I don't know, boss. I saw you looking at me like that—like cops have looked at me since I was a kid. Whenever I see someone in uniform looking at me like that, instinct kicks in, and I run. It was stupid, I know."

"*You're* a cop now, Martin," Ruby said, exasperated. "Are you gonna run every time I look at you?"

"You're different," Martin said. "You're my partner."

Lehigh pondered the situation. He didn't have a lot on Martin—just a fingerprint—and his story seemed as plausible as the alternative that pointed to his guilt. Thus far he'd kept his record clean, otherwise.

"Here's what I'm gonna do," he said. "You're on phone duty until further notice. That's your regular assignment until I say otherwise. Stay away from the files and be ready to account for every moment of your time over the past two weeks. We're gonna get to the bottom of this, one way or the other."

"Thank you," Martin said. "You'll see. It ain't me! I ain't no mole!"

He shook Lehigh's hands with both of his own and rumbled out of the office. Lehigh sighed. The number of deputies he could trust was dropping by the minute.

"What do you think, Ruby?" Lehigh asked.

She frowned and moved closer, speaking in a low voice. "It doesn't seem in character for Marty to pull something like this," she said. "But I've been wrong before about people."

Lehigh nodded. "Have you seen him snooping around the evidence vault at all?"

She shook her head. "But I haven't really paid attention. I will now. Of course, he's not likely to try anything with you around."

His stomach growled. A cup of coffee sounded good. "In that case," he said, "let me go ahead and make myself scarce for a bit. Keep an eye on him while I'm out."

She nodded. "Will do, boss."

***

Lehigh paused before entering Dot's Diner to scan the room through the glass door, left ajar about an inch by whomever last gave up on getting coffee worth drinking. The salty, greasy aroma of bacon and sausage leaked out from the gap between the door and the gap on the handle side, almost balanced by the sharp tang of burnt toast. The tables along the wall remained empty at this late morning hour, but a few hardy souls sipped weak coffee at the counter.

Nobody looked too happy with their meals, but the air leaking out around the door felt ten degrees cooler than the outside, maybe twenty, so he swung the door open and grabbed one of the many vacant booths farthest from the white-haired men who stopped talking as soon as they recognized him. Dot delivered a white porcelain mug and filled it with steaming liquid, about the color and consistency of weak tea. "Cream and sugar, Sheriff?" she asked without making eye contact.

"Lots," he said. "And a donut."

She smirked, and he realized what a stereotype he'd become, and almost changed his mind. But no, dammit. He wanted a donut. She whisked herself away and filled the men's mugs at the counter, made some small talk with them, then returned with his treat, a palm-sized confection bearing a thick coat of powdered white sugar.

"Thank you, Dot," he said, dipping the donut into the coffee. She stood by with the pot, ready to refill at a moment's notice. Coffee cups never went empty at Dot's.

"Friend of yours was in here t'other day," she said.

"That narrows it down, considering how few people admit to being my friend," he said. "Male or female?" He couldn't imagine Stacy ever stepping foot inside the greasy spoon.

"One of your old football chums. And a coupla suits. That Reverend character."

Lehigh's alarm bells sounded, and heat rose in his ears. "Well, now," he said, sipping his coffee, "I'd have a hard time believing Ray Ferguson called me his friend. Who was he with?"

"One of them politician types. Johnson? Jackson. Something like that. Big fella. Kind of full of himself, you know?" She topped up his coffee. He stirred in another packet of sugar.

"Commissioner Jackson? What the heck was he doing here? I thought he had his coffee delivered to his office." He smiled, hoping she'd catch on that he was joking, but she never met his eyes. "And I *know* he didn't call me his friend."

"Nope. 'Twasn't the suits saying hello to you. Although that's not to say you weren't on their mind, from what I gather." She eyed his half-eaten donut, as if she wanted to pour coffee directly onto it. He dipped it, chewed, swallowed.

"Dot," he said around his mouthful, "you're talking in riddles. What are you trying to tell me?"

She sighed, shook her head. "I'm saying you need to keep in touch with your old pal who *might* have overheard something he wasn't supposed to hear. You catch my drift?" She leaned closer to him and whispered. "His name's Phil. And yes, you should talk to him. Soon. Okay?" She wiped away the few drops of coffee that had spilled onto the table and slapped the rag back into her hand.

"No hints as to what they said?" Lehigh sipped his coffee. Ugh. He took a quick bite of the donut.

She leaned toward him again and spoke in a low voice. "The suits? Listen, Sheriff. Men like that don't come in here much. I could count on one hand the number of times I've seen either one of them within fifty feet of a blue plate special. So when they do, I know they're up to no good." She glanced around and leaned closer. "They want you gone, Sheriff. Something to do with that dead pervert Downey. How, I don't know. Figured you might."

Lehigh swallowed the last of his donut and washed it down with a sip of coffee. "As to how, I got some ideas. But as to why…that I still haven't figured out."

She smiled, a thin flat line with tiny upward curls near her cheeks. "The why is the easy part," she said. "Sheriff, those boys are afraid of you."

He set the mug down in surprise. She emptied the rest of her pot into it and swished away, humming.

***

Julia greeted him at the doorway to his office and followed him inside. "Sheriff? A Mr. Benjamin Wright is waiting to see you."

"Benjamin who?" He searched his memory. The name didn't ring a bell.

"He says he knows you. Says you had beers at The Stadium a few months back."

"Ben? Holy cow, what does he want?" Ben once worked for Stacy's ex-boyfriend Paul, and turned state's evidence in Paul's trial for the murder of Lehigh's predecessor, Interim Sheriff Jared Barkley. "I'm not involved with the Barkley case any more."

"He says it's a personal matter. Shall I tell him to come another time?" Julia headed toward the door.

"No, no. I'll see him." He had no idea what Ben had up his sleeve, but he figured he owed him one. Moments later, an athletically-built African-American man in a tight-fitting T-shirt appeared in the doorway. He removed his cap to reveal close-cropped black curls and a sheen of sweat trickling down his brow and temples.

"Thanks for seeing me without an appointment." Ben extended a shovel-sized paw for a handshake. Lehigh shook it, grateful the man didn't engage in foolish hand-crushing games like Ferguson and Jackson.

"What's all this about, Ben?" Lehigh pointed him to a seat. "You having trouble with the prosecutor's office on the Paul van Paten trial?"

Ben remained standing and shook his head. "Nope, nothing like that," he said. "I'm here because, well, my buddy Martin called me. Sheriff, Marty Lightfoot never double-crossed nobody."

"I see," Lehigh said. "So you're here as a character witness?"

"I guess you could say that." Ben dipped his head and lowered his eyes. "Mr. Carter, I've known Marty since we were boys. He's the most honest man I've ever met, and loyal to a fault. Kind of like you, Sheriff." Ben lifted his gaze and met Lehigh's. "That's why I was so surprised to hear you suspected him of something like this."

Alarm bells rang in Lehigh's head. He never trusted flatterers, and Ben never struck him as the type. He chose his words carefully. "Ben, I appreciate your sticking up for your friend, but I can't ignore evidence right in front of me. While it's not proof by itself, it's definitely enough that I can't ignore it."

"Fair enough." Ben finally took the seat Lehigh offered him. "But isn't it as likely he's been set up as done anything?"

Lehigh weighed the man's words. "It's possible. I don't know about likely."

"Sheriff, a lot of people in this town are saying things about you, about how you're playing favorites, just like all the old sheriffs used to," Ben said. "Now, wait, hear me out. I don't believe those rumors, because I've known you a little while. You're a man with a strong sense of justice, and I respect that about you. A lot of us do. Working folks like me, I mean. Folks who don't have a lot of money, or some big government position." He dipped his head again, his eyes on the floor. "Innocent folks who spend time in jail because of people like Buck Summers and Ray Ferguson."

Lehigh caught his breath. "Folks like me, you mean," Lehigh said. "And my wife."

"I didn't want to say it, but yeah." Ben looked Lehigh in the eye again. "Folks like us need you to do what's right. We're tired of the good old boys running everything and scaring everyone into just going along, not saying nothing. We're done with those days, Sheriff. We need you to stop it. You know what I'm saying?"

A lump rose in Lehigh's throat. "I do know what you're saying, Ben," he said in a hoarse voice. "And I promise you, I will fight for what's right. If that means Martin is innocent, he'll be reinstated with no questions asked. If he's guilty, he'll be punished. And if I can't tell, then I'll give him the benefit of the doubt and call him innocent. Those are the rules for Martin Lightfoot, Ben Wright, George McBride, anyone. Everyone. On that, you have my word."

A broad smile creased Ben's face, revealing perfect white teeth. "That's all I ask, Sheriff. For Martin, and for people like Senator McBride." He stood and extended his hand again, this time gripping Lehigh's with a firm but not painful shake. "Thank you, Mr. Carter."

After he left, Lehigh sat in his chair, pondering Ben's plea. He wanted to trust him, as he had in the past. But the whole thing might be a setup, too.

He clicked an icon on his computer's desktop that granted him access to the county's arrest records. Within minutes, he had his answer.

***

Lehigh parked his pickup on the muddy shoulder of a neighborhood street just off of Highway 279 on the edge of town and glanced at the faded house numbers on the streetside mailbox. The numbers matched, as did the condition of the house compared to what he'd expected: a modest ranch in decent enough condition to rent, but not quite as well-kept as if the owner lived there. No name on the mailbox, or anywhere. Short, sun-baked grass, not much in the way of flowers or shrubbery. In the driveway sat a ten-year-old gold Impala in much better shape than the property, the car of an honest working man who wanted to avoid another car payment. Definitely the right place.

The door opened as he walked up the gravel drive. A husky man with rounded shoulders and a receding buzz cut filled the doorway, at first with a scowl, but then his expression softened into an uneasy smile. "Hey, Sheriff," Phil said. "To what do I owe the pleasure?"

"I wondered if you and I could chat over a beer," Lehigh said. "I'm buying."

"A beer?" Phil scrunched his eyes half-shut and cleaned out an ear with his finger. "I take it this isn't official business, then?"

"To be honest, I'm not sure." Lehigh took a deep breath. Time to just plunge in. "I stopped by Dot's this morning."

Phil's expression darkened and he held onto the door handle, keeping it shut between them. Only the screen on the lower half let their voices carry through. "What'd she have to say?"

Lehigh glanced around, spotted nobody else in the

neighborhood who might be eavesdropping. "Just that I should talk to you. Said you mighta heard something I ought to know."

Phil eyed him a few moments, then pushed open the door. "Come on in. The beer's on me."

Moments later they'd each taken the first long draft from an ice-cold can of light beer, seated at a right angle in Phil's living room. A small TV provided background noise from a baseball game. Phil spoke to him in a low voice. "I don't know what you've done to get on the wrong side of the district attorney and the county chair," he said, "but for some reason, they don't like you."

Lehigh smiled. "Yeah, well. Since you're sharing your beer and we're off the record, I confess, that's mutual. But what makes you think so?"

Phil took a noisy sip from his beer and rested the can on his knee, leaving a wet circle on his cargo shorts. He took a deep breath and let out a long, noisy sigh. "I'm not sure I should repeat any of this, Lehigh. I wasn't actually part of the conversation. Kind of accidentally overheard it, and I can't be a hundred percent sure of what I heard, you know?" Another noisy sip, followed by a quiet burp.

"I get it," Lehigh said. "Look, I'm not here to grill you or put you on any witness stand. But," he said before Phil could beg off, "you and I both know, the same good old boys who've always run things for their own benefit around here don't like it when folks like me come in and rock the boat. But the best hope we have of changing things is—"

"They're out to get you, Lehigh!" Phil gripped his can so tight he bent it into an hourglass shape. "They're talking about a setup of some kind, getting some stripper girl to pretend you hired her for sex and then beat her up. Ruin your reputation, get everyone hating on you so they can—well, I don't know what-all they're after, other than getting you out of their way. I figured you'd know."

Lehigh sat back, stunned by the barrage of words from the normally quiet man. He scratched at the stubble on his chin, grimacing. "Ray Ferguson said that?"

Phil shrugged, drained the last of his beer. "I'm not remembering which one said what, but they both were in agreement. Pretty excited about it, too. Get rid of you, and your father-in-law, and Ev Downey's strip clubs all at once. I understand the last thing, and I don't care one way or the other about old George McBride, but why would they lump you in with those two? It don't make sense. Another beer?" He stood and reached for Lehigh's can.

Lehigh swirled the contents of his beverage. "No thanks. You go ahead." He followed Phil into his kitchen and leaned against the doorway connecting the two rooms. "Tell me, Phil. How confident are you of what you heard?"

Phil popped the top of a new can and took a long slurp before wiping his mouth and answering. "Pretty certain. Like I said, not word for word, but that's the gist of it."

"Did they mention a time frame for pulling this little stunt?"

Phil shook his head. "Not in my earshot. Soon, though. Long before the election."

Lehigh nodded. "No doubt about that. You're sure they weren't aware that you heard?"

Phil shrugged. "Pretty sure. They seemed pretty oblivious to my presence there. But I'd feel better if you didn't talk to anyone else about it."

Lehigh clapped him on the shoulder. "I owe you that much. But what about Dot? She knows."

Phil took a long swallow of beer and wiped his mouth. "Dot's not a problem. She loves being the only one to know something—especially something as juicy as this." He grinned. "Besides, I'm a regular who tips way better than they do."

Driving back toward town, Lehigh became less and less convinced that Dot would keep her secret for long. He'd have to do something to thwart their plans before the secret got out.

Chapter Twenty-Seven

Lehigh set the forensics report on his desk and rubbed his eyes. Stupid, stupid. How had he not seen this detail before?

The lab's report detailing whose fingerprints touched the independent ballistics analysis had listed four sets of fingerprints. They found three—his, Wadsworth's, and the author's—on the report's glossy cover. The fourth—Martin Lightfoot's—had come from the metal clasp on the envelope. None from the cover or pages of the report itself.

Just like Martin had claimed. Or, at least, consistent with his contention that he'd only held the envelope for a moment.

"Julia," he said into his intercom, "please send in Martin Lightfoot."

Martin slumped into his guest chair moments later, breathing hard. Lehigh wondered if he'd run down the hallway. "Martin, I owe you an apology," Lehigh said.

Lightfoot straightened in his chair. "You mean you believe me?" he said. "You're not firing me?"

"Should I?" Lehigh asked, suddenly unsure.

"No!" Martin's eyes grew wide. "I swear, I never went into those files! You gotta believe me!"

"Then why the crack about getting fired?" Lehigh asked.

Martin shook his head and gazed at the floor. "That's how it always is around here for people like me," he said. "Guilty until proven innocent. I swear, I never went into those files. But people always want to believe the worst about me."

Lehigh's mouth grew dry, and a lump formed right where it hurt the most. He'd done exactly what Martin described, he had to admit. "Martin, I believe you're innocent—a victim of circumstance. I admit, I jumped to conclusions. I'm sorry. It won't happen again."

"So I can go back to patrol?" Martin's eyes brightened. "Please?"

Lehigh cleared his throat. Damn lump wouldn't go away. "I have something I'd like you to help me with first."

Martin sank back in his chair. "I hope it ain't more office work. Staffing the archives is bad enough. Reception is just killing me. Sheriff, I got to tell you, I don't know how you can stand being in here all day."

Lehigh smiled. "I want you to help me find whoever is doing what I blamed you for. Who snuck into the files and leaked them? And how are they doing it?"

The deputy shook his head, mouth agape. "How can I help, Sheriff? I don't know anything."

"Unfortunately, it means no patrol just yet," Lehigh said. "But perhaps it's something better. How would you like to go undercover for me?"

"Undercover? How? What do you mean?"

Lehigh leaned forward, gesturing for Lightfoot to do the same. "I want to make it look like you're still under suspicion," he said in a quiet voice. "The cover story will be, you're suspended, pending investigation. That'll make the real mole get a little bolder, I'm thinking, and hopefully make a mistake."

"But I won't really be suspended, right?" Martin asked. "I don't want this to sound bad, Sheriff, but I got a wife, two kids—"

"Don't you worry about that," Lehigh said. "I'll make sure you don't miss a paycheck. In fact," and he smiled a little, "undercover pays better."

Martin stood and shook Lehigh's hand. "Sheriff," he said, "if you need a spy, I'm your man!"

"Perfect," Lehigh said. "Now, listen carefully to what I want you to do."

***

Executing his plan to trap the mole required more information and careful planning, so Lehigh spent a couple of late nights reviewing case files in his office. Interview transcripts, official reports, and forensics analyses filled his dreams as well as his waking hours in his search for the right tidbit to set as bait. But nothing jumped out at him.

Until he re-read the coroner's report.

The summary page noted the time of death as somewhere between eleven p.m. and one a.m. on July 25. But that didn't seem right. He pulled out his own notes from his visit to the crime scene the following morning. He'd written down "8-10 pm TOD, Doskey/Wads." His shorthand for: Wadsworth had told him that Coroner Doskey estimated a time of death being between eight and ten p.m.

Well, that had been a preliminary estimate. Maybe he changed his mind after a more thorough investigation. He read further into the report. Yes, that seems to have been the case. All of the references to time of death repeated the same revised estimate. A little after 10:30, he closed the file.

Then he reopened it. Something didn't add up.

The math.

The report was dated "July 26, 2 PM." Doskey had, according to his notes, finished his examination of the body by noon. Just over twelve hours after the estimated time of death. But his narrative stated that the condition of the body suggested a more advanced state of lividity and necrosis than that, even taking the summer heat and humidity into account. Fourteen to sixteen hours, he'd noted.

Between eight and ten p.m.

He double-checked the summary page and all of the other references to time, trying to resolve the inconsistency. And then he spotted something else.

All of the references to the time of death were listed in numeric format, exact to the minute, followed by lower-case "a.m." For example, "12:04 a.m." All other times in the report, such as when the coroner first received the alert of the potential homicide and the time he'd completed the report, were written out and rounded to the nearest hour, followed by capital "AM" or "PM." For example, he'd arrived at the scene at "eight AM." Body removed by "ten AM."

As if one person had written the times in some cases—the time that Ev Downey had been murdered—and someone else had written all other references to the time.

He picked up the phone and dialed the emergency number listed on page one of the report—Herman Doskey's personal cell number. A groggy voice answered after the second ring. "Doskey here."

"Sorry to call you so late, Doc." Lehigh winced. His computer's clock read 10:51 p.m. "I lost track of time."

"Carter, this had better be an emergency," he said. "Any other reason for waking my wife at eleven at night is liable to get you impeached."

Eleven. Not 10:51.

"Again, I apologize. I just had a question about your report on Ev Downey. The time of death—"

"Your time of death is going to be in ten minutes if that's the only reason you called," Doskey said in a hoarse whisper. "Couldn't this wait until morning?"

"It probably should have," Lehigh said. "But not if it means we put the wrong man in jail for murder."

Several seconds passed. Lehigh heard deep breaths on the other end of the line. Finally, Doskey said, "Talking on the phone is not a good idea."

"Let's meet, then," Lehigh said. "When and where?"

"Somewhere private," Doskey said. "Not in town."

Lehigh recalled the restaurant that his assistant, Julia, had enjoyed for her recent anniversary. "Wilkinson's, in Wyee Falls," he said. "Six-thirty tomorrow morning okay?"

"Make it seven," Doskey replied with an exasperated sigh. "It's a long drive. And Carter? Turn your damned phone off. It's late."

The line went dead.

***

Wilkinson's Riverside Restaurant overlooked the town's namesake Wyee Falls, one of the many gorgeous waterfalls scattered along the rocky eastern slopes of the Oregon Cascades. Modern in amenities but rustic in look and feel, its hot springs spa pampered the whims of guests and locals alike, which crowded the undersized parking lot. Lehigh parked behind the building and had to wander around to the front entrance, a hike that caused him to arrive in the lobby five minutes late. He found a white-haired, bespectacled man seated at a window table, sipping orange juice and reading a newspaper.

"Sorry I'm late, Dr. Doskey," he said, extending a handshake. "I had to—"

"I saw where you parked." Herman Doskey sniffed and set down his newspaper to accept the proffered handshake. "Smart idea. Keeps your truck out of sight."

"Uh, yeah, sure." Lehigh sat in the seat opposite the coroner and thanked their waiter for an immediate pour of coffee. After they ordered, Lehigh pushed his mug aside and leaned in, lowering his voice. "So, Doc. I have some questions about your report."

"My report, or the county's?" Doskey glanced from side to side and ducked his head. "In twenty-five years of service to the public, I've never seen anything like it. I've never had a single word of my reports changed or challenged—hell, usually not even proof-read for typos. Now, all of a sudden, every syllable gets examined under a microscope."

Lehigh raised his eyebrows. "Who's reviewing your reports?"

Doskey pushed his horn-rimmed glasses up to the bridge of his nose and scoffed. "Not my *reports*. Just *this* report. As for who…" He paused, then leaned back. "I've been ordered not to say."

"Ordered?" Lehigh scratched at his chin and lifted his mug of coffee. "You're an elected official, just like me. Who's got authority to give you orders?"

Doskey patted the air downward with open palms. "Keep

your damned voice down!" He beckoned for Lehigh to lean closer. "Never mind who has authority. It's about who can make my life miserable. I've got a wife and family, and I'm just a few years away from retirement. The last thing I need is to start a war with law enforcement."

Lehigh's heart raced, and he set his coffee mug down hard, spilling about a sip's worth onto the white tablecloth. "Doc, *I'm* law enforcement, and I didn't—"

"Forget I said that," Doskey said, waving his hands in front of his face. "I didn't mean that. I misspoke. Okay?" He fixed Lehigh with an earnest stare, his eyes blinking at a rapid rate.

Lehigh knew fear when he saw it. "Doc, who's threatening you?" he asked. "Who's telling you to change reports and—"

"*I didn't say that!*" Doskey spoke in a strained, hushed voice. "What I said was, people are *reviewing* my work. 'Quality assurance,' they call it. My version is considered a 'first draft.' That's all I'm saying."

Lehigh nodded and drew in a deep breath. The waiter arrived with their breakfast, and the conversation paused while he ensured that everything was to their liking. Once he departed, they dug in, eating in silence for a minute or two. After washing down a few bites of delicious huckleberry pancakes with a final swig of coffee, Lehigh cleared his throat.

"I understand," he said, "that you don't want to name names, for fear of retributions. But if you could just give me a hint of who's modifying your reports—"

"Nobody *said* anyone was modifying my reports," Doskey said around a bite of sausage. He kept his eyes glued to his plate and ate with methodical efficiency. A forkful of eggs, a bite of sausage, a nibble on the buttered English muffin, a sip of juice. Rinse, lather, repeat.

"Excuse me, Doc, but somebody *is* saying it," Lehigh said. "Me. And you've basically confirmed it. The only thing I don't know is who's doing it. And you do know. Right?"

Doskey stopped chewing, stared at him for a few moments, then resumed eating. "This meeting was a bad idea," he said. "I should never have come here."

"I'll take that as a yes," Lehigh said. "Someone in law enforcement. Which is my department. So—"

"You're not the only law enforcement agency around here," Doskey said.

Lehigh pushed some food around on his plate, lost in thought. "Doc," he said. "What time was Everett Downey murdered?"

"You read the report."

"I did. And I noticed some inconsistencies."

"Well, aren't you smart." Doskey shoved his plate aside, still half-full of food.

"I did the math. The time of death should have been before midnight, like you initially estimated, not after."

"Then somebody's math is wrong."

Lehigh paused and chewed another huge bite of pancake. "Mine, or yours?"

"Not mine," Doskey said.

"Whose, then?"

Doskey glared at him. "Next question."

Lehigh sighed. "I see. So, to recap. *Someone* involved in the investigation ordered you—"

A cell phone rang. Doskey pulled one out of his pocket. "Duty calls," Doskey said. "I have to go. But listen, Carter. You need to follow your instincts on this one. That's all I'm able to say right now. Thanks for breakfast." He tossed his napkin onto his plate and rushed out of the restaurant.

Lehigh sat still at the table, staring at his food long after it had gone cold. As cold as Doskey's feet, all of a sudden.

Follow your instincts, Doskey had said. Lehigh's instincts told him that somebody had either changed Doskey's report, or forced him to, and threatened him harm if he revealed their identity. Someone in law enforcement, who could make good on that threat, at least enough to frighten him. Someone who knew the actual time of death, but needed it changed to protect their own alibi—or undermine George's.

He clicked open a pen and jotted down some names on a

napkin: Buck Summers. Ray Ferguson. Clayton Maddox. Jim Wadsworth. Judge Petros Geroux, if he stretched the definition of "law enforcement."

Stretching the definition further, he added another name: Elliott Jackson. As county chair, he oversaw all executive functions of county government. Which led him to add another name: Teresa McBride, his well-connected secretary. Which led him to add one more: Bobby Wills. Wills had access to the files, and while he had no authority of his own, through Teresa he could influence actions of those who did wield power.

That thought led him to add one more name. Someone who could wield power, even without holding a government position. The power of the press. Bruce Bailey.

He looked over the list and scratched out a few names. Jim Wadsworth, out of pure gut feeling. Buck Summers, who had been in jail at the time. He hesitated over Ray Ferguson's name, then left it alone. He couldn't *prove* Ferguson did it, or not.

That left a handful of names. Still too many. He needed to narrow down that list, and fast.

Follow your instincts.

***

Lehigh arrived back in Clarkesville a few minutes before nine with a headache pounding at both temples. He blamed coffee deprivation, as he'd downed only one cup over his strange breakfast with the coroner. He'd been so preoccupied with what Doskey had revealed—and refused to reveal—that he'd forgotten to ask for the bottomless refills to which he'd been entitled. Considering how much breakfast at the posh resort had cost him, he should have emptied the pot and taken some to go.

He weighed his options and decided, against the wishes of his taste buds, to head to Dot's—a purely financial decision. Dot charged less than anyone else in town, and often comped law enforcement types. Considering how weak she made the coffee, she should have paid people to drink it.

Entering the greasy little diner, he spotted Ben Wright sitting alone in the corner, finishing a plate of corned beef hash. Ben raised a half-eaten slice of buttered white toast and waved him over. Lehigh took the seat across from him and thanked the ever-efficient Dot for immediately serving him up a cup of coffee. She cleared away Ben's dishes, then waddled back to the kitchen, humming an old George Strait tune.

"I want to thank you, Sheriff," Ben said, "for taking care of…what we talked about. Martin's a good man. You won't be sorry that you trusted him."

"No, I should be thanking you," Lehigh said. "You set me straight and kept me from making a big mistake. I appreciate that."

"There's more where that came from," Ben said with a grin.

"How's that?" Lehigh sipped his coffee. A tingling sensation trickled down his spine.

Ben shrugged. "You're making another big mistake. 'Course, I suspect you know that already."

Lehigh frowned. "I'm not sure what you mean."

Ben laughed. "Come on, now. You put your own father-in-law in jail, and you don't know what kind of mistake that is?" He laughed again, drawing stares from patrons at nearby tables.

"My wife has let me know what a mistake she thinks it is," Lehigh said. "And I've had my own doubts lately. But I had to arrest him, based on the evidence we had."

"You say so." Ben drained his coffee and signaled Dot for a refill. She showed him an empty pot, and he scowled.

"Of course, if you know something different…" Lehigh's voice trailed off, inviting Ben to finish his sentence.

Ben leaned back in his chair. "What I'm going to tell you isn't going to please your wife, or her mother," Ben said, a smile still teasing at his lips. "Are you sure you want to know?"

Lehigh sighed, working on being patient. Everybody was being so coy these days. "If it bears on the evidence of the case and the guilt or innocence of the accused, of course I want to know," he said. "Come on, man. What is it?"

Ben cocked his head, as if weighing his decision. "What time was the murder?" he asked. "Was it before midnight, or after?"

"Officially, between midnight and two in the morning," Lehigh said. "But let's just say, there may be reason for me to re-open that question. Why?"

"And old George says he was home alone all night, right?" Ben said, his smile widening. "His wife was out for the evening with friends, and he had no alibi until his wife got home around one-thirty?"

Lehigh nodded. "You know something different?"

Ben leaned forward, his hands knotted together on the table. "Sheriff, I know where George McBride was that night. *Exactly* where, from nine o'clock until almost one in the morning."

"My God, man, tell me. Where?"

"He was in the same place I was, Mr. Carter. A place he won't care to admit ever being, but I assure you, he was."

Lehigh took a deep breath. Ben was having way too much fun with this, but if that was the price to pay for the truth, let him. "Let me guess," Lehigh said. "A place where his wife wouldn't approve of him being? Say, for example, a strip club?"

"Downey's own," Ben said, nodding. "In fact, he was there *before* me. I got there at nine, and he already had a drink in front of him. Sitting with Old Ev Downey, right there in the club, in a booth in back. They were having themselves a good old time."

"George McBride? At Downey's? Seriously?" Lehigh shook his head. "Doesn't seem like him."

"Nope," Ben said. "I go there two, three times a month, have for years. Never seen him there before, not once."

"Anyone else in the club at the time?" Lehigh asked. "I mean, at that time of night, shouldn't a whole lot of people have seen them there? No one else has come forward."

Ben shrugged. "A lot of guys don't want to admit they frequent such places, and the girls, well, they've been flat-out told to never talk to *anyone*, much less cops, about who the customers are," he said. "You go in there waving a badge around, well, suddenly they can't remember who was there or who was working that night, you know what I mean?"

Lehigh nodded. "Squares with what I've seen. So, you saw George in there all night?"

Ben shook his head. "About an hour after I got there, the two old boys went back to the uh, private rooms," Ben said. "You know what I mean?"

Lehigh shuddered, recalling what Stacy described from her own time working as a waitress in the club. Had George ever ventured into Downey's club during one of her shifts, neither would have lived down the embarrassment. "How long was, er, he, uh…"

"Downey came out and sat back at his table right away," Ben said. "George was back there at least an hour. He came back out, had another drink or two, then he and Downey shook hands, as if they'd just made some sort of deal, you know? Then a waitress brought them champagne. Man, were they in a good mood."

"And then George left? Alone?"

"That's the funny thing," Ben said. "After about a half hour, and long before George left, Downey disappeared into the back rooms again. I was just coming back from the men's room and he flew past me in the hallway. I look down past him, and I see Buttercup, one of his dancers, running out the back door. Old Everett, he ran right out after her. I figured, she must be quitting or getting fired or something. Too bad, 'cause I always liked her. But some ten minutes later, she comes back, and ends up doing another set. But Downey, he never came back in. It didn't strike me at the time, but now it does. Anyway, George stayed behind to enjoy the show and that bottle of champagne. He was there a good hour or more by himself. Eventually, I guess he got tired of waiting for Downey, and he left. A little before one a.m., like I said."

Lehigh sipped his coffee, now stone cold. If the coroner's report had been changed, and the murder had taken place before midnight, then Ben's eyewitness account could vindicate George after all.

If, if, if.

But then again, if George didn't kill Ev Downey, who did?

Chapter Twenty-Eight

Lehigh rolled his truck along the long narrow drive leading up to Stacy's split-level ranch, hesitating a moment before taking the parking spot that had once been his. He peered through the wide picture window into the living room, but the dark room revealed no hints as to whether his wife was at home. He hadn't called first. Maybe a mistake.

He swung his suddenly heavy legs out of the truck and gave Lucky and Diamond a treat, then laughed as they bounded by him into the yard, one they'd run in hundreds of times over the past year. They picked up right where they left off, finding squeaky rubber toys at the base of a few trees at the side of the yard and diving into a game of chase. Their noisy barking reached ear-shattering levels in moments, and seconds later, the front door opened.

"Lucky! Diamond!" Stacy called out. The dogs ceased their insane but simple game and dashed over to her, sitting at her feet, tongues out. She grinned and mussed the fur on Lucky's head, then Diamond's, and tossed the squeaky toys they'd delivered back out into the yard.

"I hope it was okay to bring them," Lehigh said, fingers hooked through the loops of his belt a few steps away from her.

"It's fine," she said in a low, even voice. She smiled. It looked a little forced. "It's, uh, nice to see you."

"You too." He wondered if her heart ached as much as his at that moment. "I have a favor to ask of you." He squinted into the sun toward the dogs so he wouldn't have to see her response.

"Huh." She opened the front door. "Well, I'm fixing dinner.

You hungry?"

"Always. But I didn't come here to—"

"I know. A favor. But just like you, I listen better on a full stomach. Come on, there's plenty. Roast chicken and mashed potatoes. Your favorite." She held the door open for him. After a moment's hesitation, he slipped inside the house.

She set two plates on the table and pulled the cork out of a half-empty bottle of white wine. "Are you on duty?"

He shrugged. "I'd love a glass of wine, thanks." He sat and she served them both a healthy portion. Chicken breasts, potatoes, gravy, and steamed green beans filled their plates. "These are from the garden you planted," she said, indicating the green beans.

"Delicious," he said around his first bite. "I really appreciate the meal. You didn't have to."

"I know that," she said. "Just like I don't have to do you any favors. Speaking of which…or would you rather finish your dinner, just in case?"

He took a bite of the chicken, savoring the seasoning she'd sprinkled onto the skin before roasting. A little salt, some green spices, maybe some red pepper. Perfect. As was the chardonnay. He set down his fork. "It's about your dad's case," he said.

"I figured." She sipped her wine, kept the glass in her hand. "I mean, what else do we have to talk about these days?" She shook her head and looked away. "I'm sorry. I promised myself I wouldn't do that any more, and there I go again."

"It's all right." He set down his wine glass and reached out a hand to her. She stared at it a long moment, then set a tentative hand in his. He held it and waited for her eyes to meet his again. "I've discovered some things that could help exonerate your father," he said, "but it's not the type of thing you'd want spread all over town."

"I can't imagine it's any worse than being accused of murder." Her voice sounded strained. "Have you discussed it with him or his lawyer?"

"Constantine Richards refused to allow me to speak to him,"

Lehigh said. "As for the D.A.—well, let's just say I have reasons not to inform them of this just yet." His heart rate quickened. If Ray Ferguson knew he had tried to speak to George, or that he'd shared this with his wife... "Let's keep this confidential, between us for now, if we can. Okay?"

She nodded, her eyes gleaming. "So how can I help?"

"You have some history that could help your father out here," Lehigh said, drawing out his words. "I thought maybe you could use your connections to verify what I've learned. The folks there clam up when they see a badge and a uniform pull up."

"Who? Where?" Stacy clenched her napkin. "I don't understand."

Lehigh stared at the meal going cold on his plate. He'd rehearsed this conversation a billion times, and like every other time he did that, it never went according to the script. "I have reason to believe that the time of Everett Downey's death happened earlier in the evening than what's been reported in the news," he said.

Stacy shrugged. "How does that help my father?"

Lehigh took another deep breath and let it out slowly. "A witness says he saw your father at the time of the murder...in a club."

"A *club*?" Stacy's face lost all color, and she slid her chair back from the table. "Lehigh. What *club*?"

Lehigh looked away from her. "Ev Downey's place— Montgomery's Lounge. Where you used to—"

"My father would *never*!" Stacy stood and glared at him. "Who was this? Who said they saw him there?"

"I'm not yet at liberty to—"

"They're lying!" Stacy shook a finger at Lehigh, then pulled it back to her side. "I'm sorry. I know it's not you saying this. But my father never went to those strip clubs. He spent his career trying to get them closed. He still refuses to believe I ever waited tables there!"

Lehigh shrugged again and shook his head. "It surprised me, too. But it meshes with other things we've learned—his business deals with Downey, for example."

"That's it!" She brightened and tapped her palm on the table. "He was there for business. Cutting a deal. Doesn't that make more sense?"

Lehigh gave a slow nod, then shook his head. "That actually might look worse for him. Cutting secret business deals with a shady character like Downey just before he was killed gives him motive. Especially since he spent most of his political career claiming he wanted to shut those clubs down."

She folded her arms across her chest. "Maybe it's best we just leave this story alone."

Lehigh stood and stepped toward her, but stopped when she backed away. Dammit! She remained so angry at him, or at least, so wary of his intentions. "You understand," he said, "if he was there—*if*—and if this witness's story can be corroborated, it could provide your dad an alibi."

"And ruin his reputation."

Lehigh grimaced and let out another long breath. "Forgive me saying so, but I think it may be a tad bit late for that."

Stacy opened her mouth as if to object, then closed it, nodding. "Yes. I suppose that's true." She smiled, even, then the smile soured. "It would kill my mother."

"Again…"

"No," she said, "even worse. My mom could probably live with the thought of Dad being a murderer. But the idea of him hanging out at a strip club…wait. Why are you making that face?"

Lehigh wished he could kick himself for his lack of poker face. If his expression showed even a tenth of the dread he felt about telling her what Ben had revealed to him, he'd never be able to keep it from her. "I just agree, I guess. It's pretty bad."

She stepped closer to him, peering into his eyes. "I know you, Lehigh. You're holding back on something. Something even worse than him being a pervy old man. What is it?"

Lehigh spread his hands, tried to speak. No words came.

"Come on, Lee. Tell me!"

He stepped back, repelled by the force of her words. There

was no hiding it now. If she did help him, she'd find out anyway. "He may have…visited the private rooms in back."

"Impossible! My dad is not a cheat! Even with—even with—" Tears flowed down her cheeks, and she buried her face in her hands. "Oh, my God, Lehigh. Are you sure that's what they saw?"

Lehigh pressed his lips together and gave a slow nod.

"Were there witnesses? More than one?"

He churned one hand in the other, wishing his nerves would settle down. "That's where I need your help. If you could use your connections, trade upon your own history there, maybe people would talk to you who wouldn't talk to me or the D.A. Woman to woman, you know?"

"I don't know, Lehigh. It's been so long—over fifteen years. Nobody I knew then still works there." She meandered into the living room, her mind off somewhere in the clouds.

After a minute of waiting, he joined her on the sofa. "I'm not saying this is one hundred percent true, or even a little bit true," he said. "And if not, we're no worse off than before. But if it is true, and we can get at least one other person to testify that they saw him there at the time of the murder, it proves your Dad's innocence, and he goes free. Don't you think that's worth finding out?"

She stared out the picture window, tears flowing like waterfalls down her face. "I tried, all of my life, to keep my history there from my father," she said. "I probably failed, but if so, he always kept up the pretense. If I do this, all of that comes out publicly." She looked back at Lehigh. "All of it."

Lehigh reached out his hand and waited several seconds. Still in tears, she unfolded her arms and rested her palm in his. He closed his hand on hers with the lightest possible pressure. "I understand," he said. "It's not just your dad's reputation that would go down. I know this is a lot to ask. But, Stacy. I don't ask this for me. It's for your father. No matter what happens, I'll stand by you, and support you, and do whatever I can to protect you." He squeezed her hand.

She squeezed back, nodding. "I know. Thank you."

He waited a long minute while she thought, their eyes locked in the dimming daylight of the room. She reached for a tissue with her free hand, wiped away her tears, blew her nose. Fresh tears replaced the ones she'd brushed away, and she dabbed at her cheek with a fresh tissue.

She turned to him, a look of determination and grit in her eyes, her dark hair framed by the fading daylight from the picture window. She held his stare another long moment.

He waited.

Finally, she spoke. "It wasn't easy for you to come here, was it?"

He shook his head. "I knew how hard it'd be for you. And if you can't do it, I understand. I'll just have to figure out a different way, that's all."

"You would?" She cocked her head, examining his face. "You'd help out my father, in spite of everything that's happened—with him, between us—all of it?"

Lehigh surrendered a tiny smile and pulled her hand closer. "Of course. Not because he's your father, *per se*. I'd do the same for any man I believed to be innocent." He chuckled. "Not what you wanted to hear, I know, but—"

"You believe he's innocent?" Hope tinged her voice. "Really?"

He nodded. But it was a slow nod, and she picked up on it.

"There's more, isn't there?" she said.

Lehigh drew another deep breath. Telling her the rest could undo the good will she'd extended thus far in the conversation. But not telling her seemed dishonest, and she'd find out sooner or later. "The people that hate me in this town—"

"People don't hate you!"

He chuckled. "We both know that there's at least a few who do. And we both know who they are. Anyway, they apparently are recruiting someone at the club, one of the dancers, to set me up. If you could find out who—"

"We could stop it before it happens! What kind of setup?" She moved closer, growing more excited.

"She's supposed to take a punch or two and blame it on me, I guess."

"Those scumbags would beat up a woman?" Stacy's voice reached shrieking levels. "I'll tear their eyes out!"

"And I'd hold them down for you," he said. "But first, we have to prove it."

She took his hand in both of hers and squeezed. "Lehigh," she said with a smile, "you got yourself a deal. Let's do this!"

Chapter Twenty-Nine

They gave the dogs each a bone to chew in the back yard, and then Stacy drove them both to the McBride mansion. Lehigh reasoned that they'd be less suspicious if they saw her Volvo rolling up the long drive rather than Lehigh's unwelcome pickup or a sheriff's department Crown Victoria. Not that he wanted to catch George unawares. He just didn't want to be chased off the property at gunpoint.

They nodded to the armed marshals standing guard at the perimeter of the property, a condition of McBride's house arrest since his ill-fated attempt to leave the state. He also had to wear a tracker bracelet and report his whereabouts and every movement to the court every 24 hours. While a far cry from barbed wire and black bars, Lehigh had no doubt that George felt as imprisoned as Buck Summers and his co-conspirators in county lockup.

Consuela, the diminutive housekeeper, greeted them at the door with a wide grin, hugging both of them and babbling in Spanish too fast for Lehigh to translate with his high-school language skills. She broke into English after giving Lehigh a good-natured shake of the shoulders. "How skinny you are! You stay for dinner, okay?" Their half-true protests of having already eaten fell on deaf ears, and she ushered them into George's study with promises of wine for Stacy and McBride's best scotch for Lehigh.

Lehigh leaned close to Stacy and whispered, "Does she know that we, uh…?"

"The whole town knows, Lehigh," she said without moving

her lips. "We're all just very good at pretending otherwise."

Stacy's silver-haired mother, Catherine McBride, appeared in the doorway in a blue floor-length Polynesian-style dress, as if attending a formal ballroom event. "Darlings," she said. "Why didn't you call ahead? We're having dinner with Constantine Richards and his wife tonight. You'll understand if we can't include you." She pecked Stacy on the cheek, then, glaring at Lehigh, extended her hand. He took it and gave it a light squeeze, keeping his eyes on her face for any sign of emotion. She gave none.

"We won't be long," Stacy said. "Lehigh has something he'd like to ask Dad."

"Sheriff Carter knows Mr. Richards' office phone number, I presume," Catherine said with a sniff. "Drinks?"

"Consuela's on it," Lehigh said. "Yes'm, I know how to reach Mr. Richards. He also knows how to put me off, no matter how much I'm trying to help his client."

"Help? Hah!" Catherine turned her back on them and headed to the hallway. Consuela's entry with a tray full of drinks interrupted her departure. Lehigh noted that her tray included a champagne flute that slipped right into Catherine's hands. So much for her dramatic exit.

"He's right, Mother," Stacy said. "He has a lead that could help Dad's case. But Mr. Richards won't even take his calls." She glanced at Lehigh as if for confirmation, and he gave a quick nod. "If we could speak privately with him—"

"Consuela, please ask the senator to join us," Catherine said, as if asking for a glass of tea. Consuela handed Stacy and Lehigh their drinks, curtsied, and left without a word.

"I think it might be best if you weren't here," Stacy said, her eyes fixed on the coffee table in front of her.

"Pfft." Catherine took the seat at the far end of the coffee table and crossed her legs. The chair's seat reached a few inches higher than the sofa's, which, if not for her tiny frame, would have enabled her to gaze down at them with the full force of her contempt. "George and I have no secrets."

"You may have one or two," Stacy said, still not making eye

contact. Lehigh smirked behind his glass of Scotch, half-pretending to savor the light peat aroma an extra moment before taking a sip.

"We'd better not." Catherine took a healthy sip of her champagne and smacked her lips. "I should have asked her to bring the bottle."

"I second that," Stacy said, sipping her chardonnay.

"Is that my daughter's voice I hear?" George McBride's booming voice echoed from the hallway. His voluminous shock of white hair appeared in the doorway a few seconds later, capping a smile that faded into a scowl. "What the hell are you doing here?" he said, pointing a pudgy finger at Lehigh.

"I brought him," Stacy said before Lehigh could speak. "He has something important to say to you, Dad. I think you should hear it."

"It had better be an apology," George said with a scowl. Lehigh started to stand, but George stopped him with a face-out palm. "Oh, don't get up, Carter, unless you're planning to kneel and beg forgiveness."

Lehigh paused in his rise, then stood to full height. "I prefer to stand," he said. "I don't like being looked down on." In his boots, Lehigh had a good four or more inches on McBride, and he took no small pleasure in the irony of his statement. "But if it makes you feel better, yes, I am sorry I had to be the one to arrest you, sir. It was one of the worst days of my life."

"I'll tell you one that'll be even worse," McBride said, pushing his way around the furniture to stand nose-to-nose with Lehigh. "The day I'm proven innocent. Because on that day, I promise, I will run you right out of this town. Maybe out of the whole damn state! Now get the hell out of my house!" McBride waved his arm toward the door, spilling his drink all over Stacy.

"Dad! Please! Would you at least hear what he has to say? I swear, it just might help you!" Stacy pulled George away from Lehigh, then dabbed at her dress with a napkin.

"What would help me is if he resigned," George said with a growl. Then he brightened. "Wait, is that what you're here to announce? Then this *would* be a happy day!"

Lehigh drew in a slow breath. "What I have," he said, "is a witness who says he saw you at the time of the murder."

"Interesting, but impossible," George said. "The murder was at, what, two in the morning? I was home, in bed, and my wife has already attested to that. Not that anyone will listen." He finished off his Scotch and set the empty glass on the table.

"I have reason to believe the murder took place earlier than previously thought," Lehigh said. "Before midnight." He sipped his drink, letting the words sink in.

George stared at him, his expression still filled with contempt at first, but then he paled. His face drooped, his eyes widened, and his mouth fell open. "Catherine," he said, "perhaps you could find Consuela and ask her to refresh my drink?"

"You've had plenty enough to drink before dinner," Catherine said. "And I wouldn't miss this for all the chocolate in Belgium. Who is this witness? And where did he say my husband was? George, weren't you here, at home? Isn't that what you said?"

George stared open-mouthed at her. He glanced at Lehigh, then Stacy. His lips quivered, and his body crumpled into a nearby easy chair. "Perhaps I ventured out for a short while," he said. "You say someone saw me?"

"And he's willing to testify," Lehigh said. "But he's only one witness. His account would carry more weight if he was corroborating your own story. Right now, they don't line up."

"Where in thunder were you, George?" Catherine said, sitting up straight in her seat. "And why in heaven's name are you taking this so badly? Don't you see what good news this is?"

George reached for his glass, found it empty, and dropped his arm back to his side, lips still quivering.

"Dad?" Stacy leaned forward, resting a hand on his arm. "Is it true?"

"Is *what* true?" Catherine asked, her voice a sharp bark. "What the hell's the matter with you, George? Why don't you answer us?"

George gazed up at Lehigh, his eyes pleading. "Is this witness of yours a reliable one?" he asked. "Will his testimony stand up in court, or is he, you know, one of the deplorable types that…" His mouth continued to move, but no words emerged.

"So it is true," Stacy said.

"Damn it, will somebody please tell me what is so damned true and important before I scream?" Catherine shouted. "George. Answer me. *Where were you that night?*"

George glanced at her, then let his gaze fall to the floor. He maintained a still stare for 30 or 40 seconds, and finally spoke. "I went to meet with Ev Downey," he said, his eyes flickering toward his wife for a moment. "We were negotiating a land deal for that new supermarket that was supposed to go in. But there were things about that deal I didn't like. Some of the investors seemed a little shady to me."

"Shadier than Ev Downey?" Stacy asked with a little too much sarcasm. George didn't seem to notice.

"I wanted out of the deal," he said. "I offered him an attractive buy-out option. He drove a hard bargain, and in the end, he agreed."

"He agreed?" Lehigh said. "Did you draw up papers?"

"He said he'd have his people take care of that the next day," George said. "Turns out, there was no next day."

"That's great news!" Catherine said. "Not that you partnered with such a low-life, but that people saw you meeting with him. I must say, though, I don't understand why this is so hard for you to admit."

George faced her, but lowered his eyes. "We met at Downey's place. The club. You know, with the, uh, dancers." He glanced at Stacy, then averted his eyes.

Catherine made a face like she'd just bitten a lemon. "Well, that's unfortunate. But at least it was only a business meeting." She smiled at her husband, who still refused to look at her. She waited. Still nothing.

"George," she said, "it *was* just a business deal, right?"

McBride continued to stare at the floor. Catherine's face fell. "Oh, George," she said. "George, you didn't…oh, hell. You did, didn't you?"

The room went still for several seconds. Lehigh stood. "I think this might be a good time for us to leave you to your private conversation," he said. "Thank you for your time. Stacy, shall we...?"

Once outside, Stacy shivered in spite of the intense August heat. "I wouldn't want to be in his shoes right now," she said. "So, what's next?"

Lehigh smiled at her. "Next, I take you up on your offer of becoming my newest deputy investigator."

Chapter Thirty

Stacy applied the last touch of eyeliner to her already overly-made-up face and compared her image in the mirror to an old photograph she'd kept from her waitressing days. She'd caked on a thick coat of foundation with a generous smudge of blush, waxed her eyebrows, inserted hazel contact lenses, and applied enough purple eyeshadow to make Catwoman jealous. Visible through her white button-down blouse, her lacy push-up bra gave her much-needed cleavage, and the matching G-string, while unlikely to ever see the light of day, made her feel as trashy as she looked. A red wig waited nearby to complete her slutty persona.

She sighed. She hated this look—always had, even when it doubled her tips. Once she'd worn it to bed for Lehigh, but it had the opposite of the desired effect. He claimed to favor "good girls" over loose women, and while she felt like neither, she strove for the same persona he preferred.

But she was on a mission. And she was grateful that she still fit into the same outfits she'd worn half a lifetime ago.

She kept the wig and other accessories in an overnight bag, wearing jeans to drive in rather than the ridiculously short skirt she'd have to wear if her plan worked. She'd been arrested once in her underwear, an experience she never wanted to repeat.

She entered Montgomery's Lounge in a brisk walk, with the bag slung over her shoulder like she owned the place, and donned the wig before finding the manager, a rail-thin brunette with uneven teeth and oversized blue-framed glasses, staring at a computer in her office. The place reeked of tobacco ash, whether because of the manager's flouting of the indoor smoking ban or from decades of prior indulgence. A nameplate on the desk read "Cyndee Gagnon."

"Looking for work?" Cyndee said without looking up. "Dancer or waitress?"

"Table service," Stacy said. "No live action."

Cyndee snorted. "You're a bit old for that anyway. Experience?"

Stacy bit back a retort on the age jab. Keep the eyes on the prize. "Twenty years ago. A place a whole lot like this." She set her bag down on the guest chair but remained standing. No need to get the stench of this room on her clean clothes. "You need anyone?" She already knew the answer, though. If they didn't need help, that would have been the first thing out of Cyndee's mouth. That, or tobacco spit.

"Can you work swing? If so, you can start tonight. Assuming you ain't got a record." Cyndee squinted at her. "You look kinda familiar."

"My name's Bridget," Stacy said, keeping to her script.

"Bridget, huh? Sure, sure. And mine's Cinderella." Cyndee laughed at her own joke, a quick, cynical bark. "Got any references?"

"My cousin Amanda used to dance here." Her friend Amanda's brief tenure from twenty years before would raise no red flags that she knew of.

"Amanda musta been before my time," Cyndee said. "No matter, just fill out the paperwork and make sure it's legal. Charlie will show you the ropes. She gets ten percent of your tips, straight up. Got it?"

Stacy grabbed the employment application and stuffed it into her bag. "Thanks. You won't regret it." She dashed out before she burst out laughing. Everybody at Montgomery's gave birth to new regrets every day of the week.

She found the forty-ish Charlotte, or "Charlie" as she preferred to be called, cutting up limes in preparation for a busy night. Stacy guessed that Charlie had once been a dancer, given her slender frame, full array of piercings and half-hidden tattoos, and out-of-proportion bust not quite contained by her low-cut blouse. She gave Stacy the nickel tour and seemed relieved when Stacy volunteered that she already knew the ins and outs of the operation from a prior stint at Downey's. "You'll do good here," Charlie said, eyeing her, "especially if you show a little skin. Get signed in and we'll get you a couple of tables. It's already getting busy tonight, and we're short a couple of wait staff."

"Curious," Stacy said. "Why do you suppose that is? Did a lot of people quit recently?"

Charlie wiped a clean bar towel on the counter and shrugged. "Every day, lately. Seems people are spooked by old Ev kicking the bucket. Good for you, though, huh?"

Stacy nodded. "He used to hang out in the bar a lot, years ago. I heard he was here the night he was killed. Were you working?"

Charlie narrowed her eyes. "I work every night, honey. I got bills to pay. Yeah, the old man was here. As usual, he was entertaining some rich dude who was blowing a wad of dough. Good tipper, but then, they all are when they're drinking free booze."

"I like the sound of that," Stacy said. "Is the rich guy here tonight? I wouldn't mind getting his table."

Charlie laughed. "Not friggin' likely you'll ever see him around again. Not without the free booze."

"Was he famous or anything?" Stacy said.

The bar rag stopped moving on the counter. Charlie eyed her with suspicion. "Don't ever talk about who our customers are," she said. "Even among ourselves. We ever do that, we'd be out of business in a week."

"Sure, sure," Stacy said. "I was just hoping, you know, a guy like that...well, I kind of need the money."

"You'll make money," Charlie said. "Just keep selling drinks. Go on, get out of those clothes. You look like you belong on Wall Street."

Stacy headed into the changing room down the hall behind the stage, frustrated. She'd come so close to verifying George's alibi. She'd pressed too hard, too fast. This would take time.

A group of dancers waited their turns in the changing room, bouncing to the thump-thump of a disco beat that pounded through the walls. The show had begun. She tried to make eye contact with them, but they kept their distance. Just like when she'd waited tables years ago, the dancers and wait staff rarely mingled. She'd save them as a last resort in her investigation.

But the other waitresses working in the bar with her were no more forthcoming than Charlie. One had just started a few days before, and the other claimed not to have been working that night. A third rushed away after only the briefest of hellos, claiming to be swamped.

Then, a little over an hour into her shift, two men with familiar faces entered. The younger one, short and round-bellied, she recognized as Deputy Peters. The other, with his black crew-cut and athletic build, she'd remember forever. Sergeant Dale Dupont.

She cursed under her breath when the two out-of-uniform deputies took a table close to the stage in her section. Moments later, a third, even younger man, pudgy and dough-faced, joined them, a man she didn't know. She tried to flag another waitress to cover the table for her, but two begged off and the third could not be found. She sighed and hoped her disguise and the unusual context would prevent recognition.

"What can I get youse guys?" she asked them in her best Brooklyn accent, slapping cocktail napkins in front of each man. She stood opposite the stage side of their table, kept her face in shadow and faced away from them.

"Pitcher of light beer," Peters said. "Hey, are you new?"

"Just started tonight," she said. "I'm Bridget. You guys got IDs?"

"IDs?" DuPont leaned back in his chair and laughed. "We come here every weekend. Nobody ever asks us for IDs!"

"I'll be honest," Stacy said, her face burning hot, "it's this one here." She pointed to the dough-faced boy. "I need to make sure he's twenty-one."

"Show her your badge, Bobby," Peters said. "That'll shut her up." The other two laughed. After a moment, though, the boy pulled out his driver's license.

Stacy checked the date and the name. Bobby Wills. The name sounded familiar. "I'll be right back with your beer—hey!" She slapped DuPont's hand off of her thigh.

"Just testing the waters," DuPont said with a laugh. "Hey, you look kind of familiar. Are you sure we haven't met before?"

"I just got into town a coupla days ago." Stacy chomped an imaginary piece of gum. "You must know my cousin Amanda."

"If she looks like you, I want to know her," Peters said.

"You boys enjoy yourselves." She spun away before they could grab anything more substantial.

She delayed at the bar as long as she could, then returned with their pitcher. She poured their glasses about two-thirds full, swatting DuPont's hands off of her butt twice between pours. She wanted to keep her visit as brief as possible, but it occurred to her that they might volunteer information she needed. "You guys waiting for anyone else to show?" she asked at a safe distance from DuPont.

"Yeah, his wife." Bobby Wills pointed at DuPont and laughed.

DuPont thumped him in the chest. "We're just here for the show, and, you know, maybe a little company," he said with an oily smile on his face. "Maybe get some first-time action for our friend, here." He smacked Bobby's shoulder and sipped his beer.

"Hey, I ain't no first-timer!" Bobby said, perhaps a little too loud.

"So, what do you say? Help our friend out, maybe go on a 'date' after your shift?" DuPont asked. "Maybe make a few extra dollars in 'tips' for your trouble?" He grinned, and Stacy nearly puked.

"You're not asking me to do anything illegal, now, are you boys?" Stacy said.

"If it's so illegal, why do the politicians and the prosecutors in the D.A.'s office—*oof!*" Peters doubled over, clutching his belly and twisting away from DuPont, who rubbed what appeared to be sore, red knuckles on his right hand.

"I think you misunderstood me," DuPont said. "I apologize for any offense."

"So, what's your story?" Peters said. "How'd you end up in a place like this?"

Stacy shrugged. "It's a job, you know? I just need the money, like everyone else." She started to move away.

Peters draped his arm over a chair at the adjoining table, blocking her path. "Well, if you're looking to make a little extra, I might be able to help you out with that."

Her heart raced. "I, uh, don't do that kind of thing, okay? I just wait tables." She took a step back, but DuPont was there, and all eight of his giant hands. She wiggled back toward Peters.

"It's not *that* kind of work," Peters said. "Tell me, have you ever done any acting? It pays well, and it would do the community a great service."

Her heart pounded. "Tell me more," she said.

Peters patted his thighs, grinning like a wolf. She groaned, but set her tray down and sat in his lap, leaning close.

"You'd just need to 'pretend' to get into a fight with a guy," Peters whispered into her ear. "And be real believable. You know what I mean?" His hand slid up her leg. She batted it away.

"Who's the guy?" she asked in a husky voice close to his ear.

Peters giggled. "No names, but let's just say, I work for him—for now." He grabbed another thigh, and she dug her nails in to his wrist. He yanked it back.

She smiled at him, grateful that her disguise had worked so well. "Well, I bet I could do that for you," she said. "Here, I'll give you my number." She scribbled the number of a pet supply store on a napkin and stuffed it into his shirt pocket. "You call me in a couple of days, okay?"

"Sure, sweetie. And why don't you bring us another round when you get a chance?"

Stacy smirked and hustled off to another table. The three men drained a couple of pitchers over the next two hours and left cash on the table, including a meager tip. Only DuPont gave her a second look the rest of the evening, squinting as though trying to remember her. She did her best to stay away and hide her face from him.

After three more hours of avoiding grabby hands and ignoring lewd proposals from table after table of old men and sleazy ex-jocks, she was exhausted. Being a weeknight, the steady stream of customers slowed to a trickle early. Charlie dismissed her for the night at ten o'clock.

Stacy left with mixed emotions. On the one hand, she'd intercepted the setup against Lehigh, and maybe thwarted or slowed its execution long enough for Lehigh to outmaneuver them. On the other hand, she'd been unable to verify her father's alibi, with serious doubts that a return trip would yield any better results, and a lump of disgust weighed her down from within. A decade and a half after quitting this secret life, a few hours immersed back into it brought back all of the guilt and self-loathing she'd long ago hoped to leave behind. She hoped the meager results she'd obtained on her father's behalf would somehow make it all worthwhile.

Chapter Thirty-One

"I'm about at my wit's end, Carter!" Ray Ferguson fumed across the table from Lehigh, his face flushed red, his eyes narrow and dark. "Here I thought we had figured out a way to work together, and then I discover you going cowboy again!" He poked a long index finger onto the stapled sheets of paper in front of him, thumping it again for emphasis. "Interviewing witnesses—'informally' you say—and meeting with the accused without his attorney present—do you know how improper all of this is?"

Lehigh gripped a pencil in both hands, bending it almost to the point of breaking. Once again, key information had somehow reached Ferguson through informal back channels. How? And by whom? It drove him crazy. Someone in his own department was determined to embarrass him.

"Ray," Lehigh said, "the reason I haven't discussed any of this information with you is that it hasn't been verified. It's just hearsay. You can't use it, one way or the other, until—"

"I'll be the judge of what I can use or not!" Ferguson stood and planted twin fists on the table, leaning over Lehigh. "Your job isn't to decide what's usable. It's to find the evidence and turn it over to my office so we can build an appropriate legal case!"

Lehigh stood to match Ferguson's gaze. Seated beside him, Jim Wadsworth locked eyes with the blue-suited lawyer seated next to Ferguson across the table, who had started to rise out of his chair as well. Wadsworth gave his head a tiny shake and a "wait" sign with an open palm. Lehigh took it all in with a glance, recognized his deputy's wisdom in trying to avoid further escalation, and softened his tone. "Look, Ray. I'm not trying to be a pain in your butt. I just don't want to repeat every syllable of hearsay folks volunteer who want to be part of the big story. This murder case, people are fascinated by it. They want to feel important. That doesn't mean they actually know anything. They just want a little time in the spotlight. Right?"

Ferguson relaxed a little, unclenching his fists. "That may be true. But, Sheriff, you've got to trust us with the information. We're pretty good in my office at determining whether someone's testimony will hold up in court. We're trained legal professionals, each and every one of us. Can you say the same?"

Lehigh tossed his hands up in surrender and sat, waiting for Ferguson to do the same. Once they were at eye level again, he folded his hands and spoke in an even tone. "So, now that you know what we know," Lehigh said, "specifically that George *may* have an alibi after all…don't you think you ought to drop the charges?"

"Of course not," Ferguson said. "As you said, it's unverified. What's more, it's not much of an alibi. He stayed at the club until *close* to one a.m. That still leaves plenty of time for him to catch up to Downey on Brady Mountain Road and do the deed. And it strengthens his motive, if anything."

Lehigh started to object, then sighed. Had Stacy been able to find a witness to corroborate Ben Wright's story, placing George in the Montgomery Club until one a.m., he'd argue the point, but he knew that the word of an ex-con like Ben would carry no weight with Ferguson.

Then he realized the upshot of Ferguson's remark. Ray didn't know that Lehigh had discovered the discrepancies in the coroner's report—only that he'd followed up on Ben's eyewitness account of seeing George at Downey's club. That was an important clue, and one he didn't want to share with Ferguson just yet. "If what George claims is true, that they were dissolving the deal, then it weakens his motive, doesn't it?" he asked. "If George wanted out, he'd need Downey alive, at least until they signed the papers."

"Maybe he got impatient," Ferguson said. "He probably figured Downey was cheating him again, and *didn't* want the new deal to go through. When Everett refused to back out, that was his death sentence." Ferguson smiled at his wordless assistant, who mirrored the smile back at him.

Lehigh considered the district attorney's point. "What do you think, Jim?"

"It's plausible," Wadsworth said. "But so's the opposite. That's why we need to verify…everything." His eyes widened at Lehigh. Good. He'd probably just realized what Lehigh had moments before.

"We'll take that from here," Ferguson said. "Just send us the contact information for these so-called witnesses. And Carter? Please." He smiled, but it was not a friendly smile. "Leave the investigative work to the professionals, okay?" He picked up his report, returned it to a black briefcase perched on the floor beside him, and led his sycophantic assistant out of the room.

Lehigh swiveled and smiled at Wadsworth. "He doesn't know," he said.

"About the Doskey report? No, I don't think he does." Wadsworth cocked his head. "Which means whoever it is wasn't here when that came in. But they were when Ben talked to you."

Lehigh nodded. "We need to catch this son of a you-know-what," he said. "Because whoever it is, they want George McBride convicted just a little too much. And that's starting to bother me."

***

County Chairman Elliott McBride Jackson straightened his tie and checked his hair one last time before stepping in front of the TV camera next to the tall, dark-haired reporter. Bruce Bailey had promised him an "easy" interview after reading a quick summary of what he promised to reveal on-air. With the scoop he was about to get, Bailey ought to set up automatic monthly donations to Jackson's re-election campaign. Even a tiny percentage of the Pulitzer Prize money would get Jackson re-elected ten times over, if anyone was ever stupid enough to run against him. Perhaps, he mused, he should vie for statewide office.

"On in five, four, three…" A small man in short sleeves finished the countdown on his fingers and mouthed "Go!" when he ran out of digits. The camera's red light came on, and the newsman turned on his made-for-TV smile.

"Breaking news on the Everett Downey murder investigation," Bailey said in a deep baritone. "Bruce Bailey reporting from Mt. Hood County headquarters, where County Chairman Elliott Jackson has *late-breaking* news about the case. Commissioner Jackson, what's the latest?"

"Thank you, Bruce," Jackson said, turning on his kiss-the-babies grin for the camera. Then he realized how incongruous that might seem to viewers, and adopted a stern, angry expression. "We have learned that the sheriff's office has undertaken unauthorized, unofficial, and *unprofessional* independent investigations into the murder of Everett Downey, and has suppressed information vital to the case," Jackson said. "It is our understanding that this information definitively proves the guilt of the sheriff's own father-in-law, George McBride, which is why he refused to reveal his data and his sources!" He stopped when he saw Bruce take a step back from him, which Bailey had told him would be his cue to lower his voice. He came across "hot" on TV, Bailey had told him, whatever that means. Something bad. He softened his tone. "We ask the sheriff to discontinue this reckless behavior and release all of his information to the district attorney immediately."

"What sort of information is this?" Bailey said. "What do you know about what the sheriff has uncovered?"

"We can't say for certain, since we haven't seen the evidence first-hand." Jackson flushed red. So much for "easy" questions. "But we can say that it corroborates evidence already collected that identifies George McBride as the shooter."

Bruce turned to face the camera head-on. "Sources inside the department say that secondary analysis of ballistics and forensics data place McBride—and his privately owned weapons—at the scene of the crime. The individuals providing the information hesitated to appear on camera or be identified out of fear of retaliation. Chairman Jackson, you seem unafraid of such retaliation. What gives you the courage to stand up to the full force of local law enforcement in Mt. Hood County?"

Jackson beamed. For a moment he'd thought Bailey would steal all of his thunder by summarizing his revelations himself on camera, but with such a softball question as a follow-up, he had no complaints. "I've made a career out of sticking up for the little guy against ruthless, out-of-control government overreach," he said. "The fact that this particular bureaucrat carries a gun and a badge doesn't deter me one iota." His head buzzed at how good he sounded. This would play on TV like free money at the welfare office. Who could resist him now?

"Attempts to clarify these revelations at the sheriff's office have gone unanswered," Bailey said. Jackson's ears tingled. What attempts? Had the scoundrel gone behind his back already? "For now, citizens of Mt. Hood County look to their *elected* leaders for guidance. What steps, if any, can the County Commission take to rein in this rogue sheriff, Mr. Chairman?"

Jackson's heart rate steadied again and he scowled into the camera. "We have the authority—nay, the *responsibility*—to investigate these reports, and report back to our vot—er, citizens," he said. "Whether it be motivated by cronyism, improper influence, or simple ineptitude, our citizens deserve better."

"How serious are these accusations?" Bailey asked with a smirk. "Should the sheriff be worried for his job?"

"If these reports bear out, they're very serious," Jackson said. "Charges could be brought, up to and including impeachment and removal from office."

Bailey turned toward the camera again, his eyebrows furrowed. "This is Bruce Bailey reporting."

The camera light turned off and Bailey grinned at him. "Good stuff, Mr. Jackson. Now, if you decide to impeach, you know who to call first, right?" He winked and signaled for the camera crew to pack up.

"Likewise," Jackson said. "If you want more on this story, you know right where to come. For the *truth*."

His cell phone buzzed in his pocket. He checked the caller ID. Ray Ferguson. What the heck did he want?

***

Lehigh turned off the TV set and chuckled to himself. He couldn't wait until the D.A. *insisted* on seeing the actual independent forensics report. He'd have no choice but to reveal its actual contents. Had Lehigh released the information on his own, rather than "hiding" it, as Jackson had insinuated, everyone would have dismissed the report as biased.

Still no sign that anyone else knew of the discrepancies in Doskey's report.

He punched the first speed-dial button on his phone. "Julia," he said when she answered, "is Martin Lightfoot nearby?"

"Right here," she said, "looking like a puppy who just busted into the meat locker. Shall I send him in?"

Martin didn't wait for his reply, bursting through the door a moment later. "Did it work?" he asked, out of breath.

"Like a charm," Lehigh said. "But I need to verify something with you. Who, exactly, did you tell about this report, and what exactly did you tell him?"

Martin folded his arms across his beefy chest. "The only person I told was Bobby Wills," he said. "I made sure we were alone and that no one else could overhear, like you asked."

"You're sure?" Lehigh asked.

"Two hundred percent," Martin said.

Lehigh smiled. Perfect. He had his man. The source of the leaks was Bobby, after all.

***

Ben Wright sipped his icy-cold light lager alone, as usual, at the end of the bar in The Roadhouse, one eye and one ear always alert to the dangers around him. He'd long since gotten used to being the only African-American to patronize the cowboy bar, ever since his cousin Will ditched out on him the previous spring—without paying that month's rent, of course. The white folks in Mt. Hood County—those not wearing uniforms and a badge, anyway—left him alone for the most part.

A mixed blessing, that. He had few close friends in town and fewer dating prospects, but at least the sheriff left him alone. In fact, Sheriff Carter had become kind of a friend in recent days. He'd never been able to claim that growing up in the big city.

He waved his near-empty bottle at the skinny barkeep to get her attention, but she pretended not to notice him, despite his history of generous tipping. He'd been tempted to stiff her on occasion to repay her rudeness, but the guilty memory of his single mom's tireless labor at countless greasy spoons always prompted him to leave no less than twenty percent. Babs may be a jerk, but like everyone else, she had to make a living.

She flirted with a young deputy at the bar, an apple-shaped white man with a buzz cut and a growing redness in his pudgy face. His wise-cracking at the TV screen had grown louder and louder over the past hour. He either didn't care who might be listening, or was trying to attract an audience. The occasional chuckle from the fellows playing pool added encouragement on top of the attention Babs lavished on him, whose blouse seemed to lose buttons every time she refilled his shot glass. By Ben's count, two more drinks would qualify her to tend bar at Downey's place.

"There ain't no way!" Bobby shouted over the noise to the man at the bar next to him. "No friggin' way he wins the election. Not after what's going down today."

The man mumbled something back at him, and Bobby laughed. "Oh, he's going down, all right." He tossed back his drink. "They got the goods on him, big time. Old Rev Ferguson's gonna roast him like a stuck pig at the Lumber Festival."

"Best be careful about what you're saying," Babs said, shaking her head. "That's your boss you're talking about there."

Ben's ears burned. The deputy was talking about Carter? He couldn't imagine anyone in town voting for that goofy guy running against him. Everyone knew former Deputy Dwayne Latner owed his candidacy to the moneyed interests in town, the old-boy network that had run the county into the ground over the past twenty years. He'd thrown Buck Winters under the bus as a co-conspirator with Paul van Paten on the Jared Barkley murder and somehow emerged unscathed himself, so he was craftier than he looked. But the man had never come up with an original thought of his own and couldn't chew gum and tie his shoelaces at the same time.

So, what was this idiot Wills up to?

"He won't be my boss for long," Wills said, signaling for a refill.

Babs grabbed the cheap, lower-shelf whiskey and leaned over the bar to give him a slow, generous pour. "What makes you say so?" She brushed her hair back with a free hand.

"I got him dead to rights, holding back on evidence on his father-in-law." Bobby's voice slurred. "Dead to rights, I tell ya."

The man next to him asked a question. "They got proof that his father-in-law's the shooter, and Carter's holding back," Bobby said. "But I fixed him. I fixed him like a six-month-old puppy." He laughed and sipped from his glass.

"You shouldn't be talking like this out of school." Babs wiped down the bar with a rag. "You never know who's listening."

Ben's ears burned again. He hunkered down low on his bar stool, looked away and pretended not to hear. Thank God she ignored his request for a new beer. She'd probably forgotten about him.

Bobby laughed. "I don't care who's listening," he said. "He shouldn't be sheriff and in a few months, tops, he won't be. And I'll be sitting pretty, with good friends in the D.A.'s office. *Good* friends."

The man next to him laughed. "Or *you'll* be out of a job," he said, loud enough for Ben to hear. "Remember, he's still sheriff. Word gets back to him, you'll be on the streets in no time."

"Who'd be stupid enough to go against me now?" Bobby

said. "I got connections. Powerful connections. Nobody would dare!" He stood and faced the room, scanning the faces of the pool players, who shook their heads and laughed.

"Careful, Meat Loaf," one of them said.

"Right now, I'd put my money on Carter," another said.

"Against the Reverend?" asked another. "No way."

Bobby's gaze settled on Ben for a moment. Ben pretended to nurse his lukewarm beer, now mostly backwash. Avoid eye contact. Avoid…

Bobby looked away and returned to his seat. "One more, Babs," he said. "For the road."

"I think you've had enough," she said. "How about a cup of coffee?"

"I don't want no stinking coffee," Wills shouted. "Gimme a damn whiskey!" Ben winced. Bobby's piercing whine could shatter glass.

Babs crossed her arms and shook her head. "Sorry, Bobby. Now, why don't you get yourself a sandwich or some fries? On the house." She stepped toward the kitchen.

"Where you going?" Bobby yelled. "You calling the cops on me?"

"No, Bobby, I'm just—"

"Are you forgetting? I *am* the law. I could arrest you right now for serving visibly intoxicated people. Look at this place! Full of drunks, and *they* all keep getting served!"

The man next to Bobby slid off his stool and slunk off to the end of the bar. A couple of the pool players strolled over, pool cues in hand, surrounding him. "Who you calling a drunk?" one of them asked.

"Hey, guys, I didn't mean nothing—"

"I take offense at accusations like that," one of the men said in a menacing tone.

"I think our boy here needs a lesson in manners," said the first. They stepped closer.

In a flash, Bobby burst through a tiny gap between them, tripping over a pool cue that somehow got tangled up in his legs. He sprawled face-first on the floor, howling in pain. One of the pool players removed the wallet from Bobby's back pocket, emptied it of its cash, and tossed the wallet onto Bobby's head. The man slapped the cash on the bar, nodding at Babs. "That ought to cover his tab and a nice tip. Now, get out of here, you sloppy little turd, before we stuff that uniform of yours up your big fat butt!"

Ben, still at the end of the bar, blinked in surprise. Before he realized what happened, Bobby was gone.

Chapter Thirty-Two

"You gotta help me, Mr. Ferguson!"

Ray Ferguson shook his head in disgust at the rumpled, drunken figure of Deputy Bobby Wills sprawled out in the guest chair on the far side of his massive mahogany desk. Another of the county's finest, and, as a recent hire, one that Carter couldn't blame on his predecessor. He wished he could have recruited a more trustworthy insider to keep him updated on the sheriff's secretive maneuvers, but Carter's caution limited Ferguson's options.

"I can only do so much, Deputy," he said in as soothing a voice as he could muster, given his irritation. "I can't protect you from yourself if you go spilling your guts in every dirty saloon in the county. What in the devil's name were you thinking?"

"I–I–that barmaid tricked me," Wills said, near tears. "She kept refilling my glass when I wasn't looking—"

"And forced you to drink it, of course," Ferguson said in a mocking tone. "You wretch! Fools like you should be barred from alcohol. Then again, all men are fools who indulge in the devil's elixir. One drink leads to another, and soon your mouth runneth over. '*Wine is a mocker, strong drink is a brawler; whoever is led astray by them is not wise.*' Proverbs 20:1. That's you in a nutshell, young man."

Bobby's face twisted with confusion. "I ain't had no wine," he said. "I was drinking whis—"

"All we can hope now is that the ruffians who ran you out of there are as uncontrolled in their consumption as you," Ferguson said, loud enough to drown out the boy's rambling.

"And as forgetful as you are irresponsible. A tall order, of course, considering." He shook Bobby by the shoulder. "You keep your mouth shut from here on out, unless you're talking to me and only me. Am I being clear?"

"But what about the sheriff? What if he fires me?" Bobby lurched forward and nearly fell out of his chair. "Can't you do something to save my job?"

"You're still on probation," Ferguson said, his patience fading fast. "Carter could fire you even without a good reason— and you've given him plenty. No, your best bet is to go home, eat some food to absorb that alcohol, and try to get some sleep. And for God's sake, shut your damned mouth!" He picked up his desk phone and started punching in numbers.

"But Reverend—"

"*Don't call me Reverend!*" Ferguson slammed the phone back into its cradle, six digits into dialing the local taxi service. "Only my *enemies* call me that. Are you planning on becoming my enemy, Deputy?"

"N-no sir, I'm sorry—"

"Good. Because you will rue the day you cross me, boy. Now get the hell out of here. And don't ever come here again unless I summon you. Go on—get!"

***

A short while later, Ray Ferguson gave a thumbs-up to Bruce Bailey, who stood with a hand-held microphone in front of a portable news camera held by a burly assistant. "On in five seconds," Bailey said, then smiled at the camera. "Welcome back to 'Live at Five' News," Bailey said. "I'm at the District Attorney's office of Mt. Hood County with more breaking news on the Everett Downey murder case. With me is the lead prosecutor on the case, Assistant District Attorney Raymond Ferguson. Mr. Ferguson, we understand that you've uncovered some shocking irregularities in the sheriff department's handling of the case, is that right?"

"Unfortunately, that is true," Ferguson said, putting on a

somber face. "We are preparing to file charges of improper use of funds, illegal search, and misuse of police authority against high-ranking officials in the sheriff's office, based on eyewitness accounts of said behavior from within the department."

"Those charges sound serious." Bailey's surprised expression even looked real. "Can you name the persons being charged?"

"In due time." In truth, Ferguson hadn't even drawn up the charges, and wasn't sure he had much chance of an indictment. He hoped Carter would resign rather than risk being named. "Suffice to say, the persons of interest are very high-ranking. Very high."

"What are the penalties if convicted?" Bailey said.

"Those indicted would be suspended from service pending trial, and if convicted, would face serious fines and possibly prison," Ferguson said, recalling his days teaching Introduction to Law for the Layman at the community college. "The extent of the prison term would, of course, be up to the judge and jury."

"How does this affect the investigation of the Downey murder?" Bailey asked. Finally!

"Unfortunately, it's more ammunition for the defense, but I assure you, it's nothing but a smoke screen," Ferguson said, getting into a rhythm. "We're getting used to this sort of cronyism coming from this sheriff's office, and we're confident that the judge will see through it and rule appropriately on the admissibility of evidence that supports the people's case."

"And that case is that the man standing trial for this murder, Senator George McBride, is guilty of this murder?" Bailey asked.

"That is correct," Ferguson said.

"The sheriff's father-in-law," Bailey said.

"The same," Ferguson replied. He put on a sorrowful expression, as if the whole affair saddened him. Which it did, but not for the reasons viewers might conclude.

"Thank you, Mr. Ferguson," Bailey said, turning to face the camera. The cameraman waved at Ferguson, his cue to step out of the camera's view. "These revelations," Bailey went on, "come on the heels of a new poll just released today showing that Sheriff Lehigh Carter now trails former Deputy Dwayne

Latner by five percent among likely voters in the county."

The camera's red light blinked off, and a small monitor displayed some graphs being shown to viewers at home. Bailey picked up some papers and cited other figures from them by way of voice-over.

"This reverses a trend we'd noted in polls from just a month ago, where the incumbent led Latner by seven points," he said. "Our data shows Latner picking up the greatest increase in support among the business community, those with college degrees, and male voters."

Ferguson smiled. The local station's polls had accurately predicted the last five county-wide election results. Some would say they shaped those results. Fine with him.

The red light blinked back on, and Bailey faced the camera alone. "Pollsters say that the number one issue among Latner supporters is 'experience and professionalism' in the sheriff's office, followed by 'honesty and integrity' of the incumbent," he said. "It appears that recent scandals surrounding the department is starting to stain the reputation of Interim Sheriff Lehigh Carter. Back to you in the studio."

"Fascinating results on that poll," Ferguson said. "How recently was it taken?"

Bailey shrugged. "Heck if I know. I just read what they give me." He smoothed his hair back and handed his microphone to the camera crew. "I appreciate you giving me the scoop on this, Mr. Ferguson."

"Call me Ray," Ferguson said, shaking the newsman's hand. "And the pleasure is all mine."

***

The jangling of bells split the night air, jarring Stacy from a deep, dreamless sleep. She moaned and rolled over in her queen-sized bed, one that felt so enormous and empty since…

She put that thought out of her mind, aided by the repeated ringing of her stupid telephone. Her alarm clock showed 2:43 a.m. Few people, if any, dared call her this late: her parents, or best friend Donna in an emergency, or Lehigh. Anyone else would be making a mistake.

She crab-crawled on her elbows to the side of the bed and lifted the receiver. "H'lo?" She rubbed her eyes, awaiting a response.

Nobody spoke.

"Hello?" she said again, prepared to slam the receiver back into its cradle. Then she heard breathing. Heavy breathing.

"Who is this?" she said. "Speak, or I'm hanging up."

More heavy breathing. She slid the receiver away from her ear—

"You'd better watch yourself," said a man's voice. She didn't recognize it. "You're not safe."

"What do you mean, I'm not safe?" She sat up, much more awake. "From what? *Who is this?*"

"Your husband isn't there to protect you," the man said in hushed tones. It sounded odd—disguised, maybe. "Nor your dogs."

"Leave me alone, you freak!" Stacy shouted and slammed the phone down. She missed the cradle, though, and the phone rattled to the floor.

"We're coming for you, bitch!" the voice hissed from the floor. In spite of the distance, she could hear it clearly in the deep quiet of the night.

"You and what army?" she yelled back at the phone and this time was able to pick it up and slam it home. Freaks. Who would do such a thing? Probably some stupid teenagers.

Although they knew some pretty specific things, like Lehigh not being there, and that they had dogs. Stacy shivered and pulled the covers over her.

The phone rang again.

Her body went still, her limbs and neck rigid, a stiff and painful posture even if she was laying down. She gritted her teeth and waited for the next ring.

It came. Loud. Insistent. Obnoxious.

"Go away!" she shouted into her pillow.

Another ring.

Fine, then. They weren't going to go away on their own. She grabbed the phone. "Who is this?" she screamed.

"We're watching you," the voice said.

"Go away!" she yelled. "Leave me alone!" She knew she should just hang up, but—

"Your father killed an innocent man," the voice said. "Sins of the father must be repaid."

She fought to keep her voice strong and steady, but lost the battle. "What the hell do you want?"

"You," the voice said. "You are what I want. *Dead!*"

The line went still, followed by a dial tone. Stacy sat still, upright in her bed, shaking, the phone stuck to her ear, her arm unable to move to hang up. She stayed there until the dial tone stopped, switching to that annoying siren-like sound that warns of an off-hook receiver. She pressed "End" on the handset and dropped it in her lap, breathing hard.

Someone who knew her home phone number—or could find it, which was easy enough, she supposed—and knew her situation in life: separated from Lehigh, unprotected, her father standing accused of a horrible crime. And now they'd threatened to make her pay for her father's alleged deeds.

Deeds, she knew deep inside, that he'd never committed. But few knew what Lehigh had shared with her. She'd been unable to corroborate the claim that could exonerate her father, but he had to be innocent.

Still, the public didn't know anything about that. Which means the caller could be anyone. Anyone, that is, who knew Everett Downey, or cared enough to want to avenge his murder.

A cold shiver shook her again. The people that knew Downey best were the ones that worked for him—the ones to whom she'd risked exposure by working that shift at the club. Had someone identified her? Nobody seemed to recognize her at the time, but maybe her questions spurred curious minds to investigate.

She picked up the phone again, surprised to find her hands still shaking. She took a deep breath and waged an inner argument: make the call, or not? Call now, or wait until morning? Tell all, or the bare minimum?

Was she being foolish, taking any of this seriously?

The voice came back to her, haunting her. "You are what I want. *Dead*!" She had to admit, the call frightened her. Especially since they'd called back. And it didn't sound like teenagers. Not at all.

She dialed.

"Mmm-hmmm?" Lehigh's drowsy baritone filled her ears. A sweet sound, that. She loved the sound of his voice, even when angry with him.

"Lehigh, I just got a call," Stacy said. "Someone threatened me. To *kill* me, Lee."

"Could you tell who it was?" Suddenly he sounded alert, all business. "Male, female, young, old?"

"A man," she said. "I couldn't tell how old. Not a kid. He—he knew things, Lehigh. About my father. About us. It frightened me."

"I'll be right over," he said.

"No!" The word escaped her mouth before her brain could stop it. "No," she said in a softer tone, "no need. It didn't sound like they meant to kill me *tonight*. More of a warning. To scare me."

"I'll have the call traced," he said. "We'll find out who it is, and by gum, when I'm through, they'll wish they'd never heard of a telephone."

"I think I need some protection," she said. "Is that something you could arrange?"

"Like I said, I'll come over—"

"No, no," she said, again without thinking. "I don't think I'm ready for that yet. I thought maybe one of your deputies, or maybe you could bring one of the dogs...?"

"I don't have the spare manpower to post a guard," he said, "but I could bring the dogs. Of course, that means I have to come over, too."

"Drop them off tomorrow," she said. "You still have a key?"

After a long silence, he replied. "You want me to bring them when you're not there."

She sighed. How mean that sounded. "Of course you can bring them in the morning if you like. I didn't want to inconvenience you."

"Stacy, you're my wife. Even though we're separated, your safety is not an inconvenience. It's a necessity."

"Thank you, Lehigh. I really appreciate it."

Another long pause. "Stacy, are you sure you don't want me to come back for a bit? I'll sleep on the couch if you want, but I just think—"

"I'm sure," she said. "I still need some time, Lee. To think about things. But thank you for asking. It's very sweet of you."

He sighed. "You're welcome. I'll see you in the morning, before work. With Lucky and Diamond, who would *love* to see you. Almost as much as I would."

She hung up and cradled the phone to her chest. Her heart pounded, and tears crawled down her cheeks. A clear truth emerged before her. Despite his crazy ways and his odd mistakes—despite arresting her father for a crime they both knew he didn't commit—she realized that her husband was, down deep, a good man. As hard as it would be, she knew that sooner or later she'd admit to herself and to him that she couldn't live without him any longer.

But not today.

She turned off the phone's ringer, rolled over, and prayed for sleep.

***

Lehigh woke well before his 6:00 a.m. cell phone alarm after a fitful night of short sleep bursts. His mind couldn't shut off the sound of fear in Stacy's voice the night before, and he'd struggled against the urge to disregard her admonition to stay away. More than once he'd decided to drive over and park in front of her house to stand watch, armed and ready. But knowledge of how she'd react stopped him. He needed to think long-term here.

He sipped coffee by the campfire and picked at a plate of fried eggs, lit by the pink rays of sunrise climbing over the rolling hills to his left. He'd grown accustomed to the outdoor lifestyle once again, one he'd abandoned years ago after taking over the family logging business. He enjoyed the crisp night air, the soft cries of nature awakening amidst the trees, the gradual lightening of the night sky. But the pleasantness of the day came to life without his appreciation that morning. Staring off into the distance, he saw only the dark clouds emerging from within.

His wife was in trouble. Deep trouble. Threatening phone calls in the middle of the night, people stalking her to discover her vulnerabilities—and all because of him. He'd taken this sheriff's job against his better judgment, and no part of it pleased him. The bureaucracy, the politics, the constant exposure to the seamy underbelly of humanity's worst, all sucked the life out of him daily.

And now this.

He snuffed the fire, scrubbed his dishes clean, and slammed the last of his coffee. Still too early to go to Stacy's, he could at least keep a watchful eye from a closer distance. He whistled for the dogs, who bounded from invisibility in the forest into his truck, and in minutes he'd traversed the empty highway into Clarkesville.

He stopped at Shirley's Cafe and nursed a second cup of coffee. The "Good Morning" news program came on and the waiter behind the counter obliged him by turning up the volume. Minutes later, Bruce Bailey's slimy face filled the screen.

"County Judge Petros Geroux has set a trial date of September sixth for the trial of George McBride for the murder of Everett Downey," Bailey said, shading his eyes from the sun. The segment, Lehigh realized, had been taped the evening before. "Assistant District Attorney Ray Ferguson applauded the quick trial date, claiming that the defense attorneys in the case had engaged in, quote, endless delay tactics, end quote. As for their part, McBride's attorney, Constantine Richards, had this to say."

The screen shifted, and Richards' ruddy face, bright-white

shock of Einstein-like hair and long Roman nose filled the screen. "We welcome the speedy start to the trial, and contrary to the prosecution's claims, we insisted upon an early commencement of proceedings," Richards said. "We'll prove my client innocent of all charges, and clear his name from the cloud of suspicion that has arisen from these baseless allegations."

Lehigh set down his coffee and stared slack-jawed at the screen. Ferguson's desire for a quick trial made sense—the evidence, thus far, seemed stacked against McBride, and he needed to act fast before Lehigh succeeded in poking too many holes in his case. But why would Richards agree? Why wouldn't he at least return Lehigh's calls? And why would George agree, knowing, as he did, what Lehigh had discovered?

The answer struck him all at once. George would rather go to prison for murder than be exposed as a man who'd cheated on his wife in strip clubs.

Nobody, but nobody, wanted him to prove George's alibi.

Chapter Thirty-Three

Lehigh called Stacy on the drive over to her place, but the call went straight to voice-mail. No doubt she cleared out early, spooked by the late-night threats. He left Diamond outside and Lucky inside the house, knowing this would make them bark at each other and scare off intruders. He left her a note, advising her to swap their stations now and again, and somehow resisted adding anything too gushy. He did sign it "Love, Lehigh." No harm in telling her that too often.

Back in his office, he contacted a security agency to try to trace the call, and got some bad news.

"I'm sorry, but on a landline, once the call is terminated, there's little we can do to trace its origin," the security man said. "If she had pressed the star-5-7 code right away, and the caller ID was unblocked, she might have had some luck. But once she's received other calls..." His voice trailed off, the universal code for "It's hopeless."

"Thanks anyway." Lehigh hung up. He leaned back in his desk chair, rubbed his tired eyes, and cursed himself for his early morning call. Another blunder. Missteps of an amateur. He wondered if he'd ever get the hang of this job.

His desk phone buzzed him—Julia. "Deputy Wills has reported in," she said in a whisper. "Shall I send him in?"

"Ask him to wait there for me." He closed some files laying open on his desk and stuffed them into a drawer, finished off a third and final cup of coffee for the morning, and headed out to Julia's desk. No Wills. "Well, where the heck is he?"

"He said he needed to use the men's room," she said. "He

did seem to be in a hurry, though, when I told him you wanted to see him."

A flash of reflected light streamed in through the window. Lehigh peeked out as a green Crown Victoria spit gravel out of the parking lot. Car 57. "Which car is assigned to Wills?" he asked.

"Fifty-sev—"

Lehigh had his County-issue SUV rolling less than half a minute after Bobby's exit. "Car 57, this is the sheriff, come in Car 57," he broadcast over the police band. No response. He radioed dispatch, asking for the whereabouts of Bobby's car. No doubt he'd be listening in, but so what. They gave him the location and direction and Lehigh turned on his siren and lights. Cars pulled over, and once again Lehigh gave thanks for living in a small town.

"Target has turned east on Brady Mountain Road, heading toward Twin Falls," dispatch advised moments later.

"Send as many units as you can spare," Lehigh said. "I want this guy to know I'm serious."

"Sheriff," said a shaky man's voice over the radio a minute or so later. "What do you want from me?"

"I need to talk to you, Bobby." Lehigh swerved around a tight curve. "Best if we talk in the office, but I'll follow you all the way to Idaho if I need to."

"What about?" Wills' voice sounded weak and high-pitched. Definitely afraid.

"I need to verify some things," Lehigh said. "Things I heard second-hand. I want to hear your side of the story."

"About the Roadhouse?"

"Among other things." He had no other things just yet, but he wanted to get Bobby talking, see what else he knew.

"Look, Sheriff, I got a little drunk and may have said a few things I didn't mean. I was just joshing, you know?"

Lehigh took another high-speed curve and spotted Bobby's Crown Vic about a half-mile ahead of him, just before it disappeared around another bend. "Bobby, you need to take this road a whole lot slower," Lehigh said. "There's lots of blind curves, and deer, and—"

"Crap!" Squealing tires overwhelmed the sound of Bobby's expletive, then the radio went silent.

"Bobby?" No answer. "Wills? You okay?" More silence. Lehigh slowed his own vehicle for the turn, then braked harder when he spotted the Crown Vic wedged into a ditch, tires spinning. Other than being stuck, it appeared undamaged. He parked a few car lengths ahead of the deputy and grabbed the radio.

"Dispatch," he said, "get an ambulance out to Brady Mountain Road, milepost 27, ASAP." He jogged back to the sedan. Sure enough, Bobby Wills sat behind the wheel, struggling to undo his seat belt. His deflated air bag lay across his lap and the front seats, and small cuts and bruises lined his face.

"You okay in there?" Lehigh asked.

Wills glanced at him, then turned his face downward. "I'll be all right," he said. "I swerved to miss a coyote. Dang thing almost gave me a heart attack."

"We'll get you checked out to be sure," Lehigh said. "Let's get you out of there." He helped Bobby out of the vehicle. The deputy leaned against the top of the car to steady himself. Lehigh sniffed the air, detected a familiar sweet aroma coming off the deputy. "When's the last time you had a drink?" he asked.

Wills shook his head. "Late last night, I guess."

"How late?"

Wills shrugged. "I dunno. Maybe three, four in the morning?"

"Damn, boy, did you sleep?"

Wills crumpled to the ground, tears lining his face. "Sheriff, I screwed up," he said. "Bad, huh?"

"Drinking and driving's not a good way to start the workday," Lehigh said. "Why, Bobby? What's eating you?"

Bobby's tears flowed, and he tried to wipe them away, but new ones replaced the old faster than he could erase them. "My father was a drunk," he said. "I always said I wouldn't be like him, but here I am. I'm just like him, ain't I?"

"One night of partying doesn't make you a drunk," Lehigh said. "It means you made a mistake. Now, about what you said at—"

"It's like our preacher always said," Wills said through choking sobs. "The son always pays for the sins of the father. I'm doomed!"

"Sins of the father?" Alarm bells rang. Stacy had mentioned her caller threatening her with something of that sort. "Why do you say that, Bobby?"

"It's just the truth," Wills said. "Sheriff, I'm sorry. About this, about the whole Roadhouse thing. About everything."

Lehigh knelt to bring himself to eye level with the deputy. "Bobby, was it true what you said? About leaking the information to the press and all. Was it you?"

Wills glared at him through teary eyes. "I really wanted to be a good deputy," he said. "I wanted to be the best recruit you'd ever hired. But I see how you favor Ruby Mac, and Ted Roscoe, and Marty. It made me mad, Sheriff. I just wanted to be good. And then your wife…her daddy…it just ain't fair!" His words dissolved into sobs, and his body slumped sideways onto the ground, curled into a fetal position.

So, not only was Bobby the leak, as he suspected, but also, it appeared, the one placing threatening calls to his wife. All because he felt that Lehigh hadn't been fair to him.

Maybe he had a point. Lehigh still had a lot to learn about being sheriff—and about whether he still wanted to be.

***

Lehigh arched his back, shaking off the lower-lumbar pain from sitting too long in his uncomfortable chair. Another day, another month-end crime report for the County Commission. The report took hours to compile, as each satellite office reported their data in different formats. His predecessors apparently hated computers even more than Lehigh, and hadn't invested in one that enabled simple tabulations and breakdowns the way his business's accounting software did. And all for what? Single-digit totals for pretty much everything that mattered. If not for car thefts, drunk drivers, and Friday night bar fights, he could disband the entire department.

And the occasional murder, of course.

Something stirred in the vicinity of his open office door, followed by the clearing of someone's throat. The high-pitched tenor of the voice gave away the identity of his visitor-to-be.

"Come on in, Julia," he said.

She entered a moment later and stood by the door, feet together, head down. "There's a man asking for you," she said. "He says he works for the District Attorney."

"Tell him to come back tomorrow," Lehigh said. "I don't have time for—"

"Lehigh Carter?" A man appeared behind her. He stood well over six feet tall, built like a side of beef in a suit. Sweat lined his brow and his short-trimmed hairline.

"That's me. And who might you be?" Lehigh asked.

The man stepped forward, reached into his suit jacket, and placed an envelope on his desk. "Have a nice day," he said with a tight smile. He strode out of the office, never revealing his identity or affiliation.

Someone had typed Lehigh's full name on the envelope. He opened it and removed a letter with the letterhead of the District Attorney's office.

"What is it?" Julia asked.

"It says it's an 'information,' whatever the heck that is," he said. "From Ray Ferguson. Well, what do you know. He's finally sharing—oh, no." He threw the letter on the desk. Damn that Ferguson!

Julia fidgeted a moment, then asked, "What's wrong?"

"It's a notice from Ray Ferguson," he said with a heavy sigh, "that he's going to charge me with 'obstructing governmental or judicial administration' in the investigation of the murder of Everett Downey. That sumbitch wants to put me in my own jail!"

***

"This meeting is called to order." County Chair Elliott McBride Jackson banged the gavel twice on the polished hardwood block, relishing the echoes of the sharp knock bouncing off the chamber's ancient walls. As always, the sound startled his fellow commissioners, their tell-tale jerks of the head or abrupt shifts in their seats giving away their discomfort. He considered rapping it a third time, just to see them jump again, especially that dimwitted farmer from the north district, Desmond Mitchell. Old Desmond supported that redneck Lehigh Carter at every opportunity and deserved a little extra irritation for that alone. But he demurred this one time. He might need Mitchell's vote on his motion if any of the others got weak-kneed, as usual.

"The first item is a motion filed by the Chair to suspend the rules in order to consider an item out of order on our agenda, County Resolution one twenty seven," Jackson said. "Do I have a second?"

"Second," bleated one of the sheep to his left.

"Any objection? Hearing none, this motion is—"

"I object," came a soft voice to his right.

Jackson gritted his teeth. He didn't need to look. "State your objection, Desmond."

"I haven't had a chance to even read the resolution," Desmond Mitchell said. "Does the Chairman have copies to distribute?"

"It's in your packet," Jackson said, with more force than he intended. He took a deep breath and smiled at his colleague. "The chair is happy to allow a few moments for you to read the item before we proceed with a vote on the motion."

The commissioners shuffled through their papers and all six took a few moments to scan the document. Once again, Mitchell spoke up.

"Impeachment? Of the sheriff? You have got to be kidding me!"

"I most certainly am not." The skin on Jackson's neck grew

warm and his collar felt tight all of a sudden. "These charges are serious and merit our full and immediate attention."

"Dereliction of duty? Misfeasance, nonfeasance, and malfeasance?" Desmond rolled his eyes. "What evidence do you have for any of this?"

Jackson's skin grew even warmer, and his temples throbbed. This guy was always such a pain in the you-know-what. He made a mental note to find a worthy opponent to run against Desmond when his term expired. "That's what the impeachment process is about, Mr. Mitchell. Now, if we can vote on my motion—"

"Mr. Chairman, such a serious matter deserves more time to digest and reflect upon these charges," Mitchell said. A few heads nodded around them.

Dammit! The procedural vote represented a test of his strength on the commission, and Jackson couldn't afford to lose more than two votes. Suspension of the rules required a two-thirds majority—which meant five of the seven votes—the same as a vote to convict and expel from office. He couldn't afford to lose the vote and get his colleagues in the habit of voting against him.

"Of course, of course," Jackson said. "We can consider the item in its scheduled order if the members feel they need more time. It just seemed to me that we should focus on our highest priority items first, to make sure we give it the proper amount of time for deliberation, rather than rushing through it at the end of the meeting."

One of the nodding heads, Commissioner Michelle Graber from the easternmost ranching district, leaned toward her microphone. "The Chairman makes an excellent point," she said. "I vote yes on suspending the rules."

"Hear, hear," said another.

"All in favor?" Jackson said. Graber and three others raised their hands. Excellent. "Opposed?" Mitchell's hand went up.

The final member, eighty-year-old Commissioner Abram Cantrell from Twin Falls—whose district included Lehigh Carter—blinked several times. "I, uh, abstain, Mr. Chairman," he said.

Jackson breathed a sigh of relief. Under commission rules, an abstention didn't count against his required two-thirds majority. "Motion passes," he said. "The clerk will read into the record the Articles of Impeachment against Sheriff Lehigh Carter, unless I hear a motion to waive the reading…thank you, Commissioner Graber. We will consider the articles in a formal hearing next week. The clerk will notify the sheriff and request his appearance."

"Mr. Chairman!" Desmond Mitchell stood, his hands shaking. "You haven't even told him? Not even a courtesy call? My goodness gracious, did you want him to hear of this on Facebook?"

"You're out of order, Mr. Mitchell!" he shouted. "We are following *procedure* here!"

"Follow *this*!" Mitchell pointed to his backside, gathered up his papers, and stormed out of the room. Cantrell shook his head at Jackson, and a few others clucked their disapproval.

Elliott sank lower in his chair. That did not go well, and it spelled trouble. He'd either need to do some backroom relationship repair—or convince Carter to resign before the impeachment proceedings began.

Chapter Thirty-Four

Lehigh clicked the *View Document* button on his computer screen, still not sure of what he'd find in the online evidence file. The document listed the names of active members of the Twin Falls Marksman's Club in alphabetical order. Three pages in, he found George McBride's name, listed as a member in good standing for over three decades. Of course, McBride had attended meetings of the club only during election years.

He clicked on the next document, a list of award winners in the club's annual marksmanship competition. He recalled the senator's private study, a proud display of his accomplishments as a marksman and gun rights defender, and expected to find George's name on the top of the list of 2017 champions. But it did not appear on the list at all.

He scanned back to the previous year, and the one before. Same result.

He opened a new window on his computer and scanned the summary of evidence document attached to the Downey murder case. Sure enough, he found an image of the championship shooting results—the same date as his last visit to the club, dated "07-10-17." July 10th, 2017. George had won the competition less than two weeks before McBride's murder.

That struck Lehigh as odd. He didn't recall George bragging about winning that trophy recently. And McBride had insisted he hadn't been to the club in ten years.

He looked at the date again. Then he checked some other dates. The anniversary of George joining the club, for example. At first, it didn't look like a date at all: "84-06-22." Perhaps he'd misread it. The handwriting of the old Scotsman that ran the place was difficult to read. He checked again.

And that's when he realized the error.

His deputies had misread the date of George's last visit, and his big marksmanship accomplishment, by over a decade. The old Scotsman still used the old-fashioned European format for writing dates. The entry of "07-10-17" meant George won the championship not on July 10th of 2017, but on October 17, 2007.

His stomach turned into knots. While not core to the case, the error had helped add to the impression that McBride premeditated the murder of Everett Downey, to the point of practicing his aim with a rifle. The correction wouldn't prove his innocence, but it did plant more doubt in Lehigh's mind about George's potential guilt.

Odd, he thought after a moment, that Ferguson hadn't noticed the error, given his familiarity with the club's quirky manner of recording dates. Ferguson's name appeared on the membership list a page ahead of McBride's. He should have noticed the incorrect attribution. But then again, Ferguson hadn't made much of this particular piece of evidence. He was so convinced of George's guilt, in all probability, he simply chose not to publicize the error even if he had noticed it.

Lehigh sighed and closed the electronic files. More bias in the system that needed rooting out. Why didn't anyone else notice these things besides him?

***

Lehigh slammed the phone down, frustrated by call-system menus, robotic greetings, and voice mail. Since when had lawyers in Clarkesville sold out to automation? In particular, why had *his* attorney, Samantha Pullen?

"Julia," he said a moment later on the phone to his assistant, "please keep Sam Pullen on auto-dial until you reach her, okay?"

"Am I allowed to make personal calls for you like that?" Julia asked in a timid voice. "I mean, I'm happy to help, but I don't want either of us getting into any more trouble."

Lehigh sighed. "I guess we'd better play it safe, then. Never mind, I'll call her back later." He looked up another number, the one for his building contractor, who hadn't shown up at his site in weeks. They'd demolished the old structure, then informed him of an unexpected delay on obtaining permits. All that remained of his old house was a pile of ash and debris.

He dialed, and, for a change, reached the man instead of his voice-mail. "Melvin Crabb here," the gruff voice said.

"Melvin. Lehigh Carter. Wondering when I might see you back on the job site?"

After a long pause, Crabb cleared his throat. "Well, we've hit another snag," he said. "Seems that check you wrote us to get started came back. I've been meaning to call you, but I didn't want to, uh…well, let's just say, I didn't want to add to your troubles."

"Kind of you," Lehigh said, "but the number one trouble I have right now is getting my dang house built before winter comes. What's this about the check?"

"Bank said something about funds not available." Rustling sounds followed, then the muted sounds of Crabb's voice shouting at someone. "Sorry about that," he said. "Where were we?"

"This is crazy!" Lehigh made a fist, but had nothing to hit. "I have plenty of funds. Dammit! Well, you hold onto that check. I'll sort this out today. If that check clears, will you be able to start back up tomorrow?"

"Well, ah…I put my crews on other projects. Gotta keep 'em busy, you know? You let me know when you straighten that out, then call me back. Look, I gotta go. Sorry, Mr. Carter." Crabb hung up, leaving Lehigh even more frustrated than before. He buzzed Julia back. "Any luck with Sam Pullen?" he asked.

"I, uh…you told me not to…"

"Oh, yeah, that's right. Sorry." He reached out with the receiver to hang up, but heard her voice buzzing from the earpiece just in time. "What's that?" Lehigh said. "I'm sorry, I didn't hear that last bit."

"County Commissioner Mitchell just walked in," she said. "And he doesn't look happy."

Lehigh sighed. *Now* what?

***

"He *what?*" Lehigh slammed a desk drawer shut, sending a thunderous boom down the hallway, loud enough that deputies could hear it on patrol in east county.

"He impeached you," Commissioner Mitchell said. "Or, more precisely, *we* impeached you. Five members of the commission voted to take up the measure in our next meeting. I was not one of them."

"For what?" Lehigh said, pacing around his desk. "I mean, I'm not even sure what the heck a guy gets impeached for. Or even what that means. Am I out of a job?"

"Not yet," Mitchell said. "We have to have a trial of sorts— a political trial, not a legal one. You'll be called to testify, as will whomever the chairman and any member of the commission desires. If five members of the commission vote 'guilty' to any article of impeachment, you'll be removed from office immediately."

"For the love of Mike," Lehigh said. "If you guys didn't want me to be sheriff, all you had to do is ask. I hate this damned job and I'm only doing it because you all asked me to. If you want someone else, say the word. I'll quit in two seconds with no regrets. Impeachment, my butt!"

"Sheriff," Mitchell said in a gentle voice, "if you want to quit and go back to your civilian life, nobody around here would blame you. But I hope you won't."

"Why the hell not?" Lehigh stared out the window at the receding glacier shadowed by the peaks of Mt. Hood, so inviting compared to his stuffy office. "Give me one good reason not to turn in my badge and gun right now."

"Because," Mitchell said, "if you do, then the good old boys who have run this county into the ground in recent years will continue to run it like their own private casino. The people of this town deserve better. Isn't *that* why you agreed to take this job, Mr. Carter? To help clean up the corruption and cronyism?"

Lehigh spun around and glared at him. He opened his mouth to reply, and found that he had no response. He sat back in his chair, overcome by depression. "You're right, of course. That is why I took the job. But it doesn't seem folks around here are as fired up about that as they were a few months ago. Between Jackson, the district attorney, and that airhead Bruce Bailey, they've convinced people around here that I created this mess. I'm the last one they'd trust to fix it."

Mitchell shook his head, smiling. "I think if you ignore the politicians and asked the people who live and work here what *they* think, you'd find a very different answer."

"I've seen the polls, Desmond. I'm losing. To Dwayne Latner, of all people! Buck's own lap dog."

Mitchell scoffed. "I don't believe those polls, Mr. Carter, and you shouldn't either. Especially since you haven't even begun to campaign." He smiled again at Lehigh. "Talk to the people, Lehigh. Ask the ones you meet on the street, in the coffee shops, at the grocery stores. Ask who they believe. If I'm wrong, well, then you're right to quit. But if I'm right, I'd really like you to stay and help me fight these so-called leaders. Will you do that for me? For the county you grew up in and call home?"

Lehigh looked into Desmond's dark eyes, saw the honesty and desperation mixed with hope. Maybe the old man was right. He should ask around a bit, not just assume the worst. But would people answer him honestly? When asked tough questions, people tended to say what they thought he wanted to hear.

"I'll tell you what," he said. "I'll listen to the people, but it can't be me doing the asking. You go to Shirley's or Dot's and ask the first ten people you see. If six of them say I should stay and fight, I'll do it. Any less, and I go back to taking care of my trees and my dogs."

Mitchell grinned and shook his hand. "Sheriff," he said, "you've got yourself a deal."

After the commissioner left, Lehigh returned to gaze out at

the beautiful peaks visible from his office window. He doubted his one ally on the commission would find three out of ten people who'd support him, much less six. Part of him didn't mind. Most days, he wished he'd never left the forest, never took on this uphill battle of cleaning up the corrupt sheriff's department his predecessors had left behind. But he also hated knowing that he'd lost the trust of so many of his fellow county residents—people he'd gone to high school with, saw in the burger joints and grocery stores, and who rooted for the same local football team. He'd somehow lost their trust, and he had no idea how to win it back—or even if he had the energy to try.

Part IV

Conspiracy

Chapter Thirty-Five

Stacy took a deep breath outside the door of Shirley's Cafe, holding the oversized bronze handle, undecided whether to push, pull, or somehow make the door open through sheer force of will. Or run back to her car and get the hell out of there. In the meantime, the noon sun bore down on her long black hair, pulled out of its usual ponytail to flow over her shoulders, a look her mother insisted was both more attractive and more comforting to men. Usually she couldn't care less about that, but today she was on a mission. And the mission wouldn't get accomplished by standing here.

She took another deep breath.

Someone appeared on the other side of the glass—a woman pulling two pre-school-aged children toward the exit, one in each hand. She appealed to Stacy with her glance. Stacy pulled the door outward and waited for the young family to pass. The cool air from the restaurant bathed her in the comforting aromas of fried food, salt, and coffee, the three basic ingredients of every good meal at Shirley's. She swallowed hard and slid inside.

She waited a moment for her eyes to adjust to the dim light of the room, especially after the bright sunshine in which she'd just spent several minutes meditating. She spotted him in a booth near the kitchen doors—*their* booth. The one they'd sat in during their first date in high school, and their first real date after reuniting the year before. She smiled. He even sat on the same side that he always did. That silly, romantic man!

She slid into the booth, interrupting some sort of reverie, as evidenced by his faraway eyes. He snapped to attention and offered a coy smile. "Hey," Lehigh said. "Good to see you."

She smiled back, a big one. "Good to see you, too." She meant it. More than she ever had, or so it seemed. She loved his pensive side, the quiet calm that told her he was somehow figuring things out, thinking big picture in one way or another. So often he seemed to act on impulse, at times with a brashness and confidence that struck many people as cocky. She knew better: his intensity often arose from necessity, from having no other option but the current way forward, and the faster the better. "I'm sorry I'm a few minutes late. I got, um, detained."

"No problem." He smiled over her shoulder at a presence she could sense without seeing—the waitress. "We're going to need a few more minutes," he said, looking back at her. "Unless you know what you want."

"Chicken Caesar salad, extra croutons, light on the dressing," she said, "and a diet cola."

"Reuben, fries, Dr. Pepper," he said, his smile changing to one of suppressed laughter.

"What's so funny?"

He shrugged. "I don't know why we bother with menus. We always order the same thing."

She sipped at her water and captured a sliver of ice, crunching it in her teeth. "As your Pappy says, if you've got a good thing, why change it?"

"I often wonder that myself." He got that faraway look in his eyes again.

She drew herself upright, willing herself into a Lehigh-Carter-state of confidence. She didn't look forward to confronting him, but she felt she had no choice. "I uh, heard you were thinking of making a big change. Did I hear right?"

He frowned at her, his eyebrows diving into a deep valley near the bridge of his nose. "News travels fast."

"Well, it was kind of on the news. Some of it, anyway. The D.A., the county commission—"

"Yeah. Well, I guess they've got plans. Me, I'm still figuring things out. And to make things worse, my lawyer has suddenly gone A.W.O.L."

"And?"

The waitress returned, chomping on too much gum and smelling of cinnamon. "Here's your drinks," she said. "Holler if you need anything else." She disappeared into the kitchen, but the cinnamon aroma lingered.

Stacy glanced back at Lehigh, who seemed lost in thought. "Stace, I don't know if this job's worth the fight anymore," he said. "I hate it as much as I thought I would, and it seems the rest of the world hates me having it an equal amount."

Her heart sank. So the rumors *were* true: he was considering quitting. Time to turn the focus to The Mission.

"I don't know who you're talking to," she said. "Everyone I talk to thinks you're doing a fine job."

"Except you."

She gasped. That stung more than she cared to admit. "Yes, I do," she said. "Whatever gave you that idea?"

He shrugged again. "The fact that you kicked me out of the house for doing my job and arresting your father," he said. She started to protest, but he continued on. "I think that's actually kind of fair," he said. "I mean, if you were sheriff and you arrested Pappy, I'd probably be mad too. Nobody likes the bearer of bad news."

Her stomach tightened, boiling in turmoil. Damn him. Why did he have to make this so hard? "Lehigh," she said, "you're right that I'm unhappy about that. But I've had time to reflect on things, and, well, I have to admit, things kind of looked bad for him. My dad's no angel, and you have a job to do."

He blinked, but said nothing.

"I still think he's innocent," she said. "But he's not helping his cause one bit with his silly shenanigans. You're not the only one who thinks he pulled the trigger."

"Actually, I don't think that at all. I'm not sure I ever did."

She felt her muscles relax, her jaw loosen. When had she started gritting her teeth? A warm feeling passed over her. "So you really do believe."

He smiled, a wan smile. "I don't know what I believe, except that this job is ruining my life. Starting with my marriage and family. Weirdos making threats, people burning down my house—and it don't take a genius to figure out which is more important. Hint: it ain't the job."

More warmth. Her stomach felt like jelly. "Lehigh, that's very sweet. Really. But I don't think you should quit."

"Why not?"

Their food arrived amidst a clatter of plates and silverware, refills of water glasses and meaningless platitudes from the waitress. After the intrusion ended—finally—Stacy stole a French fry from Lehigh's plate and dipped it in ketchup. "Because you're my father's best hope," she said, then hung her head. "I'm sorry. That's so selfish of me. It's not just about my father." She raised her eyes again and met his, staring at her with smoldering intensity. "Lehigh, you're the best hope for everyone around here. The entire county needs you in this job to stand up to the Elliott Jacksons and Ray Fergusons of the world. To weed out the deputies like DuPont and Bobby Wills, the crooked good-old-boys that make everyone's lives miserable. Like they used to do to you." She reached across the table, resisted stealing another French fry, and grasped his wrist. "Please, Lehigh. Stay on the job. *Finish* the job. The one you set out to do." She held his gaze in hers, holding back her tears.

"Even though it's messing up our lives? Our marriage? Your own personal safety?"

She slid her hand down into his palm, intertwining her fingers with his. "I'm a big girl, Lehigh. And right now, I need you to do the big boy's job of staying on as sheriff. We all do. No matter what that means for *us*." She blinked, and the tears fell. Dammit! She glanced around, looking for her napkin, and found it, in Lehigh's hand, dabbing the tears away from her cheeks. She met his gaze, intending to thank him. But no words would form once she saw his face, and the tears that wet his own cheeks.

"Stacy," he said in a quiet voice, "I'd rather have you."

***

Long before they got back to eating, their food got cold, or at least Lehigh's did. Stacy's chicken Caesar started out cold anyway. They each took a few bites in silence, but he found it difficult to chew and swallow with the giant lump lodged in his throat.

"How will you decide?" she asked at last, a moment before he asked her about the vet clinic, when the silence grew too heavy to bear.

He bit his lip, holding his burger halfway between his plate and mouth. "Desmond Montgomery is taking an informal poll. If six out of ten say stay, I'll stay." He took a bite of the cold sandwich and chewed. The cold grease and hardening cheese nearly gagged him.

"You'll stay if a majority of random strangers ask you to, but not if I do?" Stacy's fork clattered onto her plate, and she fished it out with a herky-jerky motion and wiped it with her napkin.

"There ain't six people in this county that'd trust me with their fishing rod, much less with two dozen armed deputies," he said. "I'm pretty sure I know how this will go."

"You're wrong. You're more popular than you know."

"Then, I might have to disappoint a few people," he said. "Because my top priority right now is getting right with you. Which I can't do while wearing this badge." He tapped the star pinned to his chest, and thought about ripping it off on the spot. Something—the look on her face, perhaps—stopped him.

"If you quit," she said, "and let Dwayne Latner win the election, there will never be a fair investigation in this town. It'll go right back to the bad old days of having people like Buck Summers and Dale DuPont running wild, arresting anyone they don't like. Is that what you want?"

Lehigh shrugged. "We survived it for thirty-eight years. We can survive it a little longer."

"My father can't!" Her shrill cry split the noisy din of the dining room, which went suddenly quiet. She sat still as a statue for several moments, as if she could feel the dozens of eyes in the restaurant boring in on her. She lowered her head and her voice and picked at her salad. "What I mean is…Lehigh, you're his only hope, and if they can pin a crime like this on a powerful politician like him, what will happen to the rest of us? What hope do *we* have?"

He shook his head. George damned Lindsey damned McBride. Seemed like all of the trouble in his life stemmed from that man's presence in his life, one way or the other. "Is this about the little people of the county, or the big cheeses that always stepped on the little people, who happen to be blood relations?" he said through his teeth. "Because I don't recall George ever doing much of anything for me. Nothing good, anyway."

"He raised thousands of dollars for your campaign, introduced you to people—"

"For a job I don't want!" he hissed. "Don't you get it, Stacy? I don't want to be sheriff anymore!"

Dammit if it didn't go quiet just in time for that outburst, too. Well, so what? He meant it. He ate another cold French fry.

"So you're just going to quit, and let them win?" She jabbed her fork into a pile of lettuce.

"In case you haven't noticed, they hold all the cards, and all the chips," Lehigh said. "I've got a losing hand, or maybe no hand at all. The game is stacked against me. Why fight it?"

"Because you're a fighter, Lehigh," she said. "That's what I think of when I think of you—a man who fights for what's right, no matter what the odds and no matter what the cost. Or am I wrong about you?"

"I get into too many fights," he said, but her words stung, for some reason. Damn it!

"You have to keep fighting," she said. "One more fight, Lehigh. Fight for yourself, fight for my father, fight for whatever reason you can think of. But don't let those bastards win. Please?"

He stared at her, taking deep breaths, confused. Why couldn't she see that these fights were destroying them? That he had to stop fighting in order for them to have a chance? He exhaled all of his air, took one more deep breath. "Sometimes the bad guys win, Stacy. That's just how it is."

"Lehigh Carter." She leaned over the table and pointed a finger at his face. "If you quit now—if you leave my father's fate in their crooked hands—then you're quitting on me, and quitting on us. And if you quit on me, then we're done. All. Done."

She pushed her way out of the booth and ran from the restaurant, brushing away tears.

***

Lehigh somehow dragged himself back to his office, cursing his situation with every moment of his short drive. Stacy flat-out shocked him with her passionate plea for him to try to carry on the fight. His inability to convince her that the sheriff's job was the main problem between them—and a very fixable one, with an exit strategy that would make everyone happy—frustrated him. He walked past Julia's desk in as foul a mood as he'd been in for some time and almost didn't notice her waving at him.

"Sheriff!" she said in a hoarse whisper. "Ben Wright is asking for you. Wants you to come see him right away."

"I ain't got time," he said, growling. "I gotta go wipe this huge target off my back."

"It won't take you long." She smothered the microphone of her headset with one hand. "He's in jail."

"Jail? What the hell for?"

"Dale DuPont booked him last night on a dewey," she said. "Which I think means driving while under the—"

"I know what it means," he said. "Where's Dale now?"

She shrugged. "Back on patrol, I guess."

He spun on his heel and headed toward the incarceration unit. "Get him back in here. Now!"

He slid his security ID through the scanner and kicked the heavy metal doors as they swung open into the short hallway of jail cells. He ignored the first few inmates, men arrested months before and still awaiting trial, and checked the first cell he last knew to be vacant. Three cowboys he recognized from The

Roadhouse jeered back at him, and he moved on, past Paul van Paten, Stacy's ex-fiancé, and reached the final pair of cells at the end. One was full of brown boxes—he recognized them as archived storage from the case files. He shook his head in dismay. He'd told Roscoe to remove those a week ago.

But that left only one cell.

He turned and spied the white-haired man, seated and bent over on his cot, the former sheriff of Mt. Hood County, Buck Summers. Across the cell, on a bare mattress tucked into a corner, lay the dark, husky form of Ben Wright.

He unlocked the cell door and pulled it shut behind him, per protocol, and grunted a hello to the former sheriff. No response. He touched Ben's shoulder, then shook him awake.

"Sh-sheriff?" Ben said, sitting up and rubbing his eyes. "What are you doing here?"

"I was about to ask you the same question," Lehigh said. "Want to talk about it?"

"I was walking home from The Roadhouse last night, and—"

"Wait, you said you were walking?" Lehigh sat next to him. "How the heck did you get booked on a dewey, then?"

"A what?" Ben shook his head in confusion. "Mr. Carter, the bank repo'd my car two months ago. I *never* drive." He rubbed his head, then screamed in pain. "Dammit! Ow, that hurts!"

"What hurts?"

"My head. Damn, it feels like someone pounded me with a baseball bat."

Lehigh looked closer at the man's head, shook his head. "More like a billy club. Okay, Ben, let's get you out of here." He helped Ben up, unlocked the cell door, and guided him back to his office.

"Get a medic in here," he said to Julia as he passed her. He sat Ben in a chair, wet a wad of paper towels he found in his desk, and dabbed at the cut that bled into Ben's tight curls.

"Do you remember what happened?" he asked.

"Like I said, I was walking home. A cop car screeches to a stop right in front of me, and that DuPont guy gets out, starts giving me grief, saying there had been suspicious activity and what did I know about it."

"What kind of suspicious activity?"

Ben shook his head. "He didn't say. Just tried to get me to 'confess.' Then another car comes, and stops, and drives kind of into the drainage ditch. On purpose, I think."

"Why?"

Ben dabbed the makeshift bandage against his head. "What was really weird was, the driver gets out—it's another deputy. He had three stripes. Name began with a P."

"Peters?"

"That's it. Next thing I know, they're pushing me and yelling at me, like they want me to fight back. They tell me stuff like, 'You been drinking, *boy?*' Which I admit, I had been, but so what?"

"Then they hit you?"

Ben winced and pulled the bandage away from his head. "I guess. Next thing I know, I wake up next to that old white dude."

"Dammit. Look, Ben, I'm sorry. I'll make sure there's an investigation."

"That's what the old white dude told me you'd say."

"The one in the cell with you?" Lehigh fetched him a new wad of wet paper towels.

"Yeah. He's something else, that guy." He smiled a little. "He don't like you much."

"No, I don't suppose he does. Let me see that cut." Lehigh looked closer at the injured area. His stomach heaved a bit. "You're going to need stitches. Dammit!"

"I'll be all right. Hey, you'll want to watch out for that old white dude. He said something about how he was gonna get his last laugh at you."

"Yeah? How?"

Ben winced again when Lehigh placed some dry towels on the wound. "Said he's got friends on the force, still working for him."

Lehigh froze. "Working for him?"

"Yeah. Like, telling him things. When they bring him lunch and stuff."

Lehigh squatted down to eye level with Ben. "Did he say who they were?"

Ben shook his head. "Naw. But he seems to know everybody here."

Lehigh shook his head. "That he does, Ben. That he does."

Chapter Thirty-Six

Lehigh drove Ben to the local ambulatory care clinic, where a doctor sewed up his head wound and checked him for a concussion. He spent the next hour catching up Jim Wadsworth on the new developments over coffee at Dot's.

"I had all charges dropped against him," Wadsworth said. "He's free to go, once they're done stitching him up."

"*All* charges?" Lehigh asked. "I thought it was just drunk driving."

Wadsworth shook his head, a glum expression on his face. "DuPont piled on with an assault-against-an-officer and resisting arrest. When I find him, he's got a lot of explaining to do."

"Any luck with that?"

Wadsworth shook his head again. "Nope. He's gone AWOL. Wills and DuPont, too. Looks like all of them have been in on this thing all along."

"That explains a lot," Lehigh said. "I'd been looking for only one culprit. It didn't occur to me that they'd conspire on this."

After mapping out a search strategy with Wadsworth, Lehigh swung back by the clinic to drive Ben home. He passed at least two billboards displaying Dwayne Latner's long, clean-cut face and innocuous slogans like "Experienced and Professional." He nearly vomited.

"I sure appreciate you guys helping me out," Ben said once they were back on the road. "I thought I'd be in jail for weeks again."

"Again?"

Ben nodded. "Last time they kind of forgot about me for a month or so. I lost my job, my apartment—I thought about leaving town. But that's what they wanted, right? So I stayed. I'm a stubborn old coot, I guess." He grinned. "Ironic, isn't it, that they shacked me up with Buck Summers. Which would've been fine, if he'd have just let me sleep. But that old fart, all he does is talk, talk, talk." He laughed to himself and gazed out the window.

"What did he talk about?" Lehigh said. "Anything I should know?"

"He didn't have anything nice to say about you, if that's what you mean," Ben said. "He said you've been nothing but a pain in his backside for a year or more now. Him and his friends, that is."

Lehigh's ears perked up. "What friends? Any in particular?"

"Well, your father-in-law, for one," Ben said. "I guess those guys go back a long ways. Ran some campaigns together, stuff like that. But then George went his own way and left Buck behind, kind of a double-cross, according to Buck. But I'm sure this is all old news to you, right?"

Lehigh shook his head in awe. "Actually, no," he said. "He only recently became my father-in-law, and before that, we almost never talked. He didn't like me much. In fact, we kind of had a few run-ins of our own." Anger rose in him, thinking of his burned-down house. He'd never been able to pin it on George, or even his lackeys. For some reason the sheriff had never uncovered any convincing evidence.

For some reason, indeed.

"What else did he say?" Lehigh asked after a few quiet moments. He pulled up and parked in front of Ben's home, a tiny one-room apartment on the far end of the strip.

"He says you must really got it in for the Rev," Ben said. "All the hard time you're giving him."

"*I'm* giving *him*?" Lehigh laughed. "I think he's looking in the wrong end of the telescope."

"Buck says you're fighting the Rev hard on this whole Ev Downey thing," Ben said, his hand resting on the truck's door latch. "Holding back evidence, stuff like that. It's why he's been helping him out, I guess. They're old pals, so Buck's using his connections to all the uniforms to leak stuff out to him through his lawyer. He figures the Rev will go easy on him when his case goes to trial. Makes sense to me, you know? But, hey, you're the sheriff. You're on top of all this already, right?"

"Right," Lehigh said, realization dawning. Ben thanked him for the ride and shuffled up the walk to his apartment.

Lehigh sat behind the wheel of the truck, engine off, thinking. Of course Buck was the linchpin behind the whole situation. After everything went south between them, Buck had tried to pin his murder of Jared Barkley on Stacy, who meant the world to George. Of course that didn't work, and now he took new aim at George himself—leaking information to Ferguson, and working hard to frame George, his old political pal-turned-enemy.

But if George didn't kill Everett Downey, who did? Buck couldn't have done it, at least not alone, since he was in jail at the time. But, as Ben had revealed, he still had lots of friends on the outside—and on the inside. All of them had access to guns…and the evidence.

***

"Hello, Buck."

The former sheriff took a moment to respond, and Lehigh thought he might be asleep. But the white mane tipped back, moving as slow as a glacier, and his eyes opened to reveal just a sliver of white on each side of his bright blue irises. He stared at Lehigh through the bars, still seated on his cot. He might not have moved since Lehigh released Ben from his cell hours before.

"Carter." Summers spat the word out like an epithet. "To what do I owe the pleasure of this visit? Is it dinner time already?"

"Got a question for you."

Buck sneered and shook his head. "What kind of question? The I-should-get-my-lawyer sort of question, or should-I-draw-to-an-inside-straight sort of question?"

Lehigh smiled. "Maybe a little of both."

Summers spat for real this time, his effluent landing an inch from the drain in the center of the floor. "Hasn't anyone taught you how to do this job yet, Carter? *Never* tell a prisoner he needs his lawyer. Consider that my answer to your inside straight question." He closed his eyes and lay down on the cot.

Lehigh slid the key into the lock, slid open the door, and stepped inside, locking the door behind him. Buck remained prostate on the bed, seemingly unconcerned. Lehigh sat on the cot across from him. "It ain't gonna work, Buck."

Summers turned his head an inch toward Lehigh, his eyes opened to slits again. "What ain't?"

"You're not running me out of this job. Not you, not Jackson, not the Rev. I ain't going anywhere, at least until the voters get their say in November."

Buck hissed out a laugh between his teeth. "Suit yourself."

"And as long as I'm here, so are you."

Buck shrugged. "I've reached my peace with that."

"Have you reached your peace with letting the Rev walk while he sells you down the river for his crimes?" Lehigh held his breath. He had no proof of their collaboration, neither on the leak, nor Jared Barkley's murder, nor any of their past shenanigans against him. But he trusted his gut. Since his chat with Ben earlier that day, his gut had convinced him they all were in cahoots on at least some part of it—and that he knew about the rest.

Buck lay still, as if he'd stopped breathing, for a minute or more. Finally his chest lifted, as if he'd taken a deep, noiseless breath. "You're fishing," he said.

"Wish I was," Lehigh said. "And I wish, both literally and metaphorically, that the fish were biting right about now."

"Yeah, good luck on that, too." Buck closed his eyes and folded his hands across his voluminous belly.

"Okay, just thought I'd ask. Personally, it don't matter to me which one of you goes down for this, as long as someone does. Well, that's not *entirely* true. It seems a pity that you'd have to take the fall for a guy as arrogant as Ray Ferguson, who never misses a chance to trash-talk the sheriff's office. And not just on

TV, either. Why, just the other day—"

"I hate that son of a *bitch*!" Buck bolted upright in his cot, breathing hard, glaring at Lehigh with wide-open eyes. "Him and his Gospel verses, always spouting this holier-than-thou crap. I've never seen such a hypocrite!"

Lehigh leaned back, forced by the power of Buck's anger. He'd hoped to trigger something, but hadn't prepared himself for this sudden explosion. "What's that? The Rev's a church-going man, Buck. My maw tells me he's in the front pew, every Sunday, and is *quite* generous with his contributions."

"Generous to a fault, you mean. With his salary he could buy the damned church and feed half the poor folk in this here county without sacrificing a single steak dinner himself. Church-going man, my eye. He does it for one reason and one reason only: to be seen." Buck jabbed a thick finger at Lehigh to punctuate his words.

"Huh. I wouldn't have guessed it. Maw says—"

"Never mind what your foolish maw says! Ferguson's a liar and a cheating back-stabber, is what he is. Why he—" Buck stopped, as if catching himself, and closed his mouth tight.

"Here's the thing, Buck," Lehigh said. "The Rev's in a position to make other people pay for not only their mistakes, but his own, too. Now, I'm not saying you two have any sort of deal going—I'm not in a position to know. But what I do know is, the Rev always seems to come out of these scrapes looking awfully clean, you know what I'm saying? And the people around him, not so much." Lehigh stood. "But you, Buck, you're a man of honor and well-earned pride, and nobody expects you to utter so much as one cross word about your fellow man. No, sir, it's well-known around here, you'd fall on your sword for your loyal compatriots, even if they wouldn't do the same for you. In fact, people count on it. I do, anyway." He edged toward the door and jingled the keys, taking his time putting the key in the slot.

"*Damn* him!" The cot creaked behind Lehigh, and he spun, fearing the worst. But Buck had moved away from him, pacing in the deepest recesses of the cell. "Damn, damn, damn!"

Lehigh let him stew a minute or two, then asked in a soft voice, "When's the last time the Rev has sent word about your case? Days? Weeks?"

Buck muttered under his breath, then glared at Lehigh. "What has he told you?" he asked in a growl.

"About you? Not much. No, I take that back. He's never mentioned you once." Lehigh leaned back against the bars of the cell door. "I'd say you're not much on his mind, Buck."

Summers continued pacing and muttering. Lehigh couldn't make out the words. He tried a different tack. "The Rev's been depending on your little network to get him information from the deputies—don't deny it, there's no point," Lehigh said as Summers tried to interrupt. "Anyway, so far as I know, it ain't illegal for *you* to do that. Them, that's another matter. And we've shut them down, Buck. The flow is stopped. Those three boys are likely to be filling up the next cell before dinnertime, and your ability to feed the Rev what he needs will be all over and done with."

Buck's protests faded, and his shoulders sagged. "*All three* of them?" Sadness tinged the edge of his voice.

"Yep. Party's over." Inside, Lehigh celebrated. He'd gambled, revealing that, and he hoped his worries about the leak could end. Of course, he still had no idea where Wills, Peters, and DuPont had gone. Still, he pressed on. "So what's the Rev gonna do with you when that happens? You think he'll keep protecting you, once you can't help him anymore?"

Buck plopped back down onto the bed, defeated. Lehigh waited.

"That son of a bitch," Buck said. Lehigh said nothing. Waited. Watched his prisoner, hoping. Buck took a deep breath, let it out slowly, drew in another. Repeated that a few times, occasionally clenching and unclenching his fists. Finally he looked up at Lehigh. "All right," he said.

"All right, what, specifically?" Lehigh asked, in as casual a voice as he could muster.

"All right, I'll cooperate," Buck said. "I'll tell you what I know about the Rev, the leaks, the conspiracy, all of it. I'm not saying I know a lot, but—damn him! I know enough to take him down a notch or two." He fumed for a moment, then a tiny smile creased his face. "Yeah, I know plenty. I ain't taking this fall for him." He pointed again at Lehigh. "I'm gonna need some protection from you. And I need to speak with my lawyer. She'll know what to do."

"She?" Lehigh caught his breath. There weren't many female criminal defense attorneys in the area. "Who's your lawyer?"

Buck grinned. "You ain't gonna believe it."

***

Back in his office, Lehigh barely had time to sit before his phone buzzed. "Visitors," Julia said. "Important ones."

Lehigh sighed. Everyone considered themselves important when meeting with their elected officials. "Send them in."

The tall, slender frame of Desmond Mitchell appeared at his door. "Greetings, Sheriff," he said. "I have good news and bad news."

"Well, even having half the news be good is a welcome change of pace," Lehigh said, grinning. Then he remembered his wager with the commissioner and his smile faded. "Let's start with the good news," he said. "Just in case."

"I finished my little poll," Mitchell said. "Unfortunately, I only got around to asking seven people. That's the bad news."

Lehigh sank into his chair. "Let me guess. Five of 'em already said no to me staying on."

"Nope." Mitchell sat in Lehigh's guest chair, smiling.

"Then I guess I don't understand," Lehigh said. "By the way, I thought my assistant said I had visitors—plural. Where are the others?"

"I thought you should meet the people I spoke with," the commissioner said. "Come on in, folks!"

A short parade of Clarkesville residents filed in through the door. His old high school teammate, Phil Reardon, entered first. "Hey, Lehigh," he said. "Nice digs."

"Thanks," he said. "So, you were one of the people surveyed?"

"Yup," Phil said. "I gave you a big thumbs-up." He stood aside, and a short, older woman scooted in behind him.

"Who's that behind you—? *Dot?*" Lehigh stood and his mouth gaped in disbelief. He'd never seen the tiny, bushy-haired matron outside her cafe before.

"Sheriff, if you think you're going anywhere, you better think twice," she said. "We need you."

Shuffling in behind Dot he spied the athletic figure of a young man with short, wavy dark curls. The face and the identity of the man didn't register at first. Then, suddenly, it did.

"Jackson Pitt?" Lehigh's voice squeaked in surprise.

"Sheriff," the young man said, "I'm real sorry for the way I treated you at the hotel. My uncle Elliott put me up to it, and, well, he can be a real jerk sometimes."

"Your uncle's not going to be too pleased if he learns you support me," Lehigh said.

Jackson laughed. "He's never happy with me. And I'm just fine with that."

Next to Pitt stood a thin, forty-something woman covered with tattoos and piercings who looked desperate for a smoke. "Name's Charlotte, but you can call me Charlie," she said. "I work at Montgomery's Gentlemen's Club—Ev Downey's place. And I tell you what. Every one of the slick son-of-a-so-and-so's that rant and rave on County Council about closing down our place has been in there getting lap dances at least twice, and some are regulars. And that includes this boy's uncle." She put an arm around Jackson. The boy blushed, but didn't push away her embrace. She sneered. "And that holier-than-thou prosecutor, wagging his finger at everyone else. He's as sleazy as the next guy."

The next citizen in the room, a red-haired woman with oversized, blue-framed glasses, wore a low-cut dress that looked straight out of the 1950s. "My name's Ginger Michaels," she said. She paused and focused her attention on Lehigh. "Until two days ago, I worked for Ray Ferguson."

"And now?" Lehigh asked, the hairs on his arm raised.

She shrugged. "I quit. He treated me, and all the women in

the D.A.'s office, like sex objects. And his ethics…lower than low. Mr. Carter, I'm here to help you beat him."

Relief and gratitude washed over Lehigh. "I'm honored to have your support," he said. "I can't offer you a job or anything, but—"

"I understand," she said. "Don't worry. I've got some prospects all lined up. I even have an interview next week with a woman named Samantha Pullen. Do you know her?"

Lehigh grinned. "Well enough to help you with a recommendation," he said. "She represented me against the county a few months ago." He turned to Mitchell. "That's five. You said you had seven. Where are the others?"

A bustle of activity sounded outside the door, and a small group of uniformed deputies filled the room. Ted Roscoe, Jim Wadsworth, Ruby MacArthur, and Martin Lightfoot stood abreast, arm-in-arm, at attention. "We're here in solidarity with you, Sheriff," Ruby said, and the others all nodded. "Please stay on and continue the work you're doing. It's important!"

Lehigh grinned and shook a finger at Desmond Mitchell. "No fair asking people I hired," he said. "You can't exactly call them random citizens."

"I wasn't counting them," Mitchell said. He called out to the hallway. "Doctor?"

County Coroner Herman Doskey shuffled in and pushed between the wall of deputies. "You need to stay on, Carter," Doskey said. "The truth must come out."

"Does that mean that what we talked about—"

"Yup," Doskey said. "And I'll testify to that, no matter what that means for my retirement."

Lehigh found it difficult to speak. The group in front of him represented as broad a cross-section of the community as he could imagine, other than Ben Wright, who was probably still recovering from his injuries. Besides Phil Reardon and his deputies, he wouldn't have considered many of them allies. "Thank you all," he said, choking on his words. "Your support means the world to me."

"We've got one more, if you're ready." Desmond winked at

Lehigh. "I saved the best for last."

"I can't imagine," Lehigh said. "This is already a pretty impressive group."

He looked to the doorway, and the crowd blocking his view parted, just in time to reveal a wiry, silver-haired man in overalls, holding the hand of a tiny stick figure with a halo of gray hair tied back behind her pastel-blue housedress.

"Make that two more," Desmond said.

"Pappy?" Lehigh's jaw dropped. "*Maw?* What are you two doing in downtown Clarkesville?"

"Desmond says you're thinking about quitting," Pappy said. Maw's face twisted like she'd just bitten into a lemon, and she shook her head in disapproval.

"Well, I—"

"Carters don't quit," Pappy said, and spit tobacco into the trash can.

Lehigh opened his mouth to reply, but words failed him. Shame washed over him, pressing him into his chair. In all of his deliberations about whether to stay on the job, he'd never considered how it would disappoint his parents. They despised politics and government, and rarely ventured off their own remote property. The idea that they'd even pay attention to something like this came as a complete surprise.

"That's dirty pool, Desmond, bringing in my parents," he said.

"I admit, it's not exactly a random sampling of county voters," Desmond said with a sly smile. "But they're the ones that matter most, or ought to. Don't you agree?"

Lehigh glanced from face to face, settling finally on the hopeful, silent expression on his parents' faces. He nodded. "They are to me." He stood and opened his arms wide. "If you'll have me, folks," he said, "I guess I'll stay on and fight the good fight."

The room erupted into cheers.

Chapter Thirty-Seven

Lehigh greeted the pretty, blonde-haired attorney with a wary handshake, vowing not to let her bright blue eyes, slender 5'6" frame, and jury-wowing smile overwhelm him as she had the first time they'd met. But Samantha Pullen enveloped his hand in both of hers, smiling ear to ear. "Lehigh, we're way past formalities, aren't we?" She pulled him in for a brief hug and whispered, "Surprised?"

"I have to admit, I am," he said. "When Buck told me he'd switched lawyers, I wasn't prepared to be talking to the one who kept me out of jail when *he* was sheriff."

"Oh, the irony," she said. "I hope you understand, under the circumstances, I can't represent you in your obstruction case. But I'm happy to give you a referral."

He waved her off. "I'll find someone…if I'm still around on Monday." He opted not to express his doubts, given the circumstances.

Her jury-wowing smile faded. "Is Detective Wadsworth joining us?"

"Sorry I'm late," Wadsworth said, entering the meeting room in a frenzied rush. He carried his briefcase in one hand and, in the other, a cardboard take-out tray with three coffees. He handed one to Lehigh and one to Sam. "Greetings, counselor."

"Detective." They sat across from him at the black laminate-top table, avoiding eye contact.

Lehigh studied both of them, arms crossed. "Is there something I should know about you two before we begin?"

Wadsworth cleared his throat and glanced at Sam, head bowed. "We're fine."

Sam chuckled. "What the detective isn't telling you, Lehigh, is that we've tangled a few times in court before. I'm afraid I may have been a little aggressive cross-examining Mr. Wadsworth on occasion. If I have crossed any lines, Detective, I apologize."

"No, no." Wadsworth waved her off. "You're a strong advocate for your clients. I expect nothing less." He busied himself with pulling his paperwork out of his briefcase.

"Do either of you mind me taping this conversation?" Sam asked, starting a tape recorder.

"Shouldn't you ask before you begin recording?" Lehigh was beginning to understand why other lawyers didn't like arguing cases opposite her.

Sam paused the recorder. "Before we begin," she said, "I have to say, it's a bit unusual not to have the prosecutor in the case present for these negotiations. I understand why," she added before Lehigh could respond, "given the sensitivity of the information he has to share, but we should all understand, your ability to influence the court on my client's behalf is quite limited."

"Are you backing out already?" Wadsworth said. "Because I'm okay with letting him rot."

"No, no," Sam said. "We're still willing to discuss a deal with you. But please understand our caution—and hence, this." She tapped the recorder.

Lehigh nodded and signaled a "cool down" message to Wadsworth. "We're good with it."

"Very well," she said. "My client faces charges of conspiracy, murder one, obstruction of justice, assault, hell, half the penal code. We want all felony charges dropped—"

"Wait, wait," Wadsworth said. "We don't even know what you've got yet."

"And you won't, unless you keep Buck Summers out of prison," she said. "That's our bottom line. He can't end up in a prison yard with the dozens of men he's helped put away for the past decade or so. You know what would happen to him."

"Then he'd better have something good and solid," Wadsworth said. "No con jobs, Counselor!"

"Easy, Jim," Lehigh said. "Have some coffee." He uncapped his and waited for the detective to follow suit. Sam did likewise and toasted them before taking a sip.

"Now, why don't you give us a flavor of what you've got," Lehigh said. "No details, just the fly-over."

Sam scanned a one-page bullet-point outline in front of her. "We can name the inside leaks, with specifics about who gave what restricted information to whom." She zeroed her gaze in on Lehigh. "Including certain high-ranking officials in the D.A.'s office."

"Ferguson himself?"

She smiled. "No names yet, but it reaches that level in the department."

"What about the case itself?" Wadsworth said. "Downey's murder. Any dope on that?"

Sam swiveled to face Wadsworth. "My client has been in jail since long before Everett Downey lost his life," she said, "but, in return for immunity, he'll testify regarding a conspiracy to suppress and tamper with evidence in the case. It's all part of the same package."

"With names?" Lehigh asked. Sam nodded. "Can't hear that on tape," Lehigh said with a smile.

Sam chuckled and waved a polished fingernail at him. "You learn fast. Yes, with names. And, gentlemen, it's not an eyewitness, and it's not direct evidence at all, but once you hear what he has to say, I believe it will set you on the right path for discovering who's *really* guilty of murder in Mt. Hood County."

"If you know who killed Downey, why haven't you come forward sooner?" Wadsworth asked, near the point of exploding.

"*I don't* know who killed him." Sam sipped her coffee. "My client doesn't claim to know either. But if you follow the leads he gives you, I have a strong feeling *you'll* know very soon." She paused the recorder. "And gentlemen, it's not the man Ray

Ferguson arrested for the crime. That much I *do* know."

Lehigh glanced at Wadsworth, and the two men nodded. He pointed at the recorder, and Sam turned it back on.

"Counselor," he said, "to the extent this is within my power as sheriff of Mt. Hood County, I think we've got a deal."

***

Stacy squinted at her computer screen, her eyes tired from a full day of catching up on billing and correspondence with her growing clientele of pet lovers in Mt. Hood County. Her head pounded, and she hated to admit it, but her vision had gone a bit blurry lately. She might have to break down and make an appointment for an eye exam.

A knock on her door broke her concentration, and she tore her eyes away. She usually hated interruptions, but a never-ending run of animal emergencies had trained her to prepare for them at any time. Given how her head felt at that moment, she welcomed this one. "Come in," she called out and clicked *Save Transaction* on her screen.

The familiar face that entered was not the one she expected. Charlie, the slender forty-something bartender from Downey's, slipped inside and shut the door behind her. She wore jeans and a conservative blouse that covered most of her tattoos, with a "Carter for Sheriff" button pinned to the lapel. "Nice place you got here," she said. She smiled and took a seat.

Stacy's jaw dropped. "What are you doing here?" she stammered after a moment.

"I thought that was you at the club," Charlie said with an easy grin. "That red wig didn't fool me one bit. I guess you don't remember me, do you, *Bridget*?"

"I don't understand," Stacy said. A dizzy wave passed over her and she slumped in her seat.

Charlie chuckled and inspected her long fingernails, painted with intricate and varied designs over a red lacquer base. "I don't look the same as when we first met sixteen years ago, but you ain't changed a bit," she said. "Maybe if I give you a clue. Purple hair, lots of beads, pussycat outfit?"

Stacy gasped. "Kitty?"

Charlie nodded and grinned. "Dropped my stage name when I moved to bartending, of course. That and the hair coloring. And now…" Her voice took on a bitter tone. "Well, I guess I'll need a whole new gig."

Stacy's heart skipped a beat. "Wait. You got fired? After working there, what, fifteen years?"

"Eighteen. And yes, I am now officially unemployed. Without a dime of severance, either!" She grew animated, poking her finger on Stacy's desk. "But trust me, they're gonna pay. Are they *ever* gonna pay."

"I'm sorry to hear it," Stacy said, "but I don't understand why you came here. How can I help you?"

"You can help me by letting me help you," Charlie said in a quiet voice. "You came in asking around about whether we'd seen your daddy. Oh, cut it out, I knew that's what you were up to from the first minute you walked in the door. At the time I wanted to protect my job, so I pretended to know nothing. But honey, I ain't got no job to protect no more, so guess what?"

Stacy's heart skipped a beat. "You saw him that night?"

"Saw him? Ha! I served him all night long," Charlie said with a harsh bark of a laugh. "Except for the half-hour or so he went back with—um, are you sure you want to know all the details?"

Stacy swallowed hard, unable to speak. Half of her did want to know, and half wanted to run for the hills. The half that wanted her father out of danger of prison won out. She nodded.

"He had a 'bonus room' session with Buttercup, that cute little blonde out of Texas." Charlie seemed to be enjoying telling this tale a little too much. "Buttercup's gone now, already back to Abilene for all I know, so good luck finding her. But I know who your daddy is—hell, everybody in this town does—and he was there, all right. From nine o'clock until well after midnight. I cashed him out at 12:45. I remember because he left me a $45 tip. I told him that he could stay until 12:99 if he wanted, but I don't think he got the joke."

"And Mr. Downey, when did he leave?" Stacy asked, working hard to take a breath.

"Long time before that," Charlie said. "Said he had to go meet someone out of town. Something about a deal he was working on."

Stacy's heart raced. Finally, a break for her father! If—

"Will–will you testify to this?" Stacy asked.

Charlie shrugged. "Why the hell not? It's not like I have a job to protect anymore."

Stacy's euphoria faded a bit. "Why did they fire you?" she asked in a quiet voice. "If you don't mind my asking."

Charlie threw up her hands. "They gave me some dumb reason that didn't make any sense, saying my till was way off, and accused me of sneaking drinks on the job," she said, spittle flying. "Which is total crap. I can't drink—I got kidney problems. And I make plenty enough on tips so I don't never have to steal. But it don't help arguing. If they want you gone, you're gone. They got all threatening, saying they'd press charges, even had that county prosecutor standing there, all threatening and mean. I figure, they go to all that trouble, best if I just walk away, you know what I'm saying?"

"Which prosecutor?" Stacy asked, now on full alert.

"That fella that's always quoting Bible verses on TV," Charlie said. "What's his name?"

"Ray Ferguson?" Stacy asked in a hushed voice.

"That's him!" Charlie said. "He shows up, and the next thing I know, they're escorting me out to my car. Them bastards!"

Stacy's jaw dropped yet again. "Charlie, I'm so sorry. I'm so glad you came here today."

"Yeah, well, time's getting short. Couple of those fat deputies came in again, the same ones that were there the night you worked. Started asking if I'd take a punch and pin it on the sheriff."

"They asked me that, too," Stacy said. "The night I worked."

"You should've said something to me," Charlie said. "Anyway, I kicked 'em out, told them never to come back." She paused. "On second thought, that might've been what got me fired. We *never* eighty-six a paying customer. Yup. That explains it all, now that I think about it."

"In more ways than you know!" Stacy said. "Will you excuse me a moment? I need to make a phone call." She had to get word of this to Lehigh—and her father's lawyers—fast.

***

The meeting room door opened. Lehigh stood, hat in hand, and counted off the army of lawyers that filed into the room. The Rev led the pack, of course, strutting like a horse that had just won the Kentucky Derby. Flanking him, the two black-suited, closed-mouthed attorneys that always seemed to hover in his shadow kept up their butt-kissing ways. A pair of younger pups, a man and a woman who both looked fresh out of law school, scurried to the far end of the meeting room and set out a series of folders and papers, as if setting up a war room for a big case.

"Sheriff," Ferguson said, "thank you for reaching out to me today. I hope we can reach a quick resolution on your case. I took the liberty of asking my staff to draw up some paperwork—"

"I ain't here to cut a deal." Lehigh waited for surprise and irritation to register on Ferguson's face, then pointed to the mountain of paperwork in the hands of the young aides, who froze in mid-sort. "I'm afraid you may have wasted their time."

"I don't understand," Ferguson said. "When you asked for the meeting, I understood your intention to be, how was it phrased? An 'end-game' of some sort. Did I misunderstand?"

"I was hoping we could find a solution that didn't involve a formal plea," Lehigh said. "One that saves face for everyone." He indicated the array of assistants, both senior and junior, with an open palm. "One that wouldn't require quite so many staff members to participate...?"

Ferguson sniffed and rubbed his chin. "I see. Well, I don't see any harm starting with a little informal chat. Ladies and gentlemen?" He nodded toward the door. The attorneys and assistants filed back out of the room, casting suspicious stares at Lehigh. He kept his gaze unfocused, not wanting to give anything away. Not to them. The shock of the "news" he wanted to share had to belong only to Raymond Ferguson.

"Mr. Ferguson," Lehigh said when they were alone and seated, "I want to be honest with you." He leaned forward, and Ferguson did the same. Lehigh could feel the excitement emanating from the prosecutor, could hear his quick breaths. "I have to confess, Raymond—can I call you Raymond?—I hate this damned job." He punctuated his words with a light tap of his open palm on the table.

Ferguson's lips curled into a brief smile, then he smothered it, putting on an expression of sympathy. "I could tell the stress and frustration have been building lately," he said. "We in the county have asked quite a bit of you."

"That's very gracious of you, Ray." He expected, and got, a look of pained consternation on Ferguson's face from the use of his familiar short name. "Before I go further—I hope I can trust you with some rather personal observations?"

After a pause, Ferguson coughed out a reply. "Of course, of course," he said with too much bluster. "We're speaking informally here. Off the record, as it were." Ferguson smiled, his oily pull-one-over-on-the-jury no-teeth smile that Lehigh had never trusted.

Lehigh nodded. "Good, good. Ray, when I signed on to be sheriff, I expected to preside over the usual parade of bar fights and speeding tickets we've always found in our quiet little town. I never thought I'd be investigating a *murder*, of all things. I mean, we hadn't had one in decades, then suddenly we get two, back to back. Who'd have thunk it?"

"It is unusual," Ferguson said. "I presume this preamble is leading us somewhere?"

Lehigh sighed, drawing out the moment. He wanted Ferguson overconfident but also impatient. "But then along comes Everett Downey. A successful businessman with many partners, employees, and customers. A man of the community. Suddenly, we find the poor man murdered."

"I don't know about him being a 'poor man' at all," Ferguson said. "Not only was he wealthy, but he had made at least one enemy that we can be sure of—the man who killed him."

"A damned shame," Lehigh said.

"Well, let's not go too overboard here," Ferguson said. "His businesses were not of the kind that build a community. Strip clubs, casinos, fly-by-night hotels—"

"All perfectly legal, whether we like it or not," Lehigh said. "I mean, I know you wanted me to shut them down, but the man stayed within the law, for the most part." He paused and looked Ferguson in the eye. "I mean, we never saw any of his dancers abused, or beaten up, or anything."

Ferguson started, but recovered quickly. "*Many* in the community—me among them—would have liked you to be far more aggressive in enforcement of the laws he did break," Ferguson said, and he actually sniffed. Out loud. Lehigh suppressed a laugh.

"Still, he had his friends," Lehigh said. "Look at all those investors who were lining up to back his new shopping center. A shopping center—a very respectable enterprise, wouldn't you say?"

"I wish I knew where this was headed," Ferguson said with an edge in his voice. He fidgeted in his seat and offered Lehigh a nervous smile. "Perhaps you could paint the bigger picture for me? With, shall we say, broader strokes?"

Lehigh drew in a deep breath and let it out quietly. Had he strung Ferguson along enough? The man had almost no patience. He dared not push him too much further. "It's like this, Ray," he said. "I'm in your way. Right? We can both agree to that. We can disagree over whether I ought to be, but it's clear, you've got the upper hand, and the people around here are behind you. Am I right?"

A victory smile creased Ferguson's face. "Well, I have some advantages," he said. "Experience, legal training, a crack staff. And of course, the evidence is on my side. I'm glad you can now see how this is all going to end."

"Oh, definitely," Lehigh said. "And I don't want to be crushed by it all, you know?"

"Understandably," Ferguson said, his tone congenial. Downright friendly, even.

"I'll be frank," Lehigh said. "I know you're tired of fighting me. And I'm tired of fighting you. But if I'm going to get out of your way, I'm going to need a soft landing of some kind. You know? Some sort of job to fall into. And I don't see myself going back to chopping down trees." He focused on Ferguson's eyes and got what he wanted: a glimmer of satisfaction. He'd appealed to Ferguson's prejudices and hit a bullseye.

"I understand," Ferguson said, "but I'm afraid I don't have anything appropriate to offer you. You're not an attorney, after all, and—"

"Oh, I'm not asking you to put me on your payroll," Lehigh said. "What I would like, though, is to be able to walk out of here with a clean slate. No prosecution hanging over my head, no accusations, no besmirching of my reputation. Folks out in the business world won't be so keen on hiring me if they think I'm in trouble with the law, you hear what I'm saying?"

Ferguson sat back, as if calculating. "You want me to drop the obstruction charges in exchange for you resigning. Is that it?"

Lehigh smiled. "Sounds like a fair deal to me."

Ferguson mulled it over a moment, but Lehigh could read victory in his eyes. As he suspected, this had been Ferguson's objective all along. "Well," Ferguson said after a moment, "there are some people who might object to you walking away scot-free after all of this. But I'm willing to stand up and take the heat on that, if it clears a path to a more cooperative relationship between our departments." He stood and extended his hand. "I'll have my assistants draw up the paperwork."

Lehigh ignored the offer of the handshake and pushed his chair away from the table. "Send it on over and I'll have my lawyer give it a read-through," he said, standing.

"Carter," Ferguson said, also standing. "Do we have a deal or don't we?"

Lehigh cocked his head. "Sounds like we do, but the devil's in the details, ain't it?" he said. "And like you said, you've got all that legal training and experience. So, just to be safe, let's let my attorney help me sort all that out, shall we?"

"Fair enough," Ferguson said, deflated. Irritation tinged the edge of his voice. "One more thing, though. What sort of job are you looking to land, once you're out of office?"

"Well," Lehigh said, "those investors I mentioned? They're looking into taking over some of Mr. Downey's properties. I thought I'd try my hand at doing some development. Sort of as a thank-you for all that Mr. Downey's done for us."

Ferguson paled. "You don't mean—"

"Yes," Lehigh said, suppressing a haughty laugh. He adjusted his hat and headed for the door, unable to suppress a childish grin. "They want to build a whole string of new strip clubs," he said, enjoying the shock on Ferguson's face, "and I'm going to help them."

Chapter Thirty-Eight

Lehigh hustled out of the county building and headed for his truck. He wished he could have stayed to enjoy Ferguson's apoplectic reaction more, but he needed to be ready when the Rev responded. He felt some guilt about his fibs, and he was shocked at how easily the prosecutor had swallowed his story about wanting to quit and build a bunch of strip clubs. But if his ploy didn't work, he might have to quit and find a new job anyway, giving the truth to the fiction after all. Now he had to wait and watch. Where Ferguson went next would tell him all he needed to know about whether or not he was in on the conspiracy, and with whom.

Ferguson did not disappoint. Lehigh had just started the engine when the prosecutor hurried outside, barking something into a cell phone. Moments later his county vehicle sprayed gravel against a half-dozen other cars, and he left a cloud of dust in his wake as he spun onto the highway.

Lehigh followed at a safe distance, allowing a few other vehicles to weave their way between them. Dozens of "Latner for Sheriff" signs filled the grassy median dividing the highway into downtown, and almost as many lay on the ground, as if someone had mowed them down. Like, he mused with a smile, county road crews when they mowed the grass. A few billboards sported Dwayne's face and campaign slogans, his laconic grin making him look half-stoned. A few lawn signs dotted the parking strip in front of local gas stations and banks. None appeared in the front lawns of private homes. He reminded himself to get his own signs ordered. He'd had no time to campaign since the Downey murder, and he'd lost his two key supporters—Stacy and George McBride—who'd handled things like ads and event scheduling for him.

Ferguson turned onto the main drag into town and parked in the cramped lot of Yang's, the restaurant where Lehigh had spotted Bobby Wills with Teresa McBride. Lehigh parked in the lot of a strip mall a half-block up the road and sauntered back to the restaurant. He peeked in the back window and spotted Ferguson at a table, still on his cell phone. A moment later, the white-haired balloon-shaped figure of Elliott Jackson slid into the booth across from him. A busboy trudged by with a cart full of dishes and grimaced at two more tables loaded with dirty dishes, one on either side of Ferguson and Jackson.

Lehigh slipped away from the window and found an open door in the rear of the building, revealing a kitchen bustling with energetic busboys, cooks, and dishwashers in T-shirts and white aprons.

"Who's in charge here?" he asked the first dishwasher, a teen-aged boy with dark hair. The boy pointed to a short, thin Asian man with straight gray-and-black flecked hair, chattering to his assistants in a language Lehigh guessed as being Cantonese. Lehigh strode over to the man and pointed to his badge.

"I need your help," he said, enunciating each word.

The man frowned at him. "I speak English, sheriff," he said. "My name's Bill Yang. What do you want?"

Lehigh reddened and cleared his throat. "I need one of your staff to listen in on one of your customer's conversations and tell me what they hear."

"Are you investigating a crime?" Yang asked with awe in his voice and a proud smile forming on his face. "Like on *CSI: Miami?*"

"Yes, and you'll have to be very discreet," Lehigh said. "Preferably the customer shouldn't realize they're being overheard. Can you help me out?"

"I can," said an Asian teenage girl in a white apron. "I always wanted to be a spy!"

Lehigh pulled her aside. "What's your name?"

"Kim Yang."

"My granddaughter," Bill Yang said. "Very smart girl."

"Kim," Lehigh said, "there are two men in a booth in the back of the restaurant, in between two dirty tables. Can you take your time clearing the dishes away and report back to me?"

"*Dāngrán*," she said, and grinned. "That's Cantonese for 'Of course.' Right, Grandpa?"

"Perfect!" Yang said. He turned to Lehigh. "I'm first-generation. My parents immigrated from Guangzhou when I was a kid. I make sure all of my family knows the native language and culture."

"Can you speak only in Cantonese out there?" Lehigh asked her.

"Enough to fake it," she said under her grandfather's reproachful glare.

"Twenty bucks," the old man said, pointing to himself and to Kim. "Each."

Lehigh sighed. "Deal." He'd pay twice that if they could find anything solid on either man.

Kim grinned. "Awesome! I need it for my college fund! I'm going to study criminology." She grabbed an empty bus cart and disappeared into the dining room.

"Bad guys, eh?" Yang asked while loading two plates with fried wontons. "Is it those guys who say all that crap about you on TV? If you ask me, those guys are the ones we should be putting in jail. Crooked and crazy, every last one of them!"

"Innocent until proven guilty," Lehigh said. "But if you're asking my opinion, yeah. They're bad."

"You go get 'em, sheriff!" the old man said. "I'm voting for you. Throw the rascals out!"

Ten minutes later, Kim returned with a cart laden with dishes. "They're still talking," she said. "I left a few dishes behind, so should I—"

"Go!" Yang yelled at her. "Nail those bums!" He grinned at Lehigh. "We'll earn our twenty bucks," he said. He offered Lehigh a wonton. "It's free," he said. "Try it, you'll like it."

"I already do," Lehigh said with a grin. "I bring my wife here once a month." He dipped one into a small bowl of sauce the cook slid over to him. His mood dimmed. He hadn't brought Stacy out to dinner in well over a month. Maybe if he cracked the Downey murder case—

The girl reappeared with a refilled bus cart and started to unload it. "Let someone else do that!" Yang said to her. "Come here and tell us what they said!"

"They said something about stopping a land deal of some kind," Kim said. "Nightclubs or something." She turned to Lehigh. "Are you Mr. Carter?"

"I am," Lehigh said. "Did they mention me?"

Her expression darkened. "Not in a good way," she said. "Mr. Carter, I think your life is in danger."

"Did they threaten him?" Yang asked.

She looked back and forth at the two men. "They said, and I quote, they were going to 'chop you to pieces and feed you to your dogs.' End quote."

"Let's hope they were speaking metaphorically," Lehigh said with a laugh he didn't feel. "Did they mention anyone else?"

She nodded. "They said their 'boys' would take care of you. I heard a few names. Wills and DuPont. They said you'd be 'out of their hair' by Monday. Does that mean what I think it does?"

Lehigh pulled two twenties out of his wallet and set them on the counter. "It means I've been blind as a mole, and that they've stopped being careful. Thanks for your help."

The girl eyed the money, then glanced at her boss. Neither took the bills. Finally the old man spoke. "You keep my share of the money, sheriff," he said. "Put it toward your campaign. Kim, you earned yours. Take it."

The girl shook her head. "My parents would never let me take that money." She stared at her shoes.

A waiter scooted into the kitchen and tossed a dollar bill and some loose change into a large open jar on the counter. A hand-written sticky label stuck to the jar read "TIPS—Kitchen staff." Lehigh stuffed the two twenties into the jar. "After you graduate college," he said to her with a wink, "look me up. I suspect I'll be needing some deputies by then."

"Do you want me to listen some more?" she said, as much to her boss as to Lehigh.

"You stay near them and continue to speak only in Cantonese," Yang said. He turned to Lehigh. "We're behind you, sheriff. So is everyone I know. We're tired of the way things have been done around here. We want you to stay. I understand if you don't want to, with everything these guys say about you all the time. But I hope you'll stick it out. I really do."

Lehigh looked around the kitchen. All of the staff, from busboys to cooks, stopped and watched him, waiting for an answer, it seemed.

His chest swelled with pride—and, at the same time, shame. How could he have ever considered quitting with all of these people depending on him and pulling for him? He owed them at least a fighting chance.

"Of course, I'll stick it out." He lowered his voice to a whisper. "But we don't need to let them know that, do we?"

The grins that graced the faces in the room told him everything he needed to know about whether he'd made the right choice.

***

"You got to help me, Mr. Ferguson," the young deputy said, his face a minefield of worry. "The sheriff's got an all-points bulletin out on Dale and me, and it's only a matter of time before he—"

"Keep your damned voice down!" Ferguson scanned the area for possible eavesdroppers. He'd agreed to meet with the young fool out of fear that he'd go rogue otherwise and jeopardize everything he'd worked so hard to build, but now he wished he'd kept his distance. They'd met in an old sports bar outside Twin Falls, a place called The Stadium, frequented by ruffians and cowboys who Ferguson doubted would ever recognize him, Wills, or pretty much anyone else from Clarkesville. Given the mid-afternoon hour and the high proportion of empty tables in the place, he felt confident in the privacy of the meeting, but no need to tempt fate.

"Sorry." Wills sucked down the remaining half of his bottle of light lager beer and wiped foam from his lips. "What are we gonna do, Mr. F? We need a plan!"

"We'll start with you calling me 'Mr. Ferguson,' not 'Mr. F' or—worse," he said with a growl. He sipped on a Diet Coke, or what passed for one at this sleazy establishment. He'd call it a cup of wet ice with brown food coloring. "And of course there's a plan. You only need to know your part of it. Anything else risks breakdown, and a failure of the entire investigation. That is something we cannot have. Do you understand?"

Bobby sucked at his empty beer bottle and slammed it on the table in frustration. "But things aren't really going according to plan. It was all supposed to be under cover, but now the sheriff knows everything, and he's trying to pin it all on me. What am I gonna do?" His voice disintegrated into a pathetic whine and he slouched deep into his seat, near tears.

"We each must be accountable for our own actions, Mr. Wills," Ferguson said. He knew he sounded condescending, but this nincompoop disgusted him. No—Raymond disgusted *himself*. He'd picked the wrong man for this job, and for that, he had to hold himself accountable.

But not yet.

"What does that mean?" Wills said, his voice breaking. "Does that mean I'm going to go to prison?"

"If Sheriff Carter gets his way," Ferguson said. "Is that what you want?"

"But you wouldn't let them prosecute me, would you?" Bobby said. "I mean, I was trying to help *your* investigation."

"I never authorized illegal activity." Ferguson wagged a finger at the deputy. "If you've crossed the line into unlawful interference in an investigation, I'd be powerless to help you. In fact, I'd be duty-bound to ensure that charges were filed."

"But Reverend—"

"*How many times have I told you not to call me Reverend?*" Ferguson shouted. The few patrons keeping the bar afloat that afternoon turned their heads in his direction, and the low buzz of conversation ebbed. Luckily, country music clanged over the speakers loud enough to blur the specifics of their conversation.

Ferguson ducked his head low and covered the side of his face with one hand. "Now you listen here, Deputy. You've put us—especially yourself—in a bad situation. But it doesn't have to end badly for you. It comes down to who wins: our side, the side of truth and justice, or Sheriff Carter and his secrecy, lies, and cronyism. If Carter wins, we lose. I lose the case, you lose your badge and quite possibly your freedom, and the entire county loses, because the people here will never be able to trust the criminal justice system ever again. Do you want that, Mr. Wills?"

"N-no, sir."

"Good." Ferguson relaxed a little and leaned over the table, lowering his voice. "We're going to have to finish the job we've started, and it's going to take courage, and fortitude, and discipline. But if we prevail—*when* we prevail—we'll have restored professionalism to the sheriff's department in this county, which is essential to maintaining law and order around here."

"But what about—"

"You'll have to play your part," Ferguson said over Bobby's interruption, "in helping those of us with the higher perspective on these things and trust us to make the right decisions, even when you don't understand. Are you on board, Deputy? Will you help us remove that scar, that two-bit rogue lumberjack, from the highest seat of law enforcement authority in this County? Will you?"

He sat back, gauging the expression of fear and wonder on the younger man's face. Had Raymond been convincing, or would the little weakling crumple under pressure?

"I'll help," Wills said, his voice a tinny squeak. "I'll do my part, if you promise to keep me out of prison."

"If you do your part well," Ferguson said, "you'll have no such worries. But if you don't, there will be nothing I can do to protect you." He stood and dropped cash on the table for their drinks. He hated paying for the boy's alcohol, but he'd do it to buy the young fool's loyalty. He stared down at him, trying not to sneer. "I'll be in touch with further instructions," he said in as menacing a tone as he could muster.

He donned his rarely used cowboy hat and left the bar. He had no further use for Wills, but hopefully he'd bought himself some time.

Chapter Thirty-Nine

Lehigh logged in to the secure evidence tracking database, half-expecting his privileges to have been revoked. After a few heart-stopping moments watching the mouse pointer turn into a spinning, half-frozen hourglass on the screen, the system greeted him with a welcome message and a screen full of folders to choose from.

He went first to the forensics file and perused the key facts. A few items stuck out as unresolved. On the top of that list, the footprint in the mud he'd discovered. The forensics team had verified it as a smooth-bottomed shoe, like a dress shoe, size 8½. He then opened a new window and searched the personnel file. Security limited his access to only his own department, but that suited him fine. He wanted to see if any of his own deputies had contaminated the scene, as Ferguson intimated long before, but in this case, with a footprint that Ferguson insisted incriminated McBride. Luckily, since the county provided each deputy with uniforms, the database contained each deputy's clothing and shoe sizes.

He recalled that besides himself, only Wadsworth, Maddox, Peters, and DuPont had been present on the scene the day that the body had been discovered. None of them wore size 8½ shoes. In fact, only one deputy in the entire department wore that size shoe—Bobby Wills—and Lehigh hadn't even hired him by then. Strike one.

Next he checked the analysis of the tire treads. Forensics had verified that the treads matched that of a unique imported tire matching McBride's vehicle. He'd asked his deputies to track down where McBride had purchased the tires, and to see if they'd sold those tires to anyone else in the area. They'd discovered that the tires came from a specialty shop in Portland, who had sold only four sets of tires matching those specifications in the past ten years. McBride had purchased two of them. Another set went to a customer in southern Oregon. The other, oddly enough, went to another McBride six years before: Henry, the fire chief, who bought them for his daughter, Teresa, the woman dating Bobby Wills. The only other person driving a car big enough to support such tires.

Lehigh shook his head in disbelief. What motive would she or Bobby have had to kill Everett Downey? It didn't make sense. Strike two.

He kept digging, focusing on his own contributions to the file. The other big clue Lehigh had discovered was George's cuff link. George had claimed no knowledge of how it got there, and said he'd never been to the scene. In fact, he'd claimed that he'd lost one of them the evening of the fund-raiser and never recovered it. It seemed unlikely that if someone in the McBride household had found it, they'd have planted it at the scene. One of the guests might have, but whom? There were dozens—all friends of McBride, ostensibly. Outside of the guests, the only people present were the hired help and a few deputies.

He froze. Which deputies? He searched his memory. He'd noticed two of them standing guard outside the Great Room, but hadn't been on the job long enough to know all of them on sight. The party preceded his own hires, which eliminated Bobby Wills, Ruby Mac, Martin Lightfoot and Donnell Winthrop. He recalled both guards having buzz cuts, but that applied to eighty percent of the remaining staff. The two men were young-ish, one of them athletic, the other kind of round-bodied.

He snapped his fingers. DuPont and Peters, of course. Both of whom had since been detailed to Ferguson's team, and their tenure dated back to Buck's hiring days. They could have found it and planted it, or passed it on to someone who did. It was a leap, but not a crazy one.

Still, the question remained: who fired the shot? Someone

who shot well, and had access to an as-yet missing 30-30. Not George's, according to his independent forensics lab, but that didn't mean George couldn't have fired a different gun. But so could've some else.

He dove back into the files, and scanned the membership list at the Twin Falls Marksmanship Club. Lots of deputies on that list—nearly all, in fact. A few were pretty good shots with a rifle. But not, as it turned out, DuPont or Peters. And Bobby Wills' shooting was among the worst.

But two other names on the list surprised him. The same names also appeared on the list of finalists in the annual marksmanship competitions from years past. In fact, one of the names appeared as the runner-up in the 2007 rifle competition, the year that George McBride won Best Marksman. The other appeared as the overall winner three times since.

Lehigh leaned back in his chair, pondering this discovery. Everyone made a big deal about how good a shot George McBride had once been. Why, he wondered, had no one ever mentioned that the second- and third-best shots in the county were the county chair, Elliott Jackson, and the assistant district attorney, Raymond Ferguson?

***

Lehigh drove into the sunset up Brady Mountain Road, having worked late once again. He noticed a sudden proliferation of "Latner for Sheriff" signs dotting the highway. To take his mind off of it, he tried to piece together a coherent narrative explaining the Downey murder. He knew one thing: George didn't do it. But without a more convincing suspect, he'd never convince Ferguson to drop the charges, especially with the court date looming.

As was his own. Come Monday, he'd face obstruction charges, and if indicted, he'd be in no position to help George any further. Which meant he'd never win Stacy back. His reputation would be in a shambles, which wouldn't help him revive his forestry business, either. He could forget about getting his house rebuilt. He wasn't even sure if he'd get his dogs back, at this point. A shame, after all they'd been through together. The loss of his house, the whole Jared Barkley murder—

Something clicked in his brain. Pieces falling in place that hadn't seemed to go together before. Something Buck Summers said about not taking the fall for "all of it." Sam Pullen's remark about "who's *really* guilty of murder in Mt. Hood County." At the time, he'd assumed she meant the murder of Everett Downey. But maybe not.

Rounding a gentle uphill curve, he spotted a large vehicle on the side of the road, on the gravel parking lot adjacent to a trail head. *The* trail head, that is, where he'd found George McBride's cuff link and footprints, leading to the scene of Ev Downey's murder. And not just any large vehicle. He recognized it from the parking lot of the Chinese restaurant where he'd spotted Bobby Wills with Elliott Jackson's secretary. A brown Chrysler 300, at least five or six years old.

He parked behind the Chrysler and made a quick phone call. "Mt. Hood County Commission office," said a female voice. "How can I direct your call?"

"Teresa McBride," Lehigh said.

"Speaking."

Lehigh hung up, made sure his sidearm was loaded, and called in to dispatch. "Ted," he said to Roscoe on recognizing his voice, "has anyone spotted Wills yet?"

"Not yet," Ted said. "Ruby and Martin are working overtime to track him down, but his trail keeps running cold."

"Send them out to the trailhead on Brady," he said. "I think I've found him."

He exited his truck and felt the hood of the Chrysler. Still warm, in spite of being in the shade. Then he noticed the tracks left by the tires. Deep, V-shaped ridges flared out from a half-dozen ribs, more shallow on the side farthest from the highway. Just like the ones he'd spotted when he'd found the cuff link.

Scanning the area, he noticed some trampled grass heading to the lesser-used trail, the one where he'd found the footprint.

Could be hikers. Or not.

He checked out the inside of the Chrysler. Not much. A tube

of red lipstick and a package of sugar-free gum in the dash, and some sort of prayer book in the console. Otherwise clean.

Bobby might have abandoned the car there. Might be nowhere in the vicinity. Or, he might be watching nearby.

He considered waiting for Ruby and Martin to show up, decided against it. If Bobby was on the run, he needed to get on his trail right away. If he'd been listening on the radio, he'd know that Lehigh was close, and would only move faster.

Lehigh plunged into the forest, following the path, making as little noise as he could. After a short walk, the trees thinned, allowing him to scan a wide area into the distance, but he found no evidence of anyone ahead of him.

Until he reached the stream.

On the near side of the stream, across from where he'd spotted a footprint weeks ago, he spotted another, nearly identical impression in the mud. A man's shoe, without doubt. Size 8½, give or take.

Checking the opposite side of the stream, he spotted another print, this one deeper and a mirror image of the first, pooling with groundwater. A one-footed landing by a man who'd jumped across.

Recently, and hadn't yet returned.

Lehigh pulled out his cell phone and snapped a photo of the footprints. He took a few steps upstream and found a narrower stretch of the stream that he could step across without getting his boots wet. He regained the path and continued into the forest until he neared the clearing. He slowed his pace and hunched low into the brush until he reached the edge.

On the far side of the meadow, a round-shaped man in a beige khaki uniform sat with his back to Lehigh. His right hand rested on the ground, gripping a service revolver.

Lehigh stood, but stayed out of the clearing. "Bobby," he called out, just loud enough for his voice to carry across the quiet meadow.

Wills started and jerked his head around, as if searching for the source of the voice. "Sh-sheriff?" he said after a moment. "Stay away! I-I'm warning you, I'll–I'll–"

"You'll what? Shoot me? Not from there, you won't." Lehigh took a half-step to his side to further mask himself within the brush. "I've seen your marksmanship tests. But don't worry, I ain't no better."

Bobby scrambled up to his knees and faced in Lehigh's general direction. "You here to arrest me? I ain't going to jail!" Bobby's voice quavered, as if near tears. He waved the gun around like a crazy man.

"I'm hoping we can talk a bit," Lehigh said. "Here, downtown, don't matter. Just got a few questions for you, is all."

"I ain't talking to nobody!" Bobby got to his feet, his eyes still darting from one spot to another. His shirt fell open, unbuttoned to the waist, revealing a white T-shirt underneath soaked with sweat around his protruding belly.

"You been talking to folks already, from what I can tell," Lehigh said, facing off to his right. Sure enough, his voice echoed around the meadow, prompting Bobby to spin and point the gun to his left.

Bobby turned toward Lehigh, appearing to stare right at him. "What things?" he said. He aimed his gun at Lehigh. "You set me up!" he shouted. "You lying, rotten—"

"Easy, boy," Lehigh said, casting his voice to the left. Wills spun in that direction, gun following. "I know you want justice done, and in a professional way," Lehigh went on. "And things are all kattywampus lately. I get it."

Wills spun again, this time away from Lehigh. "Who's there?" he yelled. "How many people you got here, Sheriff? You here to hunt me down?"

"Nobody," Lehigh said. "Just me. You probably heard a squirrel, that's all. Now why don't we both calm down, put our guns down, and—"

"You got your gun out?" Bobby shouted, spinning again in Lehigh's direction. "You gonna shoot me? No, uh-uh. I ain't going down without a fight!" He straightened his gun arm and held it steady with his left hand, aiming what appeared to be a few feet to Lehigh's left—

And fell in a heap, tackled from behind by a short, stocky

blur of beige.

Moments later, a grinning Ruby Mac had Bobby pinned to the ground, her knees on his elbows, with Bobby's own gun pointed at his face.

Chapter Forty

The gunman ducked down in the brush, alarmed by Bobby shouting about movement in the woods. The last thing he needed was to be discovered by that fool of a sheriff back at the murder scene—or worse, shot by the damn-fool deputy.

He doubted that they knew of his presence there. He'd covered his tracks well—like he did that night. No one ever thought about pointing a finger back at him. Only one living soul knew who pulled the trigger, and soon that number would be down to zero.

Or so he'd planned. But then that hayseed with a badge stumbled onto the scene and put his plans on hold. He'd initially thought to run, but his better nature cautioned him not to panic, and he stayed put, discovering a much better plan: pin it on Lehigh Carter. Carter's impulsive temper, reckless public tantrums, and bar fights would make him a more than believable culprit. Plus, he had motive: everybody knew of his run-ins with Wills. That good-looking moron of a reporter had made sure of that.

More shouting from the clearing. He lifted his head enough to get a better view, confident that his hunter's camouflage hat and jacket would keep him invisible to the men in the field. Except now there were two more men—no, scratch that. A man and a woman. The big Indian fellow and that woman deputy Carter had hired. Where had they come from? That complicated things—especially his plan to pin the blame on Carter. It also made movement trickier. One of them would likely hear or see him, and then he'd be done for.

He calmed himself. Time to listen, and adapt.

***

"You two were awfully quiet," Lehigh said to Ruby Mac and Martin Lightfoot once Bobby stopped squirming under Ruby's pin move. "And fast!"

"I grew up in these woods, hunting rabbits with slingshots." Martin held his handcuffs at the ready to cuff Bobby. "You learn to run real quiet doing that."

Lehigh gazed down at Wills and registered the fear in the smaller man's eyes. "We can talk here, Bobby," he said, "or we can bring you into the jail cells, where all of the other criminals can hear you. I'm sure Buck Summers and Dale DuPont would love to know who's selling them out to save his own skin."

Martin Lightfoot blinked at Lehigh in surprise. "DuPont?" he mouthed at Lehigh. Lehigh gave his head a tiny shake to keep his question muted. He'd gambled by mentioning DuPont, hoping Bobby would bite.

He did. "Has Dale already talked?" Bobby said. "Is that how you found me?" He glanced from face to face. Ruby sneered at him, but said nothing.

Lehigh kept a poker face, but inside he celebrated. Bobby had just confirmed the identity of his accomplice. But he needed more solid evidence—a confession.

Lehigh squatted down next to Ruby so he could get a better look at Bobby while they talked. "Son, I may not be a lifelong cop, but I know not to reveal my sources. And I ain't gonna squeal on you to your buddies, either, if you cooperate. But you have to help me." He kept his face impassive, not wanting to give any clues away, waiting for Bobby to give in.

"All right," Bobby said. "But you've gotta help me. The killer, he's going to try to pin it all on me, I know he is. Help me, Sheriff!" Tears formed at the corners of Bobby's eyes and crawled down his temples.

Lehigh stood. He decided to believe Bobby, but wanted to take no chances. "Let him up, but cuff him," Lehigh said.

Ruby got off him and, with Martin's help, lifted Bobby to a

sitting position. Martin cuffed his hands while Ruby Mirandized him.

"Now, you can wait for your lawyer if you want," Lehigh said, "and face this whole thing alone. Which seems pretty unfair to me, seeing as I can't imagine you had a personal reason to take out Ev Downey. Or you can help us all out by telling us who else was involved, in which case you'll probably only be charged as an accessory. Up to you, though. What's it gonna be, Bobby?"

Bobby rubbed his eyes dry on his shoulders and sniffled. "I didn't kill nobody," he said.

"I believe you," Lehigh said, ignoring Ruby's snort of derision. "I wouldn't have hired you as a deputy if I believed you had that in you."

"I always wanted to be a cop," Bobby said. "Not just any old cop. I wanted to be the *best*. But you made it clear I wouldn't ever be the best in your eyes, Sheriff. Making me work for *her*." He shot a glance at Ruby, who grabbed her nightstick.

"Chill, Ruby," Lehigh said. "Go on, Bobby. Is that where it all started?"

Bobby laughed. "You're kidding me, right? It all started with the Rev. He got me to apply to be a deputy in the first place. Told me about your recruitment, coached me on my application, what to say. It was all part of his plan."

"To get rid of me?" Lehigh asked, confident he knew the answer. "Why?"

"Not just to get rid of you as sheriff," Bobby said. "He really wanted to know what you were up to with the investigation. He knew you'd do everything you could to get your father-in-law off the hook. That's why he wanted me on the inside."

"He wanted to plant you on my team so you could leak information?" Lehigh asked.

Bobby surprised him with his response: laughter.

"You don't think that's all he cared about?" Wills said. "Leaks? No, sheriff. He wanted *protection*."

"I'm not following," Ruby said.

"Me either," Martin said. "Protection from who? Us?"

"I think I'm beginning to understand," Lehigh said. "Bobby, why did you pick this spot to hide out?"

"Hide?" Bobby shook his head. "I wasn't hiding. I was waiting."

"Who for?" Martin asked.

"Ev Downey's killer, of course," Bobby said.

"We figured that much." Ruby pushed Bobby to the ground with her nightstick. "What's his name?"

"Cool your jets with the nightstick, Ruby," Lehigh said.

"We don't need to rough Bobby up to get him to tell us," Martin said. "We're all friends here. Right, Bobby?"

Bobby glared at Ruby Mac, then Martin, then Lehigh. "I've said enough," he said. "I ain't helping you no more."

"You'll talk, or I'll take you downtown and beat you up on the courthouse lawn again!" Ruby grabbed him by the lapels and shook him. "Is that better for you? Getting whipped in public by a girl?"

"Stand down, Mac!" Lehigh pulled her off of Bobby and shoved her into Martin's arms. "Keep her away from him," he said. "Besides, I already know who it is."

Bobby sneered at him. "Baloney. You don't know nothing."

Martin and Ruby exchanged surprised glances. "You know?" Martin asked. "Who, then?"

"Where were you the night Ev Downey was killed?" Lehigh asked. "Let me guess: right here in the meadow. Am I right?"

Bobby shook his head. "I told you, I didn't kill nobody!" he shouted. "You can't pin this on me!"

"No," Lehigh said, "and I wouldn't try to. But the district attorney would, wouldn't he?"

Wills turned white, his mouth dropping open. His gaze shot from Lehigh to the other deputies and back. Then his face crumpled, and the tears poured out of him.

"He says I'm going to prison if I don't help him pin it on McBride!" he cried. "Says he'll tell everyone I was here, that the bullets match my gun, the footprint matches my shoe, and I ain't got no alibi. I'm a goner, that's what he said! I'm a goner!" He broke down, sobs wracking his body, and slumped sideways onto the ground.

Martin knelt next to Bobby, placing a hand on his shoulder. "Nobody'd believe you'd kill Ev Downey," Martin said. "What motive would you have?"

"None! I ain't got no reason to kill Mr. Downey," Wills said through his tears. "But the Rev says I was a regular at his club. 'Maybe Downey was blackmailing you,' says the Rev. 'Maybe you owe him money.' He had a thousand reasons, he said." Wills broke into sobs again.

Martin rested his hand on Bobby's shoulder again. "It's all right, Bobby," he said. "I believe you, no matter what Ferguson or anybody else says."

Ruby sidled up next to Lehigh. "So, if Bobby didn't do it, who did?"

"Bobby," Lehigh said, "what was the reason you came here that night?"

Bobby slowed his crying and managed, with Martin's help, to sit up again. "Just to keep Downey waiting," he said, sniffling. "Keep stringing him along so he wouldn't leave. Make excuses as to why, uh, the *person* he was meeting was late. That sort of thing."

"What did you see?" Martin asked in a soft voice, still supporting Bobby with an arm around him.

Bobby shrugged. "Not much. Like I said, at first, he was right here. Then all of a sudden, Mr. Downey fell down. I swear, he fell before I even heard the gunshot. He was bleeding from the leg, real bad. I got scared and ran into the woods."

"Which direction?" Lehigh kept his voice calm, steady.

Bobby lifted his arm and pointed across the meadow, into the woods. "Over thataway."

"How far did you get?" Lehigh anticipated Bobby's answer with a glance toward the spot he'd found the bullets.

"Just–just past the edge of the field, into the trees," Wills said. "Then I fell down."

"And where was the gunman at this point?"

Bobby's tears flowed like faucets again, and his voice sounded pained. "He ran right past me, into the meadow. I was laying there, and then...it was so loud..."

"Another gunshot?" Lehigh said, still in the low, calm voice. Bobby nodded, and broke into sobbing tears again, unable to speak.

"So, you didn't take the fatal shot?" Lehigh asked him. "The one that hit him in the chest?"

"I didn't take either shot," Bobby said. "I was supposed to, but I froze. I–I couldn't do it." He ducked his head, fighting tears. "I ain't no good as a deputy, and I'm even worse as a criminal."

"Oh, boo hoo," Ruby said. "Save the crocodile tears for the jury."

"Hey, Mac, ease up," Martin said. "The guy's helping us here." He gave Bobby a reassuring pat on the shoulder. "What happened next?"

Bobby shut his eyes tight, shaking his head.

"Let me guess," Lehigh said. "The gunman left the meadow, and walked right past you, didn't he? Right where you were laying?"

Bobby nodded. "He laid the gun down right next to me. He used *my* damned gun to kill him!" Bobby's sobbing resumed.

"*Who* did?" Ruby Mac asked. "Who was the shooter?"

Bobby gave Ruby a curious stare, and his tears stopped. "You don't know?" he asked. "After all this?"

"Tell her, Bobby," Lehigh said. He knew, but didn't want to say it out loud. Even now, the shock of it still shook him.

"Tell us!" Martin said. "The suspense is killing me!" He picked Bobby up by the armpits as if righting a fallen chair and set him on his feet in front of the others.

Bobby glanced at each of them in turn, a puzzled frown forming on his face. "Why, it's the only person who ever *needed* Ev Downey gone from this county. I mean, we all kind of wanted him gone—me included, even though I went to his clubs all the time—but only one person's personal ambitions made it absolutely necessary."

"You mean, George McBride did it after all?" Martin asked.

Bobby laughed. "Don't be ridiculous. McBride's an

egomaniac, but a total coward. He could never kill anyone. Anyway, he's retiring from politics, ain't he?"

"Elliott Jackson?" Ruby Mac asked. "Is he thinking he'd take George's place in the senate?"

"That idiot?" Bobby said.

Lehigh shook his head. "He loves being the big fish in a small pond, where he can bully everybody. He knows better than to reach for anything higher than the county commission. Go on, Bobby. Name him. Tell me I'm right, as much as I can't believe it myself."

Bobby straightened his shoulders and looked Lehigh in the eye. "If I do, will you keep me out of prison?"

Lehigh exhaled through his teeth. "Bobby, I'll be honest with you. It's up to the district attorney as to what to charge you with. But I'll do what I can, and under the circumstances, I think your willingness to testify will go a long way in this case."

Bobby hung his head, tears flowing again. After several seconds, he lifted his head and gazed into the distant trees across the meadow. "I'll never forget it," he said. "It was the worst night of my life." He shook his head, as if to shake the memory free. "The man who pulled the trigger," he said, "was none other than Raymond Ferguson."

Chapter Forty-One

And just like that, Plan C flew out the window, too. Damn that Wills! Damn that idiot-savant sheriff!

Assistant District Attorney Raymond Ferguson retreated into the woods, adding distance and visual interference between himself and the gathering of uniforms in the meadow.

Up until that moment, the deputies had had no clue about what had really happened. The looks on their faces proved it. Now, anything that happened to Wills, they'd trace back to him.

Unless he could break up their party, and somehow isolate Wills and Carter from the other two. Then he could make it look like an accident, or an act of police brutality. As deputy district attorney, he'd have influence, if not outright discretion, over who got charged for what. His boss, the D.A., would certainly believe him over these rubes.

Especially if the two other deputies somehow didn't make it back either.

He retched at that awful thought, and covered his mouth to mute the sound. He hunched over on the ground and squeezed his eyes shut, forcing the black thoughts out of his mind. The body count was rising. He begged the Lord for forgiveness for even contemplating such thoughts. He'd have to beg much harder later, if he completed the awful deed.

He shook himself, forced his thoughts back to the current problem. Deal with the future later, Father always told him. He had enough problems in the present.

Such as, coming up with a plan to distract them without

getting caught.

His stomach calmed, as did his tormented soul, and he crept forward, weapon drawn.

***

"Ferguson?" Ruby Mac charged at Wills. Martin intervened just in time to prevent her from clobbering him. "You idiot!" she said. "Do you really expect us to believe such a desperate lie?"

"Ruby! Back off!" Lehigh grabbed her around the waist, with inches to spare between her swishing nightstick and Bobby's unprotected face. He finally managed to swing her around and push her back into Martin's arms. "Now hang onto her this time," he said with a growl. He lifted Wills to his feet and held on to his arm. "I believe you, Bobby. But we're going to need proof. You got any?"

Bobby sneered at Ruby Mac. "Yeah, I got proof. In fact, I got something that even The Rev doesn't know. Heh." He stood an inch taller, an expression of pride crossing his face and swelling his chest. "And it's right nearby."

"Don't believe him!" Ruby said. "He's going to lead us into a trap."

"I have to agree with Ruby," Martin said. "I mean, look where we are. He'd have no reason not to."

"The Rev has sold me out," Wills said. "It's time to turn the tables. And I have an ace in the hole. Literally!"

"You mean to say," Lehigh said, "you got something in an actual hole? As in, buried in the ground?"

"That's exactly what I'm saying," Wills said. "A key, missing piece of evidence. And I'll bring you to it. But only if you keep me out of prison."

"What missing evidence?" Martin asked. "The only thing missing so far is the—"

"Murder weapon," Lehigh said. "Bobby, are you saying you know where the 30-30 that killed Ev Downey is buried?"

Wills looked from face to face and nodded. "Of course I do. It's my own gun. I had to hide it somewhere. So, we got a deal, or what?"

Lehigh sighed, all out of patience. "Show us where it is first," he said, "And no tricks. You try anything, and I may not be able to stop Ruby from doing whatever she wants to your face with that nightstick."

Ruby cast an evil grin at Bobby. "Please double-cross us," she said. "I could use the exercise."

"I'll show you, I'll show you!" Bobby said. "Just get her away from me!"

"Good choice," Lehigh said. "Now, which way do we go?"

"East, about two hundred yards," Wills said. "If you uncuff me—"

"Not so fast," Lehigh said. "First, you show us where. When I have the weapon in my hands, then we'll chat about how much I can trust you with your hands free."

"Not at all, if you ask me," Ruby said.

Martin shook his head, his expression darkening. "I can't believe you buried evidence *here*, of all places. It's a burial ground, but for people, not murder weapons!"

Bobby's head drooped. "I'm sorry. I didn't know."

"Lead us to it," Lehigh said. He clapped a hand on Martin's shoulder and met his baleful eyes. "We'll make this right, I promise," he said to the deputy.

"Follow me," Wills said, and trudged away from the setting sun into the forest.

***

Ferguson lowered his weapon and cursed. That dirty double-crossing Wills! Unless he was bluffing, this was a very bad turn of events. Very, very bad.

He'd had one clear shot at Wills, but he couldn't take out Bobby without also engaging with Carter and his two deputies. Even on his best day, he couldn't win a gunfight with three armed cops. And if he failed, he was done for.

He'd have to bide his time. Wait for them to find the treasure, then find a way to separate them. Pick them off one by one. Or maybe just Carter and Wills. He smiled. Yes, that was an even better plan. Get rid of Carter, then blame Wills for killing the local folk hero. An escape gone bad. Then he'd make easy work of connecting him to Downey, since only Wills knew where he'd buried the murder weapon—his own gun, to boot. From what he'd seen, the two deputies would sooner believe that than some crazy story about Ray being a killer.

The four of them disappeared into the woods. Ferguson circumnavigated the perimeter of the meadow, staying out of sight but keeping them within earshot. They weren't even trying to stay quiet. This would be too easy.

***

Ruby followed Bobby down a fading path through the woods, one that hadn't been used much in recent years by area hikers. Low brush tangled their footsteps and slowed their pace. It took several minutes before Wills announced, "Left, here."

Ruby grabbed his elbow and pushed Bobby ahead of her. "I can still outrun you, so don't try anything," she said. "Just march straight to the spot. You hear?"

"I'm not running," Bobby said. "I'm telling you, I'm cooperating. No tricks."

Ruby kept her eye on the center of Bobby's back, two steps behind him. No way he could fake her out or get away from her. Still, part of her wanted him to try. She'd enjoy smacking that smug smile off his face, along with a few teeth.

Bobby slowed, staring at the right side of the path, and she slowed with him. "We're getting close," he said. "It's just a little bit...here!" He stopped and pointed with his toe. "Right there, between those ferns. I'm sure of it."

"Stay put." She circled around him to the spot. Sure enough, the ground had been disturbed there. Where the rest of the forest floor sported a thick bed of evergreen needles and other organic debris, the spot in question had only a thin, haphazard layer, and the soil underneath sagged under her weight. She turned to Bobby. "How deep is it?"

"Three, four feet," he said. "And it's covered with rocks."

"We're going to need shovels," she said to Martin and Sheriff

Carter, coming toward her from the path.

"I've got one in the back of my truck," Carter said. He turned to leave.

Martin stopped him. "I'll get it," he said. "You should stay here with Bobby." Carter nodded, and Martin hustled off.

Ruby pointed a finger at Bobby's face. "You'd better not be pulling a fast one here," she said.

"I swear, I'm not," Wills said, and his face blanched. Good. She wanted him afraid. She glanced at her boss, who eyed her with amusement. She smiled at him. He was a much better boss than the one she'd had in Wasco County, who spent most of his time trying to keep her "safe," whatever that meant.

Actually, she knew what it meant. It meant "out of the path to promotion." Not at all like Lehigh Carter.

Suddenly, a loud *Bang!* echoed through the woods, shaking her out of her reverie. A gunshot!

"What the hell?" she said. "Martin? *Martin?*"

The sheriff grabbed his radio. "Martin, you all right?" he asked in a calm voice. Like a true leader.

Ruby cursed herself and her immediate emotional outburst. She needed to learn how to keep her cool if she wanted promotional opportunities. They waited for the deputy's reply. None came.

"His radio must be off," Lehigh said.

"His radio's never off," Ruby said. "This is bad."

Another loud bang. Definitely a gunshot.

"You want to go find him, or stay with Wills?" Lehigh asked.

She gave it a half-second's thought. Maybe less. She didn't trust herself with Bobby, and couldn't bear the thought of her partner waiting alone for help, bleeding, or worse. "I'll find Martin," she said, and tore off through the trees.

***

Ferguson waited. The big Indian had broken into a run right after his first shot, then fell in a heap after the second. That surprised him—he thought he'd missed, which, at this distance and with all of the trees between them, was more likely than not.

He debated going to check, to find the body, but hesitated. What if the man was lying in wait, tricking him with an ambush? He crept toward the spot, but dared not lift his head above the brush. He listened. Nothing.

Then, rustling, and footsteps... *behind* him.

He reacted without thinking, darting to his right, back into a thicket where he couldn't be seen, a path perpendicular to the straight-line trajectory of the oncoming runner. She emerged from among the trees moments later, running at an Olympic clip. He'd never hit her, not with her running like that, and he dare not reveal his whereabouts. She zipped past him about thirty yards away. If she continued in that direction, she'd veer far from the spot where he'd last seen the big Indian, and run far past him before turning around. If he was unconscious, she'd never find him.

He doubled back in the direction from which she came. Back to where Wills had revealed his buried treasure, and the men he really needed to kill.

***

Lehigh grabbed Bobby by the shoulders. "Did you bring friends?" he asked. "Was this all a trap, as Ruby suspected?"

"No, uh-uh," Bobby said. "Like I said, I was waiting to meet The Rev—"

"Dammit!" Lehigh drew his weapon and clicked off the safety. "You said Ray didn't know about this spot?"

"Nope," Bobby said. "He tossed the rifle at me after shooting Downey and told me to get rid of it, where no one could find it. Including him."

"Plausible deniability, eh? Well, he covered his tracks pretty well," Lehigh said with disgust. "Especially since he was the one charged with *uncovering* all the tracks. Dammit. I should have seen this sooner. Tell me something. Why didn't he have you bury the body with the weapons?"

"I don't know. He had a plan, he said. That's all he'd tell me."

Another shot ricocheted through the woods. Closer.

"I can help fight him, if you take me out of these cuffs," Wills said.

Lehigh laughed. The kid had nerve. "No way," he said. "I don't trust you yet."

"But if he comes for us, I'm a sitting duck!" Bobby said.

"Better learn to quack, then," Lehigh said. "And get low." He listened, hearing only the occasional distant echo of Ruby Mac's voice, calling for Martin Lightfoot, softer each time. Soon she'd be out of earshot. He tried the radio again. "Martin? Ruby? Someone, get back to me!"

The radio greeted his plea with static.

A twig snapped behind him. He whirled about, and just in time, flattened himself to the ground. A loud report shattered the quiet. To his right, he sensed movement.

Bobby Wills had not been fast enough to the ground. Blood smeared his uniform across the midsection. Shock filled his face, and he sank to his knees.

"Wills!" Lehigh shouted at him. Another loud *Bang!*, followed by the crunch of a bullet into a tree a foot away. Lehigh sprang to his feet and flattened Bobby to the ground as another shot whizzed past his ear.

"I'm hit, Sheriff," Bobby said in a weak voice. "I think I'm gonna die."

"Not on my watch!" Lehigh grabbed Wills and rolled with him into the brush to a downed tree, then lifted the deputy over to the other side. Another shot tore into the downed tree's trunk, inches from Lehigh's hip. He turned, saw movement in the woods, and fired. The sound nearly deafened him. But the movement continued, hustling away from them. Lehigh fired again. Another miss.

He did some quick math. He'd fired twice, leaving four shots in his revolver. Ferguson had fired twice at Martin, four times at him and Wills. But how many did his magazine hold? And had he reloaded?

Wills groaned. Lehigh ducked behind the log and tore off his shirt. He opened Bobby's, nearly vomited at the sight of the all the blood. He pressed his shirt onto Bobby's wound to staunch the flow. "Hold this," he said, then remembered he'd cuffed

Bobby's hands behind him. He used Bobby's belt to secure it, then fumbled for his keys—

"Drop your weapon, Carter," said a voice.

Lehigh froze, then tilted his head back. Above him, holding some sort of cannon in two steady hands, stood a man in hunter's fatigues. A man he recognized as Assistant District Attorney Ray Ferguson.

Chapter Forty-Two

Lehigh sat up and held his arm out, dangling the weapon over the downed log. "Raymond," he said, "this is a big mistake you're making here."

Ferguson laughed and ripped the gun out of Lehigh's hand. "My only mistake was not doing you in months ago," he said. "Well, to be honest, I made another mistake. I admit it, Carter. I underestimated you."

"Welcome to the party," he said. "My own Maw and Pappy are way ahead of you on that one."

"Get away from Wills," Ferguson said. "I want you two six feet apart."

"He'll bleed to death if I let go of this bandage," Lehigh said. "I swear, I ain't gonna try—"

"*I said get away from him!*" Ferguson's voice trembled, and the force of his rage nearly knocked Lehigh back to the ground. He shook the pistol at him—whether out of nervousness or a desire to intimidate, Lehigh couldn't tell. Either way, it meant bad news. He slid away from Bobby, hoping his makeshift bandage would hold. But the blood resumed its heavy flow immediately.

"We need to get him to a hospital," Lehigh said. "You don't have to—"

"Neither of you are getting anywhere near a hospital." Ferguson shook his gun once at Lehigh's face. "Get further away. Over by that tree. Face it, hands on your head. *Now!*"

Lehigh crawled on his hands and knees toward the tree, searching the horizon for any sign of his deputies. He reached the tree and leaned against it, taking his time, putting one hand on his neck, then the other. With his head bowed, he could see Wills, unconscious against the fallen tree. Ferguson stepped over the log and swore.

"Where are the damned keys to his cuffs?" Ferguson yelled.

"On my belt," Lehigh said. He hoped Raymond wouldn't notice the ones on Bobby's own belt.

He didn't. Ferguson stepped toward Lehigh. "Very slowly, I want you to give me those keys," he said.

"Okay." Lehigh lowered his right hand—

"Left hand, Carter," Ferguson said. "Keep your shooting hand on your neck."

Lehigh nodded, raised his right hand to his head, then let his left hand drift down toward his belt. Something moved ahead of him and to his right. He didn't dare look. He could only hope. He slowed his hand's descent.

"Hurry up, damn you!"

Ferguson's shout shook him, and he started. Another explosion burst out of the attorney's gun, and the tree trunk splintered above his head. Then laughter—Ferguson's. The crazy fool! Shaking, he grabbed the keys and tossed them onto the ground to his left. Ferguson snatched them and returned to Wills. Moments later he rolled Bobby into a sitting position against the downed log and pressed Lehigh's weapon into Bobby's hands.

"End of the road, Carter," Ferguson said. "Your escaping deputy is going to kill you in cold blood to cover up his murder of Everett Downey. Isn't that elegant? I think so."

"Actually, it's kind of an awkward ending," Lehigh said. "Seeing as how we haven't yet dug up the—"

"Shut up!" Ferguson said. "We're done talking." He grunted, dragged Bobby closer, then pointed the deputy's arm toward Lehigh. He wrapped Bobby's hands around the butt end and aimed—

And fell in a heap onto the ground.

"Got him!" shouted an exuberant Ruby Mac. Grinning, she raised her weapon high: the bloody end of a dirty, round-tipped shovel.

***

"You could've just shot him, you know," Lehigh said, handing Ruby and Martin a celebratory ginger ale back at the sheriff's office. "Or, you know, hit him a lot sooner. What were you waiting for?"

Ruby toasted Lehigh, tapped her plastic cup against Martin's, and sipped the fizzy drink. "I thought it better to keep him alive, so he could confess," she said. "Besides, I'm a much better shot with a shovel. I never miss when I swing a long stick."

"It's true," Martin said. "She bats cleanup on her over-thirty-five softball team."

"Over *thirty*!" Ruby said, glaring at Martin.

"We all get old sometime," Lightfoot said. His grin turned to a frown a moment later. "Speaking of which, is Bobby Wills going to get any older?" he asked. "He was in pretty bad shape when the medics arrived."

"No word yet," Lehigh said. "He's still in surgery." The room fell quiet. Lehigh's stomach churned. He'd put Wills in greater danger by leaving him cuffed. For that matter, he'd pushed Wills deeper into Ferguson's conspiracy with his suspicions. He'd endangered his deputies, and had his own brush with mortality once again. That had to stop. He raised his own plastic cup. "To getting older," he said.

"To getting older," the two deputies said in unison.

"So, boss," Ruby Mac said, "how'd you know it was Ferguson before Bobby told us?"

Lehigh chuckled. "I didn't *know*. I guessed. But I thought it was a pretty good guess. Once Bobby said that he was meeting his co-conspirator right there at the murder scene, it all kind of fell into place—the reason for the leaks, the tampered evidence, all of it. Who else but Ray Ferguson had control of all of that? And why else would they meet there, at the murder scene?"

"What about the fact that the tire tracks at the scene matched George's car?" Ruby asked. "And how did his cuff link get there?"

"The tire tracks also match the car Bobby was driving—his

girlfriend Teresa's," Lehigh said. "Which Ferguson knew, but chose not to point out to anyone. And George lost the cuff link a week before, at my fundraiser. He'd hired two off-duty deputies as security—DuPont and Peters. Buck named both as part of Ferguson's conspiracy. They won't be deputies much longer." He sipped the ginger ale, wondering if he'd have any experienced deputies left at year's end.

"Why Ferguson, though?" Martin asked. "What motive did the deputy district attorney have to kill Everett Downey?"

"It's like Bobby told us in the clearing," Lehigh said. "Ev Downey had dirt on everyone, including Ray Ferguson. Ferguson had ambitions for higher office—rumor had it he was lining up a run for state Attorney General. But he wasn't going to get there unless he could keep Downey quiet."

"Quiet about what?" Martin asked. "Going to the strip joint? That's no big deal. Half the guys in town go there."

"Yeah, but half the guys in town aren't making public statements about shutting them down," Ruby said, finishing her ginger ale. "Damned hypocrite."

"Hypocrisy, unfortunately, isn't enough to keep politicians from getting elected," Lehigh said, "nor to motivate them to murder. But criminal activity is. And Downey knew something that few others did that could have kept Ray Ferguson from running for anything—maybe even send him to prison. That's what scared The Rev into such desperate action."

"What sort of criminal activity?" Ruby asked.

"When Buck Summers agreed to go state's evidence in exchange for a deal, he said something that didn't mean much at the time," Lehigh said, "but it came back to me later. He said he 'wouldn't take the fall for him.' At first I thought he meant just about the leaks. But he also said he'd talk about 'the leaks' *and* 'the conspiracy'. Then, his lawyer said Buck would reveal who was really guilty of murder—and didn't specify which one. When we found Bobby in the field, it occurred to me: Buck was in jail for a very different conspiracy. Only in that moment did I realize how they were tied together."

"Of course!" Martin said. "How could we have not seen it

sooner?"

"What conspiracy is that?" Ruby said. "Remember, I wasn't around in Buck's era."

Lehigh swirled the last drops of soda in his glass and downed them. "Buck's charged with conspiracy to murder former acting sheriff Jared Barkley," he said. "And I'll wager once we interview him, he'll finger a few more names that we haven't yet charged. And one of them is Assistant District Attorney Ray Ferguson."

"If Buck conspired with Ferguson, why'd Downey get plugged instead of him?" Martin asked.

"They were all in it together," Lehigh said. "Buck and Ray had made a deal that would keep Summers out of prison in exchange for keeping quiet about Ferguson's role. But Downey remained a loose cannon. The Rev had no leverage over him, but he needed to keep him quiet so he could make a run for attorney general next year."

"But why now?" Martin asked.

Lehigh shrugged. "I'm making a few leaps of logic here, but I do know a few things. Ferguson visited Downey's place the same day I did—yes, I went to meet with him about the campaign. Turns out, everybody does. Then George got cold feet and backed out of the shopping center deal, putting Ev in a bind, money-wise. I'm guessing that Downey threatened to withdraw financial support of Ferguson's campaign unless he let him put in the new strip clubs instead. One thing leads to another, and the next thing you know, Downey's threatening to reveal all. And that," he said, shaking his head, "was his fatal mistake."

Chapter Forty-Three

The office had gone quiet and dark hours before, but Lehigh remained at his desk, preparing the paperwork he needed to charge Ray Ferguson with a multitude of crimes—murder of Ev Downey, destruction of evidence, conspiracy, attempted murder of Bobby, Martin, and himself—he might as well just attach the entire criminal code to his report. Buck, with Sam Pullen negotiating, had agreed to implicate Ferguson in the Barkley murder as well, in exchange for a lighter sentence. Thankfully, they'd found the 30-30 buried right where Bobby had indicated, and ballistics testing confirmed it as the murder weapon. The lab had lifted two sets of prints, one of which matched Ferguson's, a surprising bit of sloppiness from the normally careful attorney.

Still, Lehigh was no lawyer, and he couldn't be sure the evidence was enough to convict. Raymond's boss, the district attorney, would need extensive documentation of the evidence before charging his protégé.

He sighed, hit *Print*, and closed the document. He'd done all he could do, and setting up camp in the dark wouldn't be much fun. Maybe he should just stay the night and sleep in the office again. The laser printer hummed to life down the hall, and he checked his email one final time.

"I thought I was the only one that worked this late."

Jim Wadsworth's ample frame and broad smile filled Lehigh's view over the top of his computer screen. He sat in Lehigh's guest chair and his expression changed to a grumpy frown. "I guess overtime is your only option, since you're doing all the work yourself these days," Wadsworth said.

"You want to file this report?" Lehigh said with equal mock

seriousness. "All yours."

"No, but I wouldn't mind being in on the highest-profile collar of the century around here," Wadsworth said. "On the one day I'm out on traffic patrol, you guys get into a manhunt and shootout in the woods. On second thought—next time, yeah, same thing. Don't call me," he said with a laugh.

"I couldn't have done it without your help," Lehigh said. "You set Bobby up good. That's what broke him, and the case."

"No, Lehigh. You broke the case. And, whether or not the voters around here are smart enough to realize it, the county owes you big time." Wadsworth extended a hand. "Congratulations, my friend. It's an honor working for you."

Lehigh stood and accepted the handshake. "The honor's all mine, Jim. Speaking of which, how would you like the honor of arresting Ray Ferguson?"

Wadsworth grinned. "You're too good to me. So, let me return the favor." He slid a form onto Lehigh's desk.

"What's this?" Lehigh asked, scanning the document.

"Your Certification of Eligibility, saying you're trained and qualified to be *elected* sheriff," Wadsworth said. "State requires it. I certified you on everything, but now it needs your signature. It's due tomorrow, so don't delay." He handed Lehigh a pen.

"Lee?"

The two men turned in the direction of the familiar female voice, coming from the hallway. Lehigh's heart skipped. Stacy hadn't visited him in his office since his second day on the job, when she helped him settle in. She appeared in the doorway moments later, with worry and weariness occupying her pretty, slender face.

"I'll grab that report off the printer and head out." Wadsworth slipped around Stacy and out of the room.

"Stacy, I—"

"Sh." She ambled around and sat on his desk, her legs dangling inches from his. Silence lingered for a moment. She appeared to be searching for words, and he decided to let her.

"Word on the street is that you've arrested Ray Ferguson for Everett Downey's murder," she said.

"Dammit, I thought I'd plugged all of our leaks," Lehigh said with a half-smile. "Anyway, that's a bit premature, by just a few minutes. And a bit incomplete. He's also going down with Buck and Paul van Paten for the Jared Barkley murder. When we're done with him, he's going to need a lifetime reservation in the state penitentiary, and then some."

"That's amazing!" Stacy jumped off the desk and wrapped her arms around him, crushing the air out of his lungs. He didn't mind, though.

"We haven't told the D.A. yet, so the charges haven't been dropped against your father," he said when he could breathe again. "I expect we'll be able to take care of that tomorrow."

"That's wonderful." She continued to hold him. He held her, too, and it felt good. He'd missed that feeling.

She took a deep breath, which signaled to him that she had something else to say. With reluctance, he loosened the embrace and gazed into her eyes with an expectant look. She blinked and smiled. "You know me better than I know myself sometimes," she said.

"I doubt that, but thank you," he said. "Stacy, this job. It's been bad for us. I've been thinking—"

"Don't you dare say it." She pressed an index finger to his lips. "You're a wonderful sheriff. And we need you. The county needs you—and I need you." She pressed herself close, holding him tight again. "At first, I thought different. When you arrested my father, I thought you were just out for revenge or something. But I have to admit, it did look pretty bad for him. You were in a tough place. You did your job, with honesty and integrity, no matter where the chips fell. Not many people are capable of that."

"I hurt you," he said. "I'm so sorry."

"I hurt you, too, and I'm sorry," she said, rocking a bit in his arms. "But you didn't let it stop you. You kept looking for the truth—and never gave up, even when everyone else, including some very powerful people, didn't believe you and seemed determined to stop you. You risked a lot." She pulled back and gave him a wry smile. "Maybe even too much."

"I risked losing you," he said. "That was definitely too much."

Her eyes welled up, and she brushed away the tears threatening to wet her cheeks. "Nobody else believed that my father was innocent. You kept up the fight. It's because of you he'll be proven innocent. And you did it, not because he's my father, but because it was the right thing to do." She brushed away another tear, but missed the next one, and it trickled down to the smile forming on her lips. "I'm proud of you," she said.

He pulled her in close again, and the lump in his throat kept him from trying to speak for a long time. When he finally managed words, it came in the form of a question. "So you don't think I should quit?"

"No." She shook her head against his shoulder. "Definitely not."

A warm feeling arose in his chest. She was right: the people in the town looked up to him to stand up to the likes of Ray Ferguson and Elliott Jackson. If he didn't, no one else would, and he'd suffer as much as they would.

But the work wasn't done, and it came at a high cost. Continuing meant more long hours, hard fights, and putting up with people like Bruce Bailey smearing his reputation. The thought wearied him. He fought off a yawn—unsuccessfully.

"You must be exhausted," she said, patting his shoulder.

"I'm ready to sleep standing up right here," he said. "And I still have a ways to drive, and a tent to pitch, and—"

"A tent?" She pulled back, and her eyes filled with alarm. "You've been sleeping in a tent? Where?"

"On my land," he said. "It's not so bad, really. Except when Melvin Crabb and his construction crew show up early, and—"

"Lehigh," she said, "tonight, and from now on, please. Come home, and sleep in *our* bed."

He'd never heard such beautiful words in his life.

Chapter Forty-Four

"Any word yet?" Jim Wadsworth asked Lehigh, handing him an open bottle of beer. Lehigh shook his head, having given up long before on trying to shout over the din. The expanse of the Great Room buzzed with loud conversations trying without success to drown out the chipper so-called polling analysis proffered by Bruce Bailey on the 70-inch screen above the luxurious mantel. Despite its size, the television seemed dwarfed by the crystal chandeliers hanging from the high ceilings and marble floor-to-ceiling Roman-style pillars. A guitar band occupied a small elevated stage in one corner, playing classic pop hits, contributing more volume to the chaotic rumble. Dozens of people, maybe hundreds, filled the room. George McBride had insisted on opening the party to "all of the good people who support you," including people who had never before seen such opulence.

He adjusted his tie and loosened the collar of his shirt. He'd opted to dress in his official uniform for the election night party, and Stacy, after giving up on convincing him to wear a tuxedo, had insisted on at least starching and pressing his uniform for the event. "You have to look good for the cameras," she'd said. He'd argued that it was impossible, but acquiesced.

She tugged at his elbow and pointed across the room. A cadre of deputies entered, led by Ruby Mac and Martin Lightfoot, and the room parted like the Red Sea as they made a beeline for Lehigh. "We just came from the county elections office," Ruby shouted into his ear. "They're predicting a record turnout!"

"That's good for us, right?" Stacy asked.

Lehigh shrugged. "Bruce Bailey's polls had it too close to call yesterday," he said. "With all the money behind Dwayne's campaign, they could be buying a huge get-out-the-vote effort. I heard they had fifty people knocking on doors."

"They knocked on mine," said a voice behind him. "And I threw them off my porch, physically!"

Lehigh turned to identify the speaker, and received a big hug from Phil Reardon, his old high-school pal. "I went and knocked on every door in my neighborhood after that," he said. "I made sure everyone knew to vote for you. And most said they would."

Behind Phil, the tiny, bushy-haired figure of Dot wandered by, her eyes glued to the elaborate designs on the cathedral ceilings. She spotted Lehigh and rushed over to shake his hand. "I told everyone who came into my shop to vote for you or I'd burn their eggs," she said. "Business has never been better!"

"Neither have the eggs," said a familiar voice.

Lehigh turned, not believing his ears. A moment later, he couldn't believe his eyes. The wiry frame of a silver-haired man in baggy overalls and a red flannel shirt stood next to a short, stick-figured woman with a halo of white hair.

"Pappy? *Maw*? What are *you* doing here?" Lehigh's breath left him. He wondered if his heart would start beating again.

"You invited us," Pappy said. "You *said* there'd be dinner."

"I'll show them to the food," Stacy said with a grin, hooking their arms and walking them toward the buffet table.

Lehigh spotted Ben Wright roaming the hall by himself and made his way over to him. "I appreciate you being here," he said, shaking Ben's hand.

"I appreciate you being sheriff," Ben said. "Rumor had it you were on your way out the door. I'm glad to see you sticking it out. We need someone in there willing to fight the *real* crooks." He waved at the TV, now depicting mugshots of Ray Ferguson, Buck Summers, and Paul van Paten with the caption, "Notable Arrests by Sheriff Carter."

"Hear, hear!" exclaimed a small gathering of townspeople nearby, led by the plump figure he recognized as his regular waitress at Shirley's Cafe. "Lock 'em up!" shouted another, and the group burst into nervous laughter.

The ballroom doors opened again, and the slender frame of Donnell Winthrop backed into the room. He turned, and Lehigh spotted the reason for his awkward entrance. In front of him, grinning in his wheelchair, sat Bobby Wills. Donnell rolled him over to Lehigh.

"Look who got out of the hospital today!" Donnell said, beaming. "Into my custody."

"Technically, isn't he supposed to go to jail now?" Stacy asked.

"We're on our way," Donnell said with a grin. "But I thought we'd stop for a bite to eat and a little celebration first. Tell 'em who you voted for, Bobby."

Wills blushed and extended a hand to Lehigh. "It may be the last time I get to vote in a while," he said. "And I know it doesn't get me out of any of the trouble I've caused. But you earned my vote, even if you do put me in jail."

Bruce Bailey's face appeared again on the TV screen, and voices across the room shushed each other. "They have the results of the race!" someone shouted, and the room quieted. Someone found a remote and turned up the volume on the television.

"Polls have closed in Mt. Hood County, and we have early returns and a projected winner in the sheriff's race," Bailey said, his face giving away nothing.

"That's not good," Lehigh said.

"Early returns means the big money wins," someone behind him said in a dull voice.

"Shush!" Lehigh recognized Stacy's voice admonishing the nay-sayer, and a moment later she wrapped her arms around him. "Let's go up front," she said. "People want to see you." She pointed to a raised platform where her father had gathered local notables for the cameras. Next to him, Desmond Mitchell smiled and fist-pumped, then waved him up.

"Let's wait until we hear some numbers first," Lehigh said. Knots formed in his stomach. He wasn't sure what he wanted to see on the screen. Part of him wanted to go back to logging and forestry, but another part wanted vindication for the work he'd done for the people in the room around him. He closed his eyes, holding Stacy close to him.

"Unofficial returns indicate," Bailey said, "and our exit polls confirm, a commanding lead in the sheriff's race for—"

Lehigh couldn't hear the end of Bailey's announcement, because the room erupted in a roar of shouting and table-pounding. They sounded mad. Dangerous, even. "I don't believe it!" someone said, a voice that sounded like Phil's. Stacy squeezed him and kissed him in a comforting way. He sighed, holding her tight, not wanting to open his eyes to see the result.

So, this is how it would end. He'd served his community as interim sheriff for a few months and would gracefully give way to the new incumbent, elected by the people. He knew Dwayne to be a fool, but the public loved electing fools, and he needn't be bitter about it. No, he'd work as diligently for Dwayne's transition as he had as acting sheriff, and then go back to tending his forest and selling logs to lumber mills. No indignity in any of that.

"Speech!" someone shouted, someone that sounded a lot like George McBride. "Where's our man? Let's hear a few words from Lehigh!"

Lehigh shook his head, burying his face in Stacy's soft hair. "Tell me I don't have to go up there and give a concession speech already," he said. He'd prepared one, of course—if one could call a half-dozen thank-yous jotted on an index card a speech. He'd not even gotten around to preparing a victory speech. Why bother?

"What are you talking about?" Stacy shook him by the shoulders. "Lehigh, open your eyes! Look at the screen!"

He did, and couldn't believe what he saw. In large block letters on the screen, he read:

Precincts reporting: 31%

* Carter	74%
Latner	24%
Other	2%

* Projected winner: Lehigh Carter

"Other?" he said, dumbfounded.

"You won, Lehigh!" Stacy said. "Big time! Look at that! Listen to this crowd. The people love you!"

He gazed around the room, dazed. Happy faces smiled back at him, and someone started a chant: "*Le-high! Le-high! Le-high!*"

Pappy appeared out of nowhere, wiping barbecue sauce from his lips and grinning. He extended his hand for a shake. "Congratulations, son," Pappy said. "I'm proud of you. Aren't you glad you didn't quit?"

"I won?" Lehigh said. "How the hell did that happen?"

The screen image changed to show Ray Ferguson in handcuffs at the county courthouse, captioned "Earlier today." Stacy pointed at the screen. "That's how, Lehigh," she said. "Now, get up there and give us a victory speech!"

ACKNOWLEDGMENTS

The Mountain Man Mysteries series has been in the works for nearly a decade. Many friends, colleagues, and family members –too many to count or even remember—have contributed ideas, feedback, critique, encouragement, and love. I thank you all.

But special thanks goes out to those whose support really pushed me when I needed it to get this story published. They include:

Randall Houle, Kelly Garrett, Suzie Harvey, and Rankin Johnson, all members of the Bar Noir Writers Group, whose chapter-by-chapter critiques made this story better on a weekly basis;

My Beta Readers, Richard Gray, Judith Bottorf, and Patsy Silk, for their invaluable late-in-the-game feedback;

Laura Lee Bennett and Patsy Silk, whose keen editing eyes caught many errors long after my own eyes glazed over. If errors remain, they are my fault, not theirs;

Steven Novak, for an amazing cover design;

The Willamette Writers Group, the best bunch of writers around;

Patricia and Donald Corbin, my mother and father, who made me love books, and who always encouraged my love of writing;

All of the many furry critters who have made their way into my life and heart, each of whom show up on these pages, one way or another; and,

Renée, the kindest, most patient, most beautiful person I've ever known, whose smile lights up the darkest night and brightens even the sunniest day…I love you.

About The Author

Gary Corbin is a writer, actor, and playwright in Camas, WA, a suburb of Portland, OR. His creative and journalistic work has been published in *BrainstormNW*, the *Portland Tribune*, The *Oregonian*, and *Global Envision*, among others. His plays have enjoyed critical acclaim and have been produced on many Portland-area stages.

Gary is a member of the Willamette Writers Group, 9 Bridges Writers, the Northwest Editors Guild, PDX Playwrights, and the Bar Noir Writers Workshop, and participates in workshops and conferences in the Portland, Oregon area.

A homebrewer as well as a maker of wine, mead, cider, and soft drinks, Gary is a member of the Oregon Brew Crew and a BJCP National Beer Judge. He loves to ski, cook, and root for his beloved Patriots and Red Sox, and hopes someday to train his dogs to obey. And when that doesn't work, he escapes to the Oregon coast with his sweetheart.

Connect with Gary Corbin

Keep up to date with the latest at
http://www.garycorbinwriting.com

Follow me on Twitter: http://twitter.com/garycorbin

Follow me on Facebook:
https://www.facebook.com/garycorbinwriting

Follow my Amazon Author Page (and review this book!)
http://smarturl.it/GaryCorbinAuthor

Favorite me at Smashwords:
https://www.smashwords.com/profile/view/GaryCorbin

Also by Gary Corbin

The Mountain Man Mysteries

The Mountain Man's Dog

In the small town of Clarkesville, in the heart of the Oregon Cascade Mountains, Lehigh Carter, a humble forester, stumbles into the complex world of crooked cops and power-hungry politicians...all because he rescues a stray, injured dog on the highway.

The *Mountain Man's Dog* is a briskly told crime thriller loaded with equal parts suspense, romance, and light-hearted humor, pitting honor and loyalty against ruthless ambition and runaway greed in a town too small for anyone to get away with anything.

ISBN: 978-0-9974967-1-0
Available in hardcover, paperback, audiobook, and all eBook formats at garycorbinwriting.com, and at your favorite local retailers.

The Mountain Man's Bride

In this thrilling sequel to *The Mountain Man's Dog*, the murder of popular Acting Sheriff Jared Barkley. The murder puts Lehigh and Stacy's plans to marry on hold when Stacy is arrested for committing the crime.

But evidence of a secret affair makes even Lehigh wonder if he should fight for her freedom against the corrupt local machine that accused her.

ISBN: 978-0-9974967-3-4
Available in hardcover, paperback, audiobook, and all eBook formats at garycorbinwriting.com, and at your favorite local retailers.

Lying Injustice Thrillers

Lying in Judgment

A man serves on the jury trying a man for the murder that he committed!

Peter Robertson, 33, discovers his wife is cheating on him. Following her suspected boyfriend one night, he erupts into a rage, beats him and leaves him to die…or so he thought. Soon he discovers that he has killed the wrong man—a perfect stranger.

Six months later, impaneled on a jury, he realizes that the murder being tried is the one he committed. After wrestling with his conscience, he works hard to convince the jury to acquit the accused man. But the prosecution's case is strong as the accused man had both motive and opportunity to commit the murder.

As jurors one by one declare their intention to convict, Peter's conscience eats away at him and he careens toward nervous breakdown.

Lying in Judgment is a courtroom thriller about a good man's search for redemption for his tragic, fatal mistake, pitted against society's search for justice.

ISBN: 978-06926426-8-9
Available in hardcover, paperback, audiobook, and all eBook formats at garycorbinwriting.com, and at your favorite local retailers.

Lying in Vengeance

Two months after serving on the jury trying a man for the murder that he committed, Peter Robertson's worst nightmare comes to fruition: Christine, his beautiful and charming fellow juror, knows his dark secret and uses it to blackmail him.

The price of her secrecy: Peter must kill again, this time to stop Kyle, the man who torments Christine and threatens her very existence.

Their sizzling nascent romance gets interrupted when Kyle kidnaps her. Peter's daring rescue provides him the opportunity to commit the awful deed. Peter refuses, however, only to discover that his best friend Frankie may have committed the act in his place. Or was he framed?

Peter's relentless search for evidence to clear his lifelong pal forces him to confront his demons and risk his own freedom—and his life—as he battles the ruthless, manipulative, and resourceful woman who always seems one step ahead and knows his every move.

ISBN: 978-0-9974967-5-8
Available in hardcover, paperback, audiobook, and all eBook formats at garycorbinwriting.com, and at your favorite local retailers.

Valorie Dawes Thrillers

In Search of Valor

Valorie Dawes fights an international kidnapping syndicate on behalf of a new college friend--and harbors serious doubts about her future as a police officer.

At a young age, Valorie Dawes vowed to avenge the death of her uncle, a policeman killed in the line of duty, by following in his footsteps. During her first month at college, the mysterious disappearance of a close friend's child drags her into the role of crimefighter much earlier than planned.

But Val's initial attempts to help lead to mistrust and recrimination. Self-doubts escalate, not only about Val's future as a cop, but over her ability to make and sustain the trust of a friend.

Anxious to prove herself worthy on both counts, Val puts her own life on the line--and discovers that the kidnappers will stop at nothing to get rid of obstacles like her.

ISBN: 978-0-9974967-9-6
Available in hardcover, paperback, audiobook, and all eBook formats at garycorbinwriting.com, and at your favorite local retailers.

*Read the **free sample chapter** from **In Search of Valor** at the end of this book!*

A Woman of Valor

A rookie policewoman, who had been molested as a young girl, pursues a serial child molester–and struggles to control the anger his misdeeds awake in her. Can Valorie overcome the trauma she suffered as a child and stop this dangerous criminal from hurting others like her—or will her bottled-up anger lead her to take reckless risks that put the people she loves in greater danger?

ISBN: 978-0-9974967-9-6
Available in hardcover, paperback, audiobook, and all eBook formats at garycorbinwriting.com, and at your favorite local retailers.

A Better Part of Valor

When Valorie Dawes discovers the body of a young girl who had also been sexually molested, Lt. Gibson assigns her to assist the detectives investigating the case. Then Clayton Mayor Megan Iverson, candidate for governor of Connecticut, ties her political fortunes to the case, vaulting herself into the lead in all of the major polls with her law-and-order campaign.

Iverson's meddling in the case costs them dearly when key evidence disappears and other evidence, withheld for strategic reasons, gets leaked to the press. The pressure intensifies when a former campaign aide, Val's childhood friend Amy, becomes the next victim.

Can Val find and stop the killer before he strikes again?

Expected release: Summer, 2020

Excerpt from

In Search of Valor

by Gary Corbin

Chapter One

The short, squat man shaded his eyes, as much to hide his face as to shield his vision against the intense late-summer sun. "Built like a fireplug, sweats like a pig," his football coach used to say. Mostly to get under his skin, but also to make an excuse for not letting him play quarterback. Never mind that he had the best arm on the team and could read defenses better than anyone. That he could outrun all but the fleetest of wide receivers and running backs, and every last defensive lineman who lumbered after him in parks-and-rec league. That he'd broken records for touchdowns and passing yardage in junior high ball. And—

Dammit! Focus! He cursed himself and shook his head to force the distracting thoughts away. Look for the girl. Ensure she's a safe distance from Ground Zero. And that she didn't return to her car and drive to where her kid played under adult supervision…for now.

He smiled. Such a great plan. If he didn't have such an important job to do at the moment, he'd pat himself on the back, literally. Something his coach would never do.

Movement caught his eye to the left. A tall, curvy woman with light brown skin and thick black curls emerged from the parking structure. Even wearing those stupid oversized sunglasses, he recognized her. The bitch. He'd never forget that face. That condescending stare, telling him he wasn't good enough for her.

She'd regret that decision. He'd make sure of it.

He watched her walk for a moment, striding toward the center of campus, checking her cell phone. Oblivious. Unsuspecting.

Perfect.

He tapped a message into the burner phone in his hand. "Move. Now." Hit Send. Then he walked in the opposite direction from her, tossing the burner into a garbage can on the way to his car, never looking back.

Chapter Two

Valorie Dawes averted her hazel eyes from the intense morning sun, an unseasonably warm mid-September day on the campus of the University of Connecticut. She'd dressed for the heat: shorts, running shoes, and a "Property of UConn Huskies" t-shirt. Nevertheless, sweat dripped down her back, soaking not only her skin, but also the sturdy backpack holding her books and laptop. She brushed damp, light-brown hair away from her face and stretched her wiry, five-foot-six frame onto her tiptoes to see over the heads of a few oncoming upperclassmen. Still no sign of her.

She checked the time on her cell phone. She'd arrived at 9:25, five minutes early, but that was fifteen minutes ago. Maybe she'd gotten the location wrong.

Val searched the busy sidewalks, crowded with students hurrying to their next air-conditioned classroom. Still no sign of Rhonda LeMieux's tall, curvy frame. Despite having moved to the mainland in her teens, Rhonda continued to operate on what she called "Jamaica time." Her habitual lateness had made her a favorite whipping post of their cantankerous professor of Criminology, Warren Hirsch. Doubts crept into Val's mind once again over her choice of a research partner for the Crim 101 term paper, the first class in her chosen major.

She scolded herself a moment later. Rhonda had mentioned when they'd first met that she had a daughter, and as a young single mother, she worried constantly about the girl's well-being. No doubt something had come up with the girl's care, and—

"Well, well, what have we here?" said a familiar male voice. She turned toward the glass doors of the Student Union entrance. A thin-shouldered, blond-haired man wearing khaki shorts, a Polo shirt, and deck shoes stared back at her behind expensive Oakley sunglasses. He uncrossed his arms and pushed off of his shaded perch, ambling toward her with a silly grin on his face. "If it isn't the famous Val Dawes, all by her lonesome."

"Hoping to stay that way, too, Robb," she said, sighing. If anyone on the UConn campus represented privilege and arrogance, it was Robbin J. McFarland. "Esquire," as he'd emphasized when introducing himself on the first day of classes a few weeks before. She'd joined the few women and most of the men in the classroom in a group eye roll, but Robb remained oblivious.

"What are you waiting for, the press to show up and interview you *again*?" he said with a sneer. "Oh, right. *That* hasn't happened yet. That must be *absolutely* killing you, am I right, *Val*?"

"My name's Valorie," she said, then smirked. "Only my friends call me Val."

"Well, *excuu-uuse* me." Robb stepped closer to her. "I wouldn't want to presume. I only wondered if you'd reconsidered my offer."

"Which one?" She eased away from him, squeamishness rising in her abdomen, and scanned the sidewalks again for Rhonda. "The four awkward invitations to go out with you, or the even more absurd notion of partnering with you on the Criminology paper?"

"Oh, so you do remember." He smiled, which made his face resemble a snake's, or a fully shaved weasel. He wiped sweat from his brow with a handkerchief and edged closer. His six-foot-plus frame towered over her. "Well, I thought we could kill two birds with one stone and discuss our project over dinner tonight." He reached out to touch her. Val batted it away, hard.

"Ow!" he said, rubbing his arm. "Geez Louise, Dawes. Such a slender little thing, but you sure pack a punch."

"Sorry," she said, not sounding sorry. "Martial-arts reflex. Happens every time someone misunderstands the word 'no.' Now, if you'll excuse me, I think I see my real research partner."

Sure enough, a tall, dark-haired woman sashayed up the walk with an enviable air of confidence. She appeared to be in her early 20s, with smooth, light-brown skin and a toothy smile. A bright yellow sundress hugged her curvy figure, and three-inch heels brought her eyes almost even with Robb's. Unlike Val and Robb, Rhonda seemed unaffected by the late August heat.

"Is this boy bothering you?" she asked in her island lilt. "You let me know, and I'll have my Jamaican boyfriends take care of him, eh?"

Robb blanched, edging away as Rhonda approached. "Miss Dawes and I were just discussing the potential of teaming up on—"

"*Ms.* Dawes and I," Rhonda said, her eyes hardening, "are already a team. No room for you, boyo."

"Oh, really?" Robb said. "And what do you bring to the table, *Miz* Le*Moose?*"

"De name's LeMieux. That means, de best." Her accent became more pronounced—intentional, Val guessed. Rhonda's grin widened as she went on. "And I live up to my name. Now go play on yo sailboat, or whatever you do in Martha's Vineyard." *Maw-taw's* Vin-*yawd*, to Val's ears.

"Narra-*gan*-set, please," Robb scoffed. "For Gawd's sake. Don't lump me in with the freaking Kennedys." He turned away, his nose high in the air, and strode off, muttering and shaking his head in disgust.

Val expelled a loud breath and glanced at Rhonda. "What a character," she said.

"Get used to it, my friend," Rhonda said. "These rich UConn boys think themselves to be king. And we are their pawns, no?"

"Not in my world," Val said. "So, are we a team for real, then? We have to confirm with Dr. Hirsch by Thursday afternoon."

"It would be my honor to partner with the niece of the great Valentin Dawes," Rhonda said, tugging her toward the building's entrance.

Val jerked to a stop, forcing Rhonda to halt her progress as well. "None of that, okay?" Val said. "Yeah, my uncle died a hero, and he means much more to me than anyone will ever know. But I'm not trading on his fame, and I don't expect you to, either."

Rhonda hung her head and took a deep breath. "I'm sorry, Valorie. I meant it as a joke, only. Forgive my bad taste."

Val sighed. She envied Rhonda's unpretentious, laid-back style, one that contrasted so much from hers. She needed to learn how to be like that, somehow. "Of course. Apology accepted. So, why don't we get a cup of coffee and plan our project? I'll buy."

Rhonda grinned and extended her hand. "You got it, partner!"

***

Ten minutes later, Val and Rhonda squeezed into adjacent seats at a tiny table in the crowded Student Union café. "I insist," Val said when Rhonda protested Val paying for their coffee. "I offered. Besides, don't you have a baby to feed?"

Rhonda laughed, a sound Val found infectious and charming. "Jada is only eighteen months old. She hardly eats anything." She showed Val a photo of a curly-haired girl in a pink dress whose smile seemed a miniature carbon copy of Rhonda's.

Val's heart melted at the sight of the little girl. "That's the same age as my niece, Alison," she said. "I love that little imp so much! And what a pretty name!"

"I knew I liked you for a reason," Rhonda said, grinning. "It's Jamaican, like my father, and it means 'God's gift.' And she is, to me. In fact, she is part of the reason I was late this morning. I drove almost the whole way to her day care center before I remembered we were meeting today." She checked her watch, a cheap Rolex knock-off. "I need to pick her up at day care in a half hour, so we'd better work fast. What topic should we choose?"

They opened their laptops and discussed the approved topics listed on Professor Hirsch's faculty page. "I like 'Women in Crime: Victims and Perpetrators,' but is that too predictable for us?" Val said.

"Maybe," Rhonda said. "What about 'The Rise of Hate Crimes' or 'Police Use of Force'? Same problem?"

"Those sound great to me—I love doing statistical research,"

Val said. "But what about you? As a future social worker, maybe we should choose a topic focused on families. 'Intergenerational Recidivism,' maybe, or the 'The Contributions of Poverty and Class to Urban Crime.' Are those better?"

Rhonda frowned. "Those don't sound like good fits for a future policewoman."

Val waved her off. "They're all relevant. Besides, I'm not a hundred percent decided on my major," she said. "You know, I've always thought I'd become a cop, since I was a kid. But over the last few months I've had second thoughts. I might be happier doing social work, too—helping troubled families in a more constructive way, before they get swept up by crime—as victims or perpetrators. Locking them up after they commit crimes seems kind of a negative approach."

"If you grew up like I did, you'd definitely look at cops as a negative approach," Rhonda said. "My brother spent a week in jail for a crime he didn't commit. 'Mistaken identity,' they said. Yeah, it was a mistake all right. They arrested him for being young and black."

"That's terrible," Val said. "To be honest, though, my focus would be on supporting young women and girls—victims of abuse and such." She went quiet, her heart pounding.

A silhouette filled the open doorway…the shadow of a large, overweight man, tufts of black and silver hair shining in the reflected light of the hallway. His heavy breathing filled her tiny bedroom with aromas of whiskey and sweat—

Rhonda cocked her head. "Is that motivated by personal experience, or—"

"Just something I'm interested in," Val said in a rush of words, pushing the memory out of her mind. "We'd best not get sidetracked here. You said time was short, right?"

They kicked the options around and chose the "Women in Crime" topic. "If we don't, it'll be left to the Neanderthal men like Robb McFarland," Rhonda said. "I hate to think what that paper would look like."

After dividing up the initial research responsibilities, Rhonda gulped down her coffee. "I need to get to the day care center," she said. "It's over on the west side, just off campus. Can I give you a ride somewhere?"

"I'd love that," Val said. "The surplus store is out that way, and I need a more comfortable desk chair."

"I can drop you off after we pick up Jada," Rhonda said. "It'll give us a chance to chat more about the paper."

Instead, however, their conversation shifted to more personal topics during the traffic-jammed ride across Storrs, a campus-focused village in the city of Mansfield. "Is your uncle the reason you want to go into law enforcement?" Rhonda asked.

"He definitely inspired me," Val said. "I saw how he made a difference in the community through police work. That's my real goal. I'm just not sure anymore if that's the right path for me. What about you? What motivated you to pursue social work?"

"When I first started, I wanted to make a difference in the community, like you," Rhonda said. "Now I just want to help women avoid the mistakes I made, try to keep them out of trouble." She fell silent a moment.

Val considered asking her to elaborate, then decided to steer the conversation toward less troubling topics. "You mentioned spending a year in college before you had Jada. Was that here, at UConn?"

Rhonda shook her head. "I had a full athletic scholarship to Yale," she said. "Volleyball and track. But I had to give it all up when I came back to Mansfield to take care of my mom."

"Wow!" Val said. "I have a partial scholarship—track and soccer. I didn't know women could even get a full ride for sports."

"Ah," Rhonda said. "That may be the only advantage of being a black woman in America. They assumed, correctly as it turns out, that I also had financial hardship. And finding female athletes of color with good grades is a very competitive market, it seems."

"That's awesome," Val said. "The scholarship, I mean. Will

you be running track at UConn?"

Rhonda scoffed. "Not while raising a baby and working full time. Besides, it's best if I keep a low profile. Rizzo, my baby's daddy, has threatened more than once to sue for custody…or just take matters into his own hands. I haven't even told him about returning to school. I'd rather he doesn't find out."

"He threatened to take the baby from you?" Val said, her voice hoarse. "That's outrageous!"

"You don't know the half of it," Rhonda said, pulling into the parking lot of the day care center. "A few months ago he saw me out to dinner with a man. He tried to pick a fight with the guy…until my date stood up. He was six-five and built like a steamroller. Rizzo suddenly realized that he was double-parked. I haven't seen him since."

Val laughed out loud. "You have a great way of putting things, Rhonda. Hey, is it okay if I come in with you? I'd love to meet Jada."

Rhonda enveloped Val in a bone-crushing hug. "Girl, I think I already love you like a sister," she said. "Come on! Shoot, I'm already five minutes late."

They hustled inside, and a mousy, brown-haired white woman with horn-rimmed glasses greeted them. "Are you picking up, or dropping off?" she asked with a saccharine smile.

Val and Rhonda exchanged puzzled glances. "You don't honestly think I'm her daughter?" Val said.

"Name?" the brown-haired woman responded without hesitation, fingers resting on her computer keyboard.

"LeMieux. My baby's name is Jada." Rhonda showed no surprise or impatience at the receptionist's cluelessness.

The receptionist smiled again and tapped at her keyboard. Puzzlement spread over her face. "Jada? J-A-Y-D-A?"

"No 'Y'," Rhonda said, sing-song. "LeMieux is L-E—"

"Ah, here she is," the receptionist said, but her smile evaporated. "There seems to be some confusion."

"What sort of confusion?" Rhonda said, her face forming a worried frown.

"She's already been picked up," the receptionist said. "About twenty minutes ago, by her grandmother."

"Her grandmother?" Rhonda's frown deepened. "That's impossible. Could you please check again?"

The receptionist clicked a few keys, frowning, but said nothing.

Val edged closer to Rhonda. "Are you sure your mother didn't come by and get her?" she asked.

Rhonda's eyes teared up, and she glanced at Val, her lips trembling. "I'm sure," she said. "My mother died six months ago." She paused a moment to regain her composure. "Her life insurance policy is paying my tuition."

"I'm sorry," the receptionist said. "We show that Jada left under the care of an approved guardian. The woman identified herself as Karina LeMieux."

Rhonda burst into tears and slumped into a chair, moaning. "He did it. That son of a bitch took her!"

Val drew a steadying breath and turned to the receptionist. "Miss, about the woman who took Jada. Did you get a signature, an I.D., anything?"

The woman pecked at her keyboard and stared at the screen. "I wasn't here—somebody else checked Jada out," she said. "But her grandmother is in our system as an approved guardian."

"How is that possible? She's deceased, as Rhonda just told you!" Val said.

Rhonda groaned. "I never got around to updating my records here after Ma died," she said. "Oh, my God. Oh, my God!"

Val leaned across the desk, her face inches from the receptionist's. "You need to go check to make sure that little girl isn't here," she said. "*Now!*"

The receptionist froze for a moment, then disappeared through a door behind her.

Available in print and all ebook formats from your favorite local and online retailers.